Jellybird

LEZANNE CLANNACHAN

An Orion paperback

First published in Great Britain in 2013
by Orion
This paperback edition published in 2014
by Orion Books,
an imprint of The Orion Publishing Group Ltd,
Orion House, 5 Upper St Martin's Lane,
London WC2H 9EA

An Hachette UK company

1 3 5 7 9 10 8 6 4 2

A CIP catalogue record for this book is
available from the British Library.

ISBN 978-1-4091-2796-3

Typeset at The Spartan Press Ltd,
Lymington, Hants

Printed and bound by CPI Group
(UK) Ltd, Croydon, CR0 4YY

The Orion Publishing Group's policy is to use papers that
are natural, renewable and recyclable products and
made from wood grown in sustainable forests. The logging
and manufacturing processes are expected to conform to
the environmental regulations of the country of origin.

www.orionbooks.co.uk

To Emily, Carsten and Maia, for the light in my life.

In memory of my father, Allan M. Maltarp.

I

October 2012, Seasalt Holiday Park

Jessica arrives at the caravan park sometime in the night.

'You sure this is the right place?' the taxi driver asks, staring at the closed gates, the blacked-out campsite beyond.

It belongs to my mother, she could explain, if she were able to dredge up the words. The fare shows up in sharp, red lines but the numbers slip about like oily fish in her head. She hands the driver a note, hoping it's enough, and gets out.

When he's gone, she stands in the lane surrounded by blackberry bushes that in summer whisper with a sea breeze but are now frozen still. She'd forgotten how dark it could get. She presses the night bell and waits. Minutes later, torchlight weaves through the mobile homes.

The gates rock back and her mother, nightgown brushing the muddy toes of her wellingtons, fixes the beam in Jessica's face. 'What's happened?'

'I just . . .' Her voice sounds distant, as though someone else is speaking through her. 'Woke up this morning thinking about this place.'

It's not true, but Jessica can't say about the kitchen floor; how she lay on it until the wooden boards pressed bruises like thunderclouds onto her shoulder and hip.

She follows her mother through the unlit park, the night so dense that nothing exists unless the torchlight flashes over it. It makes Jessica feel bodiless, like she could slip outside of the shivering exhaustion and aching limbs. She wants to keep going but then they reach the caravan that is both her mother's home and office.

'You could stay with me, I guess,' her mother says, 'but there's only one room.'

'How about Caravan Nineteen?'

Her mother sniffs as though the choice displeases her. She disappears into her caravan and comes back with a key. A blue enamel flower dangles from it. Her mother made it, years ago, on some course. One for each caravan and an extra one for Jessica, who stops walking, trying to remember when she last saw her key ring. The loss of it is sudden and sharp as gunshot.

'This way. You remember.' The torch in her mother's hand draws fleeting lines on the black gravel.

Inside Caravan Nineteen, her mother slaps dust and dead spiders from the sofa cushions.

'There are extra blankets under the bed.'

'I remember.'

When her mother leaves, Jessica stands in the centre of the snug sitting room, facing the sofa. She flips over one of the seat cushions then kneels before it. Her fingers trace a faint brown outline like a smudged cloud. A washed-out stain. Too old to be certain it is blood.

Hugging her rucksack, she lies down, pressing her cheek to the mark. She doesn't sleep. Before dawn, she walks out of the holiday park.

Opposite the park lies a derelict pleasure garden. A sudden moon has opened up the night, structures emerging – the boarded-up pavilion, the empty lido, her own body. She reaches a gap in the picket fence where a gate used to be. Past it, the raw edge of the cliff and a flight of rickety steps leading to a horseshoe bay. She feels her way down the stairs and onto the beach. The sand creaks with ice beneath her feet.

As she waits for first light, she takes a cuckoo clock out of her rucksack and cradles it in her hands.

From a distance, it is a perfect miniature of an alpine chalet. Up close, its plastic seams become obvious. The walls, once slaughterhouse red, have faded to a hammy pink; the roof bleached in patches like stale chocolate. Jessica no longer winds it up. It had been bought as a joke, after all.

The key is Sellotaped to the bottom. She scratches it free and winds it up. A slow tick starts inside the woodchip walls like a tutting tongue. Jessica moves the minute hand to twelve. Two windows above the clock face spring open. A peg figure appears in each, one in a white dress holding a bunch of painted-on flowers, the other in a funereal black suit. The groom's black eyes peer sideways at his bride as he hovers in his window.

Then they jerk across empty space to knock heads in a clumsy kiss beneath a scroll declaring *You'll Find Love in Longhaven Bay*.

Jessica stares at the peg-man. His eyes, with their sideways glance, now look away from the embrace, over his bride's shoulder at something – or someone – behind her. She takes hold of the little groom, making the clock's mechanism squeal and shiver as it tries to pull him back.

With her thumbnail, she scratches off his eyes.

When the sky opens up in morgue blues and purples, she lifts the cuckoo clock above her head and hurls it at the water as though she's bringing down an axe. It disappears into the ocean with a viscous gulp.

Job done.

Ten minutes later, she arrives at the park in time to see her mother leaving Caravan Nineteen, a lumpy bin bag tucked under her arm. There's a breakfast tray on the kitchen counter.

'How long will you be staying?' her mother asks.

'Just a few days, Birdie.'

They both know that isn't true. 'The Premium and Superior caravans are empty, you know.'

'Here's fine.'

Her mother strides away, the plump pads of her hips wobbling through her fisherman's jumper.

The breakfast tray contains three triangles of toast and a pot of bitty marmalade. It sparks a memory of the French toast her mother used to make on Sunday mornings – cinnamon bread, butter-gold with fried egg and maple syrup. The thought of food nauseates her. Sliding the tray outside, she locks the door.

In the bedroom, she finds her clothes are no longer on the floor where she'd dumped them before walking to the beach. The bin bag under her mother's arm takes on a new significance. Rather than crawling into the bed – narrow and comfortless as a ship's bunk – she has to go in search of her few belongings.

The deserted holiday park is picture-still as she heads to the laundry block. Jessica touches the walls of the boarded-up mobile homes, offering them comfort. The desolation of the place suits her, like stepping into water already wet.

The laundry block is a square cement building with a flat roof and slit windows for ventilation. Years back, her mother, in a flight of artistic fancy, painted one of the walls with a jungle of creepers and exotic birds. The colours have dimmed and the birds have become sinister, blurry-eyed beings among the trees. From inside comes the sound of voices and wet sheets being flapped out.

'The girl's a wreck.' Grannie Mim, her mother's best friend. Jessica recognises the slight wobble in her voice. It isn't age; she has always sounded the same. 'I saw her staggering off to the beach this morning. Dawn, it was.'

'Bit of sleep, that's all Jessica needs.' Her mother, so flat and practical. 'She's tougher than she looks.'

'Why's she here?'

In the pause, Jessica peels off a curl of paint from the body of a fat, blue bird.

'I don't know,' her mother says. 'It's none of my business.'

'But it is, Birdie. She's your youngest.'

'She's twenty-nine.'

'Still your baby.'

'She doesn't want anything from me. Never has.'

'You still have to offer it.' Despite her frail-sounding voice, there's nothing meek about Grannie Mim.

Jessica waits for her mother to respond. When she hears nothing but the accelerated snap of damp linen, she goes back to her caravan, climbs fully dressed into bed. As she drifts off to sleep, a noise startles her. She kneels at the window, convinced she heard a handful of pebbles dashed against the glass. There's no one there. Just a seagull in the sky, suspended against the wind like a kite on a string.

Birdie calls this the dead season.

Jessica sleeps away a whole day and night, waking on her second morning at the park to the blind whiteness of the room, confused, disorientated. She finds her watch on the floor where she has thrown it off at some point. It used to make him laugh, how she'd discard everything in her sleep until she was utterly naked. Her wedding ring often disappeared in that way, found days later in a crack in the floorboards or inside the pillow-case.

You trying to tell me something? he'd tease. *Everyone's honest in their sleep.*

Jessica checks her left hand, and sure enough the ring is gone. Just as she lifts her pillow, she remembers

6

where it is. Making a circle in the gathering dust of a mantelpiece far from here.

She peels off the sheets, damp with sea air and pushes the curtains open with her socked feet. Spotting blue sky, she sits up. At the far end of the park, Grannie Mim is returning from the beach, hair like brittle wool. She follows the shingle path which runs like a corpse's vein through the caravan site, heading straight for Caravan Nineteen. Hearing the front door open, Jessica pulls the sheets back over her, closes her eyes.

Mim doesn't knock; walks straight into the bedroom and grips Jessica's foot through the covers.

'Up you get.' She gives Jessica's foot a shake. 'We can't have you sleeping your life away.'

Retreating to the door, she nudges a parcel of laundered clothes into the bedroom with the toe of her walking boot. 'Your ma's done your clothes.'

Jessica waits for the door to close before getting out of bed and inspecting the bruises that run from shoulder to elbow on her left arm. The flesh feels pulpy and tender. She chooses a thick-knit jumper, loose and concealing, checking her reflection in the window as she dresses. *Clean jumper, tick. Hair brushed, tick.*

In the kitchen, the old lady hands her a mug of tea.

'It's good to come home when you're running low,' she says with a look from under her patchy eyebrows that implies layers of meaning. Grannie Mim's digging.

'It's more your home than mine,' Jessica says. 'How many years have you been at the park now?'

Grannie Mim ignores the question. 'At some point, you have to move on.'

'Someone's been talking.'

'Your ma's said nothing.' Mim sniffs, pinches her nose and wipes her thumb on her trousers. 'At seventy-six you just know these things.'

The tea tastes like milky, boiled water. Jessica drinks it in the hope that she'll be left alone once it's finished.

'I heard sobbing last night.'

Jessica has to smile. 'I haven't shed a tear.'

'Maybe you should.' Grannie Mim leaves her tea untouched. 'I'll wake you again tomorrow.'

After she's gone, Jessica thinks about crying. She pokes about in old memories to see if something might startle her into tears, finally settling on the bedsit in Threepenny Row. Where it all started.

There's a quiet knock at the door.

'Tea.' Birdie holds out a steaming mug, looking straight past Jessica into the caravan as if checking for signs of disorder, something that might need setting right. 'How did you sleep?'

'Badly.' Not her normal answer. It's Grannie Mim's fault. All of a sudden Jessica wants to feel bad. Or at least pretend to, in the hope that a real sensation will follow.

Birdie nods. 'The gale kept me awake as well. There's storm damage to some of the roof shingles.'

Jessica suspects her mother's here on Grannie Mim's insistence. 'It wasn't the storm that kept me awake.'

'Well. I guess you're used to noise from the city.'

'Did I ever tell you about Threepenny Row?'

Her mother goes straight to the cupboard under the

sink and finds a duster. 'I visited you there, if you remember?'

Once. And she'd stayed on the doorstep, refusing to come in.

Jessica sits at the breakfast bar. 'It stank of mushrooms and rancid air-freshener, that place. Eau de Plastic Peach, we called it.' Softly to herself, she adds, 'Me and Jacques.'

Her mother, noticing Grannie Mim's mugs by the sink, empties them and starts washing up. 'You can see the water from Caravan Fourteen.'

'I like this one.' Jessica hugs her elbows, looking out over the campsite. The sky is now the same mottled white as the caravans. 'Threepenny Row was a hole. I could lean out of bed and light cigarettes on the gas stove.'

Birdie's nod is the gesture of a conductor, moving things along.

'Jacques was appalled. Said he couldn't sleep at night, imagining me burned to death in my bed. I screamed at him when he moved it.'

'Well, it sounds like a fire hazard.'

'He once took a blue biro and joined up all the freckles on my back.' Jessica discovers the bar stool squeaks, if she shifts her weight. Interesting, how her mother can make her feel five years old again. 'He said I had the star constellation of a leaping salmon between my shoulders.'

Birdie turns her attention to the window above the kitchen sink, rubbing the glass with sweeping arcs that strain her coat's stitching under the arm. 'And where is he now?'

Her mother's words do the trick; Jessica stops talking.

'I could do with some help mending the roofs this afternoon.' Birdie turns to go, then stops. 'I nearly forgot. Someone was looking for you yesterday when you were sleeping.'

'Who?'

'A woman.'

Adrenalin bursts under the shallow surface of Jessica's skin. 'What did she look like?'

She tries to sound casual but it's too late. Birdie must have seen something in her face because she looks away. Her mother is the only person she knows who can pass a car crash without a glance.

'I told her you weren't here,' Birdie says.

'Did she believe you?'

'I think so.'

The tension in Jessica's neck eases, her shoulders drop. 'Thank you.'

She wants to sound grateful but Birdie's merely doing her a favour. One favour requires another in return. 'Let me know when you're going to fix the roofs.'

By the afternoon, an Atlantic gale is blowing. The caravan creaks and judders as Jessica pulls on as many layers as possible under her thin jacket. Her newly laundered clothes smell of hot-ironed soap powder.

She finds her mother balanced on a ladder at Caravan

Two, her ankle-length skirt of tropical greens gathered and tucked between her knees. Thread veins map the contours of her stout calves through beige nylons.

'That looks dangerous,' Jessica says, the ladder shaking with the vigorous jack of her mother's elbow as she crowbars broken shingles off the roof.

Birdie peers through her armpit. 'Hand me the new shingles, if you would. And some nails.'

With a steadying hand on the ladder, Jessica does as she's told. Her mother positions the shingles, humming a tune Jessica doesn't recognise and keeping time with the hammer as she drives the nails in.

'You're actually enjoying yourself, aren't you?' Jessica tries to grind the blood back into her fingers. 'Is there nothing you can't fix?'

'Cars.'

Jessica can't tell if her mother is being serious or not.

'Cars and people,' Birdie adds.

Raindrops, glutinous with unformed snow, burst on Jessica's face and hands. 'I'm not here to be fixed, if that's what you think.'

Her mother drops the crowbar and hammer into the deep pockets of her skirt, gently touching the newly positioned tiles with her fingertips like a blessing, before climbing down. Eyes on her mother's impassive face, Jessica helps gather up the damaged shingles from the sodden ground.

'Like I told you, Jessica.' Birdie straightens. 'Cars and people.'

Jessica clamps her teeth down on her tongue, looking over her mother's shoulder. Beyond Seasalt Park's hedgerow boundary, she can see the sloping roof of the house she grew up in. Purbrook Rise. Smoke wisps out of the chimney, catching and tearing in the wind. A new family in her old home.

'When was it you sold the house? January?'

'March.' Birdie glances across at the roof. 'It feels longer though.'

The thought makes Jessica dizzy. She remembers coming down from London to clear out the few remaining items of her childhood from her old bedroom. It was the day she took the sea-dragon box from its secret place in the chimney flue. If only she'd left it there, she thinks.

Which brings her to Libby. Had she already met her by then? What came first – the box, or Libby? Gnawing the tip of her thumb, she tries to sequence the events. She senses a pattern, a series of incidents that appeared random but were invisibly linked; a net waiting to catch her. If she'd only left the box in its hiding place; if only she'd never met Libby. Jessica squats down, head low to bring the blood back.

Birdie's feet stop in front of her. 'I'm surprised to be saying this, seeing as you slept the whole of yesterday away, but maybe more rest is what you need.'

It's the most her mother has said since she arrived.

'Sleep does wonders,' Jessica says. Her mother's favourite saying when she was a child. She watches Birdie stuff the tube of roofing tar and remaining shingle into her pockets and walk away, the silhouette of her skirt disfigured by sharp angles.

When she was little, Jessica used to fish her hands

into her mother's bottomless pockets, hunting for treasure. On the rare occasion she came up empty-handed, her mother would say, *Oh, but you gave up too soon*, and with a magic flourish of her hand produce a chewy sweet or a marble or a nail bent into an improbable shape.

2

Nine months earlier, January 2012, London

Every surface in the restaurant is a droning white, making Jessica's head ache. In contrast, the sprouting green of her wool dress looks vulgar and her leather boots far too earthy.

The box sits in the middle of the table. Against the starched white of the tablecloth, it too looks cheap and garish, with a swirling oil-on-water pattern of pink and silver; the product of an entire evening trawling through packaging on the internet. She should have chosen something plain.

Through long windows overlooking the restaurant's walled garden, she can see falling snow, the sky a cool metal-grey. The cold looks delicious, making the airless, overheated restaurant suffocating by contrast. The wool against her skin starts to itch.

The woman she is waiting for, Elizabeth Hargreaves – she must get her name right – is late. Five more minutes and she'll leave.

The waiter offers her a choice of rolls in a silver basket, spilling crumbs across the lid of the box. As she brushes them away, a sudden flurry catches her attention. It's not so much a noise as a ripple through the air, like something only animals sense, heads craning. Jessica's first impression is of a violent pink that seems to burn a hole in the restaurant's pristine white. A woman, whose magenta jumper is making Jessica wish she'd worn her green dress with similar audacity, studies the other diners. There's something compellingly physical about the woman's presence that keeps drawing Jessica's eyes. She is tall, wide-shouldered, and her face, framed by a black bob, is strong, almost masculine. Standing among the tables, she is clearly enjoying the attention.

Here comes drama, Jessica thinks, smiling to herself. Then, as the woman's eyes fix with sudden intent in her direction, she experiences a vague sense of panic.

This is Elizabeth Hargreaves.

'You must be Jessica Byrne.' The woman thrusts out her hand as she reaches the table.

'How did you know?' She shakes Elizabeth's cool, dry hand, aware of how unpleasantly damp her own is.

'A clever guess.'

Jessica waits for the woman to sit down, flap out her napkin and smooth it across her lap before pushing the box towards her. 'Here it is.'

Elizabeth ignores it, regarding Jessica instead. Her mouth curls in a small, secretive smile that sends another woollen prickle through Jessica. It reminds her of their telephone conversation a few days earlier. How

Elizabeth had taken her time to say who she was and why she was calling. Jessica had come away with the distinct impression that the woman had enjoyed her confusion.

'I know this must seem odd. I'm sure you've never met your other internet clients before.'

'No.' Jessica nearly adds that her website has only been live for three weeks.

Elizabeth nods. 'I am, after all, interested in your entire Deception range. I can hardly rely on internet pictures alone.'

'Of course not.' Jessica tries to match the woman's smooth, even tone. 'It's a pleasure for me to show you.'

Elizabeth signals the waiter to clear a space for her. Once her plate and cutlery have been removed, she places the box in front of her. Instead of removing the lid, she says, 'Do you know, we have quite a lot in common.'

Jessica holds back a sigh. *Open the box. Just open it.*

'I grew up in Barnestow.'

'Barnestow. I know the place,' Jessica says, trying to concentrate. 'It's about forty minutes from where I grew up.'

'I know. I read the profile on your website.' The box lies forgotten between the woman's hands. 'You must know Seasalt Holiday Park?'

Jessica straightens. 'It's my mother's. I grew up there.'

Elizabeth hides her mouth behind her hand, her eyes wide with astonishment. 'What a coincidence. I used to visit it as a child.'

Jessica smiles, her shoulders released from their tense knot. 'I used to hang out with the Caravan Kids, as my sisters and I called them.'

'Perhaps we played together.' The woman is smiling now, and Jessica is struck by how it transforms and softens her face. She is, in fact, beautiful.

Elizabeth turns her attention to the box and finally lifts off the lid.

'You've taken a lot of trouble with the packaging.'

Inside, each piece of jewellery has been wrapped in black velvet and tied at either end with orange ribbons, like oversized confectionery. Elizabeth takes them out of their nest of shredded tissue paper and lays them in front of her.

In spite of her nerves, Jessica is fascinated by the slow ritual of a client unwrapping and handling her jewellery for the first time. Last night, she had tried to explain to Jacques why she was putting so much care into the packaging when the sale was yet to be agreed.

It's the moment I always imagine but never get to see.

Elizabeth takes her time untying bows and unrolling the velvet, her face severe once more in its lack of expression. Against the pale tablecloth, the glinting oranges and reds of her necklace shout out like a battle-cry. Jessica sighs with pleasure.

It almost doesn't matter what anyone else thinks.

'May I?' Elizabeth takes off her pink jumper, undoes the top two buttons of her white blouse, pulling the collars apart, and clasps the necklace around her neck. 'Do you have a mirror?'

'Sorry, no, I didn't think . . .' Her voice trails off

as Elizabeth gets up. In a bubble of anxiety, Jessica watches her head towards the Ladies.

She studies Elizabeth's face when she reappears, but the woman is busy glancing around the restaurant, the necklace seemingly forgotten.

'According to your reviews,' Elizabeth says, sitting down, 'you're some sort of alchemist.'

'I wouldn't go that far.'

'But you take pieces of rubbish and transform them into treasure?'

Jessica nods, heat rising in her face. In a minute the woman will walk off and she'll be left alone, under the eyes of the other diners, to put it all back in that silly, whimsical container.

'So. Spill the beans. What exactly am I wearing about my neck?'

Jessica thinks she catches a fleeting look of humour, but she can't be sure.

'You want a list of the materials?'

'My friends will ask.'

She takes a breath. *What the hell.*

'Unpolished citrines and topaz. Paste jewellery from old theatre costumes, pieces of broken tile – see those swirling orange and purple pieces? Fool's gold, glazed petals of a fake rose I found in a charity shop, and those shiny yellow-brown bulbs are actually teeth from an old stag's head.'

Elizabeth says nothing. She motions the waiter over. Jessica feels an odd sense of relief. *All over now.* But instead of asking for the bill, she orders a bottle of champagne and then winks at Jessica.

'I think a celebration is in order.'

'You like it?'

Elizabeth reaches forward so abruptly that Jessica almost flinches as her hand is grasped. 'It's fabulous. I can't wait for my friends to gush over it, only to be told it's a load of old rubbish, if you'll excuse the expression.' The fingers of her other hand trail over the necklace's rough surface as she speaks, her face pink with sudden enthusiasm. 'I absolutely love it.'

'If you take it off, I'll show you why it's called Deception.'

Elizabeth hands the necklace to Jessica, who flips it over and points out the row of heart, diamond, spade and club pendants that form its base.

'Fascinating. But you can't see those shapes from the front.'

'Deception,' Jessica says. 'Its true form is hidden because the eye is distracted by all that colour and glitter.'

'Oh, Jessica. You are a genius.'

When the champagne arrives, Elizabeth proposes a toast.

'To us becoming friends.'

As they chink glasses, she adds, 'Oh, and it's Libby, by the way. My friends call me Libby.'

3

February 2012

Jessica can still taste whisky and cigarettes from the night before. Even with the sour, hollow pit in her stomach, she's happy to be propelled along by the late-morning crowd in Columbia Road Market. With Jacques holding her hand, they walk in awkward single file through trolleys of fresh-cut flowers and sculpted trees. She squints in the glare of a brilliant February sun, drifting along in a dazzled impression of bodies and foliage, full of aimless well-being. The air smells crisply green.

Neither of them knows much about plants, and Jacques is making up names as they wander through the flower market. 'Moon Roses. Fatboy Dahlias. To your left, Jessie – the greater-spotted Fernicus Flower.'

'Fornicus Flower, don't you mean?'

'Of course. The *Fornicus* Flower. A favourite of mine.' Jacques has pulled his woollen hat low over his eyes. His face – angled and drawn from lack of sleep – softens as he turns to smile at her.

'I need to eat,' he says.

They find a tapas bar at the far end of Columbia Road, away from the crowds and shouting street vendors.

'Let's buy some mini-trees,' Jessica says, once they have sidestepped their way through the busy restaurant to a table by the window.

'Olive and lemon,' Jacques agrees. 'And tomato plants for the roof terrace.'

Last night Jessica had conceded it was time to make their flat more homely. Less crash pad. She suspects this brings them a step closer to the day when Jacques will suggest converting their boxy study into a nursery.

As always, he over-orders. Terracotta bowls of chorizo, garlic prawns, spicy *patatas bravas* and oily sardines arrive; they eat in greedy silence until Jessica sits back. 'I've gone too far. Should've stopped eating ten minutes ago.'

'You need to practise, sweetheart.' Jacques forks a piece of chorizo off her plate. 'Ma Larsson is suspicious of girls with small appetites.'

Jessica pinches his thigh. 'She's had years to get used to my lack of appetite and childbearing hips.'

'She loves you the way you are, you know that.' Orange grease glistens on his bottom lip. 'She just wants grandchildren.'

Jessica reaches across and wipes away the grease with her thumb, bringing it to her mouth afterwards. 'Ma Larsson will just have to wait.'

She's smiling as she says it. Her mother-in-law's longing for grandchildren is a comfortable, well-worn carpet of conversation; perfect for hung-over Sundays when the idea of babies is nothing more than the notion of foreign lands yet to be explored.

Right now, she can't bear the thought of sharing Jacques with another living thing.

'Let's go home,' she says.

Her husband leans across the debris of half-eaten food and kisses her. He tastes of spicy sausage and stale alcohol; she opens her mouth, her hands in his hair, pulling him in.

'We mustn't kiss any more. Not after five years of marriage.'

Jacques nods. 'It's downright inappropriate.'

They grin at each other and Jessica feels a squirm of complicit pleasure, the two of them cocooned against the rest of the world.

'Look what I found.' Jacques pulls his wallet from his back pocket, leafs through old receipts until he finds a creased photograph. He holds it up for her.

A figure sits cross-legged on an unmade bed. Legs naked except for thick socks bunched at the ankles, a slight body swallowed up by a grey sweatshirt. Jacques' old walking socks and jumper; the young girl is herself.

'Where did you find it?'

'I was clearing out some of the boxes in the study.'

She decides not to ask why. 'I must have been seventeen. There's that revolting sofa bed in Three-penny Row.'

Jacques turns the photograph back towards himself;

regards it with such tenderness that Jessica feels a pang of envy for her seventeen-year-old self.

'I always loved that look on your face,' he says.

Scraping her chair closer to his, she frowns at the picture. Her face looks wide-eyed and sleepy as a child's, her mouth loose; no words waiting to be spoken. 'I look vacant.'

'Open,' Jacques says.

An electronic melody of bells sounds from under her chair. Jessica scoops up her bag and stirs its contents in search of her mobile. It takes her a moment to place the voice. 'Elizabeth?'

'Libby. I keep telling you. Only my maths teacher called me Elizabeth, and that was to conceal his lust for me.'

'Where are you? It sounds busy.'

'At the flower market,' Libby says. 'I thought you said you'd be here. With Jacques.'

'We're in the tapas bar. Come and join us.'

Jacques mouths, 'Who is it?'

Jessica ends the phone call. 'Elizabeth.' When he looks blank-faced she adds, 'The one who bought my entire Deception range.'

'Ah, yes. Your internet stalker.'

'Best behaviour, please.' Jessica nudges him with the tip of her boot. 'She's on her way now. Hope you don't mind.'

'Not at all, honey.'

'She's been wanting to meet you. Apparently you sound too good to be true.' Jessica is anticipating the look of appreciation on Elizabeth's face when she meets

Jacques. Her new friend is showy and expressive in a way that's alien to Jessica. It intrigues her.

A woman walks past the window, her white coat unbuttoned, billowing in the wake of her stride.

'In fact, that's her now.'

Jacques sits upright, twisting in his chair as though he has a sudden, sharp pain in his side. 'That's your new friend?'

There's something in his voice that makes her glance at him but then the bell above the door rings and Elizabeth walks in. She stops in the centre of the restaurant, looking about her. She's wearing a black trouser suit with a white, masculine shirt that stretches tight at her chest and huge gold earrings like autumn leaves dangling from her black bob. She's like a wave cresting over the room, everyone holding their breath, waiting to be swept away.

Jessica smiles to herself. *Here comes drama.*

'We're over here.' She waves, glances back at Jacques. There's a look on men's faces when they see Libby, she's noticed, something close to greed.

But Jacques is the only person not looking as he frowns out of the window.

'Libby?' he's muttering, and Jessica elbows him.

'Short for Elizabeth. Try to keep up.'

'Jessica, you gorgeous thing.' Libby comes over and they exchange kisses.

Jacques offers a brief handshake without standing up. He's put his hat back on as though preparing to leave. 'Nice to meet you.'

She waits for Jessica to clear their coats off the third

chair and smiles across at Jacques. 'As handsome in the flesh as your wife said you were.'

'Can I get you a coffee?' The cheery rise in his voice sounds like a stumbled attempt at running up a hill. He's looking pale again, which makes the darkness of his stubble stand out like theatre paint.

'Coffee would be lovely, thank you,' Libby says.

Jessica catches his hand as he gets up. 'Are you feeling OK, Jacqy?'

He nods, stroking his knuckles briefly against her cheek. 'Back in a minute.'

Libby gives Jacques an oblique look as he walks away. 'I was expecting a real charmer.'

'We had a messy night at a comedy club in Camden.'

'I guessed as much from the boozy haze.' She gives Jessica's arm a friendly squeeze. 'So now that I've met your husband, it's time for you to meet mine.'

Jessica watches Jacques over her new friend's shoulder, dawdling by the cakes at the counter. By the time he returns, they've agreed a date.

'We're having dinner on Friday the sixteenth,' Libby says as he approaches with a tray of coffee and cakes. 'Your lovely wife has checked the diary and you're both free.'

'Wonderful,' Jacques says but he doesn't smile. 'I'm sure my lovely wife will look forward to it.'

They both sit back. Libby looks amused; Jacques takes off his hat, ruffling his hair. Jessica has an odd sense of having missed something.

'Where shall we go?'

They both look at her blankly.

'Matthew will make a reservation somewhere,' Libby says after a beat. 'He's good at that kind of thing.'

'Matthew being your better half?' Jacques asks.

'My *other* half, yes.'

Sugar is added to coffees, followed by careful stirring and tentative sips. Jacques eats both the carrot cake and the chocolate cake while Jessica tries to think of something to say. She had imagined an instant, easy flow between the two of them.

'I can't remember if I told you, but Libby is a florist. She has her own shop. E.H. Flowers.'

Jacques nods. 'You said.'

The three of them reach simultaneously for their coffees.

When they say their goodbyes outside, Jessica worries that Libby's mouth looks a little tight. Jacques holds his hand up in a short farewell and goes to inspect a row of blue-glazed pots on a nearby stall.

Under her breath, Jessica says, 'I don't know what's got into him today.'

'I'll wear him down, you'll see.' Libby's voice is so low that it draws Jacques' attention. From the corner of her eye, Jessica sees him watching them from under his hat.

Blowing kisses, Libby heads back into the crowded market.

Jacques puts down the vase he was holding. 'Tell me again how you two met?'

'She was my first online customer. You and I disagreed on the price, if you remember.'

'All those hours you spent on it. She pretty much got it for free.'

She can't understand why it's upsetting him now. He'd been delighted when she came home from White's and announced she'd sold the whole range.

'No wonder she's such a fan,' he adds.

Jessica stops walking. 'As opposed to the quality of the workmanship?'

'Sorry.' Jacques takes her hand, still not looking at her. 'I'm sure she loves your jewellery.'

'What's bothering you, Jacqy?'

He is squeezing and kneading her knuckles. 'Why would you want to be friends with a woman like that?'

'A woman like what?' Jessica raises her eyebrows at him. Jacques is the most tolerant, easy-going person she knows.

'I just don't get it.' He drops her hand, pushing his deep into his pockets, shoulders hunched. 'You're a very different person to her.'

'Exactly. I like that.'

'She's all glitz and no substance. You can't trust someone like her.'

The way he is keeping his eyes dead ahead makes Jessica suddenly uncomfortable. 'Is it because you found her attractive?'

'What? Christ, Jessica.' It's Jacques' turn to stop walking. 'I do not find her attractive.'

'You don't have to pretend she's not.'

He shakes his head. 'Can we stop talking about her now?'

She doesn't try to take his arm again and it feels odd walking side by side, not touching. 'Weren't you the one who thought I needed more friends?'

4

March 2012

Clerkenwell Artists' Studio is hidden inside the white, anonymous flanks of a converted warehouse. It faces a water tower protected by a high wire fence. Approaching the studio, Jessica's pace increases. The narrow side street feels both deserted and watched; she always has the sense of unfriendly observation.

She steps over a fresh collection of windblown newspapers and polystyrene cups into a stairwell with white, eczema-patched walls. Skipping up the stairs to the second floor, she pushes open the glass and wire doors to the studio. Light and space envelop her as she catches her breath.

The studio takes up the whole floor, reaching high into the rafters where unbalanced pigeons flap and shit. Morgan, a painter of urban landscapes, sometimes leaves his wet canvases out overnight to catch their white splatters.

The studio is open-plan, roughly divided by the

territorial overspill of tools and workbenches. Five artists share the space. Herself and one other jeweller, Serena; Neil, a potter who looks barely old enough to shave but six years ago became one of the Clerkenwell Studios' founding artists; and two painters, Janey-Sue and Morgan.

This morning their benches are messy with interrupted work and dirty mugs. No one is in.

Jessica sits at her bench with a coffee. Shoves a pile of sketchbooks and loose scraps of unrealised designs under the desk. Today she wants to work with her fingers, to pour herself into the tiny, mundane tasks that give birth piecemeal to the trinkets in her head.

She spends the day soldering links for a charm bracelet and polishing a set of rings, barely registering Morgan's arrival sometime after lunch. As the sun drops below the skylights, she displays her work across the desk and hugs her elbows with satisfaction.

Looking across at Morgan, she says, 'Bitter shandy and a packet of peanuts?'

After such intense, intricate focus, her head feels detached from her body, as though she's viewing everything from far away. She needs the press and noise of other people to pull her back into her physical surroundings before going home to an empty flat.

But Morgan is gnawing his thumbnail, glowering at an unfinished canvas. He shakes his head without looking up.

When she gets home, she finds Jacques in the bedroom, doing sit-ups.

'You're back early.' Leaping on him, she pinions his wrists to the floor. 'Is it my birthday?'

'If only.' His damp hug squeezes the life back into her body. 'Dinner with the Hargreaves, remember?'

'It's a miracle she's not cancelled after your sulk last Wednesday.' Jessica tries not to smile.

'So, I was a little out of sorts.'

'But Jacqy, you are never out of sorts.'

'I hadn't expected to come home from a long day at work to find your new best friend settled in for the night.' He had sat at the desk, facing the window, glass of wine in hand, his silence a great boulder around which Libby and Jessica had been forced to manoeuvre their conversation.

Jessica climbs off him. 'We don't have to go if you really don't want to.'

'I'm happy to do it for you. Just don't get carried away and invite them back for coffee. There's only so much Libby I can stand in one evening.'

He runs a bath, and when it is full they both get in. Jessica hangs her legs over the side of the tub, painting her toenails while Jacques scans work notes, topping up the hot water.

'What is it, exactly, that you don't like about Libby?'

Jacques puts down his work. 'Her best-friend act.'

'Why would it be an act?' Jessica frowns down at him, stepping out of the bath.

'Just seems a bit keen.' He fills his palm with far too much shampoo and lathers up his hair. 'Does she have to see so much of you? Or drop by whenever you can't come out to play?'

Jacques slips below the surface, scrubbing his scalp with such vigour that water slops over the rim of the bath. When he re-emerges, she leans over him, dangling her wet hair in his face.

'What?' he asks, catching her grin.

She kisses his wet face. 'I don't like sharing you either, Jacqy.'

They meet Libby and Matthew in a Highbury steakhouse with long trestle tables and bull heads on the wall. Libby arrives ahead of her husband, a commotion of kisses and hugs and perfume. When they sit down, Jacques slips his foot around Jessica's, ankles touching. There's a slick of Libby's lipstick on his cheek like a small, deep gash. Jessica rubs it away with her thumb.

'A little . . . smut, that's all,' she whispers when he turns to look at her.

Matthew, having parked the car, makes his way through the diners, frowning as if he's woken up in a strange place. Half his shirt hangs over his belt and his jacket hangs boxily off his shoulders, making him appear gaunt. Beside Libby, he looks like an unmade bed. Jessica finds herself studying their casual automatism as Libby holds out her hand for the car keys and Matthew takes her coat. She wants to peek beneath the public skin of their marriage and see what binds them. Wonders how people see her and Jacques.

Once the drinks have been ordered, there's silence as they read their menus. Libby barely glances at hers. Putting it down, she catches Jessica's eye and winks.

Jessica smiles back. 'Chosen already?'

'I'm here for the conversation, not the food.'

Jacques brings his head up sharply. 'Can't live on talk alone.'

Under the table, Jessica squeezes his knee.

'Good point, Jacques.' Libby smiles sweetly at him. 'We need talk *and* kisses to sustain us.'

'I think your work is wonderful.' Matthew shifts his chair to face Jessica. 'So clever the way you use commonplace materials, a little subversive, even. So what does a day in the life of a jewellery designer look like?'

She gives him the bare bones of her day at the studio and though he makes no comment, his eyes don't leave hers. He has a knack, Jessica decides, for listening.

The waiter brings a round of vodka tonics and a bottle of Pinot Noir, after which the evening relaxes into an easier flow.

'What about first love?' Libby poses the question to the whole table. Matthew nods, giving it due attention.

'Alas, my wife's still searching.' Jacques strokes Jessica's earlobe. She loves the way he deflects personal questions.

Libby isn't satisfied.

'How about *your* first love then, Jacques?' She's talking loudly, with her mouth full, somehow making it look adorable. 'If you say Jessica I shall die of boredom.'

And even though Jessica knows it was a girl called Valentina at his junior high school, he says, 'It was Jessica.'

Libby purses her mouth. 'I've been meaning to ask you about your name.'

Jessica stiffens. Libby already knows the story behind Jacques' name. In a moment of weakness, Jessica told Libby a secret that wasn't hers to give away.

'You're American, aren't you?'

'Yes, ma'am,' Jacques says, tipping an invisible cowboy hat. His eyes flicker to Jessica's, and she manages to give him a sympathetic smile while resisting the urge to kick Libby under the table.

'Then why *Jacques*, and not good old stars-and-stripes *Jack*?'

Jessica pictures Libby's expression of scandalised delight when she explained that Jacques' mother told him the truth behind his name's origin on his tenth birthday and then swore him to secrecy. She'd named her son after her first lover, a Parisian exchange student, not – as he'd grown up believing – the famous underwater explorer, Jacques Cousteau. He was never to tell his beloved father and for this very reason, Jessica knows, her husband abhors secrets and dishonesty.

'You know us Yanks,' Jacques drawls out his accent. 'We're suckers for a bit of European sophistication.'

Libby's eyes meet Jessica's for a finger-snap second. 'It's a gorgeous name for a gorgeous man.'

She takes a slow drink of her wine, then leans across the table to stroke Jessica's sleeve.

'Seven weeks ago today I sent you an email saying how much I liked your jewellery, did you know that?' Raising her glass, she says, 'Let's make a toast to how much more fun the world is when we're together.'

Matthew takes a slim camera from inside his jacket and asks the waiter to take a photograph. Jessica pictures how the four of them might look to the outside world. A tight, closed circle. Libby bestows her friendship like a gift; she can't help but be flattered.

The next morning, Jessica potters about the flat in Jacques' green dressing gown. It's her favourite time of day, the flat full of early light, windows open to weed out the smell of sleep and exhaled alcohol. Jacques has gone running, and she has the place to herself. She makes coffee and thinks about the night before.

A touch, she remembers.

Jacques had relaxed enough to tease Libby about her series of car prangs – *Driving 'Near-miss' Daisy* – and Libby had leaned in, laughing as she squeezed his forearm, his shirtsleeve puckering under her nails. The touch fascinated Jessica; she's never been able to touch people so casually.

When Jacques comes home, he is springy with energy, his face raw with cold. He showers, dresses and starts chopping vegetables for the Sunday roast.

Jessica joins him in the kitchen with her sketchpad. 'How's the Arden Group thing going?'

'I want the walls to billow out like sails.'

'Sounds complex.'

'You have no idea.' He puts down the potato peeler so he can cup her face. His fingers smell earthy. 'Buildings don't just . . .'

'. . . grow out of the ground like trees.'

'So you do listen.' Jacques' thumb strokes her temple. 'The structure of a building is as complicated as the human body. Take your eyelashes, for example. They

35

are a particular length, placed at just the right angle to protect your eye without interfering with your vision. It's all measurements and angles.'

'And I thought you just liked green eyes.'

'I never underestimate the influence of colour.' He touches his lips to each of her eyelids then goes back to his vegetables at the kitchen sink. On a blank page, Jessica chases his moving lines in charcoal against the light of the window.

'Honey, I hate to do this but—'

Jessica closes her pad. 'The office?'

'After lunch.' He goes back to her, puts his hands on her waist. 'Don't be upset.'

She kisses his forehead. 'Upset is ripping at your shirt so all the buttons fly off, shouting "liar".' *Upset* was what her mother used to do.

Jacques smiles. 'In that case, I'm grateful you're not upset.'

She almost tells him about the little pad Birdie used to keep, noting down the length of her father's absences. Searching for a pattern.

Jessica rounds on the mess in the kitchen, scrubbing grease off roasting tins with freshly boiled water that leaves her skin red, sensitive to the touch. When the phone rings, she doesn't rush to answer, knowing it's her mother's weekly phone call.

'I'm selling Purbrook Rise.'

Birdie always opens the conversation with a particular piece of news, as if there must be a purpose to their Sunday chats.

'Have you had an offer?' She won't give her mother the satisfaction of sounding shocked.

'Not yet, but my agent says I can add twenty per cent on its actual value and one of your lot will still snap it up.'

'My lot?'

'Londoners.'

'He's probably right.'

'It always was an ugly house.'

Jessica rubs the sore skin on the backs of her hands. 'Where will you go?'

'I'm moving into one of the caravans.' Her mother pauses. 'Han and Lisa have already taken their things.'

'Can it wait for the weekend, so Jacques and I can drive down?'

'A car won't be necessary. You can probably bin most of it.'

Jessica wishes her luck with the viewings, trying to remember where she hid her emergency cigarettes.

She finds a crumpled pack of Marlboro Lights in a pocket of her winter coat. The wind rattles the bedroom window – a sound she suddenly remembers from the bedroom she and Hannah used to share. They used to stuff newspaper in the gaps of the old sash to make it stop.

Putting on the heavy woollen coat, she unlocks a narrow door hidden behind a curtain in their bedroom. It leads to a two-tier flat roof. Lit cigarette in mouth, she climbs the metal ladder to the top level. There's nothing to sit on. In summer they'd furnished it with chairs and pots of geraniums, until the neighbours informed them that planning permission was required to convert the roof into a terrace. Jessica refuses to stop using it. It's her favourite part of the flat. She does a little tap dance for the Silverstons' benefit, in full view of the lit but deserted office blocks. No one's working on a Sunday evening. Except Jacques.

When he comes home a few hours later, she's potting tomatoes in the bathroom. As he walks in, she notices the soil she's spilled on the floor. Before he can comment, she says, 'Birdie's selling her house.'

'You're kidding? Are you OK with it?'

'When did I last even visit?' Jessica shrugs. 'I am going down there tomorrow to sort through my stuff.'

'If you wait until the weekend, I can come with you.'

'Birdie insisted on tomorrow.' A white lie. White lies don't count.

If her mother searches hard enough, she'll find the sea-dragon box and the terrible memories it keeps. The thought makes her nauseous. Even now, seventeen years later, she needs to keep Thomas a secret.

5

The estate agent's yellow sign swings in the wind, standing out like a brilliant weed against the weathered fence. It isn't just the sign that makes Jessica hesitate. The swing her mother made from an old dining-room chair is gone, and the azalea bushes she once played hide-and-seek in have been replaced by neat rockeries.

A man is working at the flowerbeds with a trowel. Seeing her, he winces to his feet and disappears behind the house. Jessica has never known her mother to part with good money for outside help. Another sign of Birdie's determination to be done with the place.

She checks her reflection in the window of a parked car. Her hair is escaping its black plastic grip, falling around her face. *Hair like a firework*, Birdie used to say, tugging a brush through Jessica's night-tangles. She ties her hair back with a rubber band from the bottom of her bag.

Before she can open the gate, Birdie is standing in the front door, arms folded.

'You said the weekend.'

'I thought I'd surprise you.'

'Well. You've done that.' Her mother doesn't smile. 'I've barely touched your room.'

'That's why I'm here. To help.'

Birdie steps aside as Jessica reaches the porch. 'I'll make tea.'

As always, the wooden baldness of the house shocks her. A blue corduroy jacket – presumably the gardener's – has been slung over the banister in the hall, its vibrant colour disturbing the blank room.

In the kitchen, the gardener is washing mud off his trowel in the sink. Instead of telling him off, her mother offers him a cup of tea, her hand hovering above his sleeve, not quite touching.

As he heads out into the garden, Birdie refuses to catch Jessica's eye. They watch him from the kitchen window as he bends to deadhead a small rose bush. It gives Jessica a sudden picture of her father in his shabby red turtleneck, pushing his fringe back as he tended his plants. She turns her back to the window.

'You never mentioned a gardener.'

As her mother lays crockery on a tea tray, Jessica notices cosmetic dust tracing the fine lines of her skin. It springs another memory – of her father scrubbing a flannel across Birdie's cheeks before one of their rare nights out. *Why would you want to hide that beautiful skin?* And her mother submitting, eyes liquid with what Jessica now recognises as love.

Feeling her scrutiny, her mother looks across. 'You take sugar, don't you?'

'Three. Same as ever.'

Birdie carries a mug of black tea out to the gardener while Jessica takes the tray into the sitting room. Standing in the doorway, she tries to remember how it once looked – before her mother threw all the furniture on a huge bonfire. It hits her every time she visits. How she and her sisters adapted to such a changed home. No furniture, and no father.

She notices the apple crate has been replaced by a DIY coffee table in lemon-yellow wood. Jessica puts the tray on it and sits down on a camping stool.

Apart from the cheap coffee table, the room is as bare and unwelcoming as ever. Birdie's collection of birds' eggs has grown, glass jars lining the skirting boards, filled with fragments of blue, cream and speckled egg-shell. It wakes another uncomfortable memory; her mother coming home after one of her long walks, an empty blackbird egg cupped in her hand as tenderly as if it were a living thing. The dry sound like a tiny itch as it settled on top of the other broken shells. When no one was looking, Jessica had tipped them out and ground them into the floorboards, the delicious crispness of them under her foot.

'There was always something wrong with this house.' Birdie joins her a few minutes later, standing in the doorway, shaking her head. 'It was never a home.'

'That's not true. Though burning all the furniture didn't help.'

Her mother ignores the remark, sipping her tea. 'I should have trusted my instincts when I first saw the place, but he loved it. I let myself be persuaded.'

He. The reference to her father shocks Jessica into voicing a sudden thought. 'That's why you're selling it now because—'

'He was never coming back, in any case.'

But you hoped. She wonders what happened the day Birdie picked up her post and found the black card with embossed letters looping under the sorrowful weight of their message. A penned scrawl had been added to Jessica's invitation, begging her to attend the funeral. It was that which had prompted the fury of her reply; her words driven in, defacing the discreet gold lettering.

As far as I'm concerned, he's been dead seventeen years already. I didn't mourn him then and I won't now.

Jessica tops up her mug though she is yet to drink from it; the clink of crockery loud against their silence. 'Han, Lisa and I were born here.'

'Too much pain trapped inside these walls.' Her mother sighs. 'At least in hospital everything is scrubbed clean again.'

Birdie can still suck the air out of a room.

'You finally bought a coffee table.'

'The estate agent insisted. Said the crate and camping stools would make it difficult for potential buyers to imagine it as a home.'

'He had a point.'

Her mother lowers herself into a folding camp stool. 'I'm moving into Caravan Thirty-Three.'

Jessica nods, staring into her tea. 'I don't think I ever said sorry about the eggshells.'

Birdie looks at her. Jessica can't tell if she remembers the crushed eggs. 'I felt awful about it straight away.'

'Well.' Her mother gets up again. 'I've left your things in a box. I'll go to the tip later with anything you're not going to take.'

Jessica follows her mother to the bedroom she once shared with her older sister. Except for a large removal box, the room is bare. There are two wine-red rectangles of carpet where their beds used to be.

'The Tesco bag is also yours.' Her mother points to a bag by the doorway. 'Don't forget it. And your secret box is still in the chimney.'

Jessica crosses her arms, digging nails into her closed fists. She listens for her mother's feet on the stairs before kneeling by the hearth. The tiles shine in the pale afternoon light, their hand-painted birds lifting out of the ceramic. They've been polished; no telltale sprinkles of soot to inform her whether the box has been disturbed in its hiding place. She slides the back of her hand inside the flue until her nails touch metal. As she lifts the box off the brick lip onto her spread fingertips, it tips away, almost falling, heavier than she remembered.

The tin is coated in a layer of blackened rust and bird-droppings. The grime hides a painted sea dragon on the lid. Jessica scrapes at the grey droppings. Flakes of rust with a brilliant blue underside come away in her fingers. The sea dragon can't be saved.

'Joss and I are going to the garden centre.' Her mother reappears at the door. They both look down at the box. 'Mind you don't make a mess of the carpet.'

Jessica cradles her box, listening to the low hum of

voices in the hallway, followed by the sound of the front door closing.

A pile of newspapers, crisp with age, lies beside the packing boxes. Jessica folds a yellowed *Selcombe Messenger* around her treasure box before placing it into the bottom of her rucksack. She doesn't bother to look at the rest of her belongings in the packing box. On her way out, she picks up the Tesco bag from the doorway. Another newspaper lies just inside. Before she can discard it, the headline catches her attention.

Local Jeweller Dazzles London

Unfolding the stiff, crackling paper, she discovers a photograph of herself at her first exhibition stand, surrounded by customers craning over her necklaces, oblivious to the photographer. Her face is wide-eyed, wary, as though a noise that no one else could hear had startled her. The force of the moment returns with the flashing camera, the genial pestering of the photographer and her dizzying nerves. Then she spots Jacques, standing close, his head turned away in distraction and yet his hand lifting slightly towards her. Always taking care of her. Jessica smiles; Hannah always said his was a profile fit for a coin.

Folding the newspaper back into the Tesco bag, she draws out an item of clothing folded beneath. The material looks familiar – a man's tweed jacket with velvet elbow patches. The sight of it stops her dead.

Sliding two fingers into the breast pocket, she finds a scrap of paper. Tweezing it out, she flattens it against her knee.

A pint of cream,
streaky bacon,
1 onion,
2 bottles of chianti!!
and you.
xxxx
PS a box of Frosties while you're there!

With trembling fingers, she refolds the little shopping list along its worn lines. Squashing the jacket back into the bag, she ties the handles into a tight knot.

She's an hour early for the afternoon train, and Platform Two is empty. Opposite her, the sea wall keeps the shingle off the tracks, the beach hidden from view. She hears the water hissing against the shoreline. The air is mild and behind the seagull cries, she can hear a blackbird singing. The first sound of spring.

Taking the dragon box out of her rucksack, she holds it on her lap. She has spent all these years trying to forget its contents.

She calls Jacques. 'I'm on my way home.'

'Already, hon?'

'There wasn't much to do.'

He pauses. 'Sweetie, I thought you were going to stay the night? I'm working late, remember?'

'It's OK.' The solid fact of his voice is enough. 'Wake me up when you get in.'

'I hope you didn't let Birdie upset you.'

'I'm fine, Jacqy.' Which isn't true. Seeing Birdie makes her restless in her own skin, like the onset of fever. With a deep breath, she prises open the sea-dragon box.

Newspaper clippings spring up, threatening to over-spill. Topmost is the grainy picture of a young boy sitting on a harbour wall. The sun is hitting him sideways so half his face is in shadow. He looks so young, it hurts her.

She thinks about calling Jacques again for the comfort of his voice. Only she can't tell him about the box and its secrets. Not yet.

In the corner of the tin, she finds a collection of stones. When she scoops them up, they fall into a familiar shape – a bracelet of grey and white beach pebbles strung on blue twine. Pressing the bracelet to her mouth, she roots through loose sketches – the caravan park, cartoon winter trees – until she finds something red and hard hidden beneath the whispery paper.

A notebook bound in crimson leather – one she's never seen before.

Frowning, she flicks through it and finds a stranger's handwriting, neat and rounded, filling every page. She can't make any sense of it. Putting the book aside, Jessica returns to the picture, staring at it until the boy's face pixelates into black and grey dots.

Thomas.

6

February 1995, Seasalt Holiday Park, Selcombe

Hannah was trying to get out of walking the dog, even though it was her turn.

'I'll give you a quid.'

'Forget it.' Jessica pointed at the overcast sky. 'It's going to rain.'

'Two.'

Jessica closed her homework. 'A week's pocket money or nothing.'

'Fuck's sake,' Hannah mouthed, keeping her eyes on their mum. But Birdie wasn't listening, her hands peeling potatoes in the sink, her head somewhere else. 'Three, then.'

'Done.' What Hannah didn't know was how badly Jessica wanted to get out of the house. The thought of another evening with her mother shadowing her dad, hissing like a cat under her breath, was unbearable.

She made her sister hand over the coins before she left.

'Keep an eye out for Bloody Russian,' Hannah said, crushing a mix of twenty- and fifty-pence pieces into Jessica's palm.

'I'm not scared of that old nutter.'

'You haven't heard what he did to Leona's big sister, then?'

Despite herself, she had to know. 'What?'

Hannah shrugged, her eyes creasing into a fat grin. 'If I tell you now, you won't dare walk Kezy.'

Jessica rattled her fist of coins. 'You're the one who's too scared to go outside.'

Closing the front door on her sister, she felt better, like peeling off a wet jumper. She reminded herself that the tramp hung around the school, not the beach. Tickling the top of Kezy's head, she clipped on the leash. The terrier bounded around Jessica's feet, the flopped triangle of her ears shivering with excitement.

She headed for Crowline Avenue so she could spy on the massive houses with their swimming pools and tennis courts. The lawns had neat rockeries with prim flowers, while her garden sprouted random patches of early daffodils and crocuses. Bloody Russian wouldn't come here. Someone would call the police as soon as they saw his crusty face and broken shoes.

Jessica started to sing, making the Jack Russell glance back, doggy-grinning, flipping out her bad leg.

The last house on the avenue was the Seawitch Nursing Home. Past it, there was nothing but a wasteland of scrub and sand dunes leading to the empty coast. No one ever went there, not even the tourist coaches, because everyone knew it was haunted.

Years ago, when her mother was young, a teenager had vanished there, his body never found. Jessica couldn't bear to think of his lonely bones. She'd be the one to find them – if she ever dared walk that far. She felt it in the same way her mother always knew when it would snow.

Reaching the nursing home, Jessica sat on the low garden wall as Kezy sniffed around her feet. Suddenly the dog darted across the deserted car park.

'Hey. Come back.'

Jessica watched in horror as the terrier nosed her way under the fence and into the gorse; a flash of white wire wool racing through the scrub. By the time she'd taken a few steps past the fence, brambles plucking at her trouser-legs, Kezy seemed impossibly far away. She couldn't bring herself to shout, standing there all alone on the edge of that vast, watchful space.

She'd tell her dad how Kezy had run off, and he'd come back later and find the stupid dog. He'd understand. He wouldn't want his daughter walking alone in that place.

Then the Jack Russell gave a single, shrill bark and Jessica knew she couldn't leave her there. Biting the inside of her cheek to stop the rising tears, she tore deep into the knee-high gorse.

She ran in soundless panic, eyes on the beach ahead, afraid to look down and see what awful things might be sticking out of the ground. Something cut into her ankle, pitching her to her knees, and the silence caught her. Keeping to a crouch, she brushed dirt from her trousers and peered over her shoulder. She was deep into the wasteland, the car park as far from her as the distant stripe of sand. Kezy was nowhere to be seen. The wind made a noise like whispered voices through the dry gorse and she hunched closer to the ground, holding her breath.

Then she spotted Kezy's little brown head bobbing along the dunes and jumped to her feet. Ignoring the twinge in her left ankle, she started to run again. The tight mesh of brambles gave way to sand and seagrass. Fringe glued to her forehead, lungs shrinking, Jessica finally reached the shore.

Kezy leaped at her, paws pattering her legs as she caught her breath. She pushed the dog away. 'Bad girl. Horrid dog.'

She sat down on the cool sand, delaying the walk back across the haunted dunes. A dark hand of cloud pressed down from the sky, squeezing brilliance from the light beneath. A fisherman's boat passed close to the shore, the rumble of its engine sucked out to sea as though the gathering storm had drawn in a huge breath.

It was then that Jessica realised she wasn't alone.

Further along the beach, a boy was standing with his feet in the surf. Stomach tumbling over, she wondered how she hadn't noticed him until now. In the strange light, it was hard to see him clearly, his silhouette blurring against the water like he was made of shadow. He was too tall and skinny to be the Russian tramp.

She'd found the missing boy.

The funny thing is, she didn't feel frightened. He was oblivious to her, trapped in his own place. Standing motionless, he stared into the water that swelled around his shins.

Impressed by her own daring, Jessica watched him. 'It's OK,' she told Kezy. 'He can't see us.'

Then the ghost moved, and she noticed he was holding a stick. He raised it in a slow arc over his head, breaking the motion with a sharp flick of the wrist, and a line caught in the sea. The ghost was fishing.

'This is what the boy must have been doing, Kez. Catching fish off the beach. Then something bad happened to him.'

The ghost lifted his arm again and a large fish swam through the sky. He freed the hook from its mouth in one easy movement, his hands gentle. Then he brought the fish down hard against the surface of the beach. There was no sound.

Kezy trotted towards him before Jessica could call her back. As her dog sniffed the catch, the ghost ruffled her head. The contact shocked Jessica. If he could see the terrier, he could see her too. She sat rigid, afraid to move and catch his attention.

Picking up the fish, he started walking towards her, Kezy at his side. Jessica was furious with the dog all over again. Pushing her fingers into the sand, she watched him from the corner of her eye. As he got closer, she stopped looking, concentrating on digging pebbles from the damp sand. She couldn't help lifting her head when he walked past. He looked down at her with the palest eyes – the colour of bones under the sky.

But he was no ghost: a boy, some years older than

herself. He didn't smile, though she had the feeling he was amused. He'd known she was there all along.

A drop of blood from the fish landed on a pale stone by her shoe. She was struck by how beautiful the red looked against the white. When she was sure the boy had gone, she put the stone in her pocket.

7

Jessica tried not to think about the boy on the beach. The more she thought about him, the less real he seemed. She pictured him with brilliant evening light shining through his skin, his eyes blind-white. The drop of fish blood on the pebble had dried to a rust spot, and she wondered if it had been nothing more than a ghost trick.

She could feel the boy watching her; out in the garden at night, peeping through the crack in the cupboard door, behind her closed eyes. When her dad came to kiss her goodnight, she pressed his warm, dry palm across her eyes until the boy disappeared.

Her mother caught her late one night staring out of the bedroom window.

'What are you doing?'

'Nothing.'

'Let's go downstairs.' Birdie nodded at Hannah's

53

sleeping figure in the next bed. 'I'm making hot chocolate.'

Jessica sat at the kitchen table, thinking how long it had been since her mother had last made hot chocolate.

'Hannah says you haven't been taking your turn to walk Kezy,' her mother said as she heated milk in the pan.

'What about Lisa? How come she doesn't have to walk the dog?'

Birdie put out a single cup, spooned in cocoa powder and poured in the hot milk, slopping some of it down the sides. She sat down, ignoring the spillage. That was how she was these days; careless.

'What's worrying you, Jess?'

'Nothing.'

Her mother nodded, looking up at the clock, and Jessica realised she just wanted company as she waited for Jessica's father to come home. Birdie took a brush from the pocket of her dressing gown. Head tilted to one side, she pulled the bristles through her hair until it undulated like a silk handkerchief. Jessica wanted to wave her hand through it to feel it slip off her skin. Her own hair always split into messy waves.

'Actually I'm scared of going near the sand dunes where that boy disappeared.'

Now she had Birdie's attention. 'Has a boy disappeared?'

'The one you told me about. That boy who went for a walk and all they found were his socks and shoes.'

'That was a long time ago.' Like marbles on a tilting

plate, her mother's eyes kept sliding sideways towards the clock.

'Can you tell me the story again?'

Her mother picked loose strands of hair from the brush. 'Well. The strange thing was he'd tied his shoelaces together and walked off barefoot.'

Barefoot. Jessica shuddered. The boy on the beach hadn't been wearing any shoes either. The marbles tilted again. Then her mother sighed, dropping the brush back into her pocket and pulling her sleeves over her wrists. 'I knew him, actually.'

'You knew him? You never said.'

'Not very well.' Birdie took her knitting from a drawer in the dresser where Jessica's dad stacked his vet magazines. 'He used to help his father at the farmer's market in Brigham. He was always laughing at things that weren't funny.'

Jessica's hands had gone cold. She wove her fingers around the mug. 'What did he look like?'

'Plain. Brown hair, blue eyes. He gave me a red paper flower once. He was an odd one.' Her mother's fingers were a little machine she'd switched on and left running. Hands busy, her eyes were free to stare openly at the clock on the wall.

'I'm scared I'll find his skeleton if I take Kezy for a walk.'

'Walk somewhere else then. The forest, or Selcombe Bay.' Birdie was no longer part of the conversation. She'd put her voice on automatic, along with her hands.

'Where's Dad?'

Her mother sat up as if she'd been pinched. 'Work.

55

There's some kind of virus at the Matthews' farm. Or maybe the pub. He needs to unwind.'

Jessica left her chocolate and went to bed.

The next day the ghost found her.

He was standing under the birch tree opposite the school gates, half hidden beneath the low-slung boughs. Where a heatless February sun dropped through the branches, it lay on him like spatters of white paint. He was smoking a cigarette – a detail which made her a little less afraid. Ghosts don't smoke rollies. He was also wearing shoes. The other girls noticed him as well. His presence was like a sudden breeze through a tree; he had them all flapping and fluttering. Boys at the school gate were always big news. Jessica pretended to look through her school bag, hanging back as her schoolmates linked arms, grew bolder in their huddle and tossed looks over their shoulders.

She allowed herself a moment to study him. Everything about him was light and windblown; sand-dune hair spilling over his forehead and ears, almost reaching the neck of his t-shirt. Eyes wide and brilliant with a trace of colour, suspended in the tree's shadow with a light of their own. Like the eyes of a nocturnal animal caught in headlights – a flash of reflected light, a body concealed in darkness.

He was slim and long-limbed, arms hanging loose, cigarette smoke curling up his wrist. His stance lacked the usual, self-conscious posturing of older boys. It made him look poised; ready to run. Or pounce. Jessica shivered and gathered up her bag.

When he spotted her, he lifted his head a little. He didn't smile, so she walked on past him. Once she left the main road where the mothers who didn't work collected their daughters, it became clear she was being followed. Someone was walking behind her, whistling. They were alone now on the lane that led uphill past the rust-pocked sign to the Seasalt Holiday Park. She wasn't afraid. Bloody Russian hadn't been spotted for over a week, and he always made himself obvious when he was there, pretending to lunge at the girls, jabbering in his funny language.

Ghost Boy was following her. She walked all the way home without looking back.

Two days later, he was back at the school gates.

This time she scrabbled up a handful of stones as he followed, throwing a pebble high over her head to see what he might do. The stone never landed. So she threw another and another, grinning all the way home as he caught the stones. The next morning, there was a neat pyramid of pebbles outside the front door.

He followed her home again a week later, on a spring day of such early heat that everyone was red-faced and giddy with the foretaste of summer. She cut through waist-high fields of oilseed rape and into the woods, where she took her time picking red campion and lilac-veined wood sorrel, whose leaves her mother put in salads. There was no sound; just the lazy two-note of a distant cuckoo, and the occasional snap and rustle as Ghost Boy followed behind. Bending to pick flowers, she could see him from the corner of her eye, her heart double-bounding. The sun fell through the trees and poured through her body. She wondered if he was watching the light on her hair.

He was, she imagined, keeping her safe on the long walk to her house.

As soon as she got home, the warm, sleepy feeling vanished. It was an angry heat in her house, thick and airless. That night, with Hannah cursing and kicking at her covers in the bed beside her, Jessica lay perfectly still, listening. Her mother's raised voice seeped into their room through the floorboards like smoke.

'Why does she hate Dad so much?'

'Because she's scared he doesn't love her any more,' her sister said. 'Now shut up. I'm trying to sleep.'

It was the bad feeling in the house that finally made her confront Ghost Boy. The next time he followed her, she got halfway home and stopped dead without looking around, silently daring him. He shuffled grit under his shoes, then came and stood beside her.

'Why are you following me?'

She saw his face up close for the first time. His eyes were as grey as winter sea, and there was a scar like a comma at the corner of his mouth. She wondered how it would feel to the tip of her tongue.

He shrugged. 'I like your red hair.'

'Everyone likes my hair.'

'I'm going to keep following you.'

She smiled for the first time that day.

'I thought you were a ghost when I saw you on the beach,' she said, and he seemed to like that thought.

'I'm Thomas,' he said. 'Sometimes I am a ghost.'

8

Because of gymnastics, Tuesdays were bad days.
Jessica put her jeans over her school tights,
pulled a pair of Hannah's hockey socks on top and got
back into bed with the covers up to her chin. By the
time her mother came to see why she hadn't come down
for breakfast, her face was burning.

'I don't feel well,' was all she had to say. Her mother,
whose eyes never once missed a trick, just nodded. She
didn't even feel her forehead.

'It's changeover at the park today. You'll have to go
with your dad on his rounds.' There were three furrows
on her mother's brow like stick lines in wet sand. Jessica
wanted to rub them out with her thumb.

Before she could shimmy off her jeans beneath the
covers, her dad walked in with a glass of water. He
shook his closed fist. 'Aspirins, sweetheart.'

With a cool hand he felt the glands under her jaw,
asked her to stick out her tongue.

'Is it rabies?' she asked.

'Worse.' He shook his head, frowning. 'Badger flu.'

Jessica giggled, then remembered she was supposed to be ill.

'You're quite hot, though. You should stay in bed. I'll only be gone a few hours.'

Jessica hesitated, then kicked off her covers.

Her dad rubbed his chin. 'I see.'

'Are you going to tell on me?'

'Not this time.' He left her to get dressed.

She decided to wear her denim jacket and Hannah's brooch that said TRUE LOVE in pink, glittery letters. There'd be time to sneak it back in the drawer before her sister came home from school.

'Coast's clear, Jess,' her dad called up. 'Your mum has left the building.'

She found him at the hallway mirror, running a hand through his hair, inspecting his shaving with a funny sideways twist of his mouth.

'Mum's right. You're so vain.'

'Just want to look good for my girl.' He threw her the car keys. 'I'll be out in a moment.'

Jessica unlocked the car. Her dad, who was quite messy about the house, kept the inside of his car spotless so there were no magazines or random flyers to look at while she waited for him.

He came out, swinging his vet's case. As they drove, he fiddled with the radio, humming to snatches of music before twisting the dial again. They stopped in Spentley first, and ordered a wedge of carrot cake with an inch of butter-cream icing.

'So what's new?' Her dad pointed at Hannah's badge. '*Are* you in love?'

'I'm thirteen, Dad.'

'I was in love all the time at your age.'

Jessica rolled her eyes. 'There aren't even any boys at my school.' Then, because he was waiting with his eyebrows raised, she added, 'It's chemistry today. Hate chemistry.'

Which was partly true. She didn't want to have to explain to her dad about gymnastics and the undressing that went with it; her small breasts and long, straight boy's figure under the spotlight of judging eyes.

'But you like school?'

'It's all right.'

'You have friends?'

She thought about Lucy Trelawney, who checked her reflection in every shiny surface and Mary Mickelworth – Micky – who started off fun and quickly became irritating. Friends on the surface; better than spending break alone. 'Yes.'

'And your sisters are happy, aren't they?'

A bubble of anxiety was forming in her stomach though she couldn't say why.

'I guess.'

'Good.' He wasn't eating his share of the cake. 'Great stuff.'

Jessica finished the rest of the carrot cake in two huge mouthfuls before asking, 'Are we going to move away?'

'No love, no. I wouldn't take you out of school when you're happy there.'

'I'm not always.'

'And of course your mother would never sell Seasalt Park, would she?'

'Guess not.'

'Let's get going. Four visits to do today.' Her dad asked for the bill and Jessica studied his face, worrying he was going into one of his distracted moods.

At the car he said, 'I thank you,' and gave a little bow as he opened the door for her. 'The gift of your time is most precious.'

Jessica laughed because he was back to his jokey self again.

At each of the home visits, she was offered something to eat or drink – elderflower water, sticky aniseed balls covered in fluff, freshly baked cinnamon buns. To pass the time, she thought about Thomas. It was now their regular routine to walk through the woods, sometimes as far as the beach on her way home. No one seemed to notice her coming back later and later.

After her dad had treated their yappy dogs and nasty budgies, the pet owners patted her dad's arm, pressed his hands. It irritated Jessica, the way they pawed at him with fingers shiny and crooked as sticks washed up on the beach. How their hearts would have broken to hear him trying to make her laugh once they closed the front door.

Jessie, did you notice Mrs Greencage has got more whiskers than her cat?

It's not Rover that needs flea treatment, it's Mrs Palmer.

After the fourth visit, he rested his arm across her shoulders as they headed back to the car. Jessica tried to take graceful steps so he would forget his arm was there and leave it a while longer.

'Do you think you'll become a vet one day?'

Jessica hesitated. 'I want to be an artist. Mr Schaupetter says I'm not bad. Which is a big compliment, coming from him.'

'Follow your heart.' Her dad nodded to himself. 'That's my one lesson to you. Follow your heart.'

Later, as the car slowed for a red light, he said, 'You know what's missing in this age of modern conveniences and instant gratification?'

'Magic?' She could often guess the kind of answers he was looking for.

He smiled. 'Passion.'

Jessica turned her face to the window. 'People still fall in love.'

'They *think* they do.' The light had changed to green and he wasn't moving. 'Few people ever experience real passion. I don't just mean sex.'

Behind them, a car honked its horn.

'Da-ad.' The conversation was beginning to make her squirm. The car behind overtook them with further horn-blaring, a man's angry face, all jaw and brow, flying past.

'Life and death. The battle to survive. That's the kind of passion that's missing now. It's all too easy and comfortable.'

'What's so good about fighting and dying? Everyone gets hurt.'

'You're not living if you don't experience pain at some point.' He stroked her cheek. 'Let's walk to my next appointment.'

'You said there were only four visits today.'

'Five.'

They stopped outside a semi-detached bungalow in a quiet, tree-lined street. It had red curtains in the window and red flowers in the garden.

'You knock,' he said.

A woman, about her father's age, answered. She had long black hair with grey running through it like streaks of silver lacquer. She was wearing a tight pair of cords with a beautiful beaded belt and a low-buttoned blouse. When she moved her arms, her breasts rose and sank like waves above the stretched material. Jessica tried not to look; her own breasts felt ridiculous and slight under a starter bra that kept slipping upwards.

Unlike the other pet owners, this woman didn't try to touch her father. She stood in her doorway and raised an eyebrow. 'You've brought an assistant today.'

'Jessica,' her father said.

The woman bent forward until her eyes were level with Jessica's. 'And what a beautiful young girl you are, Jessica.'

'Not really.'

The woman laughed as if she'd made a joke and stepped aside to let them in.

There was a moment in the small hallway when everyone seemed to forget what they were doing. The woman was looking at Jessica and her dad was watching the woman, obviously too polite to rush her.

'Mr Peter's in the kitchen,' she finally said. 'Sitting on my clean ironing, as usual, the naughty thing.'

'Who's Mr Peter?' Jessica asked as her dad opened a door leading from the hallway.

'My poor little cat. A car hit him a month ago. Your dad's a miracle-worker.'

Jessica nearly said, *Really? I thought he was a vet.*

'You can wait in here.' She took Jessica's hand – something she would never have allowed Birdie to do – and showed her to the sitting room. 'Touch anything you like.'

The door closed and Jessica was left with the impression that she'd stepped into a dressing-up box.

She perched on a horsehair stool, hands shoved under her thighs, and tried to take everything in. The wall opposite was lined with blank-eyed masquerade masks, the light pearlescent on their porcelain cheeks. Below them, a glass table held a collection of crystals, peacock-brilliant. Drapes of material lay across the furniture, and when Jessica lifted a stiff hem of gold-embroidered fabric, there was something reassuring about the bland, stained sofa beneath; the kind of ordinary sofa they had at home, though the similarity ended there. She got up to inspect the trinkets clustered across a wall of shelves like the haul from an ancient tomb. A gathering of squat, pendulous women carved out of stone, their weight tested in her hand; a felt hat hedgehogged with glass hatpins; a collection of bead-wire crowns, the largest of which shivered with ruby droplets. Jessica lifted it onto her head – and heard her mother's voice.

Don't touch. You girls are always breaking things.

Suddenly the woman's careless offering of her treasures worried her. It was showing off, a kind of superiority. Feeling like she'd been patted on the head, Jessica dropped the crown onto a yellow silk cushion and walked to the window. A dreamcatcher filled most of it, a huge diamond suspended beneath, catching and throwing the light like a disco ball. Jessica took Hannah's brooch off and see-sawed it under the dreamcatcher so the pink plastic gems sparkled.

After a while she just stared at the empty road and the flower-pot gardens on the opposite side.

When the woman returned, she was carrying a black pot with fake gems on the lid and a mirror on a stand, which she placed beneath the dreamcatcher. 'I can't resist.'

She spread clips and hairpins across the sill. Then she began scooping up loose handfuls of Jessica's hair. The clips pinched as they were pushed into place but the stroke of the woman's hands was mesmerising. It made Jessica drowsy.

At one point, Jessica's dad popped his head round the door. 'I think Mr Peter would be less nervous if you were to hold him.'

'He's just fine,' the woman said. When Jessica's dad retreated, she said, 'Now tell me. Who do you take after?'

'I look like my dad.' *Obviously*, Jessica wanted to add.

'You have his colouring.' The woman cocked her head to one side. 'What does your mother look like?'

'All done.' They both ignored Jessica's dad as he reappeared in the doorway.

'Dad calls Mum his little brown robin.'

The woman turned to smile at Jessica's dad. 'How sweet.'

He wasn't looking pleased, and Jessica felt disloyal. A brown robin sounded plain. 'My mum's pretty. She has dark brown hair and blue eyes.'

'She sounds lovely.'

'And she has big boobs.'

'Jessica.' Her father marched into the room. 'That's inappropriate.'

But the woman was laughing. Her hands settled lightly on Jessica's shoulders. 'Now. Don't tell me that's not beautiful?'

'Oh.' Jessica studied the better, older version of herself in the mirror. The woman had worked some sort of magic.

'Look at those eyes.' The woman's face joined her reflection. 'How much they already know, even though you hide them behind all that hair.'

Jessica stood up, holding her neck and head stiff for fear of dislodging the hairgrips.

'No, no,' the woman laughed. 'Always walk like you're trying to shake your hair loose.'

Neither of them spoke as they walked back to the car. By the time they reached the high street, a few drops of rain had started to fall. With a sudden roar, it fell hard. They sheltered in the nearest shop, laughing as they brushed water from their hair.

'We don't have any umbrellas.' A middle-aged man behind the counter pointed at a poster with the charity shop's logo. 'People only ever donate broken ones.'

'In that case, we'd better buy coats, hadn't we, Jessica?'

The shop assistant pointed to a rail listing against the wall, one castor missing. Jessica wrinkled her nose. The shop smelled like dried-up sick.

Her dad was grinning with sudden mischief. 'You choose mine and I'll choose yours.'

So Jessica picked up a thick tweed jacket with green velvet lapels and matching elbow patches. Her dad hooked his thumbs through his trouser pockets and puffed out his chest as he tried it on. 'Quite the country squire, don't you think?'

For Jessica, he chose a white plastic mac with large navy buttons. It was too big and squeaked as she moved. When her dad turned up the collar and tied the belt around her waist, she was again struck by her reflection. The rain had flattened her hair but her better self was still visible.

She wished Thomas could see her now. Arms linked, Jessica and her dad marched down the empty street with the rain washing down. All the way home, she imagined Thomas catching sight of her and being struck by her new-found beauty.

At home, her mother watched without expression as they showed off their new coats.

'Best four pounds I've ever spent.' Jessica's dad held out his sleeve for her mum to feel the material. 'Though it smells like someone died in it.'

It was only later, when Jessica was sneaking Hannah's drawer open, that she realised she had left the TRUE LOVE brooch on the windowsill beneath the dreamcatcher.

Weeks later, her mother finally took the coat to be dry-cleaned. Her dad had worn it in the meantime, its mustiness gradually overridden by soap and aftershave. Her mother, always practical, must have checked the pockets before she handed it in because she found a note. A shopping list in a stranger's handwriting, signed with a flourish of small x's.

9

There was shouting. The slam of the front door. Regular night-time sounds that washed over Jessica until an odd hacking noise in the garden shook her from the edge of a dream. Her first thought was Thomas. Tearing back the curtains, she discovered a figure in the darkness, swinging its arms through the air. The wind scraped back the cloud and the thing in its hands caught an edge of moonlight. An axe. Her father's hands.

Jessica dropped to the floor, afraid of being seen. Poked Hannah in the back.

'Why's Dad chopping down Mum's pear tree?'

Her sister only grunted, refusing to be roused from her sleep. Concealed by the curtains, Jessica watched. She'd seen him chopping wood plenty of times – the precise way he'd line up a log followed by an economic sweep of the blade that neatly spliced the wood. This was different. Through the patchy darkness, she could see how wildly he was swinging the blade. The impact bounced the axe off at dangerous and unpredictable angles, making him stagger backwards as if struck. Before he regained his balance, he would rush at the tree again.

'Bloody hell.' Hannah was kneeling on the bed, swaying slightly as she leaned forward to peer out of the window. 'Dad's lost the plot.'

'What's wrong with him?'

'Mum's driving him mad. Something about a note she found.'

They watched him strike the tree so hard the axe was wrenched from his hand, held fast in the bark. Hannah flopped back onto her mattress and wrapped her covers around herself again. 'Hope he doesn't come after us next, like some loony axe-murderer.'

'Very funny.' Jessica could hear his grunt of effort with every hack, growing louder until he was growling. She'd never seen this blind, unthinking fury before.

Light spilled into the garden as her mother darted out in a dressing gown; a fluttering moth that hovered soundlessly before disappearing back into the house, taking the light with her. Jessica's heart was thudding so hard she could feel it through her whole body like the shivering blows to the tree.

He began kicking at the trunk between blows, and it was starting to list and crack. Jessica couldn't bear to see it fall. Getting back into bed, she pulled her covers up and squeezed her eyes shut.

When it fell, it did so quietly. A slow, sad creak of wood followed by the sound of branches brushing the earth as if to catch its fall.

Silence. Then the front door opening and footsteps

stamping up the stairs, along the corridor. Marching past her parents' room. Jessica gave a small shriek as the door flew open. Her dad stood in the doorway – hair flopping in his face, breathing hard, the axe dangling from his hand.

'You chopped Mum's tree down.' Her voice was muffled by the covers. It was as if he hadn't heard her because he didn't move. The sound of his panting filled the room. Then he dropped onto the edge of her bed.

'Do you know where . . .' Catching his breath, trying to whisper. 'Where feelings come from, Jessie-rabbit?'

She didn't want a lesson. She wanted him to go away and return when he'd brushed his hair and put the axe away and explained in his normal, calm voice the perfectly logical reason for hacking down her mother's favourite pear tree in the middle of the night.

'Come on. Think about it.'

'Your head,' she ventured because the heart was too obvious. Her covers were suddenly whipped away as her father snatched at them. She scrambled upright, hugging her ankles.

'Wrong. Emotion comes from the deep cavities inside your body. Spaces you can't control or deny any more than you could ignore a heart attack.' Fury was making his hand shake as he wagged a finger, and yet he wasn't fully present. The anger wasn't for her.

'You can't help what you feel. None of us can. Keeping it in only makes you sick.'

It made sense. The things he said always did. Her mother had changed. Never smiling or singing any more, her face sagging and white. 'It's making Mum sick, isn't it?'

He looked shocked and didn't answer. She could tell she'd surprised him. Sometimes he forgot she wasn't a small child any more.

'Perhaps we are all sick.' With a long, deflating sigh, his spine bowed. He wiped a sleeve across his brow and combed fingers through his hair. The axe in his hand seemed to surprise him; he laid it carefully on the floor behind her bed. When he looked at her this time, it was the father she knew; as if he had woken from sleep-walking and found himself in her room.

'I'm so sorry,' he muttered, and his remorse was more alien and alarming than his frenzied attack on the tree. 'I must have scared you.'

Jessica climbed across the covers and hugged his arm, leaning her face on his shoulder. He smelled of sweat and the pub – tobacco and beer – but he was normal again.

'You're a good girl.' He patted her knee. 'My favourite since the day you were born.'

Jessica glanced at Hannah's lumpish frame. Her sister was making a purring sound that meant she'd been sipping at the little bottle under her mattress. What had started as a bit of fun – Hannah helping herself to the wine and liqueurs guests often gave Birdie, tipping their contents into an empty Jim Beam bottle – was becoming a nightly thing. *My bedtime tipple*, she'd say in Grannie Mim's wobbly voice, and laugh and laugh.

'You can't have favourites, Dad.'

'It's the truth.'

He rose to his feet like an ancient man, staring at the floor. 'Everyone has secrets, even those closest to you.' He was about to walk away when he turned and pressed his lips to her forehead. His stubble prickled her skin but she didn't want to make him more sad by shaking him off. 'It's facing your own secrets that takes the greatest courage. Remember that, Jessica.'

After he left, Jessica dug her hands deep into her stomach, trying to locate the black spaces where sorrow and anger were massing. She didn't want to think about her mother or her father or Hannah.

She decided the next time Thomas came by at night and threw pebbles at her window – as he had started to do – she would climb out of the bedroom window and kiss him. That was what the black spaces in her body wanted.

The next day, her dad went to a vet's conference. So her mother said.

Only he didn't come back.

~ 10 ~

April 2012, London

Alone in the bedroom, Jessica is thinking about a story Jacques once told her.

He and Greg Lamensky had been buddies since school. They'd drunk themselves sick on Mrs Lamensky's home-brewed hooch; competed over girls – once with fists – and slit their thumbs on the triangular mouth of a beer can to become blood brothers. One drunken night while Greg was collecting takeaway pizzas, Jacques had kissed a girl called Nancy who'd been hanging around his friend recently. He didn't mention it, assuming Greg would move on to the next one soon enough. Instead, his friend announced their engagement. Jacques confessed to the kiss, knowing how badly Greg might take it. They never spoke again. He regretted that empty kiss but not his honesty.

It was this story, Jessica thinks, that had brought Jacques into full focus; as if she'd rubbed her eyes and seen him clearly for the first time. He was, quite simply, a good person.

She smooths her thumbs across the creased, red leather of the notebook she found in the sea-dragon box. She hasn't started reading it yet – resisting it has become a test of self-control, like unwrapping a Mars Bar and putting it back in the cupboard uneaten, her mouth watering.

Jessica flicks through the pages. The notebook belonged to a woman called Albertine Callum, a counsellor at Thomas's school. She remembers the name. Bertie, Thomas used to call her, saying she was a friend. Jessica remembers also the mute, clogged feeling in her throat every time he'd been to see the woman. It is only now, with the discovery of the notebook, that she realises the full extent of their contact. Bertie had been counselling Thomas; the transcripts of those sessions were contained in the book she now hugged to her chest.

Pages and pages full of Thomas.

Jacques calls her from the kitchen. 'I'm making eggs, hon. You want some?'

She'd love nothing better than to join him, slipping her arms about his waist as he scrambles eggs in the pan. Only she can't stop thinking about the night before, which is why she's sitting alone in their bedroom, trying to clear her head.

'I'll grab something on the way to work.'

Libby had insisted on a cinema trip to the Odeon in Holloway Road. She'd booked tickets and, once they arrived, engineered the seating: Libby and Jacques in the middle, flanked on either side by Matthew and Jessica. Then the permissive darkness fell as the lights dimmed, full of surreptitious movement – popcorn-eating, shifting in the seats, reaching for a drink. All those little actions occurring just out of sight. Was there a brush of hands, the contact of a straying knee? Jessica's fingers whiten against the notebook.

Something about Libby and Jacques makes her uncomfortable. Put them in a room together and the texture of the air changes. He persists in warning Jessica about getting too close to Libby, and yet the two of them have fallen into unexpected ease in each other's company. The discrepancy unsettles her.

This is Jacques, she keeps telling herself. The man who gave up his best friend rather than live with a small dishonesty.

She has seen the damage a suspicious, questioning nature can inflict on a relationship – it drove her father out of his own home. She will not emulate her mother's behaviour. She will never question.

Hearing footsteps in the corridor, she slips the note-book under her pillow.

'How about a bagel then?' Jacques asks. 'You're wasting away on that coffee diet.' He smiles at her in the mirror as he chooses a tie. 'I'm not leaving until I get proof that you do, in fact, eat these days.'

'Not sure I have time to eat. Someone's got to sort you out.' Jessica pretends to straighten his perfectly knotted tie, brushes invisible scurf from his shoulders and runs a hand through his hair. It's their little joke because he's always pristine and she's like a cat brushed backwards.

Once he's gone, she throws her share of scrambled egg in the bin. He left looking happy, she thinks. As a reward for keeping her faithless nature to herself, she'll start reading Bertie's notes.

The shops haven't opened yet as she catches the tube at Oxford Circus. She finds a seat with no obvious stains, which gives a warm sag as she sits down. The carriage is empty except for two women in identical blue tunics with brass name-tags. Their conversation winds a soft thread around the metal squeal of the track. The rocking carriage makes her sleepy. When her stop arrives, she's reluctant to get up. Perhaps she's a little afraid of the book's contents.

William Mansion's is a ten-minute walk from Green Park. Its black fascia and gold lettering stand out like an ink blot in the pastel row of shop fronts. Four years, she has worked here but every time she pulls back the iron grille and steps into the jeweller's warm, cluttered interior she experiences the same thrill of discovery. There's a good hour before she needs to crack open the shutters and run a duster over the glass counters. Jessica lingers by the confectionery display of necklaces and chandelier earrings until the greater temptation of Bertie's notebook pulls her away.

A warren of stale rooms and corridors runs behind the front of the shop. Jessica takes the narrow, un-carpeted stairs to the staffroom on the top floor – a great, musty hug of a room with mismatched furniture and mouse-droppings which trail the skirting boards. It reminds her of home before the bonfire.

Sitting on the arm of a scruffy blue sofa, she calls Birdie.

Her mother sounds harried. 'Have you forgotten it's Moving Day?'

'A quick question, that's all. Do you remember a red notebook?'

'Jessica, I've got the removal men here. What are you talking about?'

'A leather book full of handwriting.'

'Be careful with them, they're precious,' Birdie calls out, then says to Jessica, 'I gave your books to the local PDSA years ago.'

'It was in my tin with the dragon painted on the lid.'

Her mother makes an *aaah* sound. 'Your little box of secrets.'

Jessica digs her nails into her palm. 'Did you put the notebook in it?'

'If that's where you found it, I must have done.'

'Where did it come from?' The line goes quiet. 'Mum?'

'I'm trying to remember, Jessica. Maybe then I can continue moving house.'

Jessica picks at a tufted hole in the sofa arm.

Then Birdie says, 'Someone put it through the letter box. There was a note with it that said *For Jessica*.'

'A note?' Jessica stops plucking the sofa threads. 'Did you keep it?'

'Of course not. It was what . . . thirteen years ago. Shortly after you ran off.'

79

'I left home, Birdie, as you were fully aware at the time.' But this is old ground, and the conversation bumps over and past it. 'Is there anything else you can tell me?'

'Actually there is.' Birdie sounds impressed with herself. 'The note was scribbled on the back of a leaflet for a farm shop selling Christmas turkeys. I remember thinking, Well, I won't be needing a turkey this year, now that all my girls are gone.'

Jessica lets her mother return to her packing and opens the first page.

Tape 1 transcript: 22 February 1995

School Counsellor: *Albertine Callum, Sir William Weir's Grammar School*
Pupil: *Thomas Quennell, sixteen years old, Lower Sixth*
Background: *Client referred by Form Tutor Mr Andrew Skeet for initial six-week period following history of violent disturbances on school premises. Regular detention, three class exclusions. Held back a year after failing to attend his GCSEs.*

AC: *Please take a seat, Thomas. I'm the school counsellor. My name is Albertine Callum.*

TQ: *Can I call you Albert for short?*

AC: *Miss Callum is fine.*

TQ: *Miss, not Mrs. Not married then?*

AC: *Let's get started. Now, do you understand why you have been offered these sessions?*

TQ: *Because old Skeeter wouldn't dare have me round his house again.*

AC: *Mr Skeet invited you to his house?*

TQ: *For a chat. To show me . . . what did he say? That not everyone had given up on me.*

AC: *No one has given up on you. The fact that your teacher made time for you out of school hours illustrates that, don't you think?*

TQ: And does him putting his hand on my leg also illustrate that?

AC: Thomas, Mr Skeet is married with three sons of his own. Do you think it's possible you misinterpreted a friendly gesture?

TQ: I gave him a friendly gesture of my own.

AC: What was that, Thomas?

TQ: I held his hand. So hard I could feel the knuckles popping. Funnily enough, he didn't invite me again.

AC: Thomas, these are serious allegations.

TQ: So forget it. Who's going to believe me anyhow?

AC: I think we need to discuss this properly. I—

TQ: I this, I that. Why've you got all these little animals on your windowsill?

AC: They're animal totems. I collect them.

TQ: My grandad collected glass eyeballs. I played marbles with them. What do you do with your animal totems?

AC: Native Americans believe each one of us has a guiding animal spirit. Now, I'd like to explain to you the purpose of us meeting here.

TQ: It's just another room to put me in. Detention, headmaster's office, now this.

AC: You sound like you feel trapped.

TQ: I like this – what did you call it, totem? – the seal.

AC: I do too. The seal is independent, sometimes fierce, sometimes playful.

TQ: Where did you get it?

AC: Someone carved it for me.

TQ: A boyfriend?

AC: I can't discuss my personal life, Thomas.

TQ: But you can stick your nose in mine, right?

AC: Is that how you see this?

TQ: What's that? Are you taping me?

AC: The tapes act as my notes.

TQ: Who else is going to hear them?

AC: No one.

TQ: Yeah, right. I'm not saying another word.

AC: What you're really asking is whether you can trust me.

TQ: I'm not asking anything. I'm juggling.

AC: You can trust me. Please don't throw the seal so high. It's quite delicate.

TQ: I can catch a minnow with my bare hands. I'm hardly going to drop a piece of wood.

AC: If you wouldn't mind sitting down again, there's still twenty minutes left.

TQ: Can I keep this?

AC: Let's forget for a moment why you're here. Why don't you tell me about something you like?

TQ: I like juggling.

AC: And seals. That makes for an interesting start, don't you think?

Here Thomas refuses to be seated. He stands with his back to me looking out of the window. I let him have this silence so he understands there is no pressure and that the sessions belong to him. He does not attempt to leave until I inform him the session is over. As he is walking out he says:

TQ: You are wasting your time. You can't help me.

II

Jessica closes the notebook and drops backwards onto the sofa, her legs dangling over the arm. This isn't the Thomas she knew. Angry, aggressive. He sounds so immature. As a thirteen-year-old, she'd been in awe of him. In reality they'd both been playing at adulthood.

She opens the book again and reads the counsellor's notes under the first transcript.

Firstly I am struck by how physically mature Thomas is. He's tall, well developed for his age. Self-esteem or aliena-tion issues among a much younger peer group as a result of his resit? The academic record suggests under-average intelligence – this is not my impression. The incident regarding Mr Skeet worries me. Though I am sure nothing inappropriate occurred, it illustrates how Thomas sees the world around him as a hostile and dangerous place. This is a boy not used to being listened to.

As with many young people labelled 'troublesome', he

acts the part expected of him. However, halfway through the session he simply stopped talking. He couldn't be bothered to continue the posturing. Encouraging.

What concerns me is the lack of visible anger. His face was blank even as he went through the motions of testing and provoking. The rage is there as exhibited by frequent, violent encounters with peers and teachers. How deeply buried is it? Is he even fully aware of it?

He took my seal.

An entire book filled with Ms Callum's tidy, considered script – fragments of Thomas captured in time. Jessica fans through the pages, reads on. Within three sessions he had dropped his act and become the Thomas she remembered. His voice comes back to her as strongly as if he'd reached across the last seventeen years and touched her.

She looks for the last entry. It was dated 20 December 1995.

The day after he disappeared.

The day passes in a blur of distraction in which she achieves nothing. She had planned to research the make of an antique fob watch booked in for repair but instead she opens random pages of the counsellor's notes, reading snippets like surreptitious nibbles of a chocolate bar.

As soon as she gets home from work, she walks straight to her bedroom and empties the sea-dragon box on the floor. A fat, wooden seal rolls away from the whispery fall of newspaper clippings.

For you, he'd said. *I carved it myself.*

She hears his laugh – that sudden, rare sound – as she picks up the seal, pressing it to her lips. It doesn't matter. His voice has come back to her.

AC: Do you remember your mother leaving?

TQ: Not really. She was hugging this vase to her chest and my dad tried to pull it out of her arms. Nathan was behind her saying, Just give it to him, just let him have it. But she wouldn't let go.

AC: Does she keep in touch with you?

TQ: She waited for me outside school one day.

AC: And what happened then? Did she speak to you?

TQ: She had a big present wrapped in green paper.

AC: What was in it?

TQ: Don't know. I threw a stone at her.

AC: You were angry and hurt that she had left you. How did she react?

TQ: How do you think? She didn't come back after that.

AC: You were just a child. A seven-year-old.

TQ: I shouldn't have thrown a stone at her.

12

April 1995, Selcombe

The next time she saw Thomas it was by the sea wall in Trough. Neither of them spoke much, watching the fishing boats rock in the harbour as a muggy spring storm crept in from the sea.

He had a gash at the edge of his mouth, his bottom lip swollen. Before she could ask what happened, he'd turned away and leaped up onto the wall, daring her to follow as he ran along its narrow length.

She abandoned her plan to kiss him – it was nothing to do with his hurt lip. It just seemed like such an airy dream.

'My dad's not been home in two weeks,' Jessica said, once they'd stopped running. As she spoke, she kept her eyes on the rain clouds hanging low over the horizon.

Thomas was whittling a stick into a sharp point with his penknife. 'Where is he?'

'Don't know. Mum won't even say his name.'

She liked the way Thomas nodded, like these things

happened. He didn't say anything stupid like *He'll be back soon.* The kind of thing people said when they weren't listening or that bothered.

'What're you doing with the stick?'

He held it up to his eye, squinting along its slim length. 'I'm going to catch a rabbit for my dinner.'

'Really?' She couldn't tell if he was serious.

'Or maybe a seal.'

'How did you hurt your lip?'

His tongue flicked over the scab but he said nothing.

'Who did that to you?'

Now he turned to look at her, his face as empty as the grey sky over their heads. 'If you're going to start asking annoying questions like everyone else, I'm not going to hang out with you any more.'

'Fine. Next time I see you, I'll be wearing rabbit ears but don't you dare ask me about them.'

Thomas stared at her, then the uninjured corner of his mouth twitched. 'You're such a jellyhead, Jellybird.'

They sat there a while longer, side by side, their hips not quite touching. She shifted closer, a caterpillar inch of movement which failed to close the gap between them. He was always just out of reach. Sometimes she imagined trying to take his hand, her fingers falling through him, finding nothing but empty air.

When it started to rain, he placed a cigarette in her open palm. 'To keep you going until next time.'

Walking home, Jessica carried the promise of their next meeting as tenderly as she caged the cigarette in her fingers, deep in her cardigan pocket. She had no intention of smoking it – her head still reeling from a last drag on his B&H. She hated the taste, the finger of smoke poking into her lungs; loved the damp filter between her lips where his had touched moments before.

With her head full of Thomas, she crossed the road to the bus stop, barely registering the man on the bench inside the shelter. It was the noise he was making under his breath that caught her attention. It sounded like he was sucking tea over his tongue then breathing out in a whispered laugh.

Ha ha ha, *wet suck*, ha ha ha.

She looked round to see a filthy man with broken shoes and a stained shirt unbuttoned down to his belly. A great gold crucifix lay on his white chest. Bloody Russian. That's what everyone called him – a homeless man with horrid sores around his mouth and chin, always hanging around the schools. Out of his mind.

Disgust must have registered on her face, because it made Bloody Russian say it louder – ha ha ha – bouncing his leg in time with it.

Turning her back to him, she leaned against the metal pole of the bus stop. She couldn't run away because nutters were like dogs and reacted to fear. If you ran, they chased you. Act like nothing.

'Freckles.' He rolled the word off his tongue. 'I lick your freckles. Taste like chocolate.'

Hot panic prickled across her forehead and down her back. She wished she wasn't wearing her school uniform with its unmistakable yellow stag-head logo. Wrapping her school coat tightly around herself, she stepped out into the road.

'Watch out, you silly little girl.' A woman in a brown mac careered across the road on her bicycle. 'You nearly knocked me flying.'

Jessica lifted a hand in hasty apology as she rushed down the street. Somehow the shouting cyclist had made her feel less scared. Until that moment, it had felt like she and the homeless man were alone in the world.

Without looking back, she ran past the chippie and arcades, heading for the next bus stop.

By the time she got home, she wondered what she'd been afraid of. Her cigarette was slightly bent where she'd been holding it in her fist. She wrapped it in cling film and hid it beneath her pillow.

It was Hannah who found the cigarette a few days later.

'Mum,' she shrieked. 'Jessica's been smoking.'

Lunging at Hannah, her nails made contact with her sister's arm as she tried to take Thomas's cigarette back. Hannah ignored the scratches, unbalancing Jessica with a shove to the chest before slamming the bedroom door. She was already in the kitchen by the time Jessica had tiptoed to the landing banisters. All she could see were their feet, her sister's school shoes almost upon their mother's bare toes. From the swirly motion of her mother's skirt, it looked like she was scrubbing the casserole pot from dinner.

'Look what I found under Jessica's pillow.'

Jessica held her breath. The skirt stopped moving but her mother didn't speak.

'Aren't you going to say something to her?' Hannah asked.

Perhaps her mother shook her head, Jessica couldn't tell. The skirt started its swirling motion again and after a brief pause, Hannah walked away.

'Give it back to me.' Jessica met Hannah at the top of the stairs.

Her sister snapped the cigarette in two, grinding it between her fingers and pushed past. 'That's for losing my TRUE LOVE brooch.'

Grabbing a jumper from their bedroom, Hannah ran back down the stairs.

'Hockey practice, Mum,' she shouted on her way out, not bothering to take her kit bag. From the bedroom window, Jessica watched her sister close the garden gate, glancing back at the house before she turned right. The wrong direction for the bus stop. Right only led to the caravan park and the booze stacked in the office cupboard among old curtains and cushions.

Jessica heaved the sash window open; it stuck and squealed, scraps of paint floating down. Her sister would snore out stale wine all night long and in the morning their room would stink of it. *Can't you smell it?* Jessica wanted to scream at her mother. Some things only a grown-up could fix.

A wave of dizziness caught her. She tiptoed to the chest of drawers. Hidden beneath her swimsuit was a spiky triangle of brown glass. Easing her school tights past her thighs, she sat on the edge of the bed, bringing her left heel to her bottom. She placed the glass's smooth face against her inner thigh and slid it down, tender and cool on her skin. A lazy stroke before she turned the sharp edge on herself. She scratched the letter T into the pale flesh – tracing over it until the skin opened up like splitting stitches.

The task swallowed her up. Tears ran down her face, dripped off her chin though she couldn't have said why she was crying. She heard Thomas call her name across a great distance and pressed the glass down harder until her forehead was cold and damp. A bloody T-shape bubbled up under her fingers. She imagined swimming with Thomas in summer. He might spot the jagged scar and touch it.

'Jessica. Are you there?'

She lifted her head, the glass shard slippery in her grip. Hot pain shot from her thigh to her stomach, the way it always hit when she stopped. Black beads dotted the bed sheet beneath her thigh.

'Can you hear me?' The voice was coming from outside.

She threw the glass under her bed. Her tights dragged her raw, cut skin. There was blood on her fingers; she crouched to lick them clean before leaning out of the window.

Thomas was standing in the back garden.

'Climb down,' he called in a low voice, stepping onto the upturned apple crate he'd pushed against the side of the house. He raised his arms.

Jessica pressed her legs together; a nauseous sting in her left thigh, the damp itch of blood prickling through her tights. Sometimes the cuts were deep, the bleeding hard to stem. 'I can't tonight.'

'There's something I want you to see.'

'Tomorrow.'

'Who says there'll be a tomorrow?'

'You're such a bugger.' Jessica hid behind the open cupboard door, peeled off her tights and bunched them in a knot, using it to wipe the cuts. Just when it looked like the blood had stopped, the T would bloat up with fresh drops. She found three crumpled plasters in Hannah's washbag, patched herself up and pulled on her jeans. Climbing onto the windowsill, her back to Thomas, she slipped one leg out at a time, the toe of her trainers scraping down the wall. Hovered a moment with her hip bones balanced on the sill.

'Come on. I've got you.'

Jessica took a deep breath as though she were about to jump into a pool and slipped downwards. Thomas's hands clutched at her clothes as she fell. They stumbled backwards off the crate, which smacked against the house. Running across the garden, they scrambled over the garden wall and dropped onto the chalk path behind.

'Where are we going?' Jessica whispered as they caught their breath.

'A secret place.'

He marched off and she had to quicken her pace to keep up with him. They followed the chalk path into the forest where the warmth of the day was still trapped in the trees. The shadows were purple and rustled with unseen life. She slowed, breathing in. At night, the woods smelled like crushed leaves, like dark secrets.

'Is it far?'

94

Thomas didn't answer, following a route in his head. She recognised that blinkered look. She might as well not have been there. It took him four strides to notice she'd stopped walking.

'What's the matter?'

Standing there with the night painting her skin purple, prickling with secrets and he didn't even know she was there. She wanted to show him the seeping T on the inside of her thigh. *Look what I did for you.* Instead, she shrugged.

He walked towards her, tilting his head to see her more clearly. 'Have you been crying?'

'No.'

'Is it your mum? Hannah?'

His concern made her feel better. 'No. I thought I heard something in the bushes.'

Thomas pinched her side. 'Little Jellybird.'

They walked on, until the trees gave way to black, gale-flattened gorse which picked at their trouser-legs. Jessica hunched her shoulders against an open palm of wind, keeping her eyes on her misstepping feet. She wondered how much trouble she'd be in if Hannah got back before her, finding her bed empty and the window open. Birdie would tear strips off her, like the time she'd skipped school to go to the cinema and been caught by Mrs Parching.

'Here we are.' They'd reached a picket fence lined with barbed wire. Tacked to one of the posts was a sign. *Danger. Keep Out.* Thomas slid his hands under the wire to grip the wooden plank. One of the spiked metal knots caught the back of his hand. 'Put your feet where I put mine.'

He leaped over and waited on the other side.

'What about the sign?'

'To scare off trespassers.'

A few metres past the fence, the ground ended abruptly and Jessica could hear the sea thundering far below it. 'But there's nothing here.'

'Trust me.' He led her to the edge of the cliff. Below them, on a rocky lip of ground perched a small chapel, its silhouette solid black against the night sky. The only way to reach it was along a steep flight of steps carved out of the cliff. Jessica pressed both hands against the rocky face as she followed Thomas, her feet sliding on the sandy surface.

'No one comes here any more. It's my place now,' Thomas said once they stood in front of the chapel. 'They're scared it will fall into the sea and take a coach-load of tourists with it.'

There were great cracks in the walls. Part of the roof gaped open to the sky and the ground was covered in bits of broken tile and stone. 'Do you think it will?'

'One day.' Thomas spoke close to her ear. 'Maybe it'll take the two of us with it.'

'That's one way of getting out of PE, I guess.'

Instead of trying the door, he walked past the chapel towards the edge of the outcrop where the wind surged up from the sea, buffeting his body. He swayed with it, careless. If he stepped out, the sea would swallow him before she could reach the edge. Jessica moved closer until she could see the water breaking against the rocks below. Foam flecks rose and spun, making her dizzy.

'If you look at the surf for too long, it makes you forget your feet. Then you fall in. That's what happened to Julie Morgan's mum.'

'Drowning's not a bad way to go,' Thomas said. 'When I've had enough of this life, I'm going to go swimming. I'll keep going until I'm so knackered I sink to the bottom.'

He sat down, dropping his legs into empty air like he was sitting on a sofa. Jessica knelt behind him, hand out, her fingertips almost touching his jumper. Ready to catch him.

Thomas plucked at the wild grass. It came away with little showers of loose rock. 'If you're in the water for long enough, your skin becomes soapy, like you're melting.'

'You hallucinate before you die.'

'Yeah, I heard that too.' He turned his head slightly, speaking to her over his shoulder. 'One guy saw an angel coming for him through the water just before they fished him out.'

Jessica studied him. The profile curve of his lips, his wrists where his jumper came up short and the hollow drape of the material from the balls of his shoulders.

'So is this what you wanted to show me? The view?' She tried to sound unimpressed, hoping it would make him get up. It worked. She followed him round to the front of the chapel.

'Have you heard of this place?'

Jessica read the sign, its edges eaten away with sea salt. 'The Chapel of St Francis of Paola. Who's he?'

'Patron saint of souls lost at sea.'

'Looks like a bloody deathtrap.'

Thomas unpicked the loop of blue twine holding the double wooden doors together. He rocked them apart and a yawn of stagnant air reached her. He turned on the threshold and smiled. Such a rare sight that for a moment he looked like a stranger. Taking a small flashlight from his jacket, he lit up the short aisle, five pews and an altar carved from a single block of stone. She followed him inside, slipping on bird shit.

'What do you think?' Thomas leaped like a mountain goat from pew to pew, slamming down his weight so the noise hit the chapel walls. Stones trickled from the cracks in the walls. In her head she kept seeing the cliff breaking into the sea, taking the chapel with it. It made her legs ache.

'I should probably get home before Hannah rats on me.'

Thomas sat cross-legged on the altar and pointed with his torch. 'Look at the wall on your left.'

Jessica followed the torch beam. A gold and azure mosaic blazed from the filthy stone, like a square of brilliant sky through a window. 'That's St Francis as he sailed to this shore. Look at the waves. They're made of little fish pulling him along by the strands of his cloak.'

The saint looked out from the mosaic with light blue eyes, his pale hair lifting in stylised waves around his head.

'He looks like you.' Jessica moved closer, tracing her

fingertips over golden tiles. They were greasy with damp ocean air. 'It must be worth something.'

'I guess. It was hidden under a load of crap. I cleaned it with Fairy Liquid. There are three more to do.'

She pictured him here, scrubbing at the walls, the way he set his top teeth on his bottom lip when he was concentrating. Imagined him stealing a bottle of Fairy Liquid out of his house, maybe hidden under his jumper. It made her want to hug him.

'I could help, if you like, after school. I could even stay late on Thursdays because that's my mum's—'

He shook his head. 'Nah. That's OK.'

Jessica pressed her finger over the sightless orb of a fish's eye. Managed a shrug. Thomas passed behind her in the narrow space between the benches and the wall, somehow not touching her, like he was made of air.

'Look at these panels.' He ran his torch over a wooden board inscribed with names and dates, nailed high on the wall by the entrance. 'Here. Joseph Quennell, 1989. That's my grandad, and here's my uncle, Nicolas Quennell, 1990.'

'Why are their names there?' Jessica joined him in front of the wooden plaque.

He stood behind her, resting the torch on her shoulder. 'It's a list of sailors who have drowned.' The beam flicked to the top of the board where the lettering was shallow with age. 'Fishermen's families used to come here to pray for their safe return during a storm. Those who didn't make it back had their names carved here so

St Francis could find their souls in the water and guide them home.'

Jessica, only half listening, was focusing on the sliver of space caught between his body and hers, growing warm. It made her shiver with delicious nerves.

'One day my name's going to be here, too.'

'Don't say that.'

'Are you cold, Jessie?'

'A little,' she said, to explain away the shivering.

'Let's get you home then.' Thomas stepped away and the chapel's icy breath moved in to fill his vacuum.

He didn't speak the whole way home, his thoughts elsewhere. Again she suffered with the rise and fall of his interest, like the sun dipping in and out of cloud. By the time they reached her house, it was close to midnight. Thomas left her at the garden wall. 'See you.'

She watched him walk away. It never occurred to him to kiss her.

Looking up at her bedroom window, she saw it was now in darkness and her heart skipped. Hannah had arrived home before her. Inside the house, all the lights were off. Her mother was in bed. Holding her breath, she crept along the corridor.

Opening her bedroom door, she found her mother sitting on the bed. Hannah lay facing the wall, covers around her ears. She could tell from her sister's silence that she was awake.

'Hannah says he's an older boy.' Her mother patted the bed.

'I just went for a walk.' Her tongue clicked drily.

Her mother leaned over and lifted Jessica's chin, their

first physical contact in months. 'Have you started your periods yet?'

Jessica bit the insides of her cheeks, eyes straining away from her mother.

'Is that a yes or a no?'

Jessica gave a stiff little nod.

Her mother's hand moved from Jessica's chin to a strand of her hair; it felt like a draught rather than a touch. 'You're so like him.'

Hannah twitched her covers lower and Jessica wanted to shout *Yes? Can I help you?* in her sister's exposed ear.

'With that red hair and those green eyes. Your father's daughter.' Her mother got up and left the room.

Jessica sat still, looking out of the window.

'Sorry.' Hannah's voice was muffled in her duvet.

Jessica took off her shoes and lay down. 'For what?'

AC: Pretend you are a stranger visiting your home for the first time. What's it like?

TQ: Like this massive shipwreck. Looters have done it over.

AC: In what way?

TQ: There's nothing left except marks on the carpet where there used to be furniture. The man sold everything that wasn't needed.

AC: Can you describe more of it?

TQ: There's no electricity. Just a wood-burner in the kitchen and the man's bedroom.

AC: What's the boy like who lives there?

TQ: Don't know.

AC: And the man, his dad?

TQ: He's in the bath because it helps his sore leg. The boy has to help him in and out of it. Sometimes he has to rub cream into his dad's leg.

AC: That's quite a chore for a young boy.

TQ: The cream makes his hands greasy. It won't come off even with soap. His dad's leg is really white with no hair because of all the scars. I hate how the skin feels.

~ 13 ~

A few days after the visit to Thomas's chapel, the T-shaped cut in Jessica's thigh began to burn. Pinching the ragged edge of skin under the bathroom light, she saw pus and tried to wash it with soap, her breath catching. She went downstairs, hoping to distract herself with television.

Moments after she'd turned on *EastEnders*, her mother ghosted in and all Jessica could focus on was Birdie's suffocating silence. She put the remote down.

'I'm going to Grannie Mim's.'

She left Birdie staring out of the window, oblivious to the shouting from the television set. On her way out, she pocketed her mother's dusty turquoise studs that had been sitting, forgotten, on the bathroom sill for months.

Grannie Mim lived all year round in Seasalt Holiday Park. Her full name was Mimosa Blue and she'd once been a West End actress; everyone called her Grannie Mim, which Jessica thought was a shame. Her caravan had three bedrooms and its own name rather than a number like the other mobile homes. *Mimosa Blue*, it said in gold letters that bobbed on scrolling waves.

Last spring Jessica's dad had planted young apple trees in a row, separating Grannie Mim's caravan from the rest of the park. *Because you're more than just a guest*, he'd told her. It was probably also to hide the clutter of boxes and furniture stacked outside. That evening, a dressmaker's dummy stood guard at the bottom of the porch steps, and Jessica had to walk sideways through the open door to get past stacks of shiny books with Elvis on the cover. Compared to her own house, it was like climbing into a toy box and rummaging for treasure.

Despite the warmth of the spring evening, Mimosa was sitting alone by the electric fire, smothered in shawls, a faded pink towel tucked around her lap. If someone unwrapped her, she'd probably be nothing more than a stick figure.

'A smiling Jessica. What a pretty sight.' Grannie Mim squeezed her hand. 'There's carrot soup on the stove, sweetness.'

'Where shall I put these?' Jessica held out the earrings.

'How lovely, dear.' Grannie Mim took the studs and put them in her skirt pocket. 'I'll find a good home for them.'

'What do you do with all the stuff you can't sell?' Jessica looked around at Mimosa's cluttered room, full of people's unwanted chairs, books and vases.

'There's a special place for everything. Same with

people.' And she smiled in a way that made Jessica think she'd missed something. 'I have something for you as well.'

From the same skirt pocket Mimosa took out five gilt horse-head buttons. 'I seem to remember you love horses.'

Jessica actually found horses quite sinister, but didn't say so. The buttons were heavy and clicked like dice in her hands. She sat down in the only place that wasn't growing a bric-a-brac stalagmite, a deep bucket of a chair which forced Jessica constantly to shift position, like a cat settling.

'How's your poor mum coping?' Mimosa was the only person who didn't pretend everything was fine.

'Fine.'

'Is she taking care of you girls?'

'We don't need looking after.' Jessica slung her legs over the armrest. The gash on her thigh felt like a hard, burning stone when she pressed her legs together.

An apple-blossom breeze was blowing in from the open front door. Grannie Mim only closed it during rain or snow. Jessica shuddered. 'Don't you get scared here? All by yourself?'

'I'm never by myself.' She winked at Jessica. 'People are always dropping in.'

'But at night? When you're in bed?'

'Of course not.' Mim's face was suddenly serious. 'There's nothing to be afraid of.'

She said it with the kind of emphasis adults use when speaking to five-year-olds. It made Jessica bristle. 'I am *not* afraid.'

'If anyone was going to see off a burglar, it would be your mum. Your dad, on the other hand, would probably have cowered under the bed.'

Jessica was about to jump to her dad's defence when it occurred to her that it was a trap. If she stood up for him, Mimosa would use it as an excuse to talk badly about him.

She shifted in the chair, aware again of the dull ache in her thigh.

'Hannah needs something for a cut. She got it when she was playing hockey.'

'Has she cleaned it?'

'I guess.'

'Bit of vinegar in water will stop it going bad.'

'It's already infected.'

Grannie Mim got up. It always surprised Jessica how easily she moved when the blankets came off. She wrapped the towel around her shoulders, poking through little tubs and jars on the windowsill.

'It's boiling in here, Grannie Mim.'

'Old people are always freezing to death,' she announced cheerfully, and handed Jessica a plastic pot with a missing lid, the label worn off. Jessica poked the greyish ointment with her little finger. It smelled like boot polish.

'It'll sting like the devil, but you youngsters can cope.'

She put it in her coat pocket. 'Hannah's pretty tough.'

'I must show you something I found the other day.' Grannie Mim disappeared into a bedroom and came back with a bundle of photographs. She held out a black and white print to Jessica. 'Me and Leonard on our wedding day.'

A young woman danced with a man in army uniform. Her black hair lay in styled waves across her forehead. Mimosa Blue smiled into her husband's face like she was looking through an open door and getting ready to step in. Jessica's mother used to look at her dad in the same way. She handed the photograph back. 'You were very pretty.'

Grannie Mim leaned forward to pat her knee. 'He wasn't my first, you know.'

Jessica's cheeks reddened. 'I guess you had lots of admirers.'

'On my wedding night I took a pin when Len was asleep and pricked my thumb so there'd be blood on the sheet. But it was such a tiny drop I had to keep going. My poor fingers.' She threw her hands in the air and laughed. 'There must be a better way, really there must.'

Jessica knew there was supposed to be blood the first time but she'd never heard of people stabbing their fingers with a pin before. Grannie Mim talked to her like she knew grown-up things; she wouldn't spoil it with a silly question. She went through the sheaf of pictures as Grannie Mim pointed over her shoulder, making comments.

'Now Lionel, there was a brilliant trumpeter. You'd have thought such talented lips could kiss a gal to sweet Friday but oh, no. And that's Franny, my cousin. Never married. Eyes only for my Leonard, though she never said.' The woman was sitting on a park bench with her ankles crossed.

'They look like movie stars,' Jessica said. She couldn't imagine her mother going about her daily jobs in a tight fitted skirt and matching jacket that gave her a waist like a Barbie doll.

'People dressed smart in those days.' Grannie Mim sat down and re-rugged herself while Jessica helped herself to a mug of soup from the pot on the stove. She felt warm and sleepy as if she could drift away and Mimosa would watch over her. She could see the sun setting, the sky like wet paper soaking up watercolours.

'Who's your best boy?'

Jessica hesitated. No one knew about Thomas and their night-time walks.

'I have a friend.' She searched for the right words to describe Thomas. 'Not really a boyfriend.'

'Of course not, sweetie. You're only thirteen.'

'Thirteen isn't how you remember it.' Jessica lifted her chin but Grannie Mim didn't smirk to herself the way grown-ups did when they thought they knew better.

Instead she said, 'Thirteen is a beautiful age. You can still dream about what's coming next.'

'My mother spends so much time dreaming she's forgotten how to talk.' Jessica was annoyed the conversation had moved away from Thomas. 'What's so good about dreaming?'

Grannie Mim sighed. 'No, I don't suppose you are a dreamer, peppermint. Not like your sister Lisa.'

'Lisa? She's working in a pub so she can save up and

leave home. Mum thinks she's having piano lessons. Not that she ever asks.'

'I hope it's not that boy giving her silly ideas.'

'What boy?'

'The one that's been hanging around your house after dark. I see him most nights cutting through the park, thinking no one sees him.'

A fish flipped in Jessica's stomach. Scared to give herself away, she asked again, 'What boy?'

'Finn Quennell's son. Looks just like his father. Handsome on the outside, empty inside. Like waxed fruit.'

Jessica jumped up. 'You've never even met him.' Her voice hissed out like fat spitting in a frying pan; it surprised them both.

Grannie Mim's eyebrows lifted. 'A boy like that preys on vulnerable girls.'

Jessica couldn't look at her. With her fist, she scrubbed at the spilled soup running down her leg.

'I've heard things about him, sweetie. You don't know—'

Still looking down, her voice quiet, Jessica said, 'I do know. He *told* me what people say behind his back.' And then the words came out in a rush. 'It's because of the disability benefit his dad gets from the council. Someone painted *Fucking Faker* on the wall of their barn but his dad can't even walk to the toilet by the end of the day. Thomas says he growls like an animal with the pain.'

'I'm not saying the boy's having an easy time of it.'

'You can't always believe what people say, Grannie Mim. You have to ask yourself *why* they're saying it.'

'That's exactly what I'm saying, Jessie.' Mimosa's voice pointed like a finger.

Jessica's throat started to burn. She ran tap water over her soup mug, her hands blurring through furious tears. She'd been wrong. Grannie Mim would never have understood about her and Thomas. Something happened to people when they got old; they started seeing everything through dirty windows.

'It's not Lisa, is it?' Grannie Mim said at the door. 'She's not the one I need to worry about after all.'

Jessica turned away; the rudeness of putting her back to Grannie Mim was both thrilling and awful. Her feet seemed to catch all the bumps in the grass as she walked away. The horse-head buttons fell through her fingers like a trail of Hansel and Gretel crumbs.

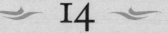

14

May 2012, London

*I*s designer Jessica Byrne having a laugh at our (quite substantial) expense? Someone a little less generous than myself might call her the practical joker of the jewellery industry. Next time I feel a bit strapped for cash, I shall be scrabbling about in my neighbour's bin (they have children – a useful source of garish junk) for precious materials, cobbling the whole lot together with superglue and calling it a necklace. For my efforts (and dry-cleaning bill) I shall make sure to stick a hefty price-tag on it.

Jessica drops the magazine onto her lap. No matter how many times she reads the damning review, the words keep their abrasive rub. She'd shown Jacques before he left for work.

Rise above it, honey, he'd said. *You and I both know better.*

A car horn blares in the street. Rolling the magazine into a tight scroll, she shoves it into the side pocket of Jacques' canvas sailing bag.

Before she leaves the flat, she writes a message on the kitchen blackboard.

Pear Tree Cottage, Bantham, TY45 2ZH. Remember – no landline, little mobile reception but it's only for three days. Good luck in Moscow xx

Libby's white-and-chrome Mini is parked on a double yellow line. 'Get in,' she shouts from the driver's seat. 'The weekend's ticking away.'

It's a full ten minutes before someone lets them out of John Prince's Street into the Friday-night traffic clogging up Cavendish Square. Water hisses beneath car wheels, the traffic like a slow trudge of debris sluicing down a great drain.

'I love this wet, filthy city,' Jessica says.

'You poor, deprived being.' Libby wrinkles her nose. 'Wait until you see Pear Tree Cottage.'

Jessica settles back and watches the city go by. The late-night delis, kebab shops and flats above are lit up – naked in the darkness – and Jessica peeks in, greedy for snapshots of other people's lives; like a child poking its fingers into sweetie jars.

'Mum and I bought the place a few months ago,' Libby's saying. 'She was going to drop by and meet you, but a friend's invited her to Prague for the weekend instead.'

'She sounds very independent.' It occurs to Jessica that Libby rarely mentions her mother.

'A bit like your mum, I'm guessing.' Libby is applying lipstick in the rear-view mirror. 'Do you think she'll marry again one day?'

Jessica pictures the gardener's coat lying across the banister. 'Who knows?'

'And your dad?'

'He's not around.' Jessica pulls her jacket tightly about herself.

'And yet, you start a lot of sentences with *My dad always says*.'

'I never mention him. You're nosing for dirt.' Jessica smiles to lighten her words but Libby's as hard and shiny as a silver globe. Words slip off her.

The traffic thins as they reach the four-storey, wedding-cake houses of Brook Green. The windows have patterned blinds to block out the surrounding red brick of Earl's Court. There's no one on the streets, nothing to see. Jessica closes her eyes.

It's the silence that wakes her. She's alone in the car, parked outside a blue timber house with large windows which are lighting up one by one as a figure moves through the rooms. Opening the car door, Jessica smells seaweed. She can't see the water through the wild rose bushes flanking the cottage but she hears it as soon as she steps out. Her heart sinks. Libby's holiday home sits directly on the ocean. With its endless memories of Thomas; the ocean, which finally claimed him.

From the doorway, Libby beckons her. 'Time for the tour.'

It isn't what she expected; all sanded wood and angled windows, so new it still smells of sawdust. Upstairs, all three bedrooms face the water. Libby flings back the curtains, saying, 'Can you imagine a more heavenly place?'

Jessica nods because how can she explain that she prefers the sound of rainwater washing through London gutters to the endless surge of surf?

Downstairs, the sitting room's floor-to-ceiling windows overlook a small garden with a globe-shaped fountain and an apple tree hanging over the low fence. A gate leads straight onto a narrow ledge of pebbled beach. Jessica sits down in a saffron-yellow armchair facing the empty wood-burner while Libby slides open the glass doors. The room floods with salty air and gull cries.

'I love your mantelpiece,' Jessica says. A single length of driftwood, long and sensual as a dancer's arm, sits above the wood-burner. Framed pictures of Libby – a single one of her and Matthew – balance along its length. One of the frames has scrolling flowers with petals of rough glass set into the pewter. It resembles an overambitious GCSE project. Frowning, Jessica picks it up.

'This is one of mine. When I was still experimenting.'

Still gazing out at the sea, Libby says, 'Told you I was a fan.'

They eat bacon omelettes and share a bottle of tanniny red in front of the wood-burner, now blasting out a sunburning heat. After the meal, Jessica curls up in the armchair feeling warm and sleepy until the review in *The Jeweller's Design* comes back to her.

'I need to show you something, Libs.' Jessica grabs her rucksack and rummages through it, looking for the magazine. A frown like a pulled thread tightens Libby's brow as she reads.

'The *outrage* of it,' Libby cries, throwing the magazine onto the floor. 'I'm going to call that woman, as one of your many delighted customers, and give her a piece of my mind.'

The vehemence in her friend's voice makes Jessica smile. 'But in a way, she's right. I do take junk and make it into jewellery.'

'What you do,' Libby is shaking her finger at Jessica, 'is far beyond the intellectual grasp of that witch. You told me how each chip of plastic or stone has its own place and meaning within the greater piece. Like the notes of a song, isn't that what you said?'

'Thank you,' Jessica says, and squeezes Libby's hand. 'You're the first person to make me feel better about this.'

'Pure spite or pig ignorance, I can't decide which.' Libby refuses to sit down as Jessica tugs at her arm. 'What did Jacques say?'

'He dismissed it. Said he believes in me, no matter what anyone else says.'

'Typical man-comment.' Libby pulls a wry face. 'Does *he* even get it?'

But you understand, Jessica thinks, and decides she will make Libby a gift; something fabulous, a pair of chandelier earrings, perhaps, or a stack of linking bracelets.

*

'You haven't told me how you and Jacques met.'

Jessica shifts in the yellow armchair where she's been drifting off.

Libby looks far from sleepy, her eyes bright, cheeks red. 'You were very young, weren't you?'

Jessica stretches for the last of her wine, wondering how Libby would know this. 'I was seventeen, and working in a café called the Tea Chest in Bridge.'

'Bridge?' Libby nods. 'Further up the coast. Studenty town?'

'It has a big architectural school. Jacques was an overseas student there.'

Libby winks at her. 'Some of the girls at my school used to travel up there on a Friday night hoping to hook up with a rich student type.'

'Couldn't have been further from my mind.' Jessica rolls her eyes. 'I just wanted to escape.'

'You didn't run very far.'

'I guess not. And you and Matthew?'

Her friend flaps the question away. 'Blind date. Or did I pick him up at a party? I can't remember.'

She empties the bottle into their glasses. 'I want details. Don't tell me Jacques chatted you up over a pastrami sandwich?'

'Something like that.'

Libby sighs. 'You, my dear, need to loosen up.'

She leaves the room, returning with a second bottle of wine and a hairbrush enamelled with ivory swans.

'My mum used to brush my hair whenever I needed a bit of TLC.' She makes Jessica sit on the floor in front of her, adding, 'Don't argue.'

She opens the new bottle, filling their glasses. Then she begins to sweep the brush through Jessica's hair until it falls back from her face like a river.

'I knew this boy once,' Jessica says. 'He was very beautiful, though no one else seemed to notice. His name was Thomas Quennell.'

Libby's hand follows the brush, stroking back from Jessica's forehead along the stream of her hair. Brush, stroke, brush, stroke. Jessica hears her own voice from far away as if someone else is telling her story. The wine has wrapped her in cotton wool.

'I haven't said his name in years.'

'What was he like?'

'When I first saw him on the beach, I thought he was the ghost of a local boy who'd gone missing years ago.'

The brush stops for a moment. 'You fell in love with a ghost.'

'He had strange eyes. Very pale, like the colour of water.'

The brushstrokes are very light now; she can tell Libby's listening intently.

'What happened with this ghost boy?'

Jessica goes quiet. She wants to tell Libby but it has sat like a stone in her mouth all these years; she's learned to talk, even laugh, around it but it won't be so easily spat out. 'We went our separate ways. Who was your first love?'

'Craig Doyle. He ate a lot of tuna fish, which was unfortunate when it came to kissing.'

'What happened to Craig?'

'I got my first period.' Libby laughs softly through

her nose. 'And realised he was just a spotty little twit. Tell me more about the beautiful Thomas.'

Jessica sits away from the brush. Awake now, full of sudden energy. She reaches for her rucksack again, her horizon tilting with red wine as she moves. Libby sees her unsteady movement and laughs, topping up their glasses.

'This is between you and me.' Jessica fishes out the red notebook.

'I'm good at secrets,' Libby says, and Jessica thinks, *Yes, I bet you are.*

She explains about the notebook but before she hands it over, she shows Libby a photograph from the sea-dragon box. 'That's Thomas. The one to my left.'

'He's got that typical teenage-boy look, all bones and angles. But beautiful, I can see that.' Then Libby snaps the photo from Jessica's fingers. 'Who's the tall guy with the dodgy Bros hairdo on your right?'

'Thomas's big brother, Nathan.'

'I know him from somewhere.' Libby looks to Jessica, who can only shrug. 'It'll come to me. Now, hand over the notebook.'

She takes her time leafing through it. 'He sounds . . . challenging. Is that the word?'

'If you read it carefully, you'll understand why. There are things even I didn't know, and I was his best friend.'

'What happened to him?'

Jessica can feel the rough surface of the sea behind her. 'He took his brother's Cornish crabber out and never came back.'

Libby covers her mouth with her hand. 'How awful.'

'They never found his body.' Jessica sighs. Looking up, she catches a glitter of tears in her friend's eyes. 'Bits of the boat washed up on the beach all winter. I was terrified of finding . . . something but I couldn't stay away.'

Libby grips her fingers but Jessica has no feeling in her body, her hand a piece of surplus matter.

'When the local papers lost interest, it was as though he'd never existed.'

'Poor you.' Libby squeezes harder. 'And poor Jacques.'

'Jacques?'

'You're still in love with a ghost after all.'

Jessica gets up, walks over to the open French doors. 'I can't bear to be near the water any more.'

In the darkness, the sea's surface rolls and bulges without breaking, like something is moving beneath it. Jessica shudders.

'Let's go outside,' Libby whispers by her ear. 'I'll go grab some jumpers.'

Jessica doesn't wait. She steps barefoot into grass wet with evening dew. Something pulps through her toes; a rotten apple. With a cry of disgust, she flings it over the fence onto the beach.

Hearing Libby behind her, she unlatches the gate and strides down to the water's edge, standing so close to the surf that it laps over her feet; the cold brings an instant, shocking pain. Picking up a handful of stones, she flings them at the sea, scrabbles up another load, throwing harder. Trying to split open the surface.

Something flies over her head. With a heavy gulp, it

disappears into the water. Jessica looks round to see Libby picking apples off the ground.

'Take that, evil, watery beast.' She lobs an apple like a grenade at the sea. 'Take that, monstrous sea.'

Jessica stares at her. 'What are you doing?'

'You want some more?' Libby shouts at the water, giggling as she catches Jessica's eye. She crouches down, gathering up an armful of small green apples. They tumble over her as she lifts her arms, trying to launch them simultaneously.

Despite herself, Jessica starts to laugh, joining in.

The two of them fighting the sea with rotten fruit, laughing so hard it makes them cry.

Jessica lies in a bath, her feet and fingers burning as the blood throbs through them. Libby has her back against the tub, flicking through a magazine. They pass a bottle of port between them.

'So you've told me about Thomas,' Libby says. 'Now I want to know about Jacques.'

Jessica lifts her head from the bath rim. 'I've already told you how we met.'

Libby flaps her hand over her shoulder. 'I'm not interested in the building blocks. Anyone can see them. I want to see the cement, the stuff that keeps you guys together.'

Jessica takes a long, slow drink of port, its sweetness catching in the back of her throat. 'I guess it's the same thing that holds most people together.'

'That's where you're wrong.' Libby plants herself on the edge of the tub.

Jessica pulls her legs into her chest. 'Pass me a towel, would you?'

Libby ignores her. 'When I was a little girl the thing that used to drive me crazy was watching people, heads together, in conversation that excluded me.'

She stops talking, waiting for a comment but all Jessica can think about is how exposed she feels, even with Libby staring through the window at the blackened sky. Having a bath with another person in the room – other than Jacques – had felt daring, like she was opening herself up to the intimacies of a friendship she'd never had before. Now she feels like a moth in a museum display with a pin through its body.

Oblivious, Libby carries on. 'Sometimes I'd lie in bed thinking about all those shared confidences, the secret interactions that I would never be party to, and it made me feel physically sick.'

Jessica gets out of the bath so quickly that she skids on the polished tiles as she lunges for the towel on the heated rail. Red-faced, she turns away from Libby and dries herself. She attempts to drape the towel over her back as she struggles damp feet through the twisted material of her knickers.

'I see the two of you in your little loved-up nest, and I want to scratch the surface and see what's going on. In fact, I want what you have.'

The towel starts to slip and Jessica gives up, shrugging it off. Pulls on her clean T-shirt and Jacques' cotton shorts and turns back to her friend.

'I guess you could say I'm greedy,' Libby is saying,

tapping her chin with one shiny, pink nail, still blank-eyeing the window.

Jessica puts her head to one side. 'I have no idea what you're talking about, but it's bedtime for me.'

'And me.' Libby gets up. 'Good God, is that really what you wear in bed?'

'I suppose you wear some kind of silk negligee with matching eye-mask?'

'You've been through my drawers.'

As they laugh, Jessica feels silly and prudish for her earlier discomfort.

Once inside her bedroom, Jessica doesn't bother with the light, bumping her way around the unfamiliar space to draw the blinds before crawling into bed. She is almost asleep when there's a soft patter against wood. Then Libby opens the door, light from the hall outlining her dark silhouette. She's wearing a long, high-necked nightie which Jessica is too sleepy to comment on.

'What's wrong?'

Her friend crosses the floor and jumps onto the bed. 'Scoot over.'

'What are you doing?' Jessica asks and turns away, hugging her pillow. She'll never sleep now.

'When I was little,' Libby says, plumping her pillow and wriggling into a comfortable position. 'I used to pretend I had a sister just like you.'

'Weed and home-made booze.' Libby grins. 'I've just placed Nathan.'

They are walking barefoot through flat surf. An

early-morning mist is blurring the divide between water and sky.

Jessica stops walking. 'You knew Nathan?'

'Everyone did. He had the local underage market cornered. Nathan's house was the first stop on a night out. I probably snogged him at a party.'

'What a crazy coincidence.' Jessica skips a flat stone across the water, hiding her face. It rankles; her past – kept private even from Jacques – somehow being shared with Libby.

'There are no coincidences. Only universal signposts.'

At which Jessica laughs. 'God, you sound like my dad.'

The silence sags under the weight of her unguarded comment. As they walk on, Jessica gazes at the water, dredging memories like sea treasure.

'Thomas taught me how to float.'

'You grew up by the sea, and you couldn't swim?'

'Of course I could swim. And float. It was just something I told him so that . . .'

'I see.' Libby looks delighted, linking her arm through Jessica's. 'Womanly wiles at such a tender age.'

Jessica smiles, looks away with her memory.

His fingers curling into her armpits as she kicked her feet off the sea bed. *Look up at the sky.* Moving a hand to cradle her head as she leaned further back, the water creeping over her ears. Shingle scratching in the current, the crunch of Thomas's feet as he moved around her, spreading out her limbs. The blissful lightness of her body.

'Do you ever get those moments of complete happiness?' she asks Libby. 'Over the most ordinary things?'

'Oh, I'm too superficial for that.' Libby squeezes Jessica's arm. 'Though this isn't bad. As moments go.'

They follow the shoreline towards Pear Tree Cottage.

'There's a man in your garden.' As Jessica says it, her stomach is flipping over, her heart vaulting behind her ribs. Something about the man's posture and his hair in the sun. Jessica starts to run.

'Why, look who it is!' Libby catches up at the gate and pushes past, arms open. 'Jacques, darling.'

Jacques returns Libby's hug with a fatherly pat, his eyes on Jessica, who is still standing on the other side of the fence.

'What are you doing here?'

Libby is laughing, an arm draped over his shoulders. 'Your Moscow trip was a ruse to catch us up to no good.'

'Honey?' Jacques disengages himself and walks towards her. 'You look angry.'

'No, no. Confused. I mean, surprised.'

'The flights were all messed up, so the meeting's been postponed. I jumped in the car. On impulse.' He looks away, rubbing the side of his nose with his thumb. A gesture, she realises with shock, he uses when he's uncomfortable.

'I thought it would be a nice surprise.'

'It is, Jacques.'

In the house, Libby has become violently animated. 'First, I'll cook breakfast and then I'll make your bed.'

'His bed?' Jessica removes her hand from Jacques', conscious of her slippery palms.

Libby bursts around the door frame, laughing behind her hand. 'What am I saying? I'm all thrown.'

'Show me to our room,' Jacques says into Jessica's hair as cupboard doors bang in the kitchen.

Jacques collects a sailing bag from the hallway on his way upstairs. It's not the case he uses for work trips; he has packed a new one for the weekend. It makes Jessica smile. 'Not quite impulsive enough to come away without clean t-shirts and casual trousers.'

He responds with a pinch to her bottom and closes the bedroom door, pushing her down onto the bed. She enjoys his kiss, open-mouthed and possessive until Libby's muffled singing rises from the kitchen, peeling them apart.

Jacques inspects the view from the window. Jessica joins him and they both dip their heads from the endless sea as Libby bustles into the garden below, spreading a tartan rug and laying out a pot of tea, glasses of orange juice and bagels. Smiling to herself. For a moment Jessica is tempted to slip her arms about Jacques' waist and lead him back to the double bed, leaving Libby with her picnic and her excitement.

When they go back downstairs, Libby flings her arms about Jacques again.

'I love a man who can master the art of surprise.'

I want what you have.

'I would have called,' Jacques says, spreading cream cheese on his bagel. 'But this place is kind of cut off from the rest of the world.'

'Deliberately so.' Libby bites hugely into her own bagel, adding through a full mouth, 'It's very liberating.'

'From what?' Jessica's voice is a jarring note in an otherwise flowing tune. Libby glances at her but makes no comment. Instead, she lies back on the rug, arms sprawled above her head, seemingly oblivious to the dangerous slide of material as her dress rides up and pools like a fallen parachute about her thighs. She closes her eyes in the sun.

'I'm so glad the three of us are together.'

They go to bed early, sun-tired and content. Jacques gives her a chaste cuddle and rolls away. She stares at his broad, naked back and feels inexplicably bereft. Trails her fingers down his spine until he shivers with goosebumps.

'You're not making this easy,' he murmurs.

'Why shouldn't we?'

'Your friend is probably still awake on the other side of the wall.'

Within minutes, he is asleep. Jessica's eyes keep pinging open. Throughout the day, she has studied Jacques and Libby: over a pub lunch, and later sipping wine in Libby's peppermint-stripe deckchairs as the sun set. Looking for what, she couldn't say. Nor did she find it. But it has left her physically uncomfortable, with an aching head and stiff neck. A Sunday-night kind of dread is swelling in her stomach though she doesn't know why.

When she finally sleeps, she dreams of Thomas.

Sitting on a fallen tree trunk, the way he was always hunched over his busy hands, feet planted wide apart, elbows on his knees. On her hands and knees, she crawls into the hollow space between his arms and legs, his chest curving over her like a roof to keep her safe. She can feel the heat of his leg through his jeans as she rests her cheek on his thigh.

She wakes to find a naked Jacques leaning his elbows on the windowsill, gazing out.

'You used to go sea-kayaking with your dad, didn't you?' Jessica clambers over the bed to wrap her arms around him. 'How's the water looking today?'

He turns, pulling her in. Over his shoulder, she catches sight of a figure on the beach by the water's edge. Libby is standing with her feet in the water wearing an emerald-green bathing suit, an old-fashioned kind that has recently become fashionable again with a cinched-in waist and corseted top. It gives her figure the glamorous curves of a 1950s starlet.

Jacques follows her gaze, craning his head over his shoulder towards the beach. 'Not what you'd call an athletic physique.'

Jessica is struck by his biting tone. Jacques, who is always so generous about everyone.

'I know you didn't come here on a whim, Jacques.'

His gaze returns to her. Sighing, he rests his head on her shoulder and for a moment, she thinks she might be sick. 'I interrupted your girls' weekend.'

Jessica swallows drily. 'You did.'

'I just don't trust her.'

'Still?'

'She's great company and all, but she plays games with people. You see that, don't you?'

'You're mistaken.' Jessica pulls away from the distraction of his stroking hand. 'We were having a lovely time. Becoming closer.'

Jacques drops his head again. 'I'll go, sweetie. Take an extra day here. I'll call William Mansion's and make an excuse for you.'

When she doesn't answer, he starts to collect yesterday's clothes from the back of the chair, folding them into neat squares.

'I'd rather go home with you,' she says.

They agree to leave after breakfast. Jessica sends Jacques to help Libby with the fry-up while she strips the sheets off the bed.

When she goes downstairs, she sees them, framed through the open doorway of the kitchen. It stops her; the way they are standing so close together that Libby's head is tilted back, their eyes bridging the narrow space between them. Jessica steps back, closes her eyes, forehead pressed to the wooden door frame as she tries to fish words out of the strained hush of their voices.

'We want the same thing.' There's a soft, entreating smile in Libby's voice.

'She mustn't be—' Jacques starts to say but she interrupts.

'—hurt. I know.'

Jessica sits on the bottom step, waiting, but the only sound comes from the rush of tap water and chink of crockery. She gets up. She will observe them, see what she can glean from the way they will now move about each other in her presence.

'Coffee, Jessie?' Libby waves a small cafetière.

Jacques strides over to the grill. 'Bacon's almost done.'

'We've burnt the toast, I'm afraid.' Libby pushes a coffee mug into her hands. 'I've put more in the toaster.'

Over breakfast, Jacques apologises again for ruining their weekend.

Libby shakes her head. 'You didn't. I had such a lovely day yesterday. With both of you.' And she takes Jacques' and Jessica's hands. 'Genuine friends are rare.'

'Showboat.' Jacques gives her hand a brief squeeze before continuing to butter his toast.

'I'm afraid Jacques has to get back to town,' Jessica says. 'It makes sense for me to go with him.'

A look passes between Jacques and Libby, so fleeting Jessica wonders if she imagined it; her doubt like the immediate darkness of the sky after a firework.

She excuses herself.

In the tiny downstairs toilet she squares up to herself in the mirror, arms gripping the bowl of the sink as though she would rip it from the wall. Her face is flushed, pupils pinprick-sharp. Feverish.

'I am not my mother.' Her voice is too quiet to lessen the pounding in her head. Picking up a silver, lion-footed soap dish, she positions her thumbnail beneath a claw and presses down. The pain is blunt and nauseating but her body starts paying attention. 'This is Jacques we're talking about. *Jacques.*'

He had written the despised origin of his name into their wedding vows, turning it into a promise. *As my name is Jacques, I will never let you down through deceit or dishonesty.*

Feeling calmer, she replays Jacques' and Libby's conversation – something about wanting the same thing and for her not to get hurt – but it could mean anything. So she considers Jacques' surprise arrival, and therein lies the clue.

He and Libby have been playing tug of war with her attention for some time, their behaviour peaking this weekend; Libby stealing her away and Jacques sabotaging her efforts.

What she must have overheard was a recognition of how harmful their actions are becoming. She witnessed a truce.

Jessica releases the bruising pressure from her thumb and nods at her reflection. She has figured it out without screaming wild accusations or tearing at clothing. She is not her mother.

A knock on the door sends the soap dish clattering into the sink.

'You OK, honey?'

Jessica doesn't reply. She takes her time replacing the soap dish and running the tap before opening the door.

'Is a moment's peace too much to ask for?' It is lightly intended but comes out flat, and Jacques steps away without a word.

As they put their bags into the boot of Jacques' old but pristine Volvo, Libby watches them from the doorway.

There's something lost and forlorn about her silence, reminding Jessica of Libby's fear of being left on the outside.

'Come on, sweetie,' Jacques is urging her. 'We're going to hit Sunday traffic.'

In the side mirror, Libby shrinks until she resembles a child, hands clasped together. Jessica kicks off her boots, crossing her legs in the seat.

Jacques clears his throat. 'I was wrong to discourage your friendship with Libby.'

'What's made you change your mind?'

'I think her friendship is genuine, after all.'

Jessica looks away with a satisfied nod. *I am not my mother.*

15

June 2012

In the hallucinatory space between her sleeping body and waking mind, she sees Thomas. Straight out of the sea; sandy-bodied, hair dark with salt water, that rare grin.

Jessica smiles up at the ceiling. Because it's Thursday – her studio day – she considers going back to sleep, chasing her fading dream.

'I've made coffee,' Jacques calls from the kitchen. 'You up yet, honey?'

Jessica spreads her limbs through the warm nest of the bed. 'Almost.'

Jacques strides into the bedroom, towel about his waist and a swipe of overlooked shaving foam along his jawline. He places a mug on her side-table, bends to kiss her forehead and doesn't notice as she reaches for him. Tucking her hand back under the covers, she watches him opening cupboards and drawers, the day already taking him away. 'Do you have to rush off this morning?'

'Today, yes.'

As if today were an exception, she thinks.

'I have a meeting with the Arden Group, which'll probably extend into lunch, and at some point this morning I have to squeeze in a fitting at the tailor's.'

A gust of wind rattles the window, rain spattering against the glass with the vehemence of a drink tossed in anger.

'I think I'll stay in bed today.' She says it quietly, not meaning it. A small test of his attention. 'It's raining.'

'I would take an umbrella, honey, it's looking pretty wet out.'

He delivers a second kiss and is gone.

Jessica puts on studio clothes; torn jeans and a pink sweatshirt, which has stiffened across the chest with polishing dust. By the time she leaves the flat, the bulging sky has burst and she has forgotten her umbrella. She joins a wet huddle of people at the bus stop. When a taxi splashes past with its yellow sign on, she can't resist flagging it down.

'Lockerstone Street, behind Clerkenwell Town Hall, please.'

She writes the letter T in the condensation of her breath on the window and considers the pieces she is working on: a serpent ring with minute scales of lacquered wood and an orchid pendant powdered in crushed glass. The thought of an unfinished item would normally fill her with energy, her head leaping to materials and processes, but today it merely fatigues her.

'I've changed my mind. Can we go to Bayswater instead? Bartholomew Lanes.'

Libby will lift her flattened mood.

The roads are clotted with buses and delivery trucks. Jessica's impatience spikes with every green light that switches to red before her taxi can reach it. She jumps out early, circumnavigating puddles, head down against the rain. Turning the corner, she looks up to check she is in Bartholomew Lanes and sees Libby's pink-fronted florist's halfway along the row of shops. As she wipes rain from her eyes, she catches a blurred image of a man leaving Libby's under a pale blue golf umbrella. Within a few strides he has vanished into the alleyway opposite the florist's. She is left with the impression of slim, navy trousers and a green mackintosh.

'Jacques?' She breaks into a run, slipping on the wet cobblestones, calling his name.

The alley is empty and there are no pedestrians on the adjacent road. Shaking, Jessica leans against the wall, ignoring the filthy sheet of water washing down the brickwork. She can watch the florist's from here without being seen. Five minutes pass without so much as a glimpse of Libby through the bay window. No one walks in or out of the shop. She's not even sure what she is waiting for.

In a shivery daze, she teeters on the pavement edge, searching for a taxi.

Rain drums against the studio skylights like a giant carwash. Only Serena is at her workstation, the silver halo of her curls shivering with the motion of her hands. When she looks up, the youthful plumpness of her face is always surprising under the premature grey of her hair.

'Byrney. Good to see you.' Serena inclines her head back over a tiny file pinched between thumb and forefinger. Jessica mutters a greeting and heads for the kitchenette at the back of the studio. The smell of sardines and turps is comforting in its familiarity. She stares through the unbarred window at a small church with flint-embedded walls. Hemmed in by warehouses, their shadows circle it like a sundial with the passing day. Closing her eyes, she leans her forehead against the cool glass.

The man leaving Libby's shop was half hidden by the umbrella, disappearing before she could study the way he walked – without these clues, he is just one of many faceless men in neutral clothing. Jacques is in a meeting with the Arden Group. He wouldn't drop in on Libby's shop without telling Jessica. It just isn't him.

Then she thinks of his distraction and how it had all but rendered her invisible as he prepared for his day ahead.

Opening her eyes, she spots a man in an oversized raincoat standing beside the church wall. Staring up at her. She pushes back from the window, watching as he covers his face, pulling his hood up, and stalks away.

Recognition flips in Jessica's stomach – the man looks like Matthew.

'I'm losing my mind,' she mumbles, pressing cold palms to her cheeks.

Back at her desk, Jessica forces her attention to the

miniature landscape before her. Brassy stacks of mock-up rings; plastic chips, aqua-hued, pooling together; opaque sea glass. Incidental placing of materials can spark unexpected chemistry. A fake cabochon ruby – smooth as a drop of fossilised blood – has found an intriguing counterpart in a torn sheet of sandpaper.

The rough with the smooth, Jessica thinks. Trying to remind herself that Jacques wasn't a man of contrasts – his words and actions as constant as the rising sun.

The rain keeps Jessica company long after Serena has wheeled her bicycle out of the studio. When her mobile rings, she ignores it, fending off the outside world. She barely registers the creak and shuffle of the door opening behind her.

A hand on her shoulder makes her jump, her cry spiralling two pigeons off the steel girders above. Matthew bends over her, dripping water from his raincoat onto her workbench.

'What are you doing here?' She glances past his shoulder. 'Is Libby with you?'

'No, it's just me. I'm so sorry I startled you.'

Jessica stands up, folding her arms about her. Asks again, 'Why are you here?'

'I hope this isn't inappropriate, my arriving at your studio like this. I tried to call.'

'What's wrong, Matthew?'

He brushes back his wet hair with both hands, grave eyes roaming the studio. A shaft of evening sun has broken through the rain, slanting across his face. It accentuates his pallor and the dark smudges beneath his eyes. 'May I?' He indicates the chair beside him, fingers stretched and precise as a salute, his formality clashing with his baggy-kneed cords and slouching coat.

'Of course. You don't have to ask.'

Before he sits, he unfolds a square of paper from his trouser pocket. A sketchy necklace has been drawn in blue biro. 'I designed it myself. Badly, of course. I was hoping you could make it as an anniversary present for Libby.'

'You want me to make her a pendant?'

Matthew sits forward to point out various scribbles and arrows. 'It's a hollow, filigree globe which was popular with court ladies during Marie Antoinette's time. They used to fill them with pot pourri or secret charms.'

'Libby calls you the Human Encyclopedia.' Jessica smiles, tracing her nail across the design. Twists of silver thread and secret catches start to take shape under the motion of her finger. 'What shall we put inside?'

'A glass flower, I was thinking. Or a tiny figure of a guardian angel.'

Jessica shivers. 'I've never really understood the appeal of guardian angels. That idea of being invisibly watched.' A beat of silence passes as they study the picture. Matthew is staring at her when she looks up. Something about his stiff posture and the awkward knot of his fingers makes her touch his arm. 'What is it?'

'French courtiers sometimes sealed a tiny lock and key inside as a charm to keep their lady-love faithful.'

A chill sweeps through her. 'Is that what you want to put inside?'

'You know she has affairs?' Even though the studio is empty, he is whispering. She leans in, their bodies forming a conspiratorial triangle over the diagram.

'Since the second year of our marriage.'

'Who?' Sees again the man under the blue golf umbrella leaving Libby's shop.

'That's not relevant.' Matthew draws back, breaking the triangle. 'It's my fault, you see, so I don't interfere.'

'How can it be your fault?' Outrage raises her voice. Seeing him away from Libby's shadow, in his own light, Jessica is struck by how gentle and kind he is. Handsome, even, in an accidental fashion. If she were better at expressing herself, she would tell him so. 'I don't understand.'

'No man had resisted her before I came along. I could see she was beautiful and exciting and vivacious, but I'm simply not equipped to deal with all that drama.'

Here comes drama. Jessica encourages him with a nod and Matthew sighs.

'You can imagine what a red rag *that* was.'

'But she won.'

He spreads the folds of paper with his palms. 'Not really. It hurts her, knowing she is not my perfect fit.'

'And yet her affairs are hurting you. If you're jealous, it's because you care.'

'I do love her.' Matthew pulls his coat back on. 'I just don't worship her, and that's what my wife craves.' He shakes his head, combing his fingers through his hair again. 'She is much sweeter and calmer when she is not in the grip of some passing infatuation. So yes, I'd like her affairs to stop.'

Jessica walks him to the door and surprises them both by suggesting a drink.

The Floss and Junket is a crooked, black-beamed pub squashed between converted warehouses. Its smoke-stained interior is empty apart from two men at the billiard table; one in a pinstripe suit with stripes too fat to be conventional City-wear, his companion with a foxy red beard and harem pants in grey wool.

As Jessica sits down at a battered table held together by what looks like the pewter wheel rim of a cart, something tugs at her sleeve. A splinter of torn metal is lifting away from the table's edge. Plucking at her snagged thread, Jessica wonders what she and Matthew will talk about without Jacques and Libby dominating the conversation. When he returns with two large vodkas, she asks if he passed her building earlier.

'Ah. I wondered if you'd seen me.'

'Why didn't you come in then?'

'You looked,' here he shrugs, embarrassed, 'as though you might have had things on your mind.'

Jessica doesn't answer. Swallows a large mouthful of her drink, the tonic fizzing sweetly acid in the back of her throat.

'So how did you and Libby meet?'

Matthew smiles, shaking his head. 'I was at a restaurant with a new girlfriend. On the table beside us was this striking woman with a couple of friends. I was rather mystified by the way she kept making eye contact with me. When my companion went to the Ladies, she leaned over to me and said, *Why don't you send your little friend home now so we can stop wasting our time?*'

'You have to admire Libby's boundless confidence.' Jessica shifts in her seat, her arm catching once again at the ragged table-edge. 'I assume you complied?'

'I admit I let her take my phone number.' He shrugs one shoulder, no longer smiling. 'Of course then I felt ashamed and refused to return her calls. I was quite unprepared for the aggression – no let's call it the vigour – of her pursuit.'

Jessica takes a spiky gulp of vodka. Looks down at her lap, fighting an overwhelming desire to tell him she saw Jacques leaving Libby's shop this morning. Or thought she saw. The metal splinter has a beautiful shape, she notices; the edge rippling into a lethal apex. With the pad of her thumb she discovers its pleasing slice.

'You and Jacques seem to get on well.'

Matthew, mid-drink, points with his glass, slopping liquid over his fingers. 'I like that man of yours. He's decent, straightforward. Exactly what it says on the tin.' He leans forward, elbows bumping onto the table, almost knocking Jessica's drink sideways. 'And the thing that makes me chuckle is that my wife is fairly taken with him and he doesn't even notice.'

A delicious, red-embered needle of pain slides under Jessica's nail and deep into her arm as she pushes the metal splinter into her thumb. It makes her breath catch, bringing tears to her eyes. Matthew's eyebrows rise in concern. He digs a creased handkerchief from his pocket.

'I've upset you. I only meant Libby expects a certain male reaction. A bit of harmless flirtation.'

A polished bead gathers on her thumb-tip, swelling until it spills like melted candle wax down to her wrist. 'Jacques would never want to hurt me.'

'I've noticed how protective he is of you.' Matthew nods in vigorous agreement, and the shadows of his face are released. 'Libby and I have often commented on your . . . togetherness, for want of a better word. It's a rare thing these days.'

Jessica's injured thumb begins to throb, her heartbeat slowing to match its pulsing ache. Blood-letting, she thinks. Letting the bad blood flow away.

'You have no idea what your friendship means to Libby.' Matthew blinks, looks away, embarrassed perhaps at having said too much.

Jessica sits back in her chair, noticing how the lights in the pub are leaving streaks in the air. She hasn't eaten since a mid-morning snack of stale pretzels, and the double vodka is singing in her head. She fixes her wavering gaze on the solid bulk of the bar. 'I managed to avoid the best-friend thing throughout my childhood. It's funny, really . . .'

They finish their drinks in silence before Matthew offers to get a second. Jessica inspects her thumb as his back is turned and realises she has been staunching it with Matthew's handkerchief, which is now wet with blood. Scrunching it into a ball in her rucksack, she hopes he will forget to ask for it back.

By the time they leave the pub, the streetlights are on and a rinsed breeze makes the night smell organic and pure. As they walk to the tube, bumping companionably, Jessica says, 'I know exactly what we'll put inside Libby's pendant.'

'Tell me.' Matthew's head looms unsteadily towards her.

'A smaller globe, and then another one inside that, and another, like a Russian doll.' The idea elates her. 'It's perfect, don't you see?'

He is nodding but frowning.

'It's about layers, Matthew. Secret layers.'

By the time Jessica gets home, her actions feel thick and swollen but her mood is buoyant. The first thing she sees is a bright red umbrella with a white Arden Group logo leaning against the wall. Not a pale blue golf umbrella. Running her hand along the material, she catches a last few drops of rain. The television is on. Jacques has waited up for her. Light with relief, she skips along the hall. At the sitting-room door, she realises it's not the sound of the television but murmuring; a low voice and a light one threaded together.

She tries to pick out individual words over the sousing blood in her ears but it's like trying to scoop leaves out of rushing water. With the pads of her fingers, she nudges the door open, knowing exactly what she'll see.

On the sofa, Libby sits cross-legged facing Jacques, who has an arm slung over the back of the cushions above her shoulders but not touching. Not touching.

The scene is so comfortable, so natural, it feels as if she's seen it before, or imagined it into being.

'There you are.' Libby rushes towards her. A moment's hesitation as she tries to read the look on Jessica's face before smothering her in a hug. 'We've been waiting hours for you.'

Jessica catches Jacques' eye over Libby's shoulder.

'I've been calling,' he says, claws of exhaustion under his eyes.

'I was working. I turned my phone off.' Aware that she is swaying in the middle of the room as Libby moves away, Jessica adds, 'I went for a few drinks afterwards.'

Jacques gives her a flat look, but how can she tell him the truth in front of Libby without giving away Matthew's anniversary surprise? She needs Libby to leave. Immediately.

'So how come you're here, Libby?' Her tone more accusing than she'd intended. In the corner of her eye, Jacques is shaking his head in disgust.

'I'm going to bed.' He skirts around her outstretched hand and she notices for the first time that he is wearing slim, navy trousers.

It means nothing because the umbrella in the hallway is red, not pale blue.

'Matthew's gone AWOL,' Libby chirps. 'I thought he might be here, getting drunk with Jacques.'

Jessica presses her lips together. Matthew will have to make his own excuses. Her earlier clarity has vanished. She is sinking beneath a rolling surface of vodka, where nothing makes sense.

All she can see is Jacques and Libby on the sofa. With a single, kaleidoscope turn, it has become the two of them together with her on the outside.

Layers and lies.

~ 16 ~

The sea-dragon box has brought with it forgotten dreams like stowaways. Every night she is a child again, searching for her dad or pulling splintered wood from the mouth of a monstrous sea. At the core of even the most surreal nightmare lies a forgotten nugget of memory, which persists into daylight. One morning she catches herself wondering which churchyard her father lies buried in. She punishes the thought under an icy shower.

The dreams, unwelcome as they are, still infect her with a longing to revisit old haunts; the secret bays and ragged clifftops. Thomas's chapel. She needs time and space – the freedom – to remember Thomas properly.

That's when she thinks of Nathan.

Thomas's older brother by five years, he was already a grown-up when she first met him. Or so it seemed to her thirteen-year-old self. Tall, sporty and clean-shaven. She'd been instantly drawn to his expression of perpetual amusement as if he couldn't quite get over the antics of the human race. He loved his brother as fiercely as she did. Apart from Hannah, he was the only other person who had known about her and Thomas's friendship.

She needs to show him the red notebook.

Jessica tells Jacques she is going to visit her mum, to see how Birdie has settled into the new caravan. He takes her to Paddington Station and as they wait for the train, she turns to him.

'Do you think I should have gone last year?'

'To where?'

Jessica scans the departures board. 'The funeral.'

It takes him a moment, then he pulls her into a fierce hug. 'No, Christ no, sweetie.'

She pushes back so she can see his face. 'You seem so certain.'

'Honey, think back. As soon as you opened that damn card your reaction was so . . . strong that I – we – can trust you made the decision that was right for you.'

She presses her forehead to his jumper again, unwilling to read in his face the memory of the days that followed. First, how the anger had made her shake so violently and persistently that for a whole day she dropped and broke everything she touched. The next day, as if a giant hand had swatted her down, she lay in bed; couldn't eat, couldn't sleep and wouldn't talk.

'Is this why you're going down there?'

Now Jessica looks him in the eye. 'No. Absolutely not.'

As the train pulls out of Paddington, she pictures his

open, trusting face – *Go do the dutiful daughter thing*. When she's ready, she will show him the counsellor's notebook and tell him about Thomas. Just not yet.

Settling back into her seat with Ms Callum's notes, she whiles away the hours with Thomas's voice in her head.

After a six-hour train journey, she catches a bus to Morley-on-Sea – the nearest village to Nathan's old house – and disembarks at the Pit-Stop Café. It hasn't changed; the same red and white chequered tablecloths and the promise of an all-day brekkie chalked onto an A-frame board on the pavement.

The three of them used to come here all the time – she, Thomas and Nathan – sitting at the back, drinking stewed tea and eating buttered toast.

Sitting down with a tuna melt and a tea she has added too much sugar to, she wipes a spyhole in the window's condensation. The flat seafront features a plait of cropped, ornamental bushes and a merry-go-round covered in dirty, transparent tarpaulin. Paint curls off the frozen horses.

Everything needs fixing in this place, she once remarked to Thomas.

Everything and everyone, he'd answered, and she thought he was talking about the hurt her dad caused by abandoning her. It had made her feel cherished, like Thomas was going to put her back together.

Now, remembering what was to come, she knows he was talking about himself.

The door opens. A thin man with dirty-blond

dreadlocks walks in. He stares at Jessica, who returns to her spyhole.

'Jessica?'

She frowns up at the man as he approaches her table.

'Little Jessie. All grown up.'

His voice is familiar. 'Did we go to school together?'

'It's Nathan.' He waves a hand over his head. 'With a little more hair.'

And then she sees him, the clean-shaven Nathan she'd known, now with dreadlocks and a short beard.

'It *is* you.' She stands up. They face each other, unsure what to do next, until Nathan holds out his hand and they laugh over their awkward handshake. 'The hair suits you, even the facial stuff.'

Nathan beams.

Spliffy, Thomas used to say, rolling his eyes at his older brother. *That stupid ganja grin.* Libby's comment about the local underage market comes back to her.

'Visiting your mum?'

'Actually,' Jessica pushes a chair out for him, 'I came to find you.'

Nathan nods because nothing ever seems to surprise him.

'Let me just grab a tea.' As he places his order, he inclines his head towards the waitress in a way that stings Jessica with familiarity. She'd never noticed how similar the brothers' movements were. A pressure like a threatened migraine throbs in her head; she presses the heels of her hands to her eye sockets.

'Are you OK?'

'You looked like Thomas just now.' Then she wishes

she hadn't said his name, unsure how Nathan will react, but he just nods, grins.

He hadn't been smiling the last time she saw him. The memory is sharp like she's turned a page in a magazine and found it there. A bright morning on top of Hasleborne Hill where a group of people are huddled together in their dark Sunday best, making black holes against the white sky. Jessica had stared at the marble plaque with its gilt words.

Beloved Son and Brother.

The pastor – with a perpetual sniff that kept making her lift her head, thinking he was about to cry – spoke intimately about a boy he'd never met. Nathan insisted she come, holding her hand throughout, she remembers. He was the only one who had wept openly. Jessica had been too angry for tears. Thomas had been gone for less than three months and there was nothing but mud and worms beneath that fancy headstone; they were giving up on him. Thomas's memorial sat on the ground like a shrug: *We tried.*

'So. You were looking for me?' Nathan smooths the fine hair of his moustache past the corners of his mouth. It is an unconscious gesture that strikes her as a measure of the time that has passed since she last saw him; long enough for new tics to develop.

'Are you still at Frotherton West Farm?'

'I run the shop now.' He sips his tea, strokes the sides of his mouth again. 'Still do the odds-and-sods stuff as well.'

Jessica's heart skips. 'Do you remember someone called Albertine Callum?'

'Bertie.'

'You knew her?'

'She was a good friend once.'

Jessica sits back in her chair. 'Did you know she was giving Thomas counselling at school?'

'That's how we got to know her, yes.' Nathan studies her like she's a circuit of wires that he's trying to connect.

'I found her notebook with transcripts from every session. I wondered if you might want to have a look at it.'

'That's OK,' he says, shaking his head. 'I already read it.'

'It was you, then. You put it through my mother's letter box.'

'A long time ago now.' Nathan fiddles with a twist of hair. 'Bertie gave it to me before she moved to Spain. I thought you might want it.'

Jessica looks at her forgotten sandwich, the paper wrapper sticking to the cheese as it cools plastically. 'It's shaken me. Because they're not *my* memories, it feels like he's stepped out of the past. A new him.' She can't tell if Nathan is following what she is struggling to explain. How she has reclaimed a piece of Thomas.

He says, 'I'm guessing there's no one you can really talk to about Thomas these days.'

She'd forgotten his talent for plucking out small truths the way some people always find coins on the ground. Jessica nods.

Nathan hesitates. 'I found some of his stuff the other day when I was having a clear-out.'

'Like what?'

'A few photos. That tatty blue jumper of his.'

That tatty blue jumper. Whenever she thinks of Thomas, he's in that jumper, the roll neck fraying against the stubble of his chin. She wants to see it, to clench it in her hands so badly it makes her stomach ache.

17

Nathan's open-back Land Rover is parked behind the Pit-Stop. She's surprised by how clean it is, and catches herself looking for signs of a woman – there's not so much as a sticker on the windscreen.

He drives more carefully than he ever rode his scrambler. There's something about the deliberate way his hands move as he changes gear, like he's reading the things he touches. Thomas's hands had that same expressiveness. Jessica turns her head to the passing countryside instead.

Everywhere seems to hold a memory of her and Thomas, their friendship rooted in marram dunes and pine forests. Snippets of his voice are caught like balloons in trees.

. . . if anyone ever hurts you, I'll find them and hurt them worse.

Has anyone ever kissed you, Jellybird?

Nathan turns off the B312 onto a forested path which opens into a gravel yard, fringed by overgrown leylandii. It takes her a moment to recognise his house. She and

Thomas would sometimes wind up here on one of their nightly wanderings but they never stayed long; Nathan was rarely on his own. On a quiet night, a body or two might be sprawled on his sofas; closer to the weekend there'd be huddles of people puffing bongs made of plastic lemonade bottles and empty biro cylinders. She hated coming here, never knowing what to do with herself in front of all those strangers intent on getting stoned. She wonders if Libby had been among them – the same age as her but more sophisticated, blending easily.

'Do you know anyone called Libby? Elizabeth Hargreaves?'

Nathan shrugs. 'Should I?'

'She used to come here, years ago.'

'Ah,' Nathan says, and nothing more. He slows for a hobbling turkey and parks beside the crooked makeshift shed that once housed the home-made wine he sold for two pounds a bottle. 'Welcome to Nathan Country.'

He takes her on a tour. The Moonshine Shed, as everyone used to call it, now houses tomato plants. He points out fastidious rows of vegetables, an apothecary of herbs growing in a rusted bath and his hen coops – three mismatched cabinets whose doors have been replaced with chicken wire.

'Total self-sufficiency,' he says, indicating solar panels on the roof.

As they return to the front of the house, Jessica listens for voices and music from within but it is dark and silent. Nathan pushes the front door open and steps aside for her.

'Still don't lock your door, then?'

'No one comes here,' he says, as she wonders what happened to all those casual drop-ins, the impromptu parties.

Jessica chews on a desiccated segment of tangerine while Nathan runs upstairs to get the photographs of Thomas. The bowl of citrus fruit offers a tiny relief of colour against the sitting room's hand-me-down furniture and bland seascape paintings. She'd had to look away as he hunched over the small hearth, fiddling with damp matches, the sight suddenly filling her with loneliness. Self-sufficiency, he'd called it.

Nathan bounds into the room and places two photographs face down beside the fruit bowl. He flips one over like a magician's trick. Jessica's hand falters in mid-air.

'I never saw the two of them together.'

It must have been one of the last photos of Thomas; she recognises his jeans with the ripped-out knees. His father is leaning on a walking stick, an arm about his son's shoulders. Support or embrace, she can't tell; Thomas's wiry frame bending like a green twig under his father's weight. The fingers gripping the walking stick have long, rounded nails like a lion's claw. Neither son nor father is smiling.

'It's me,' she says, surprised, picking up the second picture. She can't remember the moment but recognises the sea wall overlooking Selcombe Harbour where she and Thomas used to watch fishermen mending nets. She studies her teenage self.

154

'I had hair like a witch.'

'Thomas said you were the colour of autumn with your red hair and green eyes.' Nathan strokes the peel off a tangerine with his nimble fingers. 'I ragged him about that, obviously. Getting all poetic.'

Jessica hugs her knees, staring into the fire. 'Who took the photo?'

'Must have been Thomas.'

Something about the way she is gazing straight at the photographer – at Thomas – with such fierceness of feeling, full of laughter and challenge, makes her agree. She's missed that feeling, can almost feel a hole in her body where it used to be. She wonders if it was still there when she first met Jacques. Perhaps it's what drew him to her.

She gets up. 'I need to make a quick call.'

Outside, the clearing has grown long shadows and the first stars are out. An owl is calling from the invisible branches of a tree. It doesn't sound real, like someone whistling in imitation. Her mobile has no signal and she can't call home. She experiences a pang of guilt, imagining Jacques' face if he saw her now, in the house of a stranger. She tries one last time without success.

'Can I see his jumper?' she asks, going back inside.

'I left it in the kitchen.'

Before he can move, she rushes across the room. 'Don't get up. I'll grab it.'

The jumper is lying in a heap on the kitchen counter. Her arms feel lead-weighted as she reaches for it, hands shaking. Turning her back to the sitting-room door she pushes her face into it, breathing in, then drops her arms in disgust. The wool has a greasy texture as though it's been damp for so long it has started to melt. It gives off a powerful fungal smell. Forcing it back to her nose, she inhales deeply, trying to get beyond the stench to catch a trace of Thomas. Finds none.

It is a piece of dead material.

'Where are you staying?' Nathan's voice in the doorway makes her jump. She drops the jumper by the sink, ghastly with embarrassment.

'My mother's. I think.'

'You could stay here, if you like. We haven't really talked about Thomas yet, have we?'

She considers this. 'If you're sure?'

She accepts an offer of tea, fishing about in her rucksack for Ms Callum's notebook as he pours her a cup. They both stare at it as she lays it on the table.

'Not a light holiday read, is it?'

'I haven't finished it yet.' She needs to break it up into manageable snippets or risk being overwhelmed by the resurfacing loss of him. 'Some of the sections aren't clear. It's like they're talking in code.'

'Yeah, there's a lot of stuff referring to conversations outside of the sessions. They became friends.'

Jessica nips the inside of her lower lip. Those unrecorded moments in which the roots of a friendship spread and took hold, fed by words and looks and physical presence. Safely lost in history where they can never be held up to the light.

'Does this bit mean anything to you?' She flicks

through the notebook and her fingers feel their way to the right page. 'Callum asks if he's afraid of anything and he says, *I bet you never knew a whisper could scare you to death*.'

The perpetual smile at the corner of Nathan's eyes is gone. 'My father.'

She wipes her palms on her trousers, finding them slippery with dread. 'Sometimes his face would be bruised and bloody but he wouldn't talk about it.'

Nathan sighs, shifting his feet apart, stooping over his knees as he peels another tangerine. A Thomas posture.

'That wasn't my father. That was Thomas.'

'What do you mean?'

'He used to hang around pubs at closing time and say something stupid to the biggest lad he could find. He'd let the guy really punch the shit out of him before he even raised his fists. Once he started to fight back, it was hard for him to stop.'

Jessica is shaking her head. 'If I was hearing this from anyone else I'd call them a liar. I know it was your father . . . doing that to him.'

Thomas with his face and hands swollen and newly scabbed. *Did your father do this?* He'd deny it every time; sometimes wearily, often with a sour laugh. *He wouldn't dare*. She'd taken it for bravado and found his courage devastating.

Nathan is staring straight ahead. 'The marks my dad left on Thomas couldn't be seen on the outside.'

'Is that the whispering?'

Nathan blinks like he's trying to clear the film of his

eye. 'It started when Thomas was little, being too loud or lively. My dad would bend his head right down next to Thomas's and speak in his ear. Thomas's face would go blank like the life had been sucked out of him.'

'What was he saying?'

'I don't know. I knew not to cross him. Thomas never had that kind of survival instinct.'

They sit quietly for a moment, listening to the hiss of the fire.

'I can still see him. This little, wild four-year-old climbing out of the attic skylight. Whooping with excitement until my dad came into the yard. Then he went quiet. I swear he was working out if he could jump down and crush the old man. I think my dad saw it too.'

Jessica doesn't say anything. She wants to take the little boy Thomas in her arms and wrap him up tight and safe.

'The thing about my dad is you never see his anger, only its actions. He can do the most awful things, calm as you like.'

Jessica shudders, remembering Ms Callum's comment after Thomas's first session. *The lack of visible anger.* 'Why didn't you try to protect him from your dad?' She tries for a neutral tone, to strip it of any accusation.

Nathan sighs, rubbing his forehead. 'By the time Thomas turned fourteen he was taller than my father and believe me, the old man had started giving him a wide berth.'

Jessica gets up, all of a sudden wanting nothing more than to press herself into Jacques' warm, welcoming body. Her comfortable home, her safe life in London seems overwhelmingly far away.

'I might have an early night, if you don't mind.'

Nathan doesn't move. 'I guess it was too late by then. My father had whispered all his fury into Thomas. You can see why he went looking for trouble.' Then he stands up, his slow smile weighted with acceptance. 'At least he had us. He knew we loved him, Jessie.'

She nods for his sake and looks away. 'Perhaps I could have done more though. He needed someone to help him.'

'He had Bertie.'

'Yes,' Jessica says. 'Of course.'

Nathan takes her upstairs to a box room with a curtainless window and flocked wallpaper. A thin mattress with yellow stains like spilled tea fills most of the floor. He leaves her in the doorway and returns with a roll of bedding under his arm and a lit candle in a glass pot. It leaves a thin trail of Christmassy scent. 'The room hasn't been used in a while.'

As he sets the candle on the windowsill, she gives his arm a quick squeeze. 'It's good to see you, Nathan.'

'I see you're wearing a wedding ring,' he says softly.

She stretches out her fingers and they both study the ring.

'It's good.' As Nathan plumes the sheet through the air, black specks like peppercorns scatter from the musty folds. Jessica squats down on the pretext of tucking the sheet under the mattress and finds further mouse-droppings clinging to the cotton.

'Your life has moved on,' Nathan is saying.

'I haven't forgotten Thomas.'

He straightens, his fingers scrunching the dreadlocks at the base of his skull as though trying to free a troublesome thought lodged there.

'Don't spend too much time on Bertie's book.'

Under a stage-light moon, the trees in Nathan's front yard are so sharply delineated they resemble theatre cut-outs. Jessica turns from the window. Folding her coat into a pillow, she lies on the edge of the mattress as far from the mouse-droppings as possible. She keeps her shoes on, soles dangling over the edge. Pulling her sleeves over her hands, she tucks them between her thighs, skin itching with the thought of the dirty sheet.

Not a trace of summer warmth has been caught between the walls of the room. Within minutes she is shivering. There is still no mobile signal to call a taxi, and she can't throw Nathan's hospitality back in his face by asking him to drive her to the station. Not only is she trapped for the night, but she has learned nothing.

Being here and witnessing how far Nathan's life has moved on from those early days has only made Thomas seem even further removed. A lifetime away.

A scratching noise from behind the skirting board makes Jessica abandon the idea of sleep. The only option left is to read. Taking the red notebook from her rucksack and lifting the cinnamon candle down to the floor, she opens the book.

It takes her half an hour to read it from cover to cover.

'Well.' It's her mother's word; the one she uses when there is simply too much to express and too few ready words.

It's him and it's not him. She'd never realised before how utterly lost he was, and it shames her now. Silly, self-centred child that she was.

Pushing the notebook up onto the windowsill, she lies back and closes her eyes, exhausted suddenly. Too tired to care about mice and dirt. She is almost asleep when a noise startles her. Jumping up, she searches for the origin of the crash, unnerved to find the room unchanged.

Then she sees it – the notebook lying face down beneath the window, the stiff leather cover at an odd angle, like the wing of a pigeon flattened on the road. The paper lining has torn away, revealing a corner of turquoise card. She prises it out with thumb and fingernail.

A picture postcard. She can hardly bring herself to touch it.

On the front is a photograph of a modern office block with a pointed roof, the sun glinting off glass walls, like a giant crystal shafting out of the earth. *The Iceberg at Stollingworth* reads the caption beneath.

She turns the postcard, her heart going over with it. The handwriting is very different from Bertie's crisp script. Odd words stand out, ploughed into the card with such force that it shows through the Iceberg tower in mirror image. One of the words is *FREE*.

Dear Bertie
Yesterday I drowned but today I am FREE.
Luv from Tom

At the bottom of the postcard, the same pen has drawn a tiny fishing boat, its prow pointing skyward as it sinks into angry waves. On the billowing sail it says *The Bad Ship Thomas*.

Jessica's hands start to shake. Pressing the card flat on her lap, she reads it again.

It is postmarked 27 December. Eight days after Thomas disappeared.

TQ: No, he never loses his rag.

AC: In which case, your father must have amazing self-control.

TQ: When something makes him angry, he does something about it.

AC: Like what?

TQ: I don't know. I guess like the time Midge snapped at him . . .

AC: Your dog?

TQ: One of them. We keep ridgebacks for security and stuff. They're big dogs but if you train them well, they're softies.

AC: What happened when Midge snapped at your father?

TQ: It was because of her paw. She'd hurt it and it was making her grouchy. Otherwise she'd never have done it.

AC: What did your father do?

TQ: He hugged her and made her calm.

AC: That sounds kind.

TQ: . . . and then he wrapped a long chain around her neck. Over and over until she was making this coughing noise. Coughing all the air out of her lungs.

AC: He killed the dog?

TQ: You can't let your dog snap at you.

~ 18 ~

April 1995, Selcombe

Thomas came to see her every night.

At dinner, she shovelled her food in silence while Hannah tried to provoke and Lisa nagged and their mother looked out of the window. Plate scraped clean, she went upstairs and waited for the scuffle of sandy pebbles against her window. When it came, she climbed out of the window and followed him through forests, secluded coves and abandoned tin mines; sometimes to Nathan's. Their world the empty night.

Then one evening he wanted to make a plan.

Meet me tomorrow at the Tree, six thirty.

Can't it be later? We don't eat dinner until seven.

Six thirty or don't bother. Excuses are for cowards.

So the next evening, Jessica told Birdie she was going over to Lucy's. The lie was foolproof. Her mum and Mrs Trelawney would never meet by chance. She tried to imagine Lucy's mother in Seasalt Holiday Park, floating in her summer dress and gardening hat through beige rows of caravans. Her skin still crawled with embarrassment remembering how her mother had introduced herself to Lucy's mum last summer at Speech Day. Birdie small, dark and plump with her sharp eyes and sparky movements – the way she'd launched herself forward, arm out like a jousting pole to shake Mrs Trelawney's limply offered hand. A fizzy Coca-Cola beside a cool glass of milk. Only now her mother wasn't fizzy any more, she was flat.

Her mood lifted as she closed the front door, stepping into a pollen-dusty evening, the air full of melting tarmac and wild lilac. She took the cliff road down into the valley. When she reached a field of brilliant yellow flowers with a grove of beech trees in the middle, she climbed over the stile and onto a rutted path.

The beech-tree copse had become one of their favourite places now that the weather had turned warm. In its centre was a long-dead oak that made a perfect viewing tower. In its bare branches they were hidden from view. They spied on dog-walkers, couples holding hands and deer that Thomas potted, his arm stretched out under the length of an invisible hunting rifle.

When she reached the oak, Thomas was already there, swinging his bare feet, his trainers lying among the roots like fallen fruit. He didn't acknowledge her until she eased herself onto his branch. Then he turned to regard her through a pair of battered green binoculars.

'I was about to give up on you.'

'It's laundry day. I had to help Birdie. Where did you get those from?'

'Birthday present from my dad.'

'Your birthday? So you're seventeen now?' Seventeen. Just a few years between them but somehow it was an age that sounded far away, as though he was leaving her behind. 'I'll be fourteen soon.'

Thomas pulled a silver hip flask from his pocket, screwed off the top and took an audible gulp. He held it out to her. She sniffed the contents. The smell was sweet, catching the back of her throat like cough medicine.

'Is this also from your dad?'

Thomas fixed her in the binocular sights again. 'Do you know where he got these from?' He let them thud back against his chest. 'A box in the shed. Where they've been rotting since my uncle died. They were his.' He took the flask out of her hand. '*This* was my present to myself.'

'Looks really expensive.'

'Did I say I bought it?' Thomas gave her a grin that was more a baring of teeth, and Jessica felt her stomach knot. She didn't like it when he was in this mood. It could go anywhere.

He raised the binoculars again, leaning forward to rest his elbows on his knees, teetering as he adjusted his balance.

'Here we go.'

Jessica heard voices. Two people were picking their way towards the trees through the undulating rapeseed.

The woman walked with her face tilted to the evening sun; she was pretty with freckles and high cheekbones. Behind her, the man moved more cautiously, his head down. All she could see was his hat. Jessica sucked in her breath, her fingers scrabbling for a hold in the bark as her horizon tilted. Her father's hat, his old panama, the one he used to plonk on her head as he walked in through the front door, making the same joke about her head shrinking as it slipped down her brow. She could see his thick curls gathered under its brim and knew when he took off his hat the hair beneath would be flattened, sticking to his head.

'What's he doing here?' she choked through a dry throat.

Thomas shushed her, not listening. Jessica pulled her legs into a shaky crouch, gripping twigs for support as she turned to climb down.

'What are you doing?' Thomas held her arm. At that moment the man raised his face and she saw she was wrong. Those weren't her father's eyes – the laughter lines were missing – and the nose was too small, the mouth wide and thin. It wasn't him after all. It wasn't him.

'What's wrong?'

'Nothing.' The wind picked up, rattling through sun-parched leaves like spilling shingle. It whipped away the brief exchanges between the couple as the man stamped a space in the plants and the woman flapped out a blanket, pinning the corners with two bottles of cider.

'What are we doing here?'

'Time for you to grow up a little.' Thomas smiled, that same wolfish grimace. Jessica stayed in her crouch. Her mouth was still dry with residue shock; she wanted to go home. Below them the couple slugged from a bottle, the man's murmurs making the woman snicker. She flicked off his hat. Instead of matted curls there was a bald spot, round and shiny as a china saucer.

They finished the cider and as the empty bottle arced into the field, the man reared up on his knees and tipped the woman back onto the rug. Thomas put the binoculars in her hand, looping the cord about her neck and pushing her down into a seated position. 'Don't look so scared, little rabbit.'

The man hooked up the woman's skirt with a broken rape stalk and peered under the tented material. The wind stilled long enough to catch his words.

'Val, Val, Val. Does Marcus know you go out like that?'

Val sprawled her arms over the spread of her pale hair. The stalk flicked the skirt to her waist and poked her knees apart. Thomas placed his fingers beneath Jessica's wrist and raised the binoculars to her face. The man sat back on his heels, head to one side, regarding Val's naked triangle of curls like he was savouring his Sunday roast. Then he lowered himself with slow deliberation upon her. They kissed. Small, chaste kisses that grew deeper until they gasped and snorted for air like they were fighting over a single bubble of oxygen. The ugliness of it all fascinated

Jessica. Thomas straddled the branch, facing her with a grin, something amusing him in her face. Her neck began to ache in its rigid posture. The woman threw her face up to the sky so the man could peck at her neck. Jessica lowered the binoculars. Thomas moved closer, clasping his hands over hers so that she was caught between his arms as he lifted the lenses back to her face. Val's throat glistened with saliva snail-trails. Her lover moved his hand downwards, making it into a play gun and pushing his fingers deep inside her as she fiddled with his zip.

'Look,' Thomas whispered. 'He's wearing a wedding ring but she isn't.'

Jessica pulled a hand free and tried to tear his grip off the binoculars so the cage of his arms would open. 'We can't watch this.'

Thomas's breath was on her face. 'This is what it's all about.'

'Why are you doing this?' Jessica hissed. Furious tears blurred the writhing, moaning form beneath her.

His voice grew gentle. 'I'm the only one who will never hurt you.'

He brought his face closer. He smelled like sea air and wet grass. Not like the boys at the school disco with their sickly aftershave and fruity hair gel. If she turned her head, their lips would touch. She wanted to run away, leaving her body behind so she could watch, from a safe distance, what might happen next.

'Jellybird,' he mouthed against her cheek and she thought, *I'm going to turn my face.*

'Oh, you sweet bitch,' the man grunted below.

Jessica pushed Thomas away and scrambled down the tree.

AC: So, did you have a look at Wisborough College?

TQ: There wasn't time. My dad needed some help.

AC: But you mentioned the Open Day to him?

TQ: No.

AC: You were worried about his reaction?

TQ: Not really.

AC: Then what is it, Thomas? I can tell there's something on your mind.

TQ: The course is two years. Another two years stuck in that house with him.

AC: Ah, I see.

TQ: I plan to leave all the time but somehow I never do it. I'm stuck. I'm in prison.

AC: You can get away from him. You could even stay here if you needed to. Perhaps, Thomas, the prison is inside of you?

TQ: What do you mean?

AC: You've grown up listening to people telling you how hopeless you are, how incapable and antisocial. I think you believe them.

TQ: The prison is my blood. You can't escape your blood.

AC: Why do you say that?

TQ: Because I'm like my dad. I see him in my face when I look in the mirror. Fuck's sake, I even smell like him.

AC: *You are not your—*

TQ: *What's the point of leaving? You can't run away from yourself.*

~ 19 ~

A few days after the incident at the Tree, Jessica found herself alone in the house. Birdie was taking Grannie Mim to the midweek evening service at the Catholic church in Grantham. Han and Lisa were out somewhere.

All alone. The realisation filled her with a sense of prickly adventure. She went hunting for secrets. She walked past her mother's door – some things she simply didn't want to know – and into Lisa's room. Her search revealed nothing. Neatly stacked schoolbooks on her desk and clothes hanging in the wardrobe – no diary or secret notes squirrelled away. The bedside-table drawer was crammed with supermarket receipts. Lisa had taken it upon herself to make a note of all household expenses since Birdie had become so distant and careless. Prices had been underlined on some of the receipts, her sister's disapproval scrawled in stars and exclamation marks. Lisa's self-important red pen made Jessica furious. She grabbed two handfuls of crumpled papers and threw them in the air so they floated about the room like bleached autumn leaves. Something small and silver fell to the floor.

'No way.' A single condom still in its wrapper. A quick search through the remaining drawers revealed it was the only one. She tried to picture her sister having sex. Moaning and making those open-mouth faces she'd seen on late-night movies. She mock-gagged. 'No. Way.'

Putting the condom in her pocket, she was about to leave the room when the sight of her own reflection in Lisa's full-length mirror stopped her. Her jeans were too short, showing her ankles, and her jumper – pink with a huge strawberry on the front – was ridiculous. She looked like a baby. The condom was thrown back in the drawer.

You're still just a kid.

Thomas's words from two nights ago came back full of nasty little teeth.

He'd been late. She'd almost given up and gone to bed when he appeared in the back garden, whistling. Looking pleased with himself. For some reason, his good humour had soured her mood. It only got worse as he explained why he was late.

I was with a friend. She's helping me sort myself out.

She? She who?

Bertie. The school counsellor. If it's any of your business.

Jessica threw off her jumper. The sight of her white vest, straps drooping off her shoulders, made her even angrier. This, too, was flung on the floor. She stepped up to the mirror, glaring at her naked torso. Bones. Just bloody bones. Her ribs stuck out and her collarbones looked as if she'd swallowed a coat-hanger.

You're late because you've been hanging out with some old, do-gooding hag?

As it happens, Jealous Jelly, she is only six years older than me.

She put her hands over her breasts; what little she'd managed to grow since her nipples softened and popped out last summer. They were small but comforting with a slight weight she hadn't noticed before. She wondered if the school counsellor had large or small breasts.

A feeling caught hold of her, like a draught moving through a room. She unbuttoned her trousers, pushing them down until her hip bones poked out, and discovered that her waist now dipped in above her hips. Crossing her arms in front of her, she put her hands on her waist, closed her eyes and imagined they belonged to a stranger. Thomas's hands.

Then she slipped her trousers below her bottom, her panties with them. The hair down there was fine but enough that she no longer looked like a little girl. Lucy's big brother once asked if her pubes were red like the hair on her head, and she'd hit him. Now, in daylight, there was definitely a reddish tint but she couldn't decide if this was good or bad.

She pushed a tentative finger through the hair until it touched skin. The cool pad of her fingertip, gently pressing. Some of the girls talked about using their fingers, even a hairbrush – though everyone agreed that was gross.

Suddenly self-conscious before her own reflection,

she covered herself up and left Lisa's room feeling irritable and somehow crooked in her own skin. She flung herself on her bed. Lay there remembering how Thomas had looked at her later that same night when they were sitting on the beach, as though he was shocked to find himself so close to her. He had jumped up, grabbing a fistful of stones and skipping them across the flat sea. He always moved away.

She'd asked him, *How come you can't sit still?* *What's so good about sitting still?*

She wanted to reply, *That's when you kiss.* Instead she just glared at him and he looked away, shaking his head.

You're still just a kid, he'd said as if reading her thoughts.

Perhaps he was comparing her to his twenty-three-year-old counsellor now.

Putting her pillow over her head, she willed herself to grow. In biology they'd watched a speeded-up film of a sprouting seed. Jessica pictured her body filling out in the same way, her bones sinking behind swelling curves.

A loud crack made her jump. Another stone hit the window and she leaped up, hauling open the sash and shouting, 'You're going to break the glass, you idiot.'

Thomas made as if to throw another, laughing as she flinched back.

'Hurry up.' Then he rushed towards the house, full speed, leaping up and trying to climb the side of the wall with his feet before dropping back down.

'Stop that. Are you mad? You'll leave footmarks up the wall.'

He made another rush at the wall. 'If you don't get a move on, I'll come and get you. We've got work to do.'

'What work?'

He wouldn't say.

It was only once they'd reached the main road that she saw there was something wrong with his hand. He carried it at his waist as if suspended by an invisible sling. Two of his fingers stuck straight out, the knuckles swallowed up, the swollen flesh like a layer of putty. She stopped under the full beam of a streetlight.

'What's wrong with your hand?'

Thomas regarded it with mild interest as though it were something incidental lying on the pavement. 'I smacked against something.'

'What?' She moved around him, trying to catch a better look at the left side of his face, which looked odd and lumpy. His eye was beginning to puff out of shape.

'Nothing with an IQ of any sorts.' Thomas side-stepped her, leaving the orange circle of light. 'Come on, no time to dilly-dally, Jelly-jelly.'

'Can't you stand still for a second?' She reached for his arm but he evaded her, leaving her hand scratching air. 'Who did this to you?'

'Getting bor-ed.'

This time when she dived forward she caught a handful of t-shirt. 'Your dad did this. Admit it.'

Thomas contemplated her fist for a moment, then lifted his blank eyes. With a single explosive movement, he wrenched her hand off and spun away.

'Don't you ever grab at me again.' His tone so low

and snarling that the skin on her arms goosebumped. She had never heard that voice before.

'I . . .' She swallowed. 'I hate seeing you hurt.'

'Stop talking as if you know anything.' Now shouting, the cords of his neck pushing out. Anger distorted his features. Made him ugly, a stranger.

Jessica covered her mouth with her hand and bit her lip against the wobble in her chin.

Then his rage drained away like a punctured bag of rice. Eyes widening, he took a couple of quick steps towards her, hand out. She thought he was going to pull her into a hug but then his arm dropped away and he never reached her. 'I just don't want you to talk about my dad.' Conciliatory now, plaintive with an apology he couldn't voice. His manic energy returned, feet jiggling against the pavement. 'Come on, let's go.'

'Go where?'

He answered with a grin, his temper forgotten. 'Don't be frightened, Little Scaredybird.'

By the time they'd finished, the sun had set and the forest behind Thomas's house was full of creaking, shifting darkness. His left eye had swollen into something obscene and clam-like. Jessica tried not to look at it.

The thing stood a foot higher than Thomas, a piece of sacking for a head, stuffed with grass and leaves and forced down over the prongs of a rake. It had no face but as shadows formed across its lumps and folds, sinister features developed, shifting as she circled it. From its broom-handle arms hung a sheet of mud-splattered tarpaulin that moved with the wind; one minute sucked flat against its crucifix body, the next billowing out, rustling and hissing at her.

Thomas stood back to regard their handiwork. 'One last touch.'

'Where are you going?' Jessica asked as he turned to leave the clearing.

He grinned. 'Is Mr Scarecrow doing a good job?'

'I'm not scared, if that's what you mean.' She tried to force conviction into her voice. He stooped down behind a tree and picked up something large and dark in his good hand. It swung, boneless, from his grip.

'God, what is that?'

Black eyes and feathers. A wing opened and she nearly screamed. Thomas glanced about, raising one stiff, damaged finger to his lips.

'You're going to ruin everything if you can't be quiet.'

As he laid the monstrous, feathery thing on the ground it took shape and became two dead crows.

'Ugh. Where did you get them from?'

'Roadkill.' But they didn't look like they'd been squashed under a car wheel. With his right hand and the clumsy use of his left thumb and little finger, Thomas tied string around their necks and dangled them off the scarecrow's arms. His breathing hissed and caught with pained effort, spit flying through his teeth. 'What do you think?'

'It's horrible. Tell me why we're doing this?'

'To teach someone a lesson.'

'Who?'

But Thomas, intent on stringing the birds' wings open in a posture of attack, didn't answer.

Jessica started to shiver. The temperature had dropped with the last of the sunlight. 'Can we go now?'

He was about to say something when they heard it. A man singing, the sound heading in their direction.

'Bingo,' Thomas whispered, taking her wrist. He led her from the clearing to a thicket of brambles. 'Can you see?'

'See what?' Tension made her shiver harder.

Thomas shushed her. The singing had stopped but they could hear the crunch of approaching footsteps along the path leading from Thomas's house. Jessica gasped, clapping a hand over her mouth, as the figure of a man appeared barely a metre from where they were hiding. He stumbled over his own feet and shouted a strange word into the night sky.

'Bloody Russian,' Jessica mouthed.

'Revenge,' Thomas whispered. 'For scaring you at the bus stop.'

At that moment, Bloody Russian saw the scarecrow. He screamed, a high, constant thread of noise that kept on going as he fell to his knees. Thomas snorted with amusement. The tramp held out his crucifix, trying to ward the thing off, crying and babbling in his own language. Thomas was now clutching himself with laughter. Jessica stood up.

'It's only a scarecrow,' she shouted.

Bloody Russian fell backwards as he spun in the direction of her voice.

'What are you doing?' Thomas tried to drag her back

down but it was too late. The Russian had stopped weeping and praying. He stood up, the crucifix still held out before him, and shouted something short and rough.

'It's not real,' she added.

He couldn't see her properly; she could tell from the way he was craning his head in her direction. He began fumbling through his pockets and suddenly her eyes stung with harsh light. With the torch on her face, their roles were reversed and it was now Jessica who was exposed, the man hidden behind the glare of light.

'Is Freckles.' Bloody Russian started to laugh.

Thomas was on his feet, tearing straight through the hawthorn bush. He grabbed the torch and held it against the man's eye.

'Don't speak to her.' His voice was odd – detached and utterly calm. The tramp dropped his head and let Thomas shove past him. As he was walking away, he stopped, spun round and delivered a sharp kick to the back of the Russian's knees, and he crumpled to the ground. The man didn't make a noise or attempt to move.

Jessica felt sick as they left Bloody Russian in the clearing.

Thomas walked her home without a word. As they reached her garden wall, she stopped.

'You've started a war with him now, you know.'

'He got what he deserved.' His voice was still tight and toneless. She realised he was furious once more; his enormous effort of control like a dog straining at the leash.

You shouldn't have kicked him, she wanted to say but couldn't, for fear of a casual dismissal. She'd witnessed two men in a vocal but half-hearted scuffle at a country fair once and a fight at school with shirt-ripping and cat scratches; but she'd never seen a violent act delivered with so little emotion.

'You didn't have to take his torch.' Jessica hugged her arms.

'It's mine.' Thomas showed her the initials TQ scratched into the rubber. 'He's always nicking our stuff.'

AC: What makes you happy?

TQ: Jellybird.

AC: What's Jellybird?

TQ: Jessica. Her sister called her Jelly when she was little
     because she couldn't say her name properly. It's just a
     nickname.

AC: The two of you are very close, aren't you?

TQ: You don't like it, do you? You think she's too young.
     Well I don't like her in that way, even if she does act
     older than most girls my age. I'm not sick in the head,
     you know. She's a friend.

AC: I'm not being critical. Remember, we're trying to
     focus on positive feelings.

TQ: Right.

AC: In fact, today you walked in looking the happiest I've
     ever seen you.

TQ: It's her birthday. I made her a bracelet out of beach
     stones. Ones with holes and quartz crystals inside.

AC: Did she like it?

TQ: She was surprised you could make something
     beautiful out of everyday stuff.

~ 20 ~

May 1995

Jessica's fourteenth birthday was on a Saturday. She could tell by her mum's busy air that something was being planned. For the first time in ages, Birdie was humming. Jessica pretended to write her history project on the Great War, all the while keeping an eye on her mother's activities.

By lunch, all the furniture in the living room had been pushed to one side, stacked up against the wall. Making space for something. As her mother scrubbed the newly exposed floor, Jessica dared imagine it might be for a party.

A surprise birthday party.

Lisa and Hannah didn't help but they didn't leave the house either, mooching around pretending not to notice what was going on. They even sat down together for what Birdie used to call a Saturday pic 'n' mix lunch, finishing off the week's leftovers. Jessica couldn't remember the last time they'd all been home at the weekend.

They were pretending to have forgotten her birthday, and that's how Jessica knew for certain that something big was being planned.

After lunch she took out every item of clothing she owned and tried to put together something grown-up, something for dancing in. She wondered who was coming. The girls at school had kept it quiet. No one had even mentioned her birthday all week, which had made her feel a bit down. Until now. As she was tying a knot in a long white t-shirt to show off her stomach, Hannah walked in. She lifted the corner of her mattress by the wall and took out her Jim Beam bottle. It was full of dark red liquid.

'What are you doing?' She'd caught Hannah's surreptitious sips at night but never during the daytime.

'I'm bored.' Her sister yawned. 'Can't watch telly with all that spring-cleaning going on downstairs.'

'What's Mum doing?' Jessica couldn't resist testing Hannah's reaction.

Her sister shrugged. 'Turning into a lunatic, that's what.' Then, noticing Jessica's knotted t-shirt and tight jeans, she added, 'Hello, what's going on here? You about to scurry out the window to meet that pikey?'

'Come on, tell me why Mum's clearing a space in the sitting room.'

Hannah shrugged, shaking her head. 'She's also cleared her bedroom and the dining room. No idea why. Don't want to know.'

Jessica sat on the spread of clothes across her bed. 'It's not for my birthday then?'

'Birthday?'

Jessica saw her sister try to bite back the word, the little wave of surprise it rushed out on. She turned her head away but it was too late; Hannah had seen the tears spring in her eyes.

'Oh, Jessie. Oh shit. Are you sure it's today?' Hannah jumped up, tried to put an awkward arm about Jessica's shoulders. Her breath smelled sweetly stale. She must have been drinking the stuff during the night as well.

'It doesn't matter.' She shrugged Hannah's arm away. Fourteen. Time to grow up. Rubbing her face with the unravelled hem of her t-shirt, she went to find Birdie.

Her mum was stacking chairs by the kitchen door, singing and smiling to herself.

'What are you doing, Mum?' Her voice sounded angry when she'd intended it to be uninterested but at least the tears were gone.

'It's May, Jessica my love. What do people do in May?'

Celebrate my birthday, she nearly said. 'Don't know.'

'Spring clean. We're going to have the biggest bugger of a bonfire tonight.'

Jessica looked around the kitchen, which was bare except for the stone island which Birdie had once tiled with little blue and white schooners on rough seas. The Aga and fridge also remained. Through the open doorway, she could see the dining-room furniture precariously stacked.

'What are we burning?' Jessica already knew.

'The past,' her mother said.

Back upstairs in their bedroom, Hannah was crying noiselessly, her face wet and screwed up. She didn't seem to care that her lips were stringy with slime from her nose.

'I just want things to feel normal,' she kept saying as Jessica climbed out of the window.

She found Thomas fishing on the beach. He looked up at her but didn't speak. There were purple smudges of fatigue under his eyes and a fading bruise on his temple. The stillness around him was solid. The grin of pleasure as he gave her the bracelet that morning felt like something she'd imagined.

She sat down beside him. 'It's just you and me, Thomas. Everyone else is shit.'

She waited for him to tease her but he didn't react; she took it as silent agreement. There was nothing shameful in being sad together. When it got dark, she left Thomas on the beach.

By the time she came home, all their furniture had been piled at the bottom of the garden like the actions of an orderly hurricane. From the garden gate, she watched Hannah drag the rug that used to sit under the coffee table.

'Weh-hey,' her sister called, unsteady on her feet. 'We're having a bonfire.'

Next came Birdie and Lisa, their arms full of awkward shapes – vases and picture frames. Lisa had a beer bottle sticking out of her jacket pocket. 'We're finishing off Dad's – Daniel's – beer.'

They were each given a box of matches and told to go and play with fire.

'Do it like this.' Hannah showed her how to hold the match-head against the gritty side of the box and flick it off, making a tiny, mute firework.

'Careful you don't set your breath on fire,' Jessica muttered.

She stood to one side for a few minutes before deciding to join in. Fuck it. This is how she'd celebrate her birthday; by setting fire to her childhood. In her pocket was Thomas's bracelet. She pulled it out stone by stone, careful not to snap the string, and slipped it over her wrist. Then she pinged a lit match at Hannah, who did a hilarious, hand-flapping dance as it hit her chest.

So the fun began. The sisters flicked matches at each other, at the sky, the piled furniture. Hannah lit a cigarette and tried to set fire to the armchair with the red and green stripes. *No one sits in the telly-throne but me*, her dad used to boom in a pretend giant's voice, and then they'd all try to pile in the chair, banishing him with their socked feet.

'It's got the bubonic plague,' Lisa laughed as Hannah covered the chair in smouldering pocks. Jessica waited to see what their mother would say about the cigarette but Birdie was busy throwing match after match at her king-size mattress.

Jessica took the opportunity to burn the red jumper her mother had made for her last Christmas; the patchwork dog on the front had recently started bulging out over her breasts so that people always seemed to be staring at the lumpy dog on her chest. The pink and burgundy floral runner from the stairs smothered the fire before the flames burst through with a magician's finger-snap, and the girls cheered. Jessica coughed on burning rubber and acrid melting plastic. She wished Thomas would come to the house and see what they were doing. He would laugh and that would make it seem ordinary. The beer in her empty stomach started frothing up her neck.

She touched Birdie's fingers. 'I don't feel well, Mum.'

Her mother nodded into the fire. Jessica hugged her mother's arm to her chest, resting her head on Birdie's shoulder.

'Stop being silly.' Her mother didn't move, leaving Jessica to unwind her arms and move away from the contact.

'Hey, don't forget this.' Hannah was carrying a black leather case, big and formless as a carpet bag. It was the vet's case their dad kept for emergencies. *You never know when you'll need a spare. My friend Mike lost his case under a cow.* Jessica still remembered her dad laughing as he told her the story.

Her mother said, 'Fling it on, Han. Big sweeping arm.'

Jessica grabbed Hannah's arm, hissing under her breath 'Don't.'

'Why not?' Her sister shook her off.

'He might need it.'

Hannah laughed, the sound of Chinese burns and telling tales.

'He won't be back for it, you idiot.'

As she swung the bag back, Jessica pushed her to the ground. Birdie rounded on them, snatching the case out of Hannah's grasp, hurling it at the fire like a hand grenade. She walked to the other side of the bonfire without a word or glance. Jessica braced herself for Hannah's onslaught but her sister squashed herself into the dining-chair swing and rocked, staring at the flames. Jessica's raised fists looked stupid. She wanted to throw herself down on her bed, except it was burning in front of her.

For weeks afterwards, the sea breeze blew ashes towards the house, leaving smuts in odd places – streaked across a clean plate, or on their cheeks.

~ 21 ~

June 2012, Nathan's House

Nathan doesn't say a thing. Pinching the postcard by its edges as though it might be lined with poison. Jessica grips her arms so hard her nails dig in. She can't look at him – sitting on the top step in his baggy pyjama bottoms with his concave chest and small pudding-bowl belly resting on the elasticated waist-band.

He makes a noise as if to speak, then turns his head to the window instead.

'Look at . . .' Her voice is tremulous. Clearing her throat, she tries again. 'See the postmark?'

Then she has to sit down, her legs deboned. 'What does it mean?'

Still he doesn't speak, staring out of the window at the theatrical, constructed night. A sense of the unreal settles on Jessica, calming her. They have stepped off the world's slow-moving rotor into a nocturnal dimension. A place where Thomas might walk through

Nathan's front door once again. Jessica holds her head, palms damp against her cheeks.

It startles her when Nathan stands up and hands the postcard back to her.

'It doesn't mean anything.'

'How can you say that?' She scrambles to her feet, following him into his bedroom. He pulls a jumper over his head, stands for a moment with his hands on his hips, regarding his feet.

'What do you think it means?' His voice is soft.

'That he.' To dare to say it. 'That Thomas is alive.'

Back in Nathan's sparse guest room, Jessica props Thomas's postcard against the folded blanket and lies down, staring hard at it as though it might speak to her.

Somewhere in the forest outside his house, Nathan is walking, having refused to comment further on the postcard. *Give me an hour to sort my head*, he'd begged, and she had understood that need.

Somehow, without sensing its approach, she falls asleep.

An early sun on her face wakes her. Even as she's stirring, her hand reaches for the postcard. Bolting upright as she discovers it is gone.

'No.' She could weep as she flings away the blankets, rips the sheet from the mattress, empties her rucksack; vertiginous with the horror of having dreamed up the postcard.

Throwing open the door, she shouts for Nathan, her voice echoing in the empty house. At her feet lies the postcard – and beside it a local newspaper with a note scrawled across it in thick black pen.

Come to the farm shop. We'll talk then.

Adrenalin branches through her as she tries to leave the house. Rushing about, tripping blind, around the room. Her shoes, her coat. Leaving the house, door gaping. Racing back to close it. Stopping, steadying herself, hot face against the splintery wood of the door. Just breathe.

In her hand the postcard, clutched so tight it curls to the shape of her closed fist.

Then she starts to run, following the path Nathan took through the leylandii as he walked out in the middle of the night. It takes her into open fields. A nagging in her head says she doesn't know the way and she stops. Early-morning air scrapes through her. Birdsong is whipped from the hedgerows and away into a huge, white sky.

A stillness, like something celestial descending. When she starts to walk again, her footsteps are wide and earthed, pulling their roots out of the ground with every step. She knows these open planes and their boundary of sighing woods.

This world once belonged to her and Thomas.

By the time Jessica reaches Frotherton West Farm, she has walked off the delirious edge of adrenalin. Climbing the gentle elevation to the farm shop, she feels the delicious crunch of chalky stone beneath her feet, relishes the blood flow to the muscles of her thighs and the wind lifting away her hair.

This is strength. This is joy. This is how it feels when life shifts towards a new path.

The farm has changed since she last saw it. The out-buildings are now cornflower blue with wide windows and a cobbled courtyard. Light bounces off the glass and she heads for a dark opening in the corner. As her eyes adjust to the farm shop's muted interior, her mobile vibrates in her bag. A text from Libby, which she tells herself not to check – and does anyway.

Hurry home. If you leave your nest for too long a cuckoo will lay her eggs in it. Libs xxx

Sent at one in the morning, the signal on her phone only recovering enough to receive it now.

Jessica replies, *Perhaps I'll make an omelette. Back soon.*

And of course she hasn't called Jacques yet.

Nathan is behind a deli counter, serving a young couple with a baby in a sling. His dreadlocks are tied back with a piece of red and purple cloth, making his face look young and tanned.

She rushes to the counter, forcing the young couple to shuffle sideways. 'I got your note.'

Nathan's eyes flick to the disgruntled face of the man holding the baby. 'I'll be with you in just a tick, Jessie.'

With an iron-weighted effort of restraint, Jessica walks through the shop to pass the minutes, her head reeling with Thomas. Wandering along aisles of rough wooden shelving, tiny details spring out. Delicate, gold-edged labels; pungent twists of loose tea leaf; the salty, sexual smell of cured meat. She picks up marzipan fruits for Jacques, drawn by their chemical colours.

Back at Nathan's counter, he refuses to let her pay for them.

'Come on,' he says, giving her a double glance as though his sharp eyes have caught something in her face. 'It's quiet today.'

She follows him through a doorway behind the meat counter, into a windowless room. Cardboard boxes tower over a narrow desk with a computer and a fake tomato plant. They sit on upturned mushroom crates and he offers her tea, which she refuses. Can't think about eating or drinking.

'What do you think of the shop?' he asks.

'I've never seen pink Himalayan rock salt before.' Now that she has reigned herself in, she will take her time, an exquisite agony of self-control. 'How do you find all these amazing things?'

'Got a nose for it.' Nathan winks. 'I'm a natural-born shopper.'

'I can only imagine how popular that makes you with the ladies.'

Nathan rubs his nose. Still shy. 'I'm too scruffy for female company.'

Then she can't wait any longer. 'You sealed the postcard into the back of the notebook, didn't you?'

He shakes his head. 'That must have been Bertie.'

'But why?'

When his fingers start twisting a dreadlock behind his ear instead of answering, a flare of frustration sends her to her feet. 'And why aren't you surprised? Why hasn't this floored you?'

He looks up at her, his world-indulgent smile returning. 'I've always had a gut feeling that he was still alive.'

'But you sobbed at his memorial service, Nathan.'

He nods but makes no comment.

Jessica pulls off her jumper. The box towers are closing in, the room a sealed vacuum. Dizziness. She can't breathe.

'Also, I think I saw him.'

'Oh.' The sound is punched out of her. She steps back, heel colliding with the door. Grabs the handle so roughly, two of her fingernails bend backwards. 'When?'

'A few days after he smashed my boat on the rocks. I couldn't sleep. I was upstairs in the room you slept in last night . . . Are you OK?'

Jessica slides down onto the floor, focusing on the red crescent of blood gathering under one fingernail. She manages to nod.

'I saw a man standing under the trees in the yard. I think it was him.'

'You think so.'

'It was snowing, no moon. He was in the shadows.'

'What then?'

'Then he was gone again.'

'Didn't you call after him?' Jessica's voice cracks, she coughs. 'Chase him?'

'No,' Nathan says, as though it's the simplest truth in the world. 'That's not what he wanted.'

Yanking at the handle, she tears a blind path through

the shop until she finds a door. Once outside, she focuses on slow, steadying breaths; in through her nose, out through her mouth. Nathan stands beside her, smoothing his moustache along the sides of his mouth.

'Sorry. I feel odd. Like I can't find my balance.'

'Yeah,' he says quietly. 'Yeah.'

She stands on the hill with the world falling away from her. With each deep breath she pulls it back until the scrub, the distant trees and the blue horizon of water crystallise. With the sharpened focus comes a resolution.

She turns to Nathan. 'What was the name of the police officer?'

A blank look. 'Police?'

'Who investigated Thomas's disappearance.'

'That old bugger.' Nathan grimaces. 'Nilson was his name.'

'I'm going to speak to him.' Her heart begins to thud under her ribs.

'Don't.' Nathan stands back from her as if the suggestion bears a repugnant smell. 'From what I remember, he wasn't much interested at the time.'

'A young boy goes missing and he's not interested?'

'They had a bit of history, Nilson and Thomas. He'd done Thomas for a few minor things. Thought he was a troublemaker.'

'Thomas got in trouble with the police?'

Nathan shrugs.

'What kind of trouble?'

'Jessie, I loved that boy but there was no helping

him.' The strings holding his features snap, his face sagging.

'But don't you see? Nilson might remember something.'

He hasn't looked directly at her since she showed him the postcard. Now he faces her, arms sticking out from his sides, asking a question with his whole body. 'What difference would that make?'

'I've got to start my search somewhere.'

Nathan grabs her hand. His fingers are cold, bloodless, and there's a tremor running up his arm. So the postcard has affected him, she thinks.

'Listen to me very carefully, Jessica. He does not want to be found.'

She tries to protest but he leans closer, his fingers pressing into her palm. 'After all this time, that much is certain.'

22

Nathan asks her again not to track down the investigating officer. But his reasoning makes no sense; she doesn't understand how the length of missing years is excuse enough not to look for his little brother. She asks to borrow his car to visit her mother at Seasalt.

Leaning through the window of the driver's seat, pointing out various buttons and levers, he says, 'Take comfort in the fact that he survived the accident. He got away. Be happy for him, Jessica, and close that particular door.'

She nods and tries to mould her face into a convincing expression of acceptance. Then she turns the car towards Selcombe and the police station in the centre, silently apologising for her duplicity.

Rogue memories line the route. The posh lawn tennis club where she and Thomas once hid by the high hedge, pocketing balls that strayed over. Underage pints of cider at the Ship on the seafront. The pier, in whose dank shadows she and boys whose names she has forgotten drank dry martini straight from the bottle, long after Thomas had disappeared.

She whispers another apology to Nathan as she parks by Selcombe police station. The red-brick Victorian building is easy to locate, rising two storeys higher than the fishermen's mews houses on either side. Noting its darkened windows, she worries that perhaps rural police stations close for lunch.

But her real hesitation is fear; of trying to find Thomas and failing.

Of finding him.

If you think you can or you can't, you're right. Her dad's favourite phrase persuades her to climb the steps to the front door and press the intercom button.

'Can I help?' The voice, electronic through the receiver, sounds polite but vaguely suspicious.

'I was hoping to speak to Sergeant Nilson, if he still works there.'

Smart footsteps approach along a stone floor behind the door. A middle-aged lady in a loose-fitting policeman's shirt and trousers ushers her in.

Jessica explains how Sergeant Nilson investigated the disappearance of a friend of hers, a teenager called Thomas Quennell, seventeen years earlier. The officer makes no comment and Jessica is left alone in a square entrance hall with worn black and white floor tiles. One wall is papered with photocopies of cats and grainy, unsmiling faces, the word MISSING leaping out of the posters.

To her surprise, the woman returns a moment later

and shows Jessica into an L-shaped office that smells overwhelmingly male – stale laundry, unaired rooms and black coffee. There are three desks, each flanked by a wilting banana plant. Two of the officers in the room are on telephone calls. The third – an angular man with long, thinning hair slicked back from a high forehead – leans back in his chair, feet on the windowsill, tapping an unlit cigarette in time to a lively jazz tune from the radio on his desk.

'Sergeant Nilson?'

'Detective Inspector.' He indicates the chair opposite with a jut of his chin, palming back a string of blond hair that has shaken loose from his temple. 'So. A friend of a missing Thomas Quennell. Name rings a bell.'

'His father is Finn Quennell. He had a garage of sorts.'

Nilson swings his legs off the windowsill. Taps his cigarette on his chin. 'I know who you mean. Nasty piece of work, he was. Didn't he drown, or some such thing?'

'He disappeared in a boat accident. His brother says it was your case.'

Nilson's nodding, staring blankly at her the way people do when they are unpicking a ball of thoughts. 'It was.'

'I found something – new evidence – to suggest he didn't drown after all.' Her words trapeze into empty space without a response to catch hold of them.

His nervy fingers roll the battered cigarette back and

forth on the tabletop. 'Let me show you something,' he says. 'If you would follow me outside.'

Nilson leads her out of the police station and into the car park, where he lights his cigarette. He takes deep, panicky drags like he's sucking an asthmatic's inhaler. They are standing beside Nathan's car. Nilson rests a shoulder against the Land Rover's open-back frame and Jessica wonders if he's deliberately leaning on the car she just arrived in; a provocation of sorts.

She waits for him to speak, watching the seagulls overhead, their cawing reminder of the nearby sea.

'What do you see between the bakery and the chippie?' He points his cigarette at the row of shops on the other side of the road.

'Bins?'

'The sea.' With a glance at her wedding ring. 'Mrs . . . ?'

'Larsson. Though I normally go by my unmarried name, Jessica Byrne, the name of my jewellery brand.' *Funny*, she thinks, *this desire for utter transparency just because he's a cop.*

'Jessica Byrne.' He draws out her name like he's holding it up to the light. 'Another ringing bell.'

'You were saying something about the sea.' It's all an act, she figures, pretending to remember a case he has forgotten. He doesn't know her name because it wasn't linked to Thomas's disappearance.

Nilson squints at the narrow glimpse of water between the shops. 'Do you know how many missing boys I've had to deal with over my excruciatingly long career in the police force?'

She shakes her head.

'Young men are always drowning. They can't help themselves.'

'But he didn't drown.' She turns to face him, demanding his attention, the way Libby might have done. 'I was hoping you might reopen the case.'

'Like the telly programme?' Nilson grins, his teeth yellow-streaked between shapeless lips. '*Cold Case*, that's the one. I'm afraid that's not my department. You need the Missing Persons Unit.'

Jessica feels for the car keys in her pocket. This is a waste of time.

Nilson flicks the cigarette butt away, holding his fingers under his nose and sniffing. 'There are few things I love so much as a decent smoke.'

He bounds up the steps to the front door of the station and holds it open for her. 'Let's have a look at this new evidence of yours. Seeing as you've made the effort.'

Jessica follows him inside but doesn't sit down, handing the postcard across his desk. He studies it, a hand running his hair back from his face. 'And you're sure that this is postmarked *after* the accident?'

'I will never forget the date he disappeared.'

'Hah,' Nilson says under his breath. 'That little shit.'

His weary indifference has vanished. She holds her hand out for the postcard.

'I'll keep this,' he says. 'Fingerprints, and all that.'

'But I've only just found it.' Horrified, she stares at the postcard, feeling eight years old again, leaping in the air to grab her toy back from Hannah. 'I thought I needed to speak to Missing Persons?'

'I'll make sure it gets there.' There's something about his emphatic response that unsettles her; the grin on his ugly mouth. Nilson opens the grey cabinet beside his desk and drops Thomas's postcard into an empty sleeve.

Jessica stands up, her fingertips on his desk. 'You'll keep me informed?'

'Of course, Ms Byrne.' Nilson turns his attention to the computer, giving the mouse a shake; dismissing her.

'Shall I write my number down?' Jessica asks through her teeth.

'Leave it with Nikki on Reception.'

He doesn't look at her again, and Jessica walks out.

Nathan meets her at Gomeldon Station on his push-bike, which he shoves into the back of his car.

'How was your mother?'

'My mother's always the same.' Jessica can't muster the energy for another lie. 'Thank you for the car and for letting me stay.'

Hands in his pockets, Nathan stares at the ground, shifting his weight from foot to foot. Jessica waits for whatever it is he needs to say. When he doesn't speak, she tries to offer him a starting point. 'I'm sorry if the postcard has upset you.'

He nods, squeezes her hand before walking back to his car. Jessica is left with the sense of having fumbled the ball. There is something about the postcard he isn't telling her.

For the duration of the train journey home, the wild possibility of Thomas still alive flips over in her head like a coin spinning through thin air.

The train arrives in London just before one in the morning. She has been gone since yesterday morning without speaking to Jacques. She calls home.

'Where are you?' he asks evenly. His voice doesn't belong to someone newly woken; he's been waiting up for her call.

In the face of his level-headedness, an effusive apology seems unnecessary. She has, after all, only been visiting her mother.

Twenty minutes later, she hears the boisterous whine of his metallic green moped – the Green Beast – as he rounds the corner, her helmet dangling from one of the handles. He looks tired but there is nothing in his manner to suggest that her absence has worried him. As she thanks him for collecting her, she finds herself perversely irritated by his unquestioning trust. It lasts a matter of minutes, then she clings to him with arms and thighs as the moped's tin-can engine sounds rudely through the empty streets.

At home, he loses his fists in her hair, licks her spine, ties her in knots like a cat's cradle.

It's almost three in the morning by the time they are lying with their legs linked, heads together. Both drifting, neither allowing the other to sleep. Just to keep them there a little longer.

'Take a day off work tomorrow,' she whispers in his ear.

'Sure,' he says, but she knows he won't.

23

A week after she discovered the postcard, Jessica wakes to the sound of the phone ringing. She doesn't answer, distracted by the sight of Jacques' untouched pillow, smooth as a bar of soap. Recently he has started sleeping on the sofa after a late night, so as not to disturb her. Once again she has slept alone.

The ringing persists and she lifts the receiver to find DI Nilson on the end of the line. Her stomach skips. The hope of finding Thomas has been dimming and flaring inside her chest like the rotating beam of a lighthouse.

Nilson launches into a long preamble; though he couldn't reopen the case himself he'd been putting out some feelers, doing a bit of research on his own time to assist the overworked boys in Missing Persons.

'Have you found him?' Jessica cuts in. She had meant to say *anything* not *him*.

'You've stolen my thunder,' Nilson says. 'Now whatever I say will sound lame.'

'But you've found something?' Jessica swings her legs out of bed and stands up. 'Tell me.'

'What we know is this. The boat smashed against the Lady's Fingers. Rough bit of sea, that, with an unusual current due to the shape of the bay. So says the coastguard.'

'OK.' Her fingers are cramped around the material of her t-shirt. She releases it, smoothing out the creases against her thigh. 'Go on.'

'Every splinter of that boat washed up. You could have rebuilt it. But no body.' Nilson's voice is jovial, as though they're discussing the weather.

Through the open doorway, Jessica can hear the floorboards creaking in the sitting room. Jacques is still at home.

'The interesting thing is, he couldn't have done it alone.'

'Sorry?'

Nilson chuckles, enjoying himself. 'Again, just the coastguard's opinion, but he says it takes some effort to scupper a boat as opposed to merely disabling it. The extent of the wreckage suggests it was deliberate. You pretty much have to go down with it.'

'So what does that mean?' Her heart is beating so hard, the fine cotton of her t-shirt shivers over her left breast.

'There's no way he swam out of those waters that night. The waves were three metres high in the dead of winter. Someone was waiting for him in a boat.'

'Who?'

'I was hoping you might have an idea.'

'No.' Jessica takes a deep breath, needs to calm herself in case Jacques walks in. 'How come you didn't find this out before?'

'No one was that bothered, if I'm honest. I did what I could with the little help I was given. But his family weren't interested.'

She thinks of Nathan and his lack of response over the postcard. How he begged her not to look for Thomas. Now she is certain he was hiding something.

'I'm grateful that you are taking the time to find him.'

'This isn't just about a missing boy, Mizz Byrne.' Nilson's voice has lost its false note of gaiety. 'This is an unsolved murder case.'

'Murder?' She almost laughs. 'How can it be? Everything suggests he's alive.'

'I have something you need to see.'

He refuses to elucidate. Before the call ends, she agrees to meet him on Wednesday at William Mansion's just before closing time. Replacing the receiver, she stretches out in the empty bed and stares up at the crumbling ceiling rose.

The call has unsettled her. Nilson's insinuating tone, his deliberate air of mystery making her feel somehow implicated in something she doesn't understand. The fact that he is travelling up to meet her on his day off to discuss a case that is no longer his.

An unsolved murder.

Can't say too much at this point, he'd said before

hanging up, and she'd wanted to smash the receiver against the side-table until its wire entrails hung out.

Jessica closes her eyes. Then she hears Jacques' voice, like the hum of an untuned radio from somewhere in the flat.

Talking to someone on his mobile.

When he laughs, it's a tamped-down version of his usual laughter and she wonders whom he's speaking to. Holding her breath, she gets out of bed. Walks across the room on legs like broken flower stalks. In the doorway, she catches her reflection in the hallway mirror.

And sees her mother. Pressed against the door frame, listening with the whole of her body. The image so vivid she can see the pink rosebuds and curling lace hem of Birdie's nightie.

Who were you talking to? Pouncing on Jessica's father, her fingers digging white into his shoulder and his look of disgust that somehow seemed to include Jessica, standing a few steps behind.

There's silence in the flat as his call finishes. Jessica pulls her t-shirt over her head, flings it at the mirror, kicks off her panties.

'You're pathetic,' she hisses at her reflection.

On her way to the shower, something cuts into the pad of her foot. Skipping back in pain, she finds an earring squashed into the carpet. She hobbles into the bathroom and holds the piece of jewellery up for inspection.

It's one of Libby's. She remembers its jangling ugliness − an art deco design with sharp angles and clashing yellow and pink stones. Before she can question why it is lying outside the bedroom, Jessica throws it into the toilet and flushes it away. Foot still throbbing, she turns on the shower and meets the bracing freeze of the water face on.

By the time she gets out of the shower, she's shaking so hard she has to hold on to the towel rail to step out of the bath. But her head is clear.

Nilson is playing games; he'll explain himself in two days' time.

And the earring could have fallen off during any of Libby's frequent visits. Perhaps even yesterday when she dropped round for coffee.

'Hey, you're awake.' Jacques walks into the bathroom as she is brushing her hair. He puts his arms about her waist. 'Christ, you're ice cold.'

Putting his lips to her neck, his hot breath fans across her skin and Jessica clenches her jaw against the shivering. It makes her mouth look thin and mean.

Who did you call on your mobile? She could ask him, and he would tell her. The question wouldn't anger him. But, unlike her mother, she would never chase a cheap piece of reassurance.

'I slept through the alarm,' she says.

'Don't be mad, but I turned it off. I thought we might take a duvet day. I just spoke to the shop and my office and made terrible, flimsy excuses for us both.'

This was another thing her mother had never understood. The explanation would come in its own time; it took nerves to wait for it. Taking his face in her hands, she touches her lips to the delicate skin of his eyelids. 'I forgive you.'

He gives a big, settling sigh like he's sinking into bed. 'Hey, I heard the phone ringing earlier. Did you get it?'

'It was a wrong number.' She rakes her fingers through the hair at the nape of his neck, making him shiver. 'I fancy one of your famous cheese toasties.'

Jacques grins. 'Let's eat them in bed and roll around in crumbs all day.'

Wrapping her hair in a towel, Jessica goes back to bed and watches Jacques drag the television into the bedroom, fuss with the curtains. She waits for his light mood to lift hers, but Nilson's words have made her afraid of what she doesn't know. Then there's the earring. The irrational dread of its discovery lingers like the pain of stepping on a sharp stone but it will pass. She needs five minutes alone to make a phone call.

'You OK, hon?' Jacques puts a mug of tea and two Rich Tea biscuits on her bedside table.

'I might get a little more sleep.' She sinks down into the bed, the spine of the counsellor's notebook under her pillow running a hard ridge along her cheek. 'Why don't you go for a run? Otherwise you'll be bouncing off the walls by mid-morning.'

'Sure. I'll get the papers.'

With her eyes closed, Jessica tracks the sound of Jacques' progress; his t-shirt drawer scraping open, a slight shuffle as he grabs his trainers from among the bonfire-pile of her shoes at the bottom of the cupboard.

As soon as the front door closes she dials Nathan's number, using the telephone in the sitting room where she can keep an eye out for Jacques. Across the road in Cavendish Square Gardens, office workers are sitting on their spread jackets, basking in the petrol-scented sunshine. A man with blond, tousled hair is walking on the pavement beneath. As if sensing her gaze, he glances up and Jessica jumps back from the window. When she looks again, he's gone.

Nathan doesn't answer, and she hangs up. Covering her breasts with her arm, she leans her head on the glass. Her eyes are drawn to every light-haired man down in the street, some tantalisingly similar to her childhood love. But they are never quite him. She keeps looking, because Thomas is no longer to be found in the pages of an old notebook; he is out there, somewhere.

She calls Libby's shop next, the earring put to the back of her mind because she has to speak to someone. Libby understands about Thomas. 'I need to tell you something before my chest explodes.'

'I hope it's filthy. I love filth.'

Jessica laughs, sounding breathless. 'Remember we talked about Nathan, Thomas's older brother? Well, I went to see him and while I was there, I found something.'

'You went to see his brother?'

'I found a postcard sealed into the back of that red notebook. Thomas sent it a week after he was supposed to have drowned. When I showed Nathan, he wasn't surprised. Do you see what that means?'

Libby sucks in her breath. 'Oh, Jessica. Is this what you've been up to?'

'You're not listening.' Jessica's voice rises with frustration. 'Thomas didn't drown.'

'You told Jacques and I you were visiting your mother.'

She sits down on the arm of the sofa. 'I can't explain this to Jacques until I know exactly what it is.'

'Don't think your absence hasn't been noticed. Even when you're here, your head's somewhere else.'

Jessica sees the earring crushed into the hallway carpet. 'What do you mean?'

'You're chasing ghosts when you should be taking better care of the living.'

'Thomas is alive.'

'Listen to me, darling.' Libby's voice takes on the low, melodious quality of someone trying to coax a cat from a tree. 'I understand why Thomas seems so important. He was your first love, your big adolescent passion.'

'This is not about a childhood crush, this—'

'Let me continue. We all had that first love and got over it. But because of what happened, your feelings never had the opportunity to take their natural course. They didn't get to fade and wilt like they're supposed to as you grow up.'

'I hear what you're saying, but—'

Again Libby interrupts. Jessica lets her arm drop to her side, so all she can hear is an electronic pitch through the earpiece. Sighing, she puts the receiver to her ear again. 'Libs, I know you're concerned but there's no need. I've got to go. Let's speak later.'

There's silence on the end of the line. Jessica wonders if Libby has hung up.

Then she says, 'Call work and say you'll be a bit late. I'm coming over.'

Before Jessica can protest, Libby is gone. When Jacques comes home, she'll suggest an early brunch at Fernando's. With any luck, they'll have left the flat before her friend arrives. There is a danger that Libby, in one of her impulsive moments, might mention Thomas in front of Jacques and in that way force Jessica to end the search before it has even started.

Twenty minutes later, the entrance buzzer sounds. Jessica ignores it. There's a moment of silence in which she breathes easily again.

Then Jacques' key is in the door.

'Look who I found loitering outside,' he says, and Libby steps around him into hallway. She fixes Jessica with an angry smile which Jacques misses, taking off his trainers.

'You can't go chasing men from your past.' Libby kicks the sitting-room door shut so that Jacques, going to making cheese toasties in the kitchen, can't hear.

Jessica sighs, sitting down on the arm of the sofa. 'You have a knack for making things sound seedy, you know.'

'You're going to jeopardise everything we have here.'

There's a pause, the length of an intake of breath.

'We?' Jessica asks softly, and watches a play of expressions – dismay to composure – move across Libby's face like the shifting of a theatre set.

'Yes, we.' She juts out her chin to bear the weight of conviction. 'It won't be the same if you and Jacques split up.'

Because then you can't see Jacques. The thought catches Jessica by surprise, a malicious voice whispering in her ear. 'Split up? A bit extreme, isn't it?'

Libby crosses the room, sitting down and resting her head on Jessica's arm.

'I love the four of us together. You and me and the boys. I can't bear it to change.'

Jessica nudges her gently away so she can meet Libby's eyes. 'I will tell Jacques everything when the time is right.'

'And when will that be?'

'When I know exactly what happened and why.'

Libby nods but says nothing.

'In the meantime, Libs, you're the only person I can speak to about this.'

'And you must.' Her hot fingers circle Jessica's wrist, eyes wide with sudden energy. 'Promise me you will?'

Before Jessica can reply, Jacques comes in with a tray. Helping herself to a toastie, Libby prowls the room while Jessica chooses one of the many black and white murder mysteries she records on Sky Plus but never watches.

'When was this taken?' Libby picks up a small framed photo from the mantelpiece. 'You both look so young and awkward.'

Jacques studies the picture with Libby, heads close together, causing Jessica a pang of discomfort with the easy proximity between them. He looks back at Jessica, smiling. 'I mortified Jessie by asking the sour waitress to take our picture.'

'I didn't know whether to be charmed or disturbed.' Jessica smiles, the memory swelling and lifting the atmosphere in the room. 'That he'd brought his camera to our first date.'

'Honey, it was to take pictures of the Longhaven Pavilion for my dissertation, if you recall.'

'Ever the keen student.' Jessica grins at him, and they settle together on the sofa, plates on laps.

Libby looks away, directing her attention to a cuckoo clock in the centre of the mantelpiece. She picks it up to read the scroll above its face. *You'll find love in Longhaven Bay.*

'I bought it for Jessica as a joke.' Jacques gets up. Taking the clock out of Libby's hands, he replaces it between the photographs. 'It made us laugh.'

'You'll find love in Longhaven but no working toilets,' Jessica says.

'You'll find love but no sunshine in Longhaven.'

'Or friendly waitresses.'

Libby's gaze shifts between them.

Those ravenous eyes of hers.

24

Jessica replaces the telephone receiver and drops her head in her hands. She shouldn't have called Nathan but nerves got the better of her. Instead of dismissing Nilson's reference to the murder with one of his lazy chuckles, his voice had tightened.

Don't speak to Nilson again, Jess.

Why not?

I should have warned you what he was like. He used to hound Thomas.

What for?

Scrapping. Petty stuff.

But he's coming to see me this afternoon.

Cancel it. Don't see him. The man's a nutter.

But it's too late. And she needs to know.

A muted bell sounds in the shop floor below and Jessica leaves her desk to check her reflection in the gilt mirror on the mantelpiece. Her eyes look wide and dazed with panic. She's tempted to slap her own face.

Marni's voice calls up from the shop. 'Jessica. There's a Detective Inspector Nilson here to see you.' The shop assistant's voice lowers as she directs the policeman up the stairs to the staffroom.

Nilson appears with an A4 envelope tucked under his arm. 'Watchsmiths and Jewellers by Royal Appointment,' he says. 'How genteel.'

Glancing around, his lip curls with disdain. Damaged candelabra, awaiting renovation, sprout from the floor like stunted silver trees. A lightning-shaped crack in the window has been repaired with brown tape. Jessica offers him her hand but instead he catches hold of her elbow. The contact is light – she lifts her arm easily out of his grasp – but its imposition sends an angry shiver through her. He throws up his hands with a backtracking smile, his eyes hard and brilliant.

'You'll want to take a very good look,' he says with his mirthless smile. 'Just in case you ever find him.'

Jessica takes the envelope to the oak table that serves as her desk.

'So what's the big mystery?' She is smiling to soften her words, to seem friendly, likeable. It occurs to her that she is afraid of Nilson. He stands over her as she opens the envelope. Three photographs slide onto the table, colours jumping out at her. Browns and charcoal-blacks and dirty, naked whites.

The body of a man lies in the mud, his arms and legs crooked and angled out like a flung marionette. His shirt is ripped open to expose a long belly, the blue-white flesh like the smooth skin of a mushroom pushing through a mulch of rotten leaves and mud.

'Look closely,' Nilson urges and against her will, she does.

There is a large gash across his chest, the ragged lips of the wound packed with grit. Worse, so much worse, the blackly pooled liquid which has set in one eye socket. There is something wrong with the lower half of the man's face – the mouth a huge and bloody hole, the jaw lying slack on his neck. Tufts of grey hair are visible through a thick plaster of debris and gore. Jessica swallows on a dry throat. Nilson leans in, smothering her in stale nicotine.

'The victim was Nikolai Oleg Galitzine. That's a Russian name, by the way.' Dread waterfalls across Jessica's scalp.

'Bloody Russian. Isn't that what you kids used to call him? He was found dead at the bottom of an unused slate quarry.'

Jessica nods, remembering Hannah rushing into their bedroom, the *Mercury* held above her head like a trophy. *Bloody Russian's gone and smashed his own head in.*

Nilson's finger runs a circle around the beaten head. 'This is what's worrying me. The way his jawbone's snapped. It's quite common to fracture your jaw in a fall, but this is different. It takes leverage. According to the forensic report there was evidence of trauma inside the mouth. Cuts and scratches. So what are we supposed to make of that?'

Jessica hikes her shoulders and looks away.

'Perhaps he was screaming and fell on some twigs. Could account for the lost eye, I guess, but my feeling is it would take a weapon, a knife perhaps, driven deep into his throat, to rip such a hole in a man's face.'

Jessica presses the back of her hand to her mouth, closing her eyes. 'I can't see this.'

'But you must.' Nilson lifts the photographs closer to her face. 'It's our mutual friend's handiwork.'

'Not possible.' Shaking her head, disbelief and anger burning off the nausea. 'This was . . . was an accident.'

'And yet Thomas was seen running away, covered in blood.'

'I don't believe you.' Jessica staggers out of the chair. Putting space between herself and the hideous images. 'Who saw him?'

'A credible witness.'

'Thomas was troubled; he made enemies. I'm sure there were plenty of people with a petty gripe willing to step forward.'

Nilson watches her carefully, tapping a finger on a close-up of the man's broken head. 'Including his own family?'

Jessica slumps onto the sofa by the door. 'His father . . . ?'

'Obviously I can't share that information, but we have no reason to doubt the witness statement.'

Shaking her head, she whispers, 'It's a mistake.'

'Only one person can answer that, and it seems he has miraculously risen from the dead.'

A rush of hatred sweeps through her as Nilson tucks the envelope carefully inside his jacket, protecting his nightmarish pictures. He smiles, head to one side. 'Honestly, Ms Byrne. Did you never make the connection? Your boyfriend vanishes, and then this particular man turns up dead not far from his father's land.'

'So speak to the father about it.' Her lips are stiff and untrustworthy, distorting her words. She hugs her arms about herself. 'Thomas didn't have that kind of violence in him.'

'He became quite the hero, didn't he?' Nilson shakes a cigarette from a packet of Marlboro Red and slides it behind his ear. 'Just like that, an entire community forgot what a little shit he was. Suddenly he was everyone's son. *One of our own lost at sea.*' Nilson's voice lifts in a creaking falsetto. 'Made me want to spew.'

Smoothing loose strands of hair off his forehead, he continues in a calmer voice. 'What was your first thought when you heard about the Russian's death?'

Jessica licks her lips. 'I thought . . . a bad man had met with a bad end.'

And she had fought the urge to open her bedroom window and shout, damning Bloody Russian to hell. But God and the universe were always listening, and they might punish her by keeping Thomas hidden and never give him back. So she had read the short article in Hannah's hand and shrugged. *Stupid bugger.*

'Quite a season for accidents, wasn't it, Ms Byrne?'

'It doesn't make sense. Bloody . . . the Russian died long after Thomas had disappeared.'

'A dog-walker found the body three weeks after Thomas disappeared. Perhaps it felt longer, what with Christmas and New Year and all that guff but it ties in with the autopsy findings. It'd been there a good while.'

Jessica shifts position, her body rigid against the sofa's slouching comfort. Exhaustion hums in her head, somehow not reaching her limbs. She gets up and stands in the doorway but Nilson shows no sign of following her.

'No one made the connection between a local boy drowning and an old drunk falling down a hole. Not until your postcard turned up. Then I saw the boating accident for what it was. A great neon sign saying *Look at me, I'm dead*. And I thought, why?'

'It wasn't Thomas.'

'How can you be so sure?'

'He was desperate to start a new life.' The conviction in her voice strengthens her. It comes from her heart, from the dark space where Thomas has lived all these years. She unfolds her arms. 'I'll see you out.'

Her hand bumps over trapped bubbles in the crusty wallpaper as she steadies herself on the stairs. Nilson's tread is light and quick behind her. She finds Marni by the glass display counter, holding an emerald chandelier earring to the light for the benefit of a stooped lady. She catches Jessica's eye, a question in her raised eyebrows.

Nilson slows as he steps into the room, studying the black-lacquered panelling, the glass cabinets with mantel clocks and candelabra, the dazzle of polished metals and satiny woods. 'So much shiny stuff.' He gives a mock shudder. 'Some people are no better than magpies.'

Jessica opens the door and follows him out. 'Why are you doing this?'

Nilson's smile hitches over his gums and she thinks, *God, he's full of hate*.

'I found something interesting the other day. Something that seemed totally irrelevant until you showed up with your postcard.'

He pauses, waiting for a reaction, which she denies him.

'A police report, Ms Byrne. With your name in it.'

Jessica starts to close the door, forcing Nilson to step backwards into the street.

'What's fair and not fair. That's all anyone gives a toss about.' Nilson raises his voice. 'And getting away with murder is most definitely not fair.'

AC: You're upset about something today, Thomas.

TQ: Nothing I can't handle.

AC: You don't have to put on a front with me. We're friends, aren't we?

TQ: Doesn't mean you get to know everything.

AC: You're right. But if you need to talk, I am here to listen and never judge.

TQ: It's Bloody Russian. That filthy sod who works for my dad.

AC: The one you and Jessica played a trick on? Thomas . . . what's wrong?

TQ: He did something to her. It's my fault.

AC: What do you mean, he did something?

TQ: He waited for her outside school.

AC: What did he do, Thomas?

TQ: The scarecrow was my idea. If she hadn't been there, he wouldn't have taken any notice of her.

AC: Thomas, listen very carefully. Is this something Jessica needs to tell an adult about?

TQ: I'm going to kill him.

AC: You have a right to that anger. In fact, I'm encouraged to see it but you must get Jessica to speak to someone she trusts.

TQ: There's no one. Just me. And I'm going to kill him.

～ 25 ～

June 1995, Selcombe

As soon as she reached the school gates, she saw him hanging upside down from the branch of a tree on the other side of the road. His funny-shaped crucifix – rounded edges with a double bar and tiny rubies – dangled over his face, hiding his left eye, like the gold coins laid on dead people in the olden days. His jumper was rucked up, showing a white stomach with long black hairs and a pokey-out belly button. Black scabs crusted his chin. Bloody Russian was watching her with one eye.

Jessica stopped and waited for Micky, despite having rushed out of school moments earlier to escape her – Micky had been particularly irritating during biology, squealing and causing a scene as Ms Drew had dissected a rat. But there was no way Jessica was going to walk past the homeless man on her own. Since the scarecrow trick, he had started singling her out with his drunken babbling.

As they walked through the gates, Micky giggled into her palm, eyes popping. 'What's he doing?'

'Trying to get our attention.'

'Did you see him last week when he lay on his face pretending to be dead?' Jessica nodded. 'Until Jemima went up and asked if he was all right. She's so stupid, that girl.' Bloody Russian had leaped up, roaring like an ogre, and Jemima had stood rooted to the spot, hiding her face in her hands and bawling like a baby.

Both girls walked a little faster at the memory. In the tree, Bloody Russian started to chuckle. From the corner of her eye, Jessica saw him swing off the branch, landing neatly like a circus acrobat. Usually he staggered about, drunk and unbalanced, but today he was fast and light on his feet. Keeping to his side of the lane, Bloody Russian began walking in time with her and Micky. He had taken off his huge crucifix and was swinging it like a hypnotist's pendulum.

'Look at his cross,' Micky said in a high-pitched voice. 'It's got jewels and everything. He used to be one of them Russian kings, a Tsar or whatever.'

'Stop staring.' But Jessica couldn't help looking, either. Bloody Russian dropped his head back and dipped the crucifix into his open mouth.

'Eww,' squealed Micky, and he started laughing; a horrible, rumbling sound like something wet and slimy was coming up out of his chest.

The sound infected Micky, who started to giggle again.

Jessica shook her arm. 'Stop it.'

But it only made the girl laugh harder until she was bent over, no longer walking.

'Don't just stand there.' Jessica looped an arm through Micky's but the stupid girl couldn't catch her breath, let alone walk.

The tramp stopped walking and Jessica started to feel sick. They'd reached the end of the school lane and there was no longer anyone around. He was still waving his crucifix.

'You like?' His accent made it sound as if he was licking his words. 'Pretty jewel for pretty girls.'

He started across the road then sprang back as a red Volkswagen Golf rounded the corner, cutting him off from the girls. Jessica's legs were wobbly with relief. The woman in the driver's seat opened the passenger door and Micky, still wiping tears from her face, got in.

'Hi, Mum,' she said, chucking her school bag in the back. And to Jessica, 'See ya tomorrow.'

Jessica caught the car door as Micky tried to shut it.

'What's up, Jess?' In the safety of her car, the tramp was already forgotten.

'Say your goodbyes, girls.' Micky's mum gave Jessica a smile so quick it barely reached her upper lip. 'I've got nothing in for tea yet.'

On the other side of the road, the tramp had vanished. Micky peered past her mother to where Bloody Russian had been standing moments earlier. 'See, he's gone. He's just a bit of a laugh anyway.'

They drove away. And Bloody Russian rose from behind a bush, weaving like a snake from a basket. He stepped out onto the road.

She couldn't meet his eyes. Stared at his shoes instead. They were like her dad's best brown brogues except they were stained and the sole was coming away from the leather in places. He wasn't wearing socks, and the hems of his trousers were ragged and matted with mud. The shoes started doing a shuffling dance towards her, two steps to the right, two to the left.

Her legs ached to break into a sprint but if she ran, he might chase her and then they'd be in agreement that something bad was happening. She started walking again, her feet like awkward blocks of cement.

'Freckles.'

Bloody Russian was close enough for her to hear his breathing. Her back prickled. Any moment now, he would grab her. Tears started to run down her face; she bit her lip hard to stop from making a noise because she knew, she just knew, the sound of her crying was the cue he was waiting for.

At the end of the road she faced a choice; the longer but busier main road, or the cliff path – home in ten minutes via woods and empty fields.

As it turned out, Bloody Russian made the decision for her.

TQ: I went round to see if she wanted to go out in Nathan's boat.

AC: You don't have to talk about it unless you want to, Thomas.

TQ: I was throwing stones at her window but then I saw something moving in the bushes. I thought it was a dog. But it was her.

AC: And what did you do, Thomas?

TQ: I laughed. I thought she was playing a trick. Going to jump out at me. But then she wouldn't come out or let me take her hand. I had to climb in the bushes and pull her out. Then I saw her face, her legs . . .

AC: It's OK. She's safe now. Do you realise, Thomas, that what you are doing now is probably the hardest thing you've ever done? Voicing something so traumatic, after years of distancing yourself from your own emotions. You're actually allowing yourself to feel it.

TQ: How can you sit there and say this is great, I'm doing great, when I caused this?

AC: I can't comment on what happened to Jessica because I don't know, but your reaction to it shows me how much progress you have made.

TQ: Yeah? Well I'm going to kill him. How's that for progress?

26

Stick close to people and passing cars.

Jessica took the ring road and was about to pass the cliff path when, with a quick shuffle of grit, Bloody Russian was standing in front of her. She veered away, crossing the road to avoid his outstretched arms. But there he was again, this time managing to catch a strand of her hair, letting it glide through his fingers. She ducked away but he kept blocking her path, hemming her in.

Herding her off the road into empty scrubland.

A car passed. She threw a silent plea in its direction but the driver didn't glance at her. Not even when Bloody Russian grabbed a whole fist of hair. She shrieked and he let go. Dropping her bag, she raced into the wasteland between the road and the woods. She could outrun him. Run all the way home.

As she glanced over her shoulder, her shoe caught a rock embedded in the path. A moment of startling flight before she collided, chin and knee first on the ground. The earth and sky swapped places and she struggled to get up, head spinning. Looking wildly about, she brushed grit and loose stones from her clothes, her knee and palms scraped and bleeding. Bloody Russian was nowhere to be seen. Feeling nauseous and shaky, she hobbled as fast as her injured knee would allow. There was still no sign of him. He'd been trying to scare her; punishment for the scarecrow.

If she could just get through the woods, she could cut across to the road leading up to her house. She'd be safe there. But a noise stopped her halfway through the forest. Keeping very still, she turned to face the track behind her, scouring the trees and bushes for the slightest movement.

She didn't hear him coming. The shock of arms padlocking her waist pushed all the air out of her chest. She couldn't even scream. An arm like an iron belt gripped her stomach while his other hand pushed through her hair and clutched hard, yanking her head up to the sky. Then he sniffed her neck like a dog. He stank of dried sweat and shit.

Awkward sobs forced out of her constricted neck. There was a wet, unsticking noise as he opened his mouth. Until that moment, she'd been cowering under an animal impulse to hunker down until the danger passed but the feel of his tongue on her face brought her to life. She smashed her head backwards. He gave a muffled sound as his jaw clamped down on his tongue. For a dizzying second, his hold on her fell away and she bolted forward, only to slam down onto the path, her feet locked inside his tackling grip. He pinned her legs to the ground.

'Get off,' she screamed, twisting round. There was fresh blood in the corners of his mouth. She'd done that. But he was laughing. Lowering his chest on her thrashing calves, snaking his way up her body.

Rage burned up her tears. She stopped trying to scrabble out from under him and swung her fists over her shoulder, blindly aiming for his head. Catching hold of her wrists, he crushed them together. His other hand smacked her head down onto the path. Pain and shock made her suck dust deep into her chest. He pressed harder; the raw scrape of stones against her cheekbone, her nose squashed into the path. Couldn't get any air. Suffocating. She scraped her head sideways, just enough to free a nostril. Coughing and retching on a gritty breath.

Something hard with a heat of its own throbbed against her buttocks, jabbing her through thin layers of material. She started to sob again, tears and mucus further choking her.

The fingers in her hair loosened. The relief of being able to lift her head from the road and breathe in fully. Then she felt him fumbling with his trousers.

With all her might, she started to shriek, 'Help me.'

Her screams forced his fingers away from his clothing, his hand returning to stifle her voice against the road. He sank on top of her, rubbing and thrusting with such force that her pelvis was a raw bone sanded down against the gravel. He was growling in rhythm. Crushing her chest, eyes filling with blood, ready to burst.

She was going to die. Going.

The sound of violent, shuddering breaths brought

her back. The weight was gone. The noise, her own breathing. Rolling over, she found him standing over her. The front of his trousers had a dark, irregular stain and her hand, moving of its own accord, found wetness on the back of her skirt. She gagged once, staggering to her feet. Her face was burning with pain, dirt ground into her teeth.

When he stepped towards her, she lost her balance but he slipped a hand behind her head, making her whimper, and lifted the cross to her mouth.

'You kiss,' he said, and touched the cool metal to her ragged lips.

July 2012, London

Jessica sits alone with a vodka tonic. Fingers fretted together, still shaking an hour after Nilson's visit to the shop.

Bloody Russian's death. The girls at school had discussed it in low voices – *He fell down dead. Dead drunk, he was* – and their laughter boasted their daring and irreverence. Jessica could imagine it all too clearly, the vagrant staggering around his campsite in a mindless stupor on a black, rain-slashed December night. No moon, no stars, no streetlights. Blindly stepping out over the lip of the quarry, his foot finding nothing but air. She shivers, finishes her drink and orders another.

Looking around the restaurant, Jessica tries to empty her head of those hideous photographs by focusing on her surroundings; the mundane and everyday. The place reminds her of Selcombe village hall, with dusty evening light falling through the windows onto a scuffed parquet floor. In the corner, a man in a three-piece suit plays the piano.

Libby breezes in – twenty minutes late – and stops to admire her reflection in the entrance mirror. Her dark hair, having grown out of its bob, is serpentine and glossy but it doesn't detract from the circles under her eyes or her unsmiling mouth.

'Now, what's the big drama, darling?' She bends to kiss her, reaching for Jessica's vodka at the same time.

'I've done something stupid.'

'Tell me.' She strokes Jessica's fingers, a contrived and distracting gesture. Under the guise of taking a drink, Jessica removes her hand.

'I want you to listen. Then count to ten and respond like you're on my side.'

Libby waves the waitress over and orders a grapefruit juice. 'I know how I am, Jessica.' She folds her hands into her lap. 'I can be tricky and difficult. I chase attention like other people chase their tails. But if you're ever in trouble, I'm the one to turn to.'

She bends and shapes words like balloon animals, Jessica thinks.

'Half of me wants to tell you, and the other half is warning me not to.'

Libby nods as if this is to be expected. 'Everyone loves my flamboyance and naughtiness. The party starts with me, you could say . . . But I don't think they trust me.' She fiddles with the edge of her napkin. 'That includes Matthew.'

It's an act, Jessica thinks. *More drama*. But when

Libby lifts her head, there are tears in her eyes. It throws her.

'The thing is—' Voice trembling, she dabs at her eyes with a napkin. A credible performance. 'I would really like us to be close.'

Jessica tries to bolster herself with a dozen images of Jacques and Libby together; the earring outside her bedroom; Matthew admitting to his wife's affairs.

'You can trust me,' Libby adds.

'Can I?' Despite herself, Jessica is relenting. It is always the same. Every time they're alone together, Libby wins her over.

The waitress slips Libby's drink onto the table and retreats. After three audible gulps, Libby shakes her hair back from her face and smiles through smudged make-up. 'Do you realise I never, ever cry?'

'Things would be much easier if you were less troublesome,' Jessica says. Then Bloody Russian's lifeless, gaping mouth fills her vision; she sways, lightheaded and sick.

'Easier but duller.' From far away, Libby is laughing. She stops abruptly, catching sight of Jessica's face. 'What's wrong?'

'I saw the police officer who investigated Thomas's disappearance.'

'What did he say?'

The waitress comes to take their order, and Jessica is grateful for a moment in which to sieve through her thoughts; what she should and shouldn't tell Libby.

'He's convinced Thomas committed a crime before he disappeared.'

'What crime?'

'It doesn't matter.' Jessica grinds the knuckle of her thumb into the table's rough undersurface. 'Because he didn't do it. I know it in my bones.'

'But he must be basing his assumption on some kind of evidence?'

Jessica leans forward, her voice low. 'The point is, Nilson's suddenly interested in the case because I showed him Thomas's postcard. And there's a file.' She shakes her head, chewing the inside of her cheek. 'On me.'

Libby sits back in shock. 'What does it say?'

'I don't know. But I think I can guess. I just don't understand where it came from.'

'I swear I'm on your side.' This time, when Libby reaches for Jessica's hand, it feels honest. Her palm is damp but Jessica leaves her fingers there. 'What happened to you, Jessica?'

But Jessica can't bring herself to tell Libby about Bloody Russian.

The pianist beats out 'New York, New York', his fingers racing along the keys, flinging notes through the air where they catch in the back of Jessica's head like ringing saucepans. She drinks a third vodka tonic while Libby inspects her ruined make-up in a gilt compact.

Oversized bowls of Caesar salad arrive. Jessica chews and chews on a mouthful of lettuce and crouton, unable to swallow until she sluices it down with a mouthful of vodka.

Libby doesn't touch her food either. 'Do you think this secrecy is fair on Jacques?'

She says it so gently that Jessica bites back her angry response. In that moment of restraint, Libby's words sink in. How, caught up in the fear of his betrayal, she is guilty of betraying him in turn. She worries the inside of her lip with her teeth. The secrecy would hurt him. She can't think what to say.

'Whatever is going on with this policeman and Thomas, you need to keep us involved. You can't do this alone.'

Jessica is nodding. Looking at Libby, she finds only candid concern. Perhaps her suspicions are nothing more than her mother's voice grafted into her head. The earring could have fallen out at any time, and the red umbrella in the hallway had shamed her for imagining that Jacques had been visiting Libby in secret. 'Thank you, Libs.'

Libby winks, flips her palms to the ceiling. 'So, bring on the past.'

A bubble of excitement rises in Jessica's chest. Bring on the past. Nibbling a piece of chicken, she finds she is hungry after all.

'Did you just give me your blessing?'

They share a complicit grin and her anxiety over Nilson slips a notch like the loosening of a belt.

Jessica arrives home to an empty flat. She drops her bag, followed by her coat, onto the floor. Fumbles in her pocket for her mobile. Jacques' phone goes straight to voicemail. Next she checks the answering machine in the sitting room, and finds the red light blinking.

A man speaks, his words shaped with precision.

'A message for Mr Jacques Larsson from Paul Norsworthy at Mason and Dunthorpe's. We are delighted to inform you that your suit will be ready for collection on Thursday. Also, I believe you left your blue umbrella here at your last fitting, should you be wondering where it is. Wishing you a pleasant day.'

～ 28 ～

The sun shines out of a Greek island sky, filling the square with garish fairground light. All around her, people are laughing and lolling on the pub's benches, weekend weather on a workday evening making them punch-drunk. A hot, fried-onion breeze tickles her neck as Jessica pony-tails her hair away. It offers no relief from the heat.

Jacques has dived through the late-afternoon crowd into the black mouth of the Kingfisher's doorway to get the next round. When Matthew walks away from the busy tables to smoke a cigarette, Libby shifts along the pub bench. She frowns at him, then turns to Jessica. 'He looks unhappy, don't you think? I don't make him happy.'

Before Jessica can say something comforting, Libby's voice adopts a conspiratorial tone. 'Now, any news on the Thomas thing?'

'None. I need to go back and see Nathan face to face.

And perhaps Thomas's father as well.' The thought fills her with dread but if she confronts Finn Quennell – now surely harmless with age – he might let something slip and exonerate Thomas.

'Good plan.' Libby is nodding. 'When are you off?'

Jessica hesitates. 'I'm not sure.'

'You still haven't told Jacques, have you?' Libby is about to say more when Matthew rejoins them. She stands up.

'I'm going to give Jacques a hand.'

The thought of the two of them, concealed behind the walls of the crowded pub, safe from her eyes, makes Jessica's mouth dry. It is the reason she can't leave London to go in search of Thomas.

Matthew takes Libby's place on the bench, raising his face to the sun, his forehead already a raw pink. 'I've been meaning to ask about the progress of Libby's necklace.' He tilts his sunglasses to squint at her. 'Sorry, is it OK to ask, or does that constitute unhelpful pressure?'

'I've almost finished the outer casing.' Jessica shifts, sips her flat Corona which tastes like the cigarette smoke from the group of middle-aged women further along the bench. 'Remind me again when your anniversary is?'

'Twenty-third of September.'

'Still a few weeks away.' Her insides constrict with anxiety. Everything is slipping. A hundred times a day, she wonders whether Jacques' blue golf umbrella proves it was him visiting Libby that morning – surely there must be a million blue umbrellas in London. In this way, her thoughts tip back and forth like unbalanced scales, no conclusion to be reached. To distract herself, she thinks about Thomas but those thoughts drag with them the body of the dead Russian.

'Jessica?'

'I'm sorry, were you saying something?'

'I was wondering if I should go and help our other halves. They've been gone ages.' Matthew squints at the dark, crowded doorway.

Just then Jacques and Libby emerge, a drink in each hand. Sour-faced, they walk side by side like strangers, without a word or a glance.

'Cheer up, you two. You made it out alive.' Matthew pushes his sunglasses onto his head so that his hair tufts out behind the lenses, haloing his sunburned forehead.

'Now, where's the beer?'

Jessica wonders if Matthew has also noticed the tension between Jacques and Libby recently. They had become friendly, easy in each other's company after the weekend at Pear Tree Cottage. Now they are barely speaking.

Jacques gives a smile that doesn't reach his eyes, clapping Matthew on the shoulder and pushing a fresh Corona into his hand. Libby hands Jessica a large glass of white wine, treacle-yellow in the sunlight. 'Quite the little Texas whorehouse going on in there. Hands everywhere, and it's barely six o'clock.' Libby raises her glass to Jacques. 'Mr Larsson had to scold a man for pinching my bottom.'

Across the square, the sun has turned the large floor-to-ceiling windows of an ad agency into searing orange rectangles that burn their shape onto Jessica's retina. A sport's huddle of men in rolled-up shirtsleeves occupies a narrow shelf of blue shadow in the lee of the pub. Jessica touches her fingers to her damp hairline, feeling for droplets of sweat. Meanwhile Libby and Jacques are yet to sit down. Libby is asking Jacques about his latest project and he, in return, asks about the wedding season. Neither seems much interested; a conversation like a curtain pulled across a broken window.

Jessica closes her eyes against the tangerine glare and finds Bloody Russian's dead body waiting for her. What happened that night? She pictures Thomas the last time she saw him. Dirty and unkempt, his mood like an overblown balloon that could burst at the lightest touch. Her frightened fourteen-year-old self had been convinced he was covered in blood; something in later years she'd dismissed as teenage hysteria. Now she wonders.

Libby's laughter cracks open her thoughts. Jessica looks up in time to catch it. A smile passing between her friend and Jacques; stale, weary, but an acknowledge-ment nonetheless. Of what, though? Matthew notes their silent communication with a fleeting glance. Nothing registers in his face. He drinks his beer, equanimous as ever.

'How do you know Libby has affairs?'

He doesn't react, and she is relieved he hasn't heard. She doesn't really want the details. Taking his wallet out of his back pocket, Matthew leafs through notes and receipts. What he fishes out is an earring. Its pink and yellow gems glitter in the afternoon sun.

'Because she is careless. Deliberately so.'

The heat smacks the top of Jessica's head; she feels herself swaying. 'That's one of hers, isn't it?'

He tucks the earring away again with a surreptitious glance at Libby and Jacques. 'She left it on her bedside table.'

'Perhaps the other one fell down the side of the bed?'

His gentle smile makes Jessica look away. She cannot bring herself to tell him that she found its sister crushed into her hallway carpet.

'She likes to leave me clues. I think she longs for me to fly into a jealous rage.'

Jessica barely registers Jacques approaching.

'You look pale, honey.' Bending over her, he cups her face in his hands, kisses the tip of her nose. 'The heat is making you ill.'

When they get home, she begs some time alone.

'Go for a run, Jacques. I need a long, cool shower.'

He knows there's something wrong; she can read it in his searching eyes as she closes the bathroom door. The floorboards in the hallway creak with his indecision. Then he's gone.

Jessica crouches on the floor, hunched over her stomach. Bites down hard on the knuckle of her thumb but the pain is too blunt. Then she spots the smooth, white pebble, big as a seagull's egg, sitting on the windowsill. It sits so sweetly in her hand. She doesn't have to use much force – the stone's weight does the damage. The mirror shatters into slivers and triangles.

She sweeps up a handful of glass and grinds it

between her hands. The jagged points spike her palms and the soft skin between her fingers, random and shocking as bee stings. Bloodied glass rains into the sink but the pain is elevating. She hasn't realised the weight she's been carrying until – like a wall of sand sliding from a dune – it starts to slip away.

'Jesus Christ.' A shout behind her. Hands gripping. Jessica ducks out of the grasp, shoving her injured hands into her armpits. Her high crashes, shame flooding its place.

Jacques wrenches her hands free, holding them for inspection in his shaking grasp. He pales with horror. Puckered ridges of broken skin, welling blood. The sight sickens her as she sees it through his eyes.

'What have you done?' He grasps her face. 'What the hell is happening to you?'

'Leave me alone.' Turning away, she tries to wash out the sink but the glass splinters block the plughole. The water on her fingers has an acid bite, no longer cleansing.

His voice is pleading, hands slipping off her back as she shrugs him away.

'Jessie, please. Let me help.'

'Get out,' she screams. 'Get out. Get out.'

Later, when she has cleared the mess – walking back and forth past Jacques slumped on the floor, head in hands – she wraps long ribbons of toilet paper around her palms and then crouches beside him. 'I'm sorry.'

He doesn't react.

246

'It was an accident. I tripped holding a cup of tea and then . . .'

'Just stop.' His eyes are red as he lifts his head. 'I thought we left all that behind in Threepenny Row.'

So he'd known about the piece of brown glass all along. She straightens. 'This was a one-off . . . accident.'

'What the fuck is going on in your head?' The curse so much more ugly coming from him, who never swears. He apologises, goes to take her hand and then stops. Holds her wrist in a gentle grip. 'It's my fault.'

She holds her breath.

'I haven't made the time to sit down and discuss your father passing away and . . . well, I think you are struggling to come to terms with things that happened a long time ago.'

'I need to show you something.' She takes him into the bedroom and unearths her rucksack in which the red notebook is hidden. Beneath it is the Tesco bag. She hesitates, then pushes the rucksack to one side and extracts the supermarket bag instead.

Flaps her father's tweed coat out on the bed.

Jacques shakes his head. 'What is this?'

'My dad's old charity coat. Birdie gave it to me when I went down to collect my stuff.'

She sees it register, moving over his features like a clown's trick. *Hand goes up, smile, hand goes down, sad.*

'You remember the note she found in the breast pocket? Well, it's still there.'

Nodding, he snatches it up, rolls it into a ball and

shoves it back into the bag. 'This is your parents' history, not yours. Forget it.'

'My dad claimed the note was in the coat when we bought it, but who knows? My mum certainly didn't believe him.'

Jacques knots the bag handles together. 'Tomorrow we'll donate the coat to a charity shop. End of story.'

'Why do you think Birdie gave it to me? That note ended their marriage.'

Jacques rubs his face. 'God only knows with that woman. Hey, what's this?' The folded newspaper with the article on her first exhibition is lying on the bed, having fallen out of the bag. 'Look, Jessie. Do you remember this?'

The frown lines on his forehead vanish. She looks away as his face softens at the memory of those early, uncomplicated years. The lacerations on her hands throb with shame.

'Look how far you've come, baby.'

Jessica moves to his shoulder but before she can study the photograph, Jacques steps away. With a frown, he cranes his face closer to the photograph.

'What is it, Jacques?'

Shaking his head, he holds the newspaper clenched to his side. 'Enough nostalgia. I have something *you* need to see.'

He leaves the room, newspaper still in hand, and returns without it. Placing a glossy *Canada Travels* brochure on her lap, he says, 'I'm taking you away.'

Jessica fans through it. 'A holiday?'

'To start with.'

Canada. Pine forests, glassy shallows and kayaks gliding out over violet depths. The pictures make her thirsty with longing.

'I've been making a plan,' Jacques says. 'When I finish the Arden Group project next March, I'm handing in my notice. We'll spend the first month getting to grips with our kayak on the Connecticut River and catching up with my folks.'

She's nodding, wide-eyed as a child.

To leave everything behind.

'Then we head off to Desolation Sound in British Columbia.' He points to a wide, blue expanse dotted with rocky islands. She imagines touching the unbroken silk of water with her open palm, feeling the cool suck of the surface as it draws her in.

'I have a picture of you in my head.' He smiles; an imitation of his usual lazy grin. She has ruined his smile. 'Sitting by the campfire, your hair wet from swimming, freckles on your shoulders. Just you and me.'

There is such longing in his voice. It overrides the gnawing pain of her suspicion and she can believe – for one brief moment – that he is the same good, trustworthy person she married.

'You said to start with?'

'The plan was to spend a few months away.' He cups her injured hands. 'Now I'm not sure we should come back at all.'

TQ: He's back.

AC: Who, Thomas?

TQ: Bloody Russian. Turned up out of nowhere, knocking on the door last night. My father took the fucker back.

AC: Avoid him. Don't let him undo all the progress we made over the summer. You're so different from our first session — communicative, more connected to your own emotions, happy. Thomas, you've been happy recently.

TQ: Because he disappeared, that's why. No one's seen him in months. I can't believe he's stupid enough to show his face around here again. Now I have to kill him.

AC: Macho rubbish, Thomas. You're more intelligent than that.

TQ: It's genetics, not intelligence. When my dad gets angry, he sorts it. That's all I know.

AC: Fight it. Break the pattern.

TQ: What, turn the other cheek?

AC: No. Do the right thing. Behave like the functional, intelligent member of society that you are. What would I do, in your position?

TQ: You would . . . go to the cops.

AC: Exactly. Don't wait for your temper to get the better of you. Take control of the situation and do exactly the opposite of what your father would do.

~ 29 ~

August 1995, Selcombe

'My dad once killed a man.'
Jessica had been drifting off, her head resting on the outboard's rubber side, face in the sun, listening to the *slap slap* of waves against the hull.

Now she squinted up at Thomas. 'He killed a man?'

'In a bare-knuckle fight in some East End sweatshop. He used to make a lot of cash doing it.'

She sat up. 'How could he get away with that?'

'The man he killed wasn't supposed to be in this country. An illegal.'

Thomas cut the engine, letting the boat rock with the surf. Jessica lay back down, shading her face with her hand.

'Didn't he feel bad?'

'Could just as easily have been him.'

Jessica didn't say anything. Half an hour earlier, she'd been watching him bail rainwater from his brother's red tender, slopping it over his trainers; grinning through his curses. She'd laughed so hard her ribs hurt.

Until the man in a neighbouring skiff had complained that his six-year-old didn't want to hear such foul language. She saw his face change, emptying of all emotion. With a single bound, Thomas was on the man's boat. The little boy slipped his hand into his father's, blinking at Thomas. When the father stood up, his full height fell an inch short of Thomas's, and Jessica watched the man's Adam's apple dipping in and out of his beard, his grip making his son squirm. Jessica tried to say something but her mouth had gone dry. She had stared at Thomas's back as he silently shifted his weight between his wide-planted legs, making the skiff rock. Telling herself she knew him. There was nothing to be frightened of; and yet an adult's fear was contagious. It cracked open the ground.

Having said not a word, Thomas had leaped back onto the tender, whistling as he finished slopping out the bilge water. Jessica told herself it was a show of bravado. The man and his son quietly left.

Thomas then guided the tender out of the harbour, past seagulls bobbing like fishing floats on the still water. She'd lain down on the narrow bench, feet and head on the tender's rubber sides with the sun and perhaps – she imagined – his eyes on her face. Trying to regain some of the happiness she'd felt before Thomas frightened the man and his little boy.

And now he wanted to talk about his father beating someone to death.

'Sounds like bullshit to me.'

'You wouldn't say that if you knew him, Jells.' Thomas stood up, spread his feet and started rocking the boat from side to side. She closed her eyes, seeing the man stagger slightly as Thomas had rocked his boat. 'My dad was the same age as I am now.'

His voice gave nothing away. She couldn't tell if he was impressed or ashamed. He gave the start-cord a mighty yank and the noise of the engine tumbled the seagulls away.

'Look,' he shouted over the noise. 'Buffer Bay.'

Jessica knelt up on the slat bench and caught sight of a white fingernail of sand surrounded by flint cliffs. Her dad had promised to take her on one of the big catamaran tours – even though he loathed anything touristy – to spot seals. Instead, he'd left. This was better anyway. Just she and Thomas in their own boat. The kind of outing she'd pictured, gazing over the sports fields from the locked window of a stuffy classroom, counting down the last days of term.

Somehow that perfect summer couldn't quite get started. Thomas would run off, or fail to show up, or his face and hands would bear such an ugly stamp of violence that after a while she would leave, weary with the pretence of not noticing.

'Can you see any seals?' he asked as if they hadn't just had a conversation about his dad killing a man.

She shook her head. Thomas steered the tender through a narrow gap between the boulders guarding the bay. Behind it, the water was tropical blue.

'Isn't that your chapel?' Jessica pointed at the stone

building balanced on a slab of crumbling rock, halfway up the cliff.

'This is the only way to reach it now. They've got guard dogs on the land behind it.'

Jessica screwed up her eyes in the brilliant light. 'Thought we were looking for seals?'

'I'll take you to Harbinger Bay sometime. There are loads there.'

He let the boat run up onto the beach then grabbed his fishing rod, clambering along the rocks to a flat boulder where he cast off. Jessica lay on her stomach, pressing the shape of her body into the sand. The bruises on her hips were long gone but she was no longer comfortable lying on her front. Sitting up, she crossed her legs and tilted her head back. Somewhere under the same summer sky was her father, perhaps driving or eating a sandwich. He might even be looking up and wondering where she was.

When her neck began to ache, she got up to hunt for sea glass, filling her pockets with green, blue and white pieces like scuffed gemstones.

'What've you found?' Thomas called over to her.

'Treasure,' she said, then wished she hadn't. Sometimes he rolled his eyes when she said babyish things. She climbed over to Thomas's boulder.

'Coming to show me your treasure?' His elbow made a nudging motion without reaching her. Thomas seemed to keep himself just out of reach, shifting with the dexterity of a boxer to avoid a touch. Which was ironic, Jessica thought, given the only human contact he found acceptable was delivered with a fist.

She ignored his tease. 'Yesterday in Selcombe High Street, a car drove really slowly past me. Then it speeded up before I could see the driver properly.'

'So what?'

'I thought maybe . . . it might have been my dad.'

Thomas flicked his line out into the sea again. 'What kind of car was it?'

Jessica shrugged. 'It was silver. Quite big. The kind of car he likes. He left the old one with us, so he must have bought a new one. To do his rounds.'

'It wasn't your dad.'

'How do you know?'

'It was just some old perv.' Then he added through gritted teeth, 'Sorry.'

Jessica pretended the mention of some old perv hadn't sent a sick shiver through her. Thomas wound in his line with rough haste; tensing, reeling himself in. The thing with Bloody Russian was always there, the two of them stepping around it like roadkill.

'Why shouldn't it have been my dad?' she demanded.

'Because your dad has a white Ford Fiesta.'

'You've seen him.' Jessica scrambled up, bare feet slipping on the rock. 'Where? When?'

'I can't remember.' Thomas scowled at the water. 'Why does it matter?'

'Why? What do you mean, why?'

'I can't remember.' It came out as a shout as Thomas sprang to his feet. Flinging down his rod, he started to climb back to the beach.

Jessica squeezed her fistful of sea glass. With all her strength, she pelted them at his back.

'That bloody hurt.' He chased her as she jumped onto the sand, his face suddenly blank. With a shriek, she evaded him but he dived and caught her foot, dropping her face down. She kicked out hard, a brief spasm of panic.

'Get off.' Her voice was squeaky, her heart like a trapped bird in her chest.

'You're dead, Jellybird.'

Scrabbling to her feet, the pressed white light that always seemed to be lurking at the back of her head descended. Through a blind haze she ran for the shallow steps carved into the cliff-face.

'Stop running.' His voice reached her from far away but it was too late to reign the terror in. Her body locked into a forward plough, feet slipping on steps treacherous with salt and sand. Thomas came chopping up behind her. He caught her at the top of the stairs, grabbing her wrist.

'It's me, Jellybird.' Holding his face close to hers, trying to catch her eyes. 'It's only me.'

With shuddery breaths, Jessica's head began to clear. 'I thought I saw Bloody Russian yesterday. Near the caravan park.'

Thomas released her arm. 'You saw him near your house?'

'But it can't have been him.' Jessica dropped down onto the long grass. 'No one's seen him since . . . you know.'

'Next time you see him, come and find me. OK?'

The blood drained from her face, chilling her as though a cloud had crossed the sun. 'He's back?'

'Come on, let's go to the chapel.'

She let Thomas take her hand – docile as a whipped dog and full of shame because he'd seen how damaged she was. And Bloody Russian was back.

He led her along a path, tightrope-narrow, which hugged the cliff. Seagrass knotted between her toes as she shuffled forward, a sheer plunge, inches to her left, trying to tug her over the edge. She was empty now, too drained to experience a new fear.

When they reached open ground, Thomas swung her into a fireman's hold.

'We made it, we made it,' he sang and Jessica broke into hysterical giggles, head and arms lolling as he ran to the chapel. She was still bent over, convulsed with laughter as he opened the wooden doors and pushed her inside the dark cave of the chapel.

Damp and dust filled her nose. There was a story she'd heard about a girl who breathed in poisonous fungi spores and died. A great flapping noise made her jump. Thomas was shaking out a blanket and laying it in a corner. Beams of light shone through gaps in the roof and walls. One of them fell on an alcove with candle stubs and photographs. Ignoring the grit sticking to the soles of her feet, she crossed the floor to look at them, afraid they might be pictures of another girl. Instead they were of a woman reading in a garden deckchair; looking out of a window; chasing two boys in a hallway, laughing. She was pretty and sad at the same time.

'My ma,' Thomas said from the corner. He'd pulled a

sleeping bag out of a crate in a cupboard and was laying it on top of the blanket. 'Do you think I look like her?'

The woman was slight, her legs as thin as a child's. Her hair was long and very straight. Thomas, in comparison, was tall and broad, his hair falling in thick, unruly waves.

'You have her eyes.'

'And her hands.' Thomas stretched out his fingers. 'Look at her hands.'

Jessica nodded, but his mother's hands looked small and fluttery as bird's wings, where his were wide and powerful. There were deep, red cuts on his fingers. More like the hands of a bare-knuckle fighter.

'Sit down with me.'

She perched on the edge of the sleeping bag, which suddenly seemed too small. Thomas started fidgeting, a hand under his t-shirt as if he were trying to reach an itch on his back. Then he grinned and held out his hand. Three pieces of sea glass sat on his palm.

Jessica picked up the blue piece. 'When my dad first left and I used to think about him all the time, it was like holding broken glass.'

'And now?'

'Now I've rubbed it smooth with all my thinking.'

'That's how it feels to grow up.' He looked straight at her in a way that made her face grow hot. Then his eyes drifted down to the scar on her chin and his face went blank.

She needed to distract him. 'What made you follow me, you know, before we knew each other?'

'I saw you on the edge of all those dumb, giggling girls and I thought, *She's like me. She does her own thing.*'

Jessica shrugged. 'So what?'

'And I thought you were pretty.' With a sigh, he dropped back onto the sleeping bag. 'I sleep here sometimes.'

'It feels lonely.'

'Lie down.' He crossed his arms awkwardly over his stomach and she lay back, head on the sleeping bag, body on the filthy floor. The light-haired saint stared at her from his sea of silver fish, his face full of sorrow as he searched for drowned sailors.

Thomas squinted at her. 'Don't be silly. You can't sleep like that.' Slipping his fingers inside the waistband of her trousers, he jiggled her towards him. He can't have meant to, but his fingers hooked beneath her underwear so his knuckles were against her naked hip.

Mortified, she pushed his hand away. 'Sto-op.'

Even so, she shifted closer until their sides were touching. Her breathing was all wrong, too loud and fast.

'I'll take better care of you from now on, Jellybird.' Reaching out, he stroked the rough scar running along the bottom of her chin. 'I promise.'

She watched the muscles in his jaw jumping. 'It wasn't your fault.'

'I told my dad about that fucking bastard.' Thomas was speaking through his teeth, caught up in the memory. 'He didn't care. He said cheap labour had more value than a useless son.'

Her skin was beginning to feel tender under the

pressure of his thumb. She lifted her chin away. 'It doesn't matter.'

With a growl of anger, he pushed his fists into his eyes. 'Then he said you'd stop making stuff up to get my attention if I . . .'

'What?' Jessica sat up.

Thomas grabbed her hand. Rolling onto his side, he pulled her arm around him, tucking her hand between his ribs and the floor.

'Who cares what that stinking old git thinks. You and me. That's all that matters.'

With her body pressed against the length of his, she could feel the hard wrap of muscle over bone and the subdued heat of his skin through his T-shirt. What shocked her was how slight he seemed, how easy it was to circle him in her arms.

Jessica lay very still, his heartbeat in her palm.

30

Jessica sits, eyes closed, in a column of drowsy sunlight from the skylight above, eating a home-made tuna sandwich. The desk fan ripples the pages of her sketchbook as it paddles currents of stuffy air around the quiet studio. When the phone rings, she can barely muster the energy to answer it.

'You're going to a party,' Libby trills. 'You'll love it.'

But Jessica loves going home to the leather-shoe smell of the sitting room as the carpet heats in the sunlight. She has made a collage of aquamarine water, pebbled shorelines and seals, blue-tacked to the wall. Jacques comes home early these days and checks the collage for new additions. Holding on to their escape plan as keenly as she is.

'Come dressed in purple or gold.' There's a forced note of confidence in Libby's voice. Soon, Jessica thinks, she can release the dragging remains of this friendship for good. Until they board the aeroplane, she will keep Libby close, where she can watch her.

'I don't have anything purple to wear. Let alone gold.'

'You're a goldsmith, for God's sake, drape yourself in your work. Six thirty at mine, please.'

Her drama no longer intrigues Jessica; it has a staged, needy quality now. Libby can feel her pulling away. It's why she keeps coming round, as if she's afraid that one day, Jessica will simply drop out of contact. Or perhaps it is an excuse to bump into Jacques. She wonders if Libby has told him about this purple-and-gold party of hers.

'Live a little, darling.'

Jessica rips the page out of her sketchbook. Her concentration is shot. She can't risk Jacques going without her.

At six thirty, Jessica arrives at a four-storey Victorian terrace, its scrolled portico pillars twined with climbing roses. Libby greets her on the doorstep in an evening dress the colour of antique gold, a purple fur stole around her shoulders. She takes in Jessica's studio jeans and the red polishing dust caked under her fingernails.

'Luckily I've thought of everything. As always.'

In the guest room, a purple wrap dress with a deep V hangs from the cupboard door. When Jessica puts it on, the top sags open showing the ridges of her breastbone. She presses her fingers to the fine skin, feeling her ribs.

'I look like a chicken carcass.'

'That's the spirit.' Libby drapes a heavy gold coil around Jessica's neck and hands her a pair of black velvet stilettos that tie at the ankle with a bow.

'You could seduce the Pope in those shoes. There, beautiful again.'

A brief pang of guilt over the nasty thoughts she's been cultivating in the dark glasshouse of her head. The guilt doesn't last long.

She manages to say, 'What would I do without you, Libs?'

'Die of boredom.' And Libby drops a light kiss on her bare shoulder. 'Taxi'll be here in fifteen.'

The minicab drops them at Bartholomew Lanes.

Jessica frowns. 'We're going to your shop?'

Libby smiles, linking her arm through Jessica's. A small group of people wearing purple and gold stand outside the florist's. Libby stops before she reaches them, pointing up at an old-fashioned shop sign with gold lettering and a purple, droop-headed flower.

'I've had the whole place rebranded. E.H. Flowers is now . . .' She waits for Jessica to read the sign aloud.

'Belladonna.'

'Deadly nightshade. Beautiful on the outside, poisonous on the inside.'

Libby sends her off to inspect the newly decorated shop while she catches up with her PR agency. 'Remember to think nice thoughts if you speak to a journo.'

The shop is crowded. Waitresses with golden paper flowers in their hair serve purple cocktails, which Jessica avoids, accepting a glass of champagne instead. She hardly recognises the interior. Gone are the dusty, whitewashed shelves and black plastic buckets; in their place stand pedestals of exotic flowers in gold, wide-mouthed vases. A chandelier above the new marble counter casts triangles of confettied light across the crowd.

Her first visit to the shop had been in February; over half a year ago. She remembers the smell of pollen and wet soil, and how the orange street light was sliced into tiger stripes as it fell through the plants. Libby had charmed her. She'd come home to Jacques and declared that her new friend was unlike anyone she'd ever met. Libby had a way of making her feel chosen. The flower shop became their regular haunt, a place for a quiet drink once the shop closed, with leaves tickling their legs and the air-conditioning grizzling in the corner.

Jenny – one of Libby's shop assistants – waves across the room at her. Jessica returns her smile but keeps wandering. A hand-tied bouquet by the counter catches her eye. She's never seen black tulips before, their petals so lustrous they look as though they'd leave a velvet smudge if touched. There's a note among the flowers. It's the handwriting that makes her stop, squat down and hold the message in fingers like crumbling leaves.

Black is for the days I cannot see you.

Written in Jacques' steady hand. Pushing the note back into the bouquet, she steps back. The door is sealed by a tight wall of bodies, and she bites back a panicky urge to hurtle through them.

Libby appears at her side, cheeks flushed. 'Un-recognisable, right?'

Jessica can't look at her. The bouquet has been left where she might find it. *Deliberately careless*, Matthew had said.

'I'm so glad you're here.' Libby squeezes her hand. 'I was expecting another excuse.'

'Work's been busy.'

Libby nods, working her mouth the way she does when something is bothering her. 'You're up to something, Jessica. I know it.'

Her voice is so flat, it breaks their light pretence. 'You're just feeling left out.'

'I'm not the only one.'

'You mean Jacques.' Jessica's voice is bitter with accusation; she hears her mother.

'He's a friend. We talk.'

Jessica slips her hand inside her bag and finds the hard cover of the counsellor's notebook. It gives her strength. Thomas is alive, and she will find him. This moment shrinks until she can step outside it.

A bald man with a purple flower behind his ear steps between them, speaking in a low, melodic voice that excludes Jessica from the conversation. As she places her glass on the counter, a lock of her hair curls forward. Libby reaches past her companion and tucks it behind her ear. 'You're not leaving?'

'I'm not in the mood for a party.'

Libby follows her to the door, the man with the purple flower trailing behind. 'I know what you're doing.' Stepping closer, her voice lowers to a hiss. 'You're running away.'

Libby's companion pretends not to listen.

Jessica wants only to be gone. 'Let's not ruin your big night.'

'Mysterious Jessica with all her secrets. Does Jacques even know you?'

'What about you? Smiling at my face, winking at my husband behind my back.'

Libby dismisses her words with a furious snap of her wrist. 'I had to tell Jacques, you know.'

She starts to feels dizzy. 'Tell him what?'

'About your quest to find your long-lost lover boy.'

Taking a step back, Jessica's heel catches the back of a man's leg, who curses, scowling at her as he rubs his calf.

'You told Jacques about Thomas?'

'He's beside himself with worry. He knows something's going on.' Libby's voice rips a hole in the polite conversation around them. People stare, their collective interest like a tightening noose.

'Sometimes a true friend has to put herself on the line,' Libby adds.

'Friend?' For one giddy moment Jessica allows herself to say the most awful thing she can think of. 'I don't trust you any more than this bunch of sycophants. You're absolutely correct, Libby. No one wants to risk a friendship with you.'

'Why are you being so awful, Jessica?' Libby lifts her chin. 'Is it because I mentioned Jacques?'

'You just can't help yourself.' Jessica turns away, upsetting a flower pot which lolls on the floor, spilling water and white lilies. 'Don't call me, don't turn up at my house and you can tell Matthew I will no longer be making your anniversary present.'

Libby crouches to pick up the lilies. The petals shake as she places each flower back in the pot, the water soaking into the hem of her dress. There's a light, dizzy feeling in Jessica's head, something close to a deep, clean cut.

'Did I mention that Jacques and I are moving to Canada?'

'Your precious Jacques.' Libby doesn't move, hunched over the spilled vase. 'Ask him the truth about me, Jessica. I dare you.'

'Nothing you say touches me.' Her limbs loose and awkward as a broken doll, Jessica stumbles towards the door. Following the street lamps like beacons, she makes it to the end of the row of shops before staggering down a side alley, retching and miserable.

When she feels utterly and painfully empty, she straightens. Rummages through her bag until her fingers touch something cold, metallic. A penknife with a flame pattern of reds and oranges. It had been a present from Jacques, years ago, after she left Threepenny Row to move in with him. *To sharpen your charcoals with*, he'd said, but what he was really saying was *I trust you*.

It fits beautifully inside her hand. She presses the tip into her palm until the skin puckers without breaking. Saliva floods her mouth, anticipating a spear of clarifying pain.

With a tremendous effort of will, she snaps the knife

shut. Pictures instead how she will remove every scrap of her Escape Plan collage from the wall and burn it.

Her father used to say, *As one door closes, another always opens.*

She is now free to search for Thomas.

~ 31 ~

Jessica walks all the way to Shaftesbury Avenue before the pain in her feet becomes excruciating. Untying the bows of Libby's stilettos, she places them neatly on the pavement and continues barefoot to a McDonald's on Tottenham Court Road. She buys a milkshake for her empty stomach and finds a corner to hide in, blankly observing the throng of youngsters. There's an occasional glance at her elegant party dress and filthy, naked feet; nothing more than a passing flare of curiosity. When custom thins enough for her to become self-conscious, she walks home. Even at this late hour, the day's heat – hard and manufactured – radiates from the buildings. Her back is damp, Libby's dress clinging to it by the time she reaches her front door.

The foyer is stuffy with dust-trodden wood and lemon cleaner. Its familiarity drops her onto the first step. A space of sweet, domestic memories: her and Jacques struggling up the stairs with supermarket bags; the two of them coming home late, their erratic footsteps thudding upwards, arms about each other; and the time he pressed her up against the wall on the first-floor landing, hand between her legs, the stairwell like a sail swelling with the sound of their breathing.

She climbs the stairs, looking back. Noticing for the first time how cramped and dingy it is. Nothing is the same. She's already leaving it behind.

It is past one o'clock in the morning and the flat is unlit, dead.

'You're back.' Jacques appears in the doorway of the sitting room.

Jessica jumps, hand on chest. 'You scared me.'

'I was about to go looking for you.' He's wearing a coat over his tracksuit bottoms.

'When exactly did you become my keeper?'

And it hurts, hurting him. It has a different resonance, this pain, so different from that of a metal blade or an edge of glass.

He can't speak, holding out his hands as if to catch the first drops of rain.

'I was at Libby's shop opening. I left a message on the answering machine.'

'Libby got home two hours ago.' He's taking in her bare feet and gaping dress.

'Libby.' She puts the name between them like a cat dropping a dead mouse on the carpet. She can't bring herself to say more than that; the dread of his confession more than she can bear at this moment.

Jacques is squinting as if he can't quite bring her into focus. 'What about her?'

The caution in his voice shoots a feverish prickle along her spine.

'Forget it.' Walking past him, she tenses against the grasp of his hand but it doesn't come. She wishes it would. The relief of fingers digging bruises into her arms, the burn of dragged skin and scratching nails. Wishes just once he would hurt her and break the water skin they are skating across. She stops by the doorway. 'You've always been so unquestioning. I always took it as proof of trust and love.'

'I *trust*, Jessica, that when you are ready to talk to me, you will.' In his anger, he sounds like a stranger, his accent always more pronounced under stress.

'Nice pat on the head, Jacques. The truth is, you let me keep my secrets so you could keep your own.'

She sees it then. A calculation in his eyes. Wondering what she knows.

'You're right. There's too much unspoken crap between us.' He looks so pained, his eyes blacked out with fatigue that she pinches the soft underside of her arm, punishing the urge to cradle his head.

'Tomorrow we'll sit down and talk.' Softly, he adds, 'You can tell me anything, you know.'

It's too late, she thinks.

In the darkness of the bedroom, she spills Libby's dress in a heap, the gold necklace coiling on top like a possessive snake. The airing-cupboard door creaks as Jacques makes himself a bed on the sofa.

AC: *A police officer, Sergeant Nilson, came here yesterday asking about you.*

TQ: *Yeah?*

AC: *He said you've been starting fights in public.*

TQ: *He doesn't like me, that's all. His youngest brother Mike tried to take my lunch money at school so I broke his nose. Nilson's had it in for me since then.*

AC: *But Thomas, I can see from the state of your face you've been involved in some kind of violence.*

TQ: *It's nothing.*

AC: *What does your father say when he sees you like this?*

TQ: *Nothing. He wouldn't fucking dare.*

AC: *You're looking for an outlet for your anger and frustration, but it's harmful. Not just physically but also in terms of your mental and emotional health. Focus on something you long for instead. There must be something.*

TQ: *To drown.*

AC: *I'm sorry?*

TQ: *Somewhere on the bottom of the English Channel there is a mountain of iron railings.*

AC: *Iron railings?*

TQ: *My grandad said the government asked people to donate iron as part of the war effort. So they cut down the railings around their houses. It turns out it wasn't needed so it was dumped out at sea.*

AC: *What a terrible waste.*

TQ: *I can see it. Like rusty bones deep in the water. I think about swimming through the railings and getting tangled up. At first I struggle, then I just let go. Drowning's peaceful, like falling asleep.*

32

October 1995, Selcombe

Micky, Lucy and Jessica were sitting on the cemetery wall in the shadow of an oak tree when the cars started to arrive. Jessica was glad of the distraction, fed up with Lucy's endless talk of who fancied her. It wasn't enough to check out her face and skinny figure in every shop window or parked car; now she was obsessed with how she appeared to other people – specifically boys.

'Look – they're all wearing black. It must be a funeral.' This for some reason made Micky giggle and Jessica sighed, throwing back her head to look up through red and amber leaves. Snatches of sunlight dazzled her eyes as the wind stirred the branches.

'Let's gatecrash it.'

Both Micky and Jessica stared at Lucy.

'It's not a village disco, sicko.' Jessica slid off the wall. She wondered where Thomas was.

'Yes, but look.' Lucy had also jumped off the wall.

Despite the chill in the air, she was determined to show off her fading tan in a denim skirt that flared above her knees. She stepped out of the tree's shadows, hands in her jacket pockets, pretending to study the church rather than the group of young men hunched together in ill-fitting black suits, their hair slicked and shining.

'Lucy's got a point.' Micky said. 'Funerals are normally full of wrinklies.'

'Maybe the person who died was young.' Jessica shivered and leaned against the wall, hoping to catch some warmth from the stone.

Micky gasped, eyes wide over her cupped palm. 'I know who it is.'

Her squeal turned heads among the mourners. Lucy pointed the toe of her trainer into the grass, swinging her knee in a lazy arc to make her calf flex.

'This boy drowned trying to swim the Lady's Fingers. My mum read it in the papers.'

'What boy?'

'I don't know.'

'What was his name?' Jessica grabbed Micky's arm.

'There's no need to pinch me.' Micky rubbed her arm, her voice shrill as ever. 'My mum said he was seventeen years old and a local boy, that's all.'

Jessica spun away. She pressed her stomach to the church wall, feeling dizzy and sick. Lucy came to stand beside her, pressing her side against Jessica's, her head leaning conspiratorially close. 'What's wrong?'

Not trusting her voice, Jessica shook her head.

'It's not your boyfriend, is it?'

Swallowing, she managed to say, 'He's not my boyfriend.'

Lucy's eyes widened. She snapped her fingers at Micky, beckoning her over with a panicky flap of her hand. 'Micky, you idiot. We think it might be Jessica's boyfriend.'

Hemmed in by the sudden thrill of their excitement, Jessica fought the urge to scramble over the wall and run away. Instead she turned back to the church. The last of the mourners had gone in.

Of course it wasn't him.

Lucy pushed her arm through hers, the silver petals of her ring scratching Jessica's side. 'When did you last see him?'

'Ages ago.' Jessica chewed her lip. Their cloying concern was making it hard for her to breathe, to concentrate. When had she last seen him?

She thought back to the summer holidays. They had made so many plans; camping – with fried gull eggs for breakfast; seal-spotting, swimming in Selcombe Bay. None of it happened. Not once Bloody Russian reappeared. After that, Thomas lost interest in everything. In her. Minutes into a walk he'd lose interest, his mood swerving from blank distraction to manic energy. Then he'd rush off, leaving her behind.

Looking back to the day they had lain down together on the chapel floor, Jessica could see it was a goodbye of sorts. The Thomas she knew had slipped away.

'I told you, he's not my boyfriend,' she muttered. 'I bumped into him a few weeks ago.' Wearing stained trousers, his hair splitting into ragged, unwashed locks.

At the corner of his mouth a livid, crusty sore that his tongue kept poking at. She'd wanted to ask what was happening to him but couldn't think how.

'Did he say he was going to try and swim the Fingers?' Micky wanted to know, picking moss off the stone wall, already bored.

'Of course not.' Instead they'd spoken about her father.

He was at my house. He bought his car from my dad's garage.

Are you sure it was him?

Yes, because he spoke to me.

What did he say?

Tell Jessica I will always watch over her. I'll be her guardian angel.

And she'd laughed in anger. *Great job he's done so far,* she'd shouted. She shouldn't have run off. She should have calmed down and stayed with Thomas and behaved like a proper friend.

Jessica took a few steps forward. 'I'm going to find out whose funeral it is.'

Lucy was at her side again. 'Good idea.'

'Alone. They'll notice if three of us try to sneak in.'

'Come on.' Micky yawned, plucking at Lucy's sleeve. 'Let's go to the shops.'

No one spoke inside the church. Their clothes and service sheets rustled as they moved carefully through the pews, hunched over a collective stomach ache. The air was choked with flowers, a queue of wreaths lining the aisle.

At the altar stood a white coffin on a black velvet plinth. Blue and purple flowers fountained from its lid, framing the picture of a young man. Jessica gripped the back of the first pew, staring without blinking at the photograph until her eyes watered and she was certain it wasn't him.

It wasn't Thomas.

AC: How are you, Thomas? I haven't seen much of you recently.

TQ: I'm all right.

AC: You don't look all right. I'm worried about you.

TQ: OK, I'm angry.

AC: Has something happened?

TQ: No. It's just how I feel all the time.

AC: It's OK to be angry. It's progress to admit it.

TQ: You keep saying that but when my father lost his temper, he killed a man.

AC: You're not your father, Thomas.

TQ: You'll see.

AC: I'm going to say something, and it's going to sound unprofessional, but I truly believe you should break all contact with your father.

TQ: I barely go home as it is.

AC: Then move away from this area, Thomas. Find somewhere new to live.

TQ: Just like that?

AC: In fact, I'm going to help you. I'm going to give you some money.

TQ: I can't take your money.

AC: Two hundred pounds in exchange for your promise that you'll get as far from this place as you can.

TQ: You make it sound easy.

AC: Just go, Thomas.

33

Another three weeks had passed without sight of Thomas. At night Jessica couldn't sleep until she had recreated the photograph of the young man in her head and reassured herself it was not Thomas lying in the coffin.

She criss-crossed the inside of her thighs with the brown glass shard as she waited for the sound of pebbles against her window.

He'd needed her – but all she'd done was go on about her father.

She found new, untouched parts of her body for her piece of glass. Armpits, the soles of her feet and once, inside her mouth, where cheek met gum.

Then one evening, there was a thud against the bedroom window, a noise her heart echoed in sudden hope. Pulling the curtains open, she found a round, oily imprint, circled in feathers. A bird had flown into the window. Resting her head on the pane, she looked down into the garden. She could just make out the feathery mound of a wood pigeon on the grass below.

'Stupid bird,' she said through her teeth. 'Stupid, dead bird.'

Then a figure rose from the dark lee of the garden wall. Fumbling with the rusty window catches, she heaved open the sash. Would have called out his name, if Thomas hadn't put a warning finger to his lips.

'Where've you been?'

With his face in shadow, she couldn't read his mood.

'Hurry up. You want your mum to catch me here?' he called up in a voice she hadn't heard in a long time – light, excited. The way he was in the days when every evening brought them adventure.

She skinned her knees in a hasty, downward slide, the thin rubber of her plimsolls hitting the frozen ground with jolting force. Without a coat, the cold was shocking.

'Poor little thing.' She stepped over the dead bird. 'Did you see it hit my window?'

'Yeah.' Thomas chuckled. 'Because I threw it.'

Jessica gaped at him. 'What's wrong with pebbles?'

Thomas lunged, gripping her about the waist and swinging her round and round, legs flying out as though she were a small child. He released her, laughing.

'You've gone crazy.' She gave him a tentative smile, wanting to trust this happy, larking Thomas.

'I have a plan.' Grabbing her hand, he broke into a run, stopping only once they reached the huddle of pine trees by the cliff path. 'You and me are going to run away.'

'You what?'

'I can't be here any more. I can't . . .' Thomas ran a

hand through his hair, his breath pluming in the air. 'Be near that bastard any more.'

'Your dad?' She knew he meant Bloody Russian.

'Him too.' Thomas stepped closer, his grin rising and dipping across his face. 'We'll leave them all behind.'

She and Thomas. Far away. She saw them sitting on a train, or maybe a ferry crossing misty water. 'When?'

'Really soon. First I have to sort someone out.'

'Sort them out how?'

'There's nothing to worry about. You'll see.' He was hugging his hands in his armpits, nodding to some internal voice. Wearing less than she was, in a T-shirt and jeans ripped at the knees. Noticing her shiver, he took her hand and led her through the trees.

He heard the sound before she did, standing very still, a finger to his lips.

A snarling squeal, metal-shrill, followed by vigorous rustling.

'What's that?' The horror on her face made him grin. Motioning her forward, he crept towards the noise. Where the forest opened onto a gorse field, two foxes were snapping at each other.

'Look, the smaller one has something in its mouth,' Thomas whispered. As they watched, the larger fox with scabbed tufts of fur attacked, digging its teeth into its opponent's neck and wrenching hard.

Jessica looked away but Thomas was transfixed. 'Shit. It's still alive.'

'The little fox?'

'No, the rabbit they're fighting over. It moved when the fox dropped it.'

In spite of herself, she looked up and saw the hunched rabbit, eyes liquid bright in the moonlight. The foxes tumbled over and around it.

'Why doesn't it run away?'

'It's done for, Jells. There's no point trying to escape.'

Jessica jumped up and ran into the clearing, waving her arms and shouting. The scrapping animals froze; one lolloped away, the other scrutinising her before trotting off. The rabbit still didn't move and she couldn't bring herself to go near it.

'I'm cold,' she told Thomas, who was laughing, shaking his head. 'I'm going home.'

His shoulders dropped. With huge strides he covered the empty ground until he reached the cliff edge. Didn't even look round to see if she was following.

'I went swimming last night,' he said as she caught up. 'To see how far I could go.'

'Are you mad? Don't you know someone drowned a few weeks ago trying to swim the Lady's Fingers?' She pinched his arm but he was too absorbed with the sea crashing against the boulders to notice.

'The water was so black I couldn't even see my arms.'

'Liar.'

'I almost kept going, you know.' His voice was wistful, weary.

She didn't like the way he was staring, mesmerised, at the sea, as though it was singing in his head. Urging him over the edge.

'I couldn't see the beach.' His hand slipped up her arm, his eyes leaving the water to follow its progress. 'The water pulled me under.' His palm weighed down on her shoulder, fingers curling into a grip when she tried to shake it off.

'You're just trying to scare me.'

'It was peaceful. One day I'll keep going.'

This was the real Thomas now, she thought. Sad and lost. Jessica pulled her sleeves over her cold hands, wrapped her arms about herself. Sea-foam fell like snow in their hair.

'You said you had a plan.'

His grip loosened, fingers slipping from her shoulder, bumping lightly over the small pinnacle of her breast. She had his attention now.

'I do.' She could see him trying to shake off the dragging weight of the sea. 'First, I'm going to sort out that Russian bastard, and then—'

'Don't,' Jessica interrupted. 'Every time you go near him, you make it worse for me.'

Eyes widening, his hand shot into the space between them. Arresting it before it could strike her or fend off her words, she couldn't tell which. His breath hissed through his teeth. 'This time I'm going to do it properly.'

'No, please, don't.' She tugged his sleeve but his expression was set, reminding her perversely of her father; how he used to watch her, patiently confident that she would eventually understand his point.

'After tomorrow he will never, ever come near you again.'

Jessica scuffed the toe of her trainer in the loose grit and thought about the injured rabbit, frozen in defeat while the foxes fought over it. She understood then the sense of submitting to forces stronger than yourself. 'And then?'

'I will tell my father exactly how it feels to be his son.'

She followed him back to the clearing, watching him bend low, sweeping aside the long grass. When he found the rabbit, he held it up for her to see. It struggled once, feebly. Then sat in his hands, its side palpitating with the rapid burst of its heartbeat. Thomas jacked his knee up, bringing the rabbit down hard against it; the thin snap as its neck broke.

He didn't seem to hear Jessica's cry. Sitting down on the frozen ground, Thomas pulled his knees to his chest and tucked the dead rabbit in the space between, wrapping his thin arms around his legs. 'All better now,' he murmured, keeping his eyes on the horizon's black water.

A crowd had gathered in the playground. Mrs Arlbrook and the new chemistry teacher everyone called Beanpole were manning the closed gates. They weren't letting anyone leave the school. Jessica pressed her head against the first-floor window, craning for a better view. A police car was parked in front of the gates, its blue lights silently round-housing. A man in uniform walked over to the head teacher and spoke so quietly that Mrs Arlbrook leaned towards him, a hand cupped about her ear.

Jessica's first thought was that a girl had been run over – there were frequent notices sent home asking parents to reduce their speed on the school lane. Mrs Arlbrook nodded at the policeman and scanned the bobbing heads before her. Opening the gate a fraction, she let the girls leave one by one. They all twisted their heads to get a better look at the police car. Some of them stopped further down the lane and pointed, ducking their heads like grazing animals as they whispered to each other. Jessica could see the outline of a person in the back seat, face obscured by the cold, crystalline sky mirrored in the window.

She made her way downstairs, and was about to walk into the tarmacked forecourt when she heard her name. Raising her voice, Mrs Arlbrook addressed the waiting girls.

'Has anyone seen Jessica Byrne from Three F?'

The group stirred and shuffled, her name tossed from girl to girl like a ball. Shaking heads and shrugs.

Jessica flung herself back behind the door, heart like a runaway train.

'Jessica Byrne, are you there?' Mrs Arlbrook had her trumpety voice on; the one that announced the shit was going to hit the fan for someone.

Jessica bolted up the stairs to the third floor, tearing past the empty science labs until she reached the long, spiral steps leading to the sports field behind the school. Sheltering in the doorway, she caught her breath, checking the fields and shingle pathways were empty. Then she ran a straight diagonal across the hockey pitch and into the trees that concealed the outdoor pool from the road. The stone wall behind the changing rooms was low enough to climb over, though it scraped a hole in her tights. She took a moment to calm down before slinging her bag over her shoulder and starting the walk home.

Having escaped, she needed to figure out what was going on. The police were looking for her. Something bad had happened. Isn't that what you saw on TV? The police officer at someone's door, all sorry-eyed, and a woman fainting away.

Perhaps she shouldn't have run away.

The police car was beside her before she even heard it. Her feet, of their own accord, planted themselves in the pavement but the vehicle didn't stop. In the back seat, Bloody Russian pushed his face to the window. His head swivelling like an owl, keeping her in his sight.

34

Jessica leaves the flat just before six a.m. She doesn't write Jacques a note on the blackboard because she doesn't know what to say.

Ask him the truth about me, Jessica. I dare you.

She takes the Volvo and drives for five hours without a break. Directing all attention to the road and other traffic, she keeps her thoughts reigned in.

Thomas's childhood home is as she remembers it. An austere, two-storey building with oversized chimneys and windows, its white face marbled with cracks. The windows are plastered over with newspaper.

His father's probably dead, she thinks, following the gravel path to the house. Truck innards are still taking root in the front garden and behind it the vast, open-sided barn where Thomas's father and Bloody Russian used to fix buses and lorries.

The doorbell gives a shrill ring. She imagines it blasting through cobwebs, stirring up dust. The silence, as she strains to catch the sound of approaching foot-steps, swells in her ears.

A crunch on the gravel makes her jump. A short, plump woman with feathery grey hair and smart tailored trousers has stopped halfway along the path, scowling at the toe of her shiny, patent-leather Mary Jane. She stamps up to the door, peering at her shoes over the cardboard box in her arms.

'Every time I come here,' she says. 'Blasted scuff marks.'

From inside the house, Jessica thinks she hears a scrape. A shoe shuffling over gritty floorboards.

'Family, are you?' The woman eyes Jessica's short skirt and favourite leather flip-flops, loose string and gaps where the turquoise beading has torn away. As if her clothes link her to the neglected house.

'No, I'm making an enquiry.'

'You wouldn't mind taking this in, would you?' The woman holds out the box. 'If I'm honest, the old man gives me the creeps.'

The cardboard box says *Meals On Wheels*.

'I don't think there's anyone in,' Jessica says.

'Mr Q never leaves the house. The food'll need a good hour in the Rayburn.'

It occurs to Jessica it might be easier this way; playing a role. She takes the box.

'You won't get much out of him.' The Meals On Wheels woman rubs the scratch on her shoe and straightens, tugging the hem of her red jacket as it threatens to lift up over her belly.

'Why not?'

'You know how old men get.'

'Does he ever mention any family?'

The woman shakes her head, leaning past Jessica to rap the door knocker. 'Mr Q,' she bellows. 'Your lunch is here.'

Lowering her voice, she adds, 'I went to the pictures with him once. But I was a silly thing in my twenties. Looking for a bit of danger.'

The shuffling sound comes from behind the door this time. 'Danger?'

'They're an old family, the Quennells. Been in this area for ever, and always had a reputation.'

'For what?'

'They're just not right. Like a bad gene, or something.'

Jessica's hands are clammy against the side of the box. When she turns back to the door, she sees it has opened a couple of inches. Someone is standing there, watching her. A dark shape on an even darker background.

Holding up the food box, she says, 'Your lunch.'

'You're not Betty. Where's Betty?' His voice is deep and smooth. It has strength and melody where she was expecting the tremulous reed of old age.

'I'm Jessica.' She steps into a hallway so dark it's like dropping into the sea at night. Her foot slides on loose dirt. Mr Quennell towers over her before standing aside and pointing at a doorway to her left. As she heads towards it, his walking stick raps out a surprisingly quick rhythm behind her.

A powerful farmyard smell swamps her as she enters

a large, sparsely furnished sitting room. Ring marks in the navy carpet and the outline of missing paintings on the faded floral wallpaper leave a ghostly imprint of the home it once was. It reminds her of her own house after the bonfire, and the semblance shakes her.

We come from the same place, you and I, Thomas.

Thomas's father lowers himself awkwardly into a single armchair, one leg stiff and unbending. In the light of a large sash window – the only one not plastered in newspaper – his face has aged like an orange rotting from the inside, collapsing in on itself. The back of his bald head puckers as he leans forward to pick a *National Geographic* off a stack of yellow-spined magazines. She stares at the hand clutching a mahogany dog-head cane. Ridges of bone push up through the skin, the knuckles no longer aligned where old fractures have gnarled together.

The hands of a street fighter. A man who killed another with his naked fists.

Her heart is beating too fast. She clears her throat and tries to play her role.

'My father used to collect *National Geographic* as well.' Her voice infuriates her, thin and stuttering as a dripping tap.

Quennell sniffs and points his cane towards another doorway. 'The kitchen.'

To reach it, she has to step over a mattress with two badly folded rugs and a pair of blue, overwashed pyjamas. Trying not to look at the stains on the bottom sheet like the outline of orange flowers.

The kitchen is even cooler than the sitting room, the

heatwave unable to shift the stubborn cold ingrained in the building's thick walls. She can see why Thomas and Nathan were happier outdoors.

A draught whips away any heat which might have been coming off the red Rayburn. She shivers, looking for an open window, and finds instead that the door leading onto the backyard has rotted away, leaving a foot-long gap above the floor.

Pushing a cluster of used mugs to one side, Jessica places the Meals On Wheels box on the solid kitchen table. As she opens the packaging, she tries to gather herself. There's a danger she will lose her nerve, dish up his meal and leave, having never said a word.

This is the man who poisoned his son with whispers.

She takes a foil container out of the cardboard box. Someone has written *Shepherds Pie* in red biro across the lid. Opening a door in the Rayburn, she pushes the meal onto a black-crusted shelf. A weak heat touches her face.

The cupboards, she discovers as she hunts for a plate, are unexpectedly full of crockery, jugs and vases but their dust coating suggests they haven't been touched in years. Spiders trickle out of sight every time she opens a door.

Thomas as a little boy in this house. The thought makes her shudder.

'It'll be about sixty minutes,' she says, walking back into the sitting room. Mr Quennell doesn't look up. Jessica sits opposite him, on a green leather sofa stretch-marked with age.

'Do you have much family locally?'

He sniffs again, closes a magazine on his lap and looks at her. With the light behind him, she can't tell the colour of his eyes but she feels their sudden focus, gun-dog alert.

'Who are you?'

'I brought your lunch.'

'You've made the mistake,' he taps a finger to his temple, 'of assuming the brain is as decrepit as the body.'

'I'm sorry?'

'I watched you and Betty before she drove off in her little white van. So who are you?'

'I knew Thomas.' For a tiny beat his searching, probing energy recoils. 'I want to know the truth about his disappearance.'

Suddenly he's moving, rocking once, twice to hoist his weight out of the chair and onto his bad leg. Stabbing his stick across the floor, bearing down on her with the force of a collapsing wall. He drops onto the sofa, twists his torso to face her, chest heaving. Gripping his stiff leg, his breath hisses out like a leaking gas tap.

'The truth?' His voice, strangled with pain, has lost its melody.

She forces herself to remain seated. 'About the boating accident.'

Quennell's face shows no expression as he stares at her. Jessica shifts further into the arm of the sofa. 'You have red hair.'

The man has lost his mind, she thinks.

Wagging a thick twig of a finger, he adds, 'I know exactly who you are.'

Jessica shakes her head. 'We've never met.'

The heavy paw of his hand comes to rest on her wrist, his thumb stroking her bare skin. 'Ah, but I knew your dad.'

'I doubt that.' She tries to inch her hand away but the caressing thumb tightens against the tendons of her wrist.

'Daniel Byrne. The red-headed ladies' man.' His face is so close she thinks he might plant his red, watery lips on her mouth. The urge to burst out from under the weight of his proximity is overwhelming. *But if you run, they follow.* That's when it hits her – the acute memory of Bloody Russian grabbing her hair on a busy main road. A buried fear snakes into her head like lava through a fissure. The skin on her arms stipples into painful goosebumps. She wrenches free of the old man's grasp but his legs are stretched out, blocking her in and she baulks at the necessity of straddling them to escape. 'How did you know my father?'

Quennell is nodding his bald head. 'Was a time when he used to pop round for a chat. Keeping tabs on his wayward daughter and my wayward son. Ah, the trials and tribulations of parenthood.'

'I need to check the—' She gets up, awkwardly butting his legs with her shin. With a tiny pincer motion – perhaps an accident – he manages to trap the heel of her flip-flop between his shoes as she steps over his feet. She staggers forward and Quennell hooks a hand into her armpit, steadying her. His strength shocks her.

'Clumsy.' Quennell's voice has regained its low thrum. 'But such confidence. To come here on your own.'

Jessica tugs at the hem of her denim skirt and stalks to the kitchen. Leaning over the sink, she sucks deep, slow breaths into her lungs. Focuses on the metal rim of the sink, pressing her hips hard against it until its solidity steadies her.

She tries the rotting kitchen door which leads onto the yard. It is locked and unexpectedly sturdy in its frame. The windows have been painted shut.

Finn Quennell is an old, incapacitated man, she tells herself. She is permitting this intimidation. Shame marches her back into the room. 'I have a postcard from Thomas. I know he's still alive.'

'A postcard?' This time he rocks to his feet with such force it almost pitches him to his knees. Staggering, he prods the carpet with his cane, feeling out his balance. A sudden rage takes him in a strangling hold, voice strained, his face and bald head suffused with blood. 'You've been snooping through my things.'

'Pardon?'

Quennell lunges forward and Jessica backs up against the sofa. He knocks her shoulder as he brushes past. When he is out of sight, his footsteps slow to leaden thuds, sandwiched by grunts of exertion.

She can't bring herself to follow him into the unlit confines of the hall. Peering through the doorway, she sees Quennell halfway up the staircase, leaning against the bare plastered wall.

Adrenalin hobbles her movements. She trips towards the front door, numb fingers fumbling with the handle. Locked. Through the dim light of panic she can't locate the catch. His head cocks to one side at the sound of the rattling handle.

'The key is in my pocket,' he grunts through laboured breath. 'You'll have to ask me nicely.'

He starts to lower his bad leg onto the step behind him, feet slipping in the dust. His cane falls as he grips the banister with both hands.

'My cane,' he shouts, thrusting his hand behind his back and waggling his fingers.

She hesitates, then, afraid of his worsening temper, places the dog-head handle into his open palm. His grip snaps shut like a trap.

'You've been upstairs.' Spittle flecks his chin as he reaches the floor. 'Rifling through my possessions.'

'How could I? You only just let me in.'

Muttering to himself, he limps back to the sitting room. Jessica glances at the stairs. Wonders what he is hiding.

'Is there something you wanted to show me upstairs?' She returns to the living room, where Quennell is sitting on the cracked sofa leaning on his cane, which wobbles like a single pole supporting a tent.

He turns his head away, jaw working. An old man chewing his gums. Missing the monster of his own youth, she thinks. Trapped in the collapsing cage of his body.

He wipes his mouth. 'It's your fault.'

'What is?'

'It ate away at him until he couldn't control himself any more.' In one swift movement, he drops back from his cane and swings it through the air. Jessica leaps away. 'You pushed him to do it.'

'Do what?'

'Monster or not, I loved that boy. I did what any other father would do.' This time when he rises to his feet, it is a more fluid movement; his feebleness perhaps nothing more than an act.

Nilson's photographs rising like flood water before her eyes. It's not true. It's not possible. She glances towards the kitchen. Something heavy, a pot perhaps, anything to smash the window and escape. 'Thomas wasn't a monster.'

'He beat that Rusky pig and then he shoved his fancy crucifix all the way down his throat.' Quennell's voice rumbles through her. He takes a step closer and she backs away, unable to stand her ground.

'Tell me where he is.' Her voice thin as a vapour trail.

His laughter shocks her, roaring like a gale through a cave, never touching his features. 'You think you're brave enough? To witness what you've done to his life?'

'Why do you keep saying it's my fault?'

With shuffling footsteps, Quennell crosses the space between them. Jessica retreats until her head and heel bump against the wall.

'I don't know what you think you're . . .'

So close she can smell the decay on his breath. His

eyes are fixed on her mouth as he encases her little finger in his bone-mangled fist.

'Get back. Don't . . .' Her protests break against him like brittle sticks.

'My son told me what Nikolai did to you.'

Tries to stop breathing so hard, knowing it is feeding his interest. She can't speak.

'Disgusting.' The word sizzles over his tongue.

'Enough.'

It comes out as a shout just as Quennell is stepping away, shaking his head. 'I'm too old for such fun and games.' He waves over his shoulder as he heads for the kitchen. 'I'll get my own lunch, shall I?'

Jessica watches him leave the room before running into the hall. This time she notices the deadbolt pulled shut. It slides back without resistance and the door swings open. Quennell had lied about the key.

Hearing his muffled voice singing in the kitchen, she hesitates. The door is open, her escape route clear. She stares up at the stairs disappearing into the blacked-out recess of the first floor.

There is something up there he didn't want her to see.

Clenching her fists, she bounds up the stairs on feet as light as dust. The darkness on the landing blinds her, ears straining for the sound of Quennell moving below. Teeth clenched, panicky breaths skimming thin air, she grasps the nearest door handle. It doesn't budge. The next one, also locked. Forgetting to be silent, she throws her weight against the last door as she slams the handle down. It bounces open onto a bedroom of rotting carpet and dead moths. Yellowed newspaper blocks most of the light but she can make out a four-poster bed, two bedside tables and a dresser cluttered with bottles and pots.

Above one of the side-tables, a small dark rectangle is nailed to the wall.

A postcard.

Snatching it, she tears downstairs. Quennell is waiting for her in the hall. A barrier between her and the door. 'Caught you,' he whispers.

'Is this from him?' Terror makes her voice high and breathy as a child's. She tries to scan the words but there's not enough light. 'Tell me what it says and I won't take it.'

'You think I'd let you leave with it?'

The sound of her breathing fills the hall, her palm slippery against the banister. 'My husband knows I'm here. He's waiting—'

'No one knows you're here. That's why you're shaking.' He raps his cane against the floorboards and Jessica springs backwards, stumbling up two steps, deeper into the house. Further from the door. He chuckles.

'Keep the postcard if you want it that badly.' He doesn't move, his bulk sealing her only route of escape. She takes a deep breath, gathering herself to leap down the stairs, to pit her speed against his size.

Then Quennell steps aside and a blissful rush of light and warm air reaches her from the open doorway. Jessica races past him with the same skittery terror that used to propel her from floor to mattress every night as a little girl; the unspeakable fear of grabbing hands from under the bed.

'You saw him that night.'

Jessica stops halfway along the garden path. She turns to face Quennell. He is framed in the shadow of his house. Nothing he can say will make her go back inside. 'What did you say?'

Thomas's father emerges from the concealing darkness of his porch and blinks furiously in the sunlight. He points his cane at her.

'You hid him in one of your mobile homes. You and I helped him get away with murder.'

35

Jessica drives for ten reckless minutes to distance herself from Thomas's father. Pulling into a lay-by beside a wheat field, she staggers out of the car and drops cross-legged on the ground, grabbing fistfuls of straggly verge grass. Breathing in baked earth and lemon-scented leaves. When she is calm, she takes the postcard out of her pocket. The photograph is an aerial shot of a fish market – a great industrial box of a building – on the edge of a quay. The water is flat and solid under a cold dawn.

Stollingworth Fish Market – Nothing Beats Fresh Fish.
She turns it over.

Got a job at the market and somewhere to sleep.
You and me are done now.

The postcard was sent on 19 January. A month after he disappeared. Jessica presses the card to her chest. A place of work – somewhere concrete to start her search.

He would have moved on, of course, after seventeen years, but someone might just remember him.

Jessica delays the drive back to London with a late lunch at the Pit-Stop Café. Each time the bell above the door sounds, she glances up, hoping Nathan might walk in. She heaps sugar into a cup of dishwater tea and forces down a few mouthfuls of plain omelette. The grey-haired woman behind the counter has an air of brisk and cheery efficiency, and despite the sluggish tide of customers, enquires twice whether there was something else she could get for Jessica – a verbal nudge towards freeing up the table. Jessica pays the bill, unable to procrastinate any longer.

Turning out of Morley-on-Sea, she stops beside a road she doesn't recognise. The gravel path that once led to the empty land behind Thomas's chapel has been tarmacked and named. Sandringham Avenue – a lonely stretch of road cutting through the scrub to a huddle of new housing. An inconspicuous metal sign points from a lamp post towards the sand-brick buildings. *17th Century Chapel.* Thomas's chapel. Jessica turns into the road.

The houses are spacious and double-fronted, with the soulless uniformity of new builds. Between two carpets of turfed lawn, a chalk path leads to the cliffs and the unruly sea beyond.

The barbed-wire fencing she and Thomas used to leap over is gone. A metal rail protects visitors from the cliff edge, and prevents them from using the stone steps carved into the cliff face to reach the chapel on the plateau below. In compensation, a concrete viewing point struts out over the lip of rock. Jessica hesitates before stepping onto the platform, afraid of what she will see.

For years after he disappeared she imagined Thomas living there, in St Francis of Paola's abandoned chapel. Closed her eyes and willed him to swim up from the broken bones of Nathan's crabber and onto the beach. Once, in the middle of the night, she became so convinced of the possibility, she climbed out of her bedroom window and walked all the way there. She'd faced the guard dogs by the fence and shouted his name over their rabid barking and the sea's rolling thunder.

To her surprise, the chapel is still standing, though its walls hunch together like pinched shoulders and most of the roof has caved in. One of the double doors hangs at an angle, wedged open with a gap just wide enough for a person to squeeze through. Jessica swings her legs over the railing. Shuffling sideways, she slides her hands along the metal bar behind her back and concentrates on placing each foot on firm ground. The steps are brittle with salt corrosion; she takes them one at a time, shoulder pressed to the rock.

At the bottom, she looks up at the viewing platform's solid block of cement. The earth beneath her feet feels loose and porous as though it might give way at any moment. Vertigo sends shooting pains through her legs. With a skipping rush, she covers the ground between the steps and the chapel. Her palms slip against the door, the wood seeping with rot and sea spray, as she pushes through the gap, body first.

Jessica stands in a pocket of shadow beneath the remains of the roof. The sun shines through a thin layer of cloud, filling the chapel with smoky light. The pews are covered in rubble and broken tiles. Fat-stemmed plants poke through cracks in the walls and flagstone floor, their thick, vegetative scent mixing with dust and airborne grit.

Somehow his mosaics have survived, veiled beneath a green, fungal coating. With the sleeve of her cotton top, she scrubs away at a picture she has never seen; one that Thomas must have cleaned on a solitary night many years ago.

Its beauty takes her breath away. The young face of the saint stares at her with pale eyes, his golden hair haloing and rippling in the water as he stands on the bed of the sea. He is holding out his hands as if to take Jessica's in his. Tiny, silvered fish hover by his fingers. A small tile has come loose in its setting and Jessica picks it out. It bears a scrap of silver and the black bead of a fish's eye. She puts it in her pocket.

Turning back to the door, she finds the panels with their list of missing sons and fathers still intact.

Vandals have carved jagged, angry words into the weather-softened grain and as she passes, Jessica refuses to read their mindless obscenity. But the words catch her like a familiar face in a crowd. She stops with a sharp intake of breath and traces the scored letters with her finger, catching splinters.

One last entry – a final plea to the Patron Saint of Souls Lost at Sea.

Thomas Quennell　　　　*19th December 1995*

By the time she finds a resident's parking space near her apartment block, it is almost ten o'clock at night and fatigue is making her eyes blur. Before she unlocks the main entrance, she looks up. There are no lights on in her flat.

In the hall, she kicks off her flip-flops, moving on bare feet, praying he's asleep. Before the night of Libby's shop relaunch, Jessica would have crawled into bed and pressed her face to Jacques' warm, sleeping back.

'Where have you been?' Jacques' voice is thick with alcohol. 'I thought we were going to talk.'

He's filling the entire doorway as if the drink has loosened the tight bands of his body.

'I went to see Birdie.' The lie comes from her mouth like the lines of a play.

'I don't believe you.'

With cotton-wool fingers, she undoes the buttons on her cardigan. 'In that case, I can't tell you where I've been.'

He turns, wheeling into the kitchen, where he tilts the last dregs of a bottle of cheap, supermarket Beaujolais into his glass. She follows him, catching the bedroom door before he can close it behind him. A stratum of coaly smoke hangs in the room, making them both cough. Weak flames flicker in the black grate opposite their unmade bed. Something crinkles under her foot as Jessica goes to open a window. She looks down in horror. The newspaper clippings from her sea-dragon box have been laid out like a mosaic on the floor.

'What are you doing with my things?'

'I'm helping you say goodbye to the past.'

'Have you been burning them?' Her voice rises.

'I thought about it, Jessica, I really did.'

Bertie's notebook is lying on the bed. 'You went through my rucksack.'

She scrambles up handfuls of paper until Jacques rests a single finger on her shoulder.

'It's for you to burn, not me.'

'You're putting the blame on me?' She shakes off his touch. 'It's nothing to do with me or my past.'

'Tell me then.'

But she can't. Not even for the satisfaction of seeing his bravado fall, of catching the guilt that must seethe under the calm surface of his face. That kind of satisfaction would kill her. Her hands seem small and distant as she gathers up the newspaper articles.

Jacques kicks the sea-dragon box. It hits the far wall, drops to the floor with the lid hanging off a single hinge. She tries to move past him to get her box, but he stops her, lifting her chin so she has to meet his eyes. She's never seen him so angry.

'Burn them.'

'No.'

'I knew you were running away from something when I met you, and I accepted it.' The wine is sour on his breath. 'I knew about that piece of glass you hid in the back of the drawer. I let you give me your excuses, cat scratches and whatever. But do you know how hard it was for me to sit back in the hope that one day you'd open up to me, love me back?'

He grasps her face in his hot palms, her hair caught over her left eye making her feel blinkered and trapped. 'But I have loved you, Jacques.'

'Not enough. You kept part of yourself separate.' He releases her, grabbing the red notebook off the bed and shaking it at her. 'So that one day you could run away again.'

With Thomas's postcard in her pocket, there is nothing she can say.

'Running away is in your blood,' he adds.

Shock loosens her fingers. A few papers slip from her grasp and before she can stop him, he throws them into the fireplace.

'Black,' she says, 'is for the days I can't see you.'

'What?'

'That's what your note said on the flowers. Libby left it where I would find it, you know.'

Jacques frowns, shrugging. 'Didn't she give them to you?'

'To me?'

He closes his eyes, tries to pull her to him. 'Who else?'

She bites her lip against the urge to cry. She got so close to confronting him about Libby and now this small, brief reprieve has tripped her. He lets her gather the scattered newspaper clippings. Among them is the article her mother left for her in the Tesco bag and Jessica stares at her young, rabbit-eyed face. All that hope and expectation. And Jacques, his handsome face in profile, arm reaching for her even as he glances away. Then she draws in a sharp breath. Rushes into the hallway where the light is brighter.

'What is it?' Jacques slurs.

With the tip of her nail she traces Jacques' captured gaze. To Libby.

Shorter hair, rounder face but no mistaking her. There is her proof. Jacques and Libby gazing at each other, all those years ago while she fretted, naive and blind, about her first exhibition.

Jacques is flat out on the bed. She drops the paper on his chest and removes the red notebook from his hand. He glances at the newspaper.

'This is what we need to talk about, Jessie.'

'It's too late.'

'Just what,' he struggles to his elbows, 'am I being punished for?'

'Your secrets,' she whispers and he doesn't respond, perhaps not having heard. Lying down beside him, the notebook hugged to her chest, she wishes she could cry but the tears won't come. He tries to wrap his body around her but she is as stiff and unyielding as a felled tree.

After a while, he gets up. Collects every scrap of newspaper and presses them into the dying embers until there's nothing left but ash.

'And what about *your* secrets, Jessica?'

But Jessica is picturing a bloodied and desperate boy adding his name to a list of lost sons. Declaring himself dead.

36

Jessica wakes up to the smell of ash. Beside her, Jacques has his eyes open. He doesn't move as she pulls on jeans and a white cotton shirt that she remembers, too late, used to belong to him. *It looks cuter on you, honey.*

The day outside is grey with the first taste of autumn. An ashen day. Brushing out her hair, she shouts at Jacques in her head. All the things she can't bring herself to say aloud for fear of him validating them and begging forgiveness.

From under the bed, she pulls a battered brown suitcase which hasn't been used in years. She opens the cupboard, some drawers, grabbing random handfuls of socks, T-shirts, an old scarf. Terrified he's going to stop her, or worse, that he won't.

Straightening, Jessica searches the room for the red notebook and finds it on his bedside table. He's been reading it, she is certain, while she slept. She flicks through it, but of course the pages offer no proof of readership. At the back of the book where the postcard was concealed, she notices something – the final page has been ripped out, the remaining stub so tight to the seam she hasn't noticed it before.

'Did you tear a page out?'

Jacques barely glances over; he gives a mute shake of the head.

She runs her thumb along the torn edge before putting the notebook inside the case and zipping it shut.

Which brings her to this moment – the same threshold of departure her dad must have experienced. Of stepping from one world into the next.

Jacques is still staring at the ceiling. 'You're going to find him, aren't you?'

'Yes.'

'Are you coming back?'

She doesn't answer. The way to inflict the most pain is to walk out of someone's life.

The dialling tone sounds for almost a minute before Nathan answers. 'Frotherton West Farm Shop.'

Her mobile is slippery in a sweaty palm, and no matter where she moves to on the bustling concourse, someone intrudes on her space. 'It's me, Jessica.'

He doesn't sound happy to hear her voice, so she stalls with meaningless chatter to keep him on the line; asks how he is, how the shop is doing, and then cuts him off as he starts to talk about a new range of English wines. 'I need to ask you a question.'

'What now?' His voice is barbed with wariness.

'The last page in Bertie's notebook has been ripped out. Do you know anything about it?'

A moment of silence. 'It was a note for me from Bertie. I'm sure I was supposed to find the postcard as well.'

'But why did . . .' Jessica swallows, knows she should stop before he hangs up on her, 'you rip the letter out?'

'It was private. Look, I'd better—'

'I'm on my way to Stollingworth,' Jessica interrupts. 'At St Pancras now, in fact.'

'Is that supposed to mean something to me?' The bluntness so unlike Nathan. He knows what's coming.

'I went to your dad's place and he . . . gave me another postcard from Thomas.'

'You have no idea what you're doing. You're going to ruin lives.'

Jacques, rolling away from her, a glitter of tears in his eyes as he burned the newspaper clippings.

'He didn't do it, Nathan.' She hears him suck air as though struck, then is silent. 'I'm going to find him and prove it.'

'I saw him, Jessica.'

'I know, you said. In the snow.' A tannoy announcement forces her further from the platforms into an arched side-entrance.

'Not then. I made that up. I hoped you'd take comfort in knowing he was still alive, but also consider the fact that he never got back in touch with us.'

'So when did you see him?'

'Are you listening? He wants to be left alone.' He mutters something, a whispered curse of frustration before his voice returns to her ear. 'I saw something on the night he took my boat.'

'What?' Her back prickles with nervous heat.

'My dad and Thomas were arguing outside my dad's house. Thomas looked wild, terrified. There was blood on his hands and clothes.'

The letters on the departure board flip and shuffle sideways and she realises the Stollingworth train is leaving in three minutes. Rushing back onto the concourse, she bumps blindly through oncoming passengers, their curses washing over her. The ticket in her hand shivers violently as she tries to slot it into the barrier. 'It was you, wasn't it? You're the witness.'

His silence provides the answer.

She sinks onto a platform bench opposite the open door of the train. 'How could you call the police on your own brother?'

'You don't know the full story, Jessica. You need to leave this alone.'

She watches the train doors shut. 'How could you believe he did it?'

'Because of what the Russian did to you, Jessica.'

She closes her eyes and waits for the click and tone of a dead line but Nathan carries on. 'Bertie reacted like you are now. She wouldn't believe it either. When the Russian's body was found, she got scared that the transcripts and postcard would implicate Thomas and possibly herself. That's what her letter said – the one I ripped out of the notebook. She handed it all over to me before she moved to Madrid. She trusted I would keep it secret.'

And Jessica reads the accusation in his tone. *If only you'd done the same.*

Just as the guard raises his whistle, Jessica pounds the door release and leaps onto the train. Dropping into the nearest seat, she opens her suitcase and scrabbles the counsellor's notebook from its trappings of t-shirts and socks.

Wrong. They are all wrong. Thomas did not kill Bloody Russian.

She tries to recall what Bertie looked like – long brown hair and curves accentuated by hippy skirts and blouses; a woman whose advantage of age and maturity had added a sheen of sophistication in Jessica's young eyes. She'd hated Bertie for it. Now the picture shifts and she sees how young the counsellor had been; how out of her depth. But her confidence in Thomas had never wavered.

At that moment – with the train pulling out of the station, extracting her from her life, from Jacques – it makes Jessica feel less alone.

Bertie never doubted Thomas's innocence, and nor will she.

TQ: The police let him go.

AC: What happened?

TQ: They picked him up outside Jessica's school last week. Then my dad got him out.

AC: Your father bailed him?

TQ: He hadn't been arrested, only brought in for questioning. My dad went mad. He wasn't about to lose his cheap labour.

AC: Have you told your dad what that man did?

TQ: I tried, but he wasn't listening. Maybe he just doesn't care.

AC: What about Jessica in all this?

TQ: I haven't seen much of her. I think maybe I scare her.

AC: Has she said so?

TQ: No. It's just the way she looks at me. I thought if Bloody Russian was locked up, things would go back to being how they used to be with her and me.

AC: You've done all you can, Thomas. It's up to her now.

~ 37 ~

December 1995, Selcombe

On the last day of school before the Christmas holidays, Jessica and Hannah arrived home and kicked their satchels into the cupboard under the stairs. They had just opened the packet of Toffee Pops that Hannah had shoved under her coat at the newsagent's, when the doorbell rang.

Thomas stood in the doorway, clothes slicked with mud, his hair – wet with sweat – steaming in the icy air. She smelled him as soon as the door swung back; sharp and meaty, like the stewing beef Birdie sometimes forgot in the back of the fridge.

'What have you been doing?' Jessica covered her nose.

'I need to see you.' He sounded like he'd been running, taking short, light breaths as he swayed in the doorway. Leaves and black grit were twisted in his damp hair.

'What's happened?'

Thomas grabbed her sleeve, twisting the material in his fist as though she might run away. His hands were crusted with muddy streaks, their stench overpowering. 'I tried to do the right thing, you know.'

She bit her lip, afraid to ask what that might be. 'You have to come back later. My mum's on her way home.'

Tugging free of his grip, she saw that his fingers had left deep red smudges on the white cotton. She flung her arm away from herself, staring at her school shirt in horror. 'What is that?'

Thomas raised a filthy finger to quieten her, eyes pleading. The crusted muck on his fingers rose up his wrist and onto his jacket cuff, where it glistened like drying ink. Stains splashed the length of both his arms, shifting from earthy blacks and browns to red wine where it thinned and feathered outwards. Dotted among the streaks were splashes of liquid matter so thick and viscous it had pocked the material as it dried.

'Fu-ucking hell.' Hannah's voice made Jessica start. 'What happened to him?'

Thomas tried to grab her hand. 'Come with me.'

She recoiled. 'I can't.'

'You shouldn't be out in public looking like that.' Hannah mock-gagged.

His shoulders had started to twitch and spasm, eyes wide, mouthing something that might have been *Please, Jellybird*.

'Don't let him in,' Hannah was saying in her ear. Jessica turned to her, light-headed with horror, while Thomas sank to the floor, his back against the door frame. 'Get him out of here.'

Thomas's fingertips were feeling through his hair as though searching out bits of glass. Hannah elbowed Jessica out of the house, slamming the front door with such force it bounced Thomas's head forward. The porch window opened and Jessica's denim jacket and wellington boots came flying out.

'You two better run,' Hannah shouted.

Thomas wouldn't go near the road, which suited Jessica as she scanned the crest of the hill for her mother's headlights. Despite the stinging wind, she suggested the beach but Thomas shook his head. Pushing his hand into a gap in the caravan park hedgerow, he peered in.

'What about one of the caravans?' He was shaking so hard his words stuttered out.

'No way.' She took a few determined strides onto the bay path but he wouldn't move, still staring into the park. She saw how he might appear to someone who didn't know him. A tramp. A criminal. She'd be in so much trouble if her mother caught her with him.

'I need to lie down for a bit, Jells.'

Jessica pictured the caravans' pristine, ironed sheets; was about to shake her head when she caught the sound of an approaching car. 'Fine. Quick. Follow me.'

A gust of wind hit them sideways on as if a giant door had opened to let the weather in. Brittle leaves and road grit tornadoed around them as they skirted Seasalt Park's perimeter. Opposite the derelict council gardens a narrow door, oily with rot, was half submerged in the pine hedge. It was locked but Jessica knew if she barged it with her shoulder enough times, the catch would give.

The winter light had sunk into twilight. Jessica's eyes took a moment to adjust in the shadow of the hedge. She led Thomas to Caravan Nineteen, which only got bookings in peak season due to its view of the shower block. Jessica made him hide behind the mobile home as she groped for the spare key under the top step. When she turned to beckon him, he was bent over his knees as though dizzy. Muttering under his breath.

'I can't hear what you're saying,' she called above the pitched whine of the storm. 'Come on.'

He shook his head, his fingers worrying at his scalp again. Receding deep into himself; something she'd never seen before.

'Is that blood on your hands?' Her raised voice brought him back.

'There's no blood.' A violent shake of his head made him stagger, losing his balance. 'Oh, Jellybird.' He ground his palms into his eyes, a scabbed flake catching in his lashes. 'Why didn't you speak to the police about Bloody Russian?'

'How do you know about that?'

'The whole bloody county knows.'

Panic zipped through her. Hannah had sworn on her life to tell no one. That's it. She was going to tell Birdie about the bottle under Hannah's mattress.

'The stupid pigs picked him up outside your school. Of course everyone knows about it,' Thomas added, arms waving in erratic, angry circles.

She couldn't understand what he was getting so upset

about. 'The police came to my house the next day. Did you know that, too?'

'No.' He stopped moving. 'And?'

'I sent them away.'

Hid, crying upstairs, begging Hannah to tell them she was never, ever going to speak to them.

'Why?' Tendons lifted on his neck, his anger rising.

She pictured Hannah sitting on the bed after she'd sent the policewoman away, clutching her secret bottle, twisting the screw top – on, off, on, off – as though it were a magic lamp that could make everything better. She'd been angry as well. *Why do the police want to talk to you, Jessie? Is it to do with Bloody Russian getting arrested?*

'Because I want to forget it.'

Thomas covered his face, keening, *Why oh why oh why?*

The wind funnelled through the park, lifting off the ground in an inverse wave and snapping a branch off the beech tree above Thomas's head. It landed at his feet, cutting dead his rant. Jessica unlocked the door and ushered him in.

It was colder inside Caravan Nineteen than out. Jessica plugged in the small electric heater from the cupboard under the kitchen sink, keeping Thomas in the corner of her eye. He'd crouched into a tight ball beneath the window, shuffled sideways and wedged himself beneath the breakfast bar. Every time a fresh blast of wind boomed against the side of the caravan, he jumped. She knelt beside him, clenching her jaw against

320

a reflex gag as his smell wrapped around her. 'Thomas? Are you all right?'

He shook his head, rubbing his fingers together as if testing fabric. Without a word, he lurched past her towards the narrow cubicle between the kitchen and bedroom. The taps went on full, water spattering, and Jessica worried about the mess he was making.

He came out wringing his hands on the small towel that would have been folded into a neat triangle and stacked with three bars of soap on the sink. 'Can I stay here for a few hours?'

She nodded, staring at the towel he'd dropped and stepped on.

'Will you wait with me?'

'I can't. My mum . . .'

She didn't finish because he was nodding, blank distraction falling across his face, fingers picking through his hair again. 'Sometimes I feel like I'm looking through a window at myself. I get confused about stuff that I should know without thinking.'

'You just need some sleep.' It's what her mum used to say when she was wrestling with homework or grumpy with Hannah.

'People say I'm not a good person.'

'That's not true, Thomas.' Jessica took his damp fingers and led him to the sofa. Changed her mind about sitting on it and pulled him to the floor instead. Biting back her revulsion at the filth on his clothing, she pressed her side to his. Like pieces of Lego, she thought, holding each other up.

'I can't say if they're right or wrong. I don't know any more.'

Jessica lowered his hand from his scalp and worked her fingers through his. 'But I know.'

His face was expressionless. 'My dad kept shouting, *Look what you did, look what you did*. He was trying to make me believe it.'

Jessica swallowed. 'What did he mean?'

Thomas pushed himself upright with unexpected energy, slamming his hand with its filthy cuff down onto Birdie's spotless sofa. Whirling round and tapping the side of his head harder than seemed necessary. 'But I'm not confused tonight.'

Jessica stared at the dark smudge he'd left on the seat, like a storm cloud with a solid, brooding centre and wispy edges.

She climbed into the corner of the sofa, squeezing a cushion to her chest and wishing she was at home. Even with Hannah shouting, Lisa scolding and her mother slipping between them, a silent ghost. She knew how to deal with all that.

'You see, Jells, all these years he's been trying to turn me into him.' He stared out of the window at the rolling clouds. 'I'm going to go swimming.'

'How's that going to help?'

'I'll swim until I'm clean again.'

She looked at him. Trying to see through the dirt on his clothes and the spatters on his trainers that, no matter how she squinted at them, could only be blood. The real Thomas was lost in his own nightmares. He was never going to find his way out.

Tears rose through her vision. 'Shall I get you something to eat?'

He shook his head. 'Whatever people say, I was the one who did the right thing.'

'What did you do?'

'Remember that.'

An urge to lie down crept over her; to pull the covers over her head and wake up as an adult. *That's how the rabbit felt as the foxes fought over it*, she thinks. *Just waiting for the scary stuff to pass.*

He said something so quietly she missed it. When she asked him to repeat it, his fingers tightened on his coat sleeves, knuckles whitening.

'Will you kiss me? Just once.'

She'd forgotten those dreams; the countless different scenarios she'd conjured in her head, mapping out every detail until it seemed so plausible it was just a matter of time.

He didn't wait for an answer, pressing the broken frill of his lips to her closed mouth.

20 December 1995

Thomas was supposed to move in yesterday. We agreed on the last day of school but I've heard nothing from him. I don't believe it's because he's changed his mind. When I offered him the room, I saw the gratitude on his face.

I am prepared to face the inevitable questions of propriety because this boy is in desperate need of help and no one else seems to feel responsible for him. If – by offering him a clean, safe place to stay over Christmas and New Year – I offend the small people of this community, then so be it. I will put him on that train myself, having made sure he is clean and fed and ready to start a new life far from here.

Something is preventing him from coming to me as planned, so I shall have to find him.

I went to see Finn Quennell this morning. When I asked after Thomas, he flew into a frightening rage and chased me out of the gate. He kept shouting that he hadn't seen his son. He blamed me. He said I'd messed with Thomas's head so that he wasn't right any more.

I went to Nathan's afterwards, but he wasn't home. His boat is not in the harbour, either. I found Thomas's friend Jessica there. She denied having seen Thomas but she wouldn't look me in the eye.

I can't stop thinking about Mr Quennell's reaction when I asked after Thomas. I'm beginning to think something has happened. I feel sick with dread.

~ 38 ~

Jessica woke the next morning on top of her bed-covers, still dressed. She could hear her family eating breakfast – the muffled chink of cutlery against plates where once it was voices laughing, talking over each other. Without bothering to change, she climbed out of the window.

The caravan was stifling, the heater still on.

'Thomas?' She opened the bedroom door and found the bed empty, its sheets in messy ripples. On the floor beside the bed lay a small plastic-handled chopping knife from the cutlery drawer, its blade twisted, the tip bent in on itself. Unable to make any sense of it, she kicked it under the bed.

He was gone.

Though it smelled like something dredged off the ocean floor, Jessica crawled into the bed where Thomas had been lying just hours before. The sheets were gritty, dirt trickling like squashed ants into the bedding's folds as she moved.

A brilliant drop of red stood out against the dirty

snow of the sheets. She inspected it under the bath-room's strip light and discovered it was a gemstone, the shape and colour of a globule of blood. She held it up to the mirror, entranced.

And found his message written in soap across the glass.

Gone swimming it said, in crumbly white letters.

But of course he wouldn't. Not when he reached the water and felt the icy spray like acid across his cheeks. She lay down on the bed and watched the trees bending under the weight of the gale, heavy and slow as though everything were underwater. Rolling away from the window, she stared at her shoes on the floor, pictured herself springing out of bed and running off into the storm. He could be anywhere by now. She'd never find him. In any case, he wouldn't be so stupid. Jessica closed her eyes.

She must have fallen asleep because the sound of foot-steps brought her bolt upright, dizzy and disorientated.

'Thomas?' she tried to say but her throat was dry. The silhouette in the doorway was the wrong shape.

'Did you sleep here last night?' her mother asked.

Jessica nodded and an idea bloomed. 'I don't want to share with Hannah any more.'

'Why's that?' Birdie was frowning about the room, her eyes returning to the filthy sheets. Perhaps her mother's instinct, long dormant, was stirring.

Jessica cleared her throat. Without looking at Birdie, she said, 'You need to look under Hannah's mattress.'

Her mother didn't ask why. She stared at Jessica for a

long, uncomfortable moment and then sighed. 'We're out of milk and bread. Would you mind getting some from the shop?'

It had been so long since Birdie had bothered about such things that Jessica got up without protest and started putting on her shoes. 'OK.'

'Wear an extra layer,' her mother added. 'It's been blowing a gale since last night.'

She couldn't remember the last time her mother had noticed what she was wearing. She walked to Selcombe with the hope of things getting better.

Outside the newsagent's a tall, bony-faced boy was wrestling with the shop awning which had ripped free from its steel arm and was flapping violently in the wind. Ian, his name was, an ex-boyfriend of Lisa's who used to think he was being hilarious by waving Jessica away with his hands and saying *shoo little fly* whenever she walked in on them snogging on the sofa.

'Woah, woah,' he was shouting, as if the awning could be tamed like a bucking horse. As Jessica approached, he flapped limp fingers at her. 'Stay back.'

Her collar around her ears, she rocked with the gale blasts, waiting for him to wind the awning in. When he finally let her into the shop, Jessica grabbed a pint of milk and a sliced white loaf.

'How's your sister?' he asked when she brought her groceries to the counter.

'Hannah?' She busied herself counting out coins so he wouldn't see her grin.

'Lisa.'

'She's fine. In love again.'

Ian's mouth twitched down at corners. 'Who's the unlucky fellow?'

'A sailor. He's twenty-five and has his own car,' Jessica said, making up a story.

'Let's hope he doesn't get himself drowned in this weather.'

Jessica grabbed her shopping and opened the door, which caught in the wind, nearly ripping out of her hand.

Gone swimming, Thomas's message had said. She ran across the road to the harbour, her head dizzy with Ian's comment.

A chewy winter swell was butting the sailing boats by the pontoon against each other, their rubber buoys squealing. Nathan's crabber had a berth at the end of the jetty. Before she even reached it she could see the gap where it should have been, startling and unnatural among the jostling vessels like a missing tooth. The red tender was still there. Whoever had taken the crabber out wasn't intending to reach dry land.

Seawater washed over the surface of the jetty, almost sweeping her off her feet. With a stumbling jig, Jessica steadied herself and scanned the horizon. Not a single boat was braving the monstrous bulge and trough of the ocean. With the wind shrieking through the masts, she didn't hear someone walking up behind her. There was a light touch on her shoulder.

'Are you Jessica, by any chance?'

It took her a moment to register who the woman was. The wind was making a wild mess of her hair, but with her blouse tucked neatly into the waist of a long blue skirt she looked like a teacher. She had that kind of voice. Jessica went cold.

'Yes.' She hugged her arms about her waist, the milk bottle knocking against her hip. And though she knew full well, she added, 'Who are you?'

The woman held out a hand which Jessica pretended not to see, turning her face back to the empty mooring.

'Albertine Callum. A friend of Thomas's.'

Jessica chewed the inside of her cheek. 'He's never mentioned you.'

The woman didn't answer but when Jessica risked a sideways glance, Bertie's expression was thoughtful, kind rather than offended.

Together they stared at the space where Nathan's boat should have been. 'Have you seen Thomas today?'

Jessica shook her head.

'Do you remember when you last saw him?'

'Why are you asking?' Jessica kept her face turned away from the counsellor.

'I'm worried about him.' Bertie leaned in, searching Jessica's face as if secrets were like tears that might leak out unexpectedly and give you away. 'And I think you are too. That's why you're here.'

'I was looking for Nathan, actually.'

Bertie drew back, craning her head at the swollen sea beyond the harbour wall. Her eyes were red-rimmed, gory in her pale face. 'The thing is, Nate would never take his boat out in this.'

Nate. Like she, Thomas and Nathan were all best

mates. Jessica hunched her arms tighter about herself. She would say nothing more.

Another wave swelled over the pontoon lip, the water swallowing up her ankles so that for one giddy moment, she appeared to be stranded in the middle of the sea with its black depths and the colliding boats. The bag of groceries dropped from her fingers and Bertie caught her arm as she reached for it, the receding wave already sucking it out.

'We can't stand here any longer.'

Jessica shrugged her away. 'I'm fine where I am.'

'I think it's been hard on you, hasn't it?' The gentle tone in Bertie's voice made Jessica glance round, despite herself.

'What has?'

'You've been such a good friend to Thomas. I can only imagine it has been tough and made you feel sad. And perhaps a bit frightened.'

Jessica's eyes filled with tears. She didn't need to blink them back because the rain would hide them.

'I think you've been trying to help him as best you can.' The counsellor slipped her arm through Jessica's and started to lead her away from the jetty's edge. 'Did Thomas say anything about taking Nathan's boat out?'

She shook her head, the wind hiding her face in her hair. The urge to tell Bertie about Thomas and the mess he was in last night was overwhelming; the relief of handing it all over to a grown-up to make it better. She stopped walking.

Bertie whipped round to face her, grabbing Jessica's

hand. Her fingers were cold and thin and squeezed too hard. 'It's down to you and me, Jessica, to save him.'

Jessica nodded, licked her lips, tasting salt. She was just thinking where to begin, how far back she needed to go to explain how lost Thomas had become, when Bertie added, 'We just need to find him and everything will be fine. Thomas and I have made a plan.'

Thomas and I have made a plan. Said with a nod and a smile of teacherly confidence. *Thomas and I . . .* As though he belonged to her, not to Jessica.

Freeing her hand from Bertie's grip, Jessica stepped back and raised her chin. 'I don't know where he is.'

She started to walk away.

'Are you sure?' The counsellor's voice was shrill above the wind. 'Because he was planning to see you. To say goodbye.'

Jessica started to run.

39

The journey to Stollingworth takes almost five hours. Unwilling to use their joint account, Jessica allows herself nothing more than a cup of scalding peppermint tea and a cheese sandwich. For the time being, she'll rely on her sole account – tidal at the best of times – swelling with sales, depleting with the purchase of raw materials. Her hunger pleases her, a symptom of recovered independence.

Just after five o'clock, she steps off the train and books into the Midway Hotel, a modest Victorian terrace with a view of Stollingworth Station and a communal playground. The air smells foreign: chimney smoke and industrial metals.

Reception is tucked beneath the stairs, half hidden by a dusty yucca plant on a plastic pedestal. Behind it, Jessica can just make out of the head of a man in his early twenties. He doesn't look up until she dings the countertop bell.

'Can I help you?' He peers out of an overgrown fringe resting in his eyes. She pictures him spending an age in front of the mirror combing it into place with both hands.

On the registration form, she provides her mother's address.

'I like your look.'

Jessica glances up from the form. 'Sorry?'

'I only meant in an aesthetic sense.' He shapes invisible tumbling curls with his hands. 'Very Titian.'

Jessica signs the form and pushes it back to him.

'I'm doing an Open University course in Art Appreciation. That's the Titian link.' He gives a slanty grin. 'On holiday?'

'No, my boyfriend's been offered a job here. I'm helping him move in. Place is a dump at the moment, so here I am.' Out it popped. The same lie she had told to the overfamiliar landlord of Threepenny Row before Jacques came along and made everything better. She clears her throat. 'Is there Wi-Fi in the room?'

'What do you reckon?' The boy rolls his eyes at Reception. He hands her the keys but as she reaches the stairs, adds: 'Actually, the manager's not in. You can use the computer out back.'

Johnny Boyzie – as the receptionist introduces himself – lifts the counter flap and shows her into a cupboard-sized room behind the front desk. He settles himself on the edge of a table that takes up most of the space while Jessica googles Stollingworth on the ancient Mac. Then he takes out a half-empty bottle of Jägermeister from the drawer, along with a mug for Jessica and a shot glass for himself. 'Crazy juice. Against the boredom.'

She takes in his narrow chin with its splash of pimples, his wide-set blue eyes and the diamond stud in his ear. Smiles to herself as she takes a sip from her mug. The brown liquid tastes like cough syrup, warming her all the way up from her stomach, giving a little zing as it hits her head. 'I see what you mean.'

'So, does anyone actually buy the boyfriend job story?'

She laughs. 'Not since I was seventeen.'

Her internet search reveals little about the town Thomas escaped to. The only photos she finds are of a power station and the Iceberg Tower – in sunlight, at night, viewed from a plane or from the ground up.

'How far are we from the sea?' she asks.

'Dunno.' Johnny Boyzie shrugs. 'There's a canal in the old part of town. Must start somewhere.'

He goes to top up her drink but Jessica holds up her hand. 'Are you trying to get me drunk?'

'Yes.' Another crooked grin.

Jessica smiles, shaking her head. 'Go pick on someone your own age.'

'I've dated most of my big sister's friends.'

'Now there's a CV.'

Boyzie laughs, leaning forward to top up her mug, but Jessica's attention is distracted by a website – a single page only – for Stollingworth Fish Market. It offers little more than the opening times and a list of wholesalers and their produce. She thanks the receptionist, who offers to show her to the room.

'I can find number five all by myself, thank you.'

Room five is at the top of the second flight of stairs. Switching on the bedside lamp, she finds a small, sparse room with a tiny television set and fake tulips in a cut-glass vase on the desk. She gives her surroundings a moment to settle upon her, anticipating their depressive pull. Instead, she feels energised. All those months wondering where Thomas was, the slow rake of time like fingernails across her skin as she waited for the right moment, and finally it is here. She strips, throwing her clothes on the green poplin armchair, and climbs under sheets that smell of lavender and laundry powder. She falls asleep following a brick-lined canal to the sea.

In the morning, she switches on her mobile and messages flood in. She deletes them without checking and rings Birdie.

'Jacques has been calling.' Her mother's angry tone surprises her, a shiver dropping through her like a slot-machine coin, landing in her stomach.

'What did you tell him?'

'What could I say? I don't know where you are.'

'I can't explain yet.'

'Running away doesn't fix anything.' Birdie sniffs. 'It's how you ended up in that God-awful squat all those years ago. And it's what your father did.'

Jessica's throat dries. She replaces the receiver as quietly as she can. Birdie could voice her hoarded-up bitterness to a dead line.

After a long shower, she heads down to breakfast and

overfills her plate from the buffet. She's not hungry, but as it's included in the price she can no longer afford the luxury of leaving it. She manages a coffee and a few mouthfuls of egg.

After breakfast, she picks up a local map and asks Boyzie for directions to the fish market. As the receptionist draws a route in blue biro to the bus station, she is still raging at her mother in her head. *When will you stop punishing me for being my father's daughter?*

Jessica folds the map. Sunlight shines through the frosted glass of the front door. 'I don't suppose I could have another slug of that stuff? For energy?'

His face breaking into a huge grin, Boyzie glances about the empty reception area before retrieving the bottle of Jägermeister. 'Jägi before eleven. I'm loving it.'

Jessica drinks straight from the bottle.

40

The bus outside the hotel takes her to a large terminus in the centre of Stollingworth. Buses roar and belch around a concrete roundabout with a wooden bench where Jessica sits down to wait for the number thirty-two, as instructed by a chatty female bus driver.

Beside the seat is a signpost with arrow-shaped place names pointing in the direction of their location. According to the London arrow, she has put two hundred and thirty-eight miles between her and Jacques. The distance between one life and the next.

She wonders if Thomas sat on the same bench, bus fumes smoking the sea air out of his chest as he wondered what to do next.

The number thirty-two attracts a small group of people bound for the fish market; a father with young twins, three elderly ladies and a sallow-faced, middle-aged man who barely lifts his head from his guidebook. Jessica sits at the back, as far from them as possible, too anxious for small talk.

It takes fifteen minutes to leave the grey-faced city behind and reach flat, heavily farmed countryside. As the bus swings, bottom-heavy, through twisting lanes, Jessica catches an occasional glimpse of the canal, glittering opaquely in a low autumn sun. The bus follows a tarmacked road through the metal grille gates of an industrial estate, which ends abruptly with the ugliest view of the sea Jessica has ever seen – a wide, soiled expanse of water full of oil tankers. A fleet of large fishing vessels are docked alongside the pontoon. The market itself is a huge industrial block, windowless and besieged by diving seagulls. Men in white overcoats mill in and out of the market entrance with trolley-loads of crated fish. Jessica's heart is beating so hard she barely hears the bus driver announcing their final destination.

'This is it, young lady. The famous Stollingworth Fish Market.' He peers round from his seat. When she doesn't respond, he adds, 'I have to turn back in five mins, just so you know.'

Jessica thinks she nods but she's not sure. Suddenly she's afraid to get off. Every time a porter walks out of the huge building, her pulse explodes in her head. Then the driver's standing over her, his frown a mix of concern and irritation. 'A bit of fresh air, perhaps?'

As soon as she leaves the bus, the air clears her head. It's a smell she recognises; fish – fresh and rotting – and the sea itself. She slips past her fellow passengers, who are grouped around a man in a straw boater, and in through the market's cavernous doorway. The main hall is brilliant under a neon glare; it bounces off floors, shimmery with water and fish slime, catching the opalescent scales of the day's catch. The light makes her feel exposed, spotlit. There's a constant criss-cross of male banter and laughter between the merchants and porters. The assault on her senses is so vivid she almost scurries back outside. Then she notices the row of white plastic tables and chairs at the back of the hall and heads for the café.

Calm yourself, she thinks. He is not here.

The man behind the counter at the small café gives her such a beaming smile that she relaxes. 'What'll it be, love?'

His face is plump and stubbled with fair hair, the skin around his eyes puckered with humour.

'Just a black coffee, please.'

The man gives a theatrical double take. 'You're in a fish market, love, not Costa Coffee. How about a little smoked salmon? No? Some potted shrimp?'

Jessica shakes her head. 'Think I'd better line my stomach first.'

'Fair enough.' He pours tarry coffee from a thermos into a flimsy plastic cup which scalds her fingers.

'How long have you worked here?'

'Couple of years now. Used to be a postman but that was the loneliest job in the world, let me tell you. Stolly Market's best place I've ever worked, with the camaraderie and all that.'

She pays for the coffee and sits facing the hall. Feeling more at ease, she can take it all in. The displayed seafood is glossy with freshness, in hues of visceral pinks and reds, pulpy whites and intestinal browns. She takes small, fast sips of her coffee, hoping the caffeine will burn away her slight nausea.

'Is it a job you're after, love?' The man behind the counter asks.

'I'm looking for someone, actually.'

'Ah, the plot thickens.' He comes out from behind the counter and squashes himself into a chair opposite. 'You obviously weren't here for the fish.'

'Thomas Quennell. He was a porter here about seventeen years ago.'

The man sits back. 'Well before my time, but ask Greg at Mikkelson and Sons. He knows everyone. Worked here since the dawn of time.'

As she finishes her coffee, she watches porters disappearing through a curtain of thick plastic strips and returning with stacked polystyrene boxes brimming with fish. Young men with dark pony-tailed hair and the pale, fine features of Eastern Europeans. She studies their faces as they throw crumbs of broken English into the general banter.

Glances reach her, quick and curious as butterfly kisses, but nothing lingering. Except for one man in the opposite corner, hosing a section of floor. With a stocky build and blond, unstyled hair, he stands out from the other porters. His constant gaze makes her shift in her chair. She glances over. He doesn't seem to notice the water from his hose gushing over his rubber boots. Simple but harmless, she decides, and heads over to Mikkelson and Sons.

Greg is a tall man with a single grey plait under his stallholder's hat. He is discussing sea bream with a customer. A single, arachnid claw waves from a box of spider crabs. As the customer leaves, Jessica introduces herself.

'I was told you've worked here the longest, and know everyone.'

'Aye.' He's clearly pegged her as a non-sale.

'I'm looking for a boy, a man, I mean, who used to work here as a porter.' A movement behind Greg's shoulder catches her eye. The light-haired man is now standing by the doorway. The sun has broken through the grey sky and slants through the curtain strips. It catches his hair, and the gleaming fish scales in the polystyrene crates surrounding him, and ripples along the newly hosed floor. A wavering flux of brilliance like sunlight viewed from the seabed.

He is still watching her.

'Who is that?' Jessica points past Greg's shoulder. But she doesn't hear the answer as her pulse fills her ears, blood rushing to the surface of her skin. Before her head can catch up, her body has recognised him.

Thomas. Her lips shape his name, and she sees a matching certainty snap into place. Now he knows her too.

Thomas, grown into a man. His body and face thickened with years. She would have passed him by on the street. Nearly walked out of the market, dismissing him.

Greg looks around and addresses him sharply. Thomas stares back with the bemused eyes of someone waking from a deep sleep. Then something quickens in his face, but he doesn't move.

She picks her way carefully past the close-packed displays and across the slippery floor, never taking her eyes off him. Expecting him to bolt through the doorway and disappear once more. He doesn't move, frozen in the light.

Face to face, she suffers another moment of hesitation. Thomas, and yet not Thomas. She finds him in his eyes again.

'It's me. Jessica.'

His head drops, forehead almost touching her shoulder. For a moment they catch their breath.

'I found you.' Her words come out in spasms, her whole frame shaking violently.

He reaches for a lock of her hair, lifting it free from beneath the collar of her jacket and rubbing it lightly between his fingers. A tattoo like mermaid's hair runs between his thumb and forefinger down to his wrist. 'You found me.'

She closes her eyes because his voice – unchanged – brings the seventeen-year-old Thomas back. Her Thomas.

41

They don't speak as they follow the canal towards his home. Jessica lifts out of herself, following the two of them like a kite in the air. They walk like strangers, the woman with her arms wrapped about herself, the man's gait tight, reined in. A steady arm's length of space maintained; silence like a bag of stones between them.

Jessica studies the canal in minute relief. Grass sprouting through brickwork, clotted algae on the brown water, an empty crisp packet on the path with a mouthful of rainwater. Thomas stops suddenly, squatting down. He rubs his eyes, his face, brings a hand over his cropped hair. When he looks up, he's grinning.

'Jellybird,' he says, shaking his head. 'Jellybird.'

And she smiles back. One of them starts to laugh, the other joining in. She makes herself stop because her mouth starts to tremble, loose and untrustworthy. When they walk on, his hand finds hers and Jessica knows, with perfect clarity, that this moment will never be bettered.

Thomas's house is the last in a terrace of red-brick bungalows, facing a patch of stubbled grass with a bench. Beside it lies a child's tricycle, but other than that the place feels deserted.

He searches in his white coat for a single key and unlocks his door.

Thomas's home, Jessica thinks, and is overwhelmed once again by the enormity of having found him. When he walks through the door, she doesn't recognise the broadened shape of his back, or his head without its blond straggles.

She has to relearn him.

He doesn't invite her in, falling into a routined sequence of homecoming; boots placed on the porch step, coat removed, squashed into a ball and thrown into a washing machine inside the hallway cupboard. She follows him into a narrow kitchen, where he dispenses an egg-sized dollop of liquid soap into his palm from an industrial bottle, scrubbing his hands under steaming water until they are red and raw. The smell of fish reeking off his clothes catches the back of her throat in the confined space. Wiping his hands on a kitchen towel, she sees tiny filaments of blood where his over-washed skin splits with the bend of his fingers.

It's only after he's filled the kettle and switched it on that he looks at her.

'Tea?'

'Yes. Please.'

He takes two blue-striped mugs and a bag of sugar

from a kitchen cabinet. 'I can't remember how you have it.'

'Milk.' She wishes there were some background noise to relieve the self-conscious clink of cups, the sound of her swallowing and his breathing. 'And three sugars please.'

He dips his head in acknowledgement and she can't tell if he is remembering how he and Nathan used to tease her. *Want a little tea with your sugar?* He keeps his eyes on the kettle, which starts to rumble and whine. Jessica steps out of the kitchen. The house is unheated. She keeps her coat on, taking a seat on the brown suede sofa in the living room. Trying to take it all in, to find something typically Thomas which might bridge the time gap. By her feet, and scattered across a small table by the window, lie neatly scissored pictures of deer, owls and wild boar. The shelves on either side of the electric fire are stacked with magazines whose pages hang out in lacerated strips.

Thomas hands her a mug of tea and again she is assaulted by the smell of discarded scales and disembowelled viscera that have adhered to the fibres of his jeans and blue sweater.

He collects his animal pictures and piles them on the desk. She wants to ask about them, but there's something protective about the careful way he stacks them to prevent any crumpling. Sipping her tea, she glances between the brown, leafy pattern of the carpet and Thomas; trying to unwrap the years that have coarsened his features and find the boy she knew.

'Gabbler,' Thomas says between gulps of tea. 'My nickname at the market.'

'Your nickname?'

His eyes flick away as soon as she meets their pale stare. 'It's a joke because I don't say much.'

'I don't have a nickname any more.' *Not since you left*, she almost adds.

He nods, still looking everywhere but at her. 'I fell out of the habit of talking.'

'Why did you leave?' She regrets her words immediately. They are too sharp for the fragile veil of connection that hangs between them. 'Sorry. Don't answer that yet.'

'Let's go out for a walk,' Thomas says, getting up. Still happier outside than in. It makes her smile. Some things remain true.

The further they walk, the easier they become in each other's company.

'Like the old days,' Jessica comments, and is then embarrassed by his silence.

They cross open parkland of yellow grass and lone oaks. Mottled red and brown leaves blow about their feet, and Jessica has the odd sense of having lost time. When she left London it was late summer; here, autumn is already giving way to winter.

Thomas stops walking and points into the bare branches of a towering oak. 'See the little blue bird? A nuthatch. Only woodland bird that can climb head first down trees.'

Jessica smiles. 'I know. You told me.'

For a moment he looks bewildered. 'When?'

'When you and me used to do this.' She sweeps her arms at the countryside.

'You remember about nuthatches?'

She notices for the first time the frown lines like the mark of a two-pronged fork between his eyebrows.

'I remember everything, Thomas.' *I remember you and your beautiful grey eyes*, she thinks.

'You were just a girl.'

'And?' It occurs to her that he's afraid. It makes her less so.

'And . . .' Shaking his head, he lets his eyes move over her face, her hair. She sees them catch, a momentary stalling, on her breasts, and heat floods the pit of her stomach. Then he turns away, scouring the oak branches again.

'You look different,' he says. 'I don't know you.'

She finds herself digging her nails into her palms. Takes a deep breath, eyes closed, feeling the wind sweep off the ground and move through her hair. 'You don't know the details of my life, Thomas. But you know *me*.'

'Details?'

'Like baubles on a Christmas tree. They don't change the tree.'

Jacques, London, her jewellery. Baubles on a fallen tree.

Thomas starts walking again. 'There's a pond near here, full of Canadian geese.'

The rusty *chuck chuck* of a pheasant catches his attention as a brown-feathered flurry bursts from the undergrowth. He stretches his arm out like a rifle and follows its flight through the air, squinting along a pointed finger.

'Shall I fill you in on my life? Just the bare bones?' Jessica asks.

'The bare baubles, don't you mean?'

She smiles but he doesn't respond, studying her expression with the same sober intensity with which he fixed the tiny nuthatch.

When they reach the lake, he lays his sweater on the ground between the long reeds at the water's edge. The cotton of his t-shirt is almost transparent with wear beneath his armpits, but unlike the last time she saw him, it's clean and he had insisted on showering before they left the house. A tattoo of barbed wire snakes up both his forearms. Another change.

They sit on his jumper; protected from the wind by the long grass, their sides almost touching, a cocoon of warmth surrounding them. Jessica rolls up her sleeve and clinks her pebble bracelet at him. Thomas raises his eyebrows, acknowledges it with a huff of air through his nose.

'Want to know what I do for a living?' she asks.

Chewing on a stem of grass, he nods. So she tells him a story. All about a girl called Jessica who studied design in London and landed a part-time job in a prestigious jeweller's, which is helping fund her growing jewellery-design business. The tale is full of her successes and achievements – first sales, exhibitions, glowing reviews – but she never mentions Jacques. Without him, her story is so obviously pared down, its missing facts like new holes cut into paper snowflakes, obscuring the original shape.

His unquestioning acceptance of her story surprises her. Then she catches him considering her wedding ring. Until that moment, she hadn't thought of it. It was simply part of her finger. She can't bring herself to remove it.

'It's good,' he eventually says. 'Your life sounds full.'

'How about you?' she asks, as his silence settles on them again.

'It goes along as it should.'

'What about all the little clippings in your front room?'

As soon as the question's out, she regrets it, afraid it might be a symptom of some peculiarity that has developed in the passing years.

'I make collage packs for kids and sell them at local fairs and school fetes. Parents buy them in the hope their kids will make pretty pictures of animals or beaches instead of playing on their DSes.'

Hugging her legs, Jessica says, 'I wouldn't really know about kids.'

A breeze flattens the grass around them and he rubs his arms. Jessica traces a fingertip along his forearm, following the barbed-wire tattoo. Wanted to touch him to see what would happen. He doesn't move away but his eyes are sharp on her face.

'What do they symbolise?'

'Nothing.'

A fine rain forces them to their feet. Thomas stays two steps ahead, his head darting to catch movement in the undergrowth and skies. Trailing behind his unfamiliar frame, Jessica has never felt so lost.

Thomas goes out to get pizzas. Having no car, it will take forty minutes on his pushbike. Jessica puts the oven on to reheat the pizzas and hunts through his kitchen for plates and glasses. She finds his cupboards crammed with tinned soups, vegetables and pies and packets of pasta, biscuits and cereals; as though in anticipation of a natural disaster which might render him the last man on earth. It makes her smile; how typical of Thomas to be so self-sufficient and separate. The corroboration pleases her, until the rows of neatly positioned tins overwhelm her with loneliness.

She turns on the television in the sitting room and sees Jacques' favourite sports quiz – in front of which the two of them have often shared a takeaway pizza. Switching the set off again, she lets the silence wrap around her as the alien strangeness of the situation, and their attempts to dress it in everyday life, hit her. Perhaps it's the chill in the house, but she starts to shiver and once started, it won't stop.

In the bathroom, she inspects the avocado-coloured tub and finds it clean. Hesitates before turning on the taps, worrying about its appropriateness and the fact that the door has no key. Then the temptation of a hot, cleansing bath is too much. She barricades the door with her rucksack and boots, filling up the tub. Sinking beneath the surface with only her face above water, the shaking eases.

When she hears him come home, she sits up, arms crossed over her breasts, watching the bathroom door.

'Jessica?' His voice muffles as he walks into the kitchen. 'Are you here?'

She catches the slight rise of his voice, and reads it as a sudden fear that she has gone.

'I'm in the bath.'

Silence. 'I'll put your pizza in the oven,' he says after a pause.

As she washes her hair with his lime shampoo, she wonders if he's listening to the sound of water against her naked skin in his quiet, quiet house.

By the time she is dressed, he has turned the electric heater on and cleared his cuttings out of sight. They eat pepperoni pizza and drink Heineken straight from the bottle. She can feel his eyes on her. When she meets them, he doesn't look away but wears a frown of concentration as though he's puzzling out a mystery. They don't speak, the noise of the television providing a layer of lagging to fill their silence.

'Pizza and beer. All that's missing is the Friday-night video.' An inane, clumsy effort to interrupt the stillness emanating from Thomas.

'I don't have a DVD player,' he answers, and there is not a trace of humour in his face.

When the pizza box is empty he disappears into his room at the rear of the house, returning with a pillow and duvet. Again, that sweet-salty whiff of fish. She suspects they are his own covers and tries to refuse.

'I'm afraid there's only one room.' He makes a bed for her on the sofa, and suddenly she is so tired the room tilts. After a brisk goodnight, he closes his bedroom door with quiet, almost surreptitious effort.

Within minutes, she is asleep.

42

Sometime in the night Jessica wakes up. She tries to roll over and back into sleep but she is wide awake. An orange moon, as bright and low as a street lamp, is framed in the window, its light poking her eyes open.

Thomas's bedroom door is pushed to but no longer shut. She takes a few cautious steps into the hall, curious for the sound of him in his sleep. Silence. Perhaps the moon has woken him, too.

She taps on his door with two knuckles. It glides open enough for her to see the foot of a bed. There's still no noise from within. Pushing the door a little wider, it is almost a shock to see him sprawled on the mattress, no covers or pillow, wearing a pair of grey jogging bottoms.

Heart thudding, she moves a little closer, knowing she should leave; but there he lies in moonlit relief for her finally to study him. Face relaxed in sleep, he bears a stronger resemblance to his younger self. An exaggerated version of the boy she knew. Stronger chin, wider face, the same brow. Perhaps if she asks him, he'll grow his hair again.

His body is a different matter. A stranger's chest and shoulders shaped by tough, physical work. His fingers look too long and delicate for his muscled forearms. She searches his face again for the Thomas she knew. The harder she looks for him, the more he disappears. A temporary image sunburned onto the retina, always fading.

She doesn't recognise this sleeping stranger. Her Thomas is never coming back.

Out of nowhere the tears come. Those golden days are gone, when the world was as intimate as the branch of an oak tree, peopled only by her and Thomas. She clamps down on her jaw but she can't stop. She finds herself crying for everything she's ever lost. Her father, who effectively took her mother with him. Thomas, the friend she clung to like a lifebelt. Her life in London, the promise of babies like future Christmas presents.

Jacques. Letting her walk away.

She buries her head in the basket of her bent elbows, hands in her hair. Takes a deep breath and wipes her face. Looks up to find him still lying there, eyes now open. Turning away, she manages three steps before he's on his feet. He stops short of touching her.

'It's OK,' he mumbles, groggy with sleep.

Faces him. It's not OK at all. 'How could you have done it?'

The blank look on his face infuriates her. 'You let me think you'd drowned.' Her words spitting out like bitter seeds. 'Did you never think what that would do to me?'

'Hey.' He steps closer, palms outwards as if fending her off. There's a look in his eyes – a look she saw only once, outside Caravan Nineteen when he shouted at her for not talking to the police. 'Stop.'

She slaps his hands away, heart catapulting as his arms slowly drop. His eyes recede as though he's stepping back into himself, a cat settling on poised haunches. A curl of fear in her stomach. She has no idea who this man really is.

The sound of their breathing seems to reach them simultaneously, untwisting the air between them.

'You were the one who kept me going when my dad left. I still remember the love I felt for you. If I close my eyes and picture you on the beach, I can still feel it.'

Thomas sits down, leaning his elbows on his knees and holding his head. 'There's no going back once you leave a place,' he says. 'Same with people.'

'You say that because you're scared.'

'It was a different life, Jessica. It happened to different people.'

Without knowing she was going to do it, she drops to her knees in front of him, plants herself in the safe haven between his legs, as she has done so often in her dreams, and raises her face. 'Look at me properly.'

He gazes down at her for a moment before closing his eyes. His fingers lift to her face, gently tracing her cheeks, her jawline and brow. Her lips. Before his hands can drop away, she snakes her fingers behind his neck and brings his mouth down to hers. He freezes – a single, blank moment – then his arms come up and he's pressing his full force against her lips. Hands in her hair, he moans into her mouth as their lips open and his tongue slips along hers. Then the tension returns to his body.

'No,' he mumbles against her lips. She falls onto her heels, the back of her hand to her mouth. He shakes his head in a short, rapid motion, a shiver more than a gesture. 'There's something you need to see.'

Outside, she fills her lungs with sharp, wintry air. It smells of smoke and damp bracken. With the moon now behind cloud, they follow the canal towpath through an unseen landscape. A tree materialises in her path, shocking Jessica with its unexpected size and bulk. Thomas seems unaffected by the poor visibility, his feet tracking the canal edge.

He grabs her hand to quicken the pace, and his urgency makes her nervous. She begins to drag her footsteps. 'Where are you taking me?'

'I can't explain. You'll see.'

Leaving the towpath, they cross open fields. Jessica stumbles over frozen knuckles of earth. The moon is out again and she can see a forest silhouetted against the sky. They reach a signpost for Bishopshigh at the side of a road leading under a canopy of laced tree branches. Beneath it, the darkness is solid. Jessica shuffles forward swinging her arm like a machete. After a few minutes, without warning, Thomas scrambles up a bank of roots and into the woods. Jessica remains on the road.

'We're going into the woods?'

Thomas's voice comes from a little way above her on the bank. 'Yes.'

She licks her lips, finds her mouth has gone dry. 'Surely it's too dark to see anything?'

'It'll start getting light soon.'

She hears him moving away, leaving her alone with no idea of where she is.

'Shit,' she mutters, and follows the crashing sound of his progress through the undergrowth. When he appears at her side, she almost screams. He grabs her wrist to pull her along. If he left her now, she would never find her way back. Gripping his hand, she stumbles, feet catching stumps and fallen branches camouflaged in the black slurry of shadow lining the forest floor. Thomas twists around trees, pushes his way through straggling bushes, never hesitating.

'Are you sure you know where we are?' A nagging suspicion. This can't be a route; he is deliberately getting them lost.

'It's not far,' is all he'll say.

She digs her heels in, wraps her arm around a damp branch and anchors herself.

'What is it now?'

This snapping impatience is not something she recognises. Here, in the dark, Thomas is a complete stranger.

'It's too dark and cold. I . . . I want to go back now.'

'It's just through those trees. In the clearing.' He tries to take her hand again but she shrinks out of his reach, still clinging to the branch. Thomas steps back, regarding her in silence. Then he walks on without her, pushing his way through a tangle of thicket and leafless bush. His head ducks down on the other side and disappears. She listens for a clue as to what he is doing. Rustling. Trees cracking and sighing in the wind. It is much worse not to see him. She moves forward and finds Thomas squatting down to muck out twigs and mud from what looks to be the entrance of a badger's set beneath the exposed roots of a beech tree. With his head and shoulder close to the ground, he pushes an arm deep inside, gropes about and then pulls something out.

Despite herself, Jessica moves closer. He holds up a dirt-crusted casket of plain wood with a simple catch, like a jewellery box. As he balances it on his out-stretched palm, his hand is shaking.

'What is it?'

'You open it.' His voice sounds rusty, as though he hasn't spoken for a long time.

A feeling of dread comes over her. 'What's inside?'

'You'll know when you see it.'

She takes it from him, the wood slippery with mud so she has to crouch down and rest it on her knees.

'You have to know this, Jellybird,' she hears him say through a humming in her head. Holding her breath, she flicks the catch open and drops back the lid. Something gold gleams dully in the dusk. It makes no sense; her panicky brain can't decipher it so she picks it up.

In her hand is a heavy golden crucifix embedded with rubies. Dry-slicked with black matter. With a gasp, she drops it.

'No, Thomas, no,' she cries.

The cross lies half buried in fallen leaves. He fingers it out of the mulch and loops it over his head. Drops down onto the ground as if floored by the weight of it. Jessica staggers back, trying to distance herself from Bloody Russian's crucifix.

'My cross to bear.'

She stumbles onto a fallen log at the edge of the clearing and covers her face with her hands, too dizzy and numb to arrange thoughts into words. What horrifies her almost as much as the sight of the cross is that her instinct has been so skewed. She had never once doubted his innocence.

And if she was so badly mistaken about this, how can she trust her judgement in anything else? What else has she misunderstood?

Her hands drop to her lap. With her thumbnail she scrapes at the mud smeared in her palm from handling the box. Thomas is speaking, his words aimed at the crucifix dangling from his neck, and she has to push aside the noise in her head to concentrate.

'. . . still alive when I found him.'

'What did you say?'

Thomas won't lift his head. 'Though it could just have been when . . . I . . .' He makes a strangled noise, halfway between a cough and a choke. 'When I pulled it out of his mouth.'

'Pulled what?' Jessica approaches Thomas on unsteady legs, bends over him, straining to catch his words.

He is still gazing down at the soiled cross on his chest. 'His cross had been shoved deep into his throat. Blood was coming out of his mouth. I heard it gurgling up his throat.'

Bloody Russian's broken, jack-levered jaw. Jessica feels sick, hears herself moan in protest. Oblivious to the mud and waterlogged leaves, she slumps to the forest floor beside Thomas. 'You found him like that?'

He dips his head and relief like a hot, narcotic bloom flushes through her. She throws her arms around his neck, clasping hard, the cross embedded between them. He rests his face against her neck, heavy in her arms. This is the silence in him, a deep well that has swallowed him up.

Into his hair, she whispers, 'I knew it wasn't you.'

It is Thomas who stands up first, helping Jessica to her feet. As they walk, he starts to speak, his voice more tangible in the darkness than his body. She listens with her whole being, the forest receding, her feet finding their own path through the matted undergrowth. His story comes out in halting sentences, and she realises he has never told it before.

'When Bloody Russian disappeared I thought that was the end of him. Then one day there he was, in the garage with my dad. I wanted to kill him – you have no idea – but instead I did what was right. I went to the police.'

The knowledge startles her. She had never questioned how the police found out about Bloody Russian's attack.

'You told them what he did to me . . .' So here is the origin of the police file with her name on it.

'They couldn't charge him though because you wouldn't . . .'

361

Jessica worries the inside of her lip with her teeth. 'I'm so sorry.'

'But why, Jessica?' The fact still haunts him after all these years. She owes him an explanation.

'When the police picked him up outside my school, that's all anyone could talk about. One of the Year Sevens had a cousin or a boyfriend in the police and it all came out. Exaggerated, of course. What they said he'd done. I couldn't bear them to know it was me.'

She stops speaking, the memory returning in vivid, sensory waves – the cloying steam of breath and wet coats as girls funnelled through the corridors after break. Screeching like starlings about Bloody Russian.

'Then someone remembered I'd come in looking all beaten up a few months earlier.' Girls sidling up in small groups, pecking at her with questions, their eyes communicating conclusions above her head. *What happened to your face, again? Summer term, wasn't it? Fell off your bike? Really? You must have been going a hundred miles an hour.*

A twig catches her coat sleeve. Thomas waits as she tugs her arm free, careless of the material. Her hand brushes bark slick with damp, the cold bulk of the trunk looming over her. She shifts closer to Thomas, hoping to catch a trace of warmth. 'OK,' she says but he doesn't move.

'I went to confront my dad that day. I had packed a bag and was going to leave that evening.'

Without me? A forlorn echo of her lost, fourteen-year-old self.

'When I got to his house, the front door was open

but he wasn't in. I knew he wouldn't be far, so I went looking for him.'

She slips her hand in his but he doesn't seem to notice.

'In the woods I saw something lying on the ground. I laughed, you know. I thought—' His hand withdraws, the outline of his arm grey against a break in the trees. He rubs his eyes as if he could scrape away the memory. 'I couldn't understand what I was seeing. It was like he'd had some stupid accident, tripped up and landed on his own cross. Then I got closer.'

The Russian's broken-jawed, gore-streaked body joins them in the forest. Thomas grabs her wrist and they start to run.

They don't stop until they have scrambled on heels and hands down the embankment and reached the open stretch of road. Catching a dull glint at his chest, she realises he is still wearing the crucifix. The weapon.

She doesn't wait for their breath to catch up. 'Who did it, Thomas?'

'My dad.' His reply punch quick.

She swallows, nods. The old man had been trying to frighten her off Thomas's trail, knowing his murderous deed would be exposed if she ever found his son.

'I was trying to get Bloody Russian to sit up when suddenly my dad was there, shouting and swinging his cane at me. *What have you done, you monster? What have you done?*'

Jessica flinches at his sudden roar. 'Why would he say that?'

Thomas taps the side of his head. 'Because he's a crafty old bugger. I told him again and again it wasn't me. Then he said, so what? Everyone will think you did it.'

They face each other, fighting over a single rag of breath. His fingers tremble, forgotten, at his temple. She takes hold of his hand, presses it between her own; can't bear to witness the horror that has lived inside him all these years. 'And he was right, Jessica. I had a motive. My fingerprints were on him. I was fucked-up, sleeping rough and getting into fights. It didn't really matter who'd done it, they would blame me.'

'What happened then?'

'My father said my only chance was to make a run for it. He said he'd help me, but first I had to help him drag the body to the quarry.'

They start to walk slowly back along the lane, and Jessica is suddenly glad of the darkness.

'What makes you so certain it was your dad?'

Thomas's laugh is hard and bitter. 'It's the only time he ever went out of his way to help me.'

She hesitates, afraid her questions will rile him but the shock of seeing Thomas loop the soiled cross about his neck still lingers. She needs everything to slot into place, like sequencing the notes of a tune. 'But why would he do it?'

'It took me a while to work it out. He didn't care what that Russian bastard did to you, so it wasn't that. Then I remembered we'd caught him stealing tools.' Thomas nods to himself. 'It wasn't about missing hammers and screwdrivers, though. It was the fact that

Bloody Russian had taken advantage of him. After he'd bailed him out, and everything. Like how my dad killed one of our dogs for snapping at him. It was the same thing.'

'Why did you take the cross, Thomas?'

'Insurance. My father's fingerprints must be all over it.'

Nilson, she thinks. How does she tell him about Nilson?

When they reach his house, she holds back, reluctant to leave the blanketing darkness of the open fields to face each other under stark light. Thomas struggles with his boots in the hallway. Giving up, he trails mud into his bedroom. She finds him sprawled on the bed.

'Tell me about the boat.' She would rather close her eyes and sleep but this subject will never be discussed again after tonight.

'It's his feet that bother me,' Thomas says. 'Bloody Russian's shoes had come off, and his feet were white and smooth like a child's.'

Jessica's arms goosebump. 'Did your father come up with the boat idea?'

'Yeah.' In the dragging silence, she thinks he's fallen asleep, but then he continues. The plan had been simple. Thomas was to hide out until night fell. They were to meet at the harbour at one in the morning. Together they would sail to the Lady's Fingers, drill a hole in the hull and take his dad's old outboard back to shore, leaving the waves to carry and smash the boat against the pillars of rock.

'The storm nearly got us. We made it out of the harbour without being seen, but the waves . . .' Thomas shudders. 'I still don't know how we got out of Nathan's boat and into the outboard. My dad wouldn't have stood a chance with his bad leg if he'd fallen in the water.' In the unlit room, his eyes are black, opaque marbles. 'Part of me wanted that murdering bastard to sink beneath the waves.'

'Why did you agree to it?'

Thomas rises unsteadily off the bed, surprising her as his cold hands slip behind her neck. 'It was my chance to die and start over. A new me.'

'Did it work?' Her voice a whisper.

His smile brings tears to her eyes. She stops the slow shake of his head with her lips against his, and sorrow swells into a different wave.

Dizzy with him. With the rough skin of his hands along her back, his lips and breath on her neck; he twists and presses her into his bed like he's creating a mould of her body in the mattress. The smell of his skin is overwhelming, it's the deep ocean floor and beneath it the scent she knows; Marmite and toast. She licks the bare skin within reach of her mouth – a shoulder, a clavicle, a nipple.

Thomas. She has found Thomas after all these years.

With a rough movement, he draws away from her. Tugs off her trousers, his stubby nails scratching her skin, making her grind her teeth with delight. Together – his hands, her feet – they pull off his sweatpants and boots and he's lifting her legs high and wide, pushing deeply, endlessly into her.

Afterwards, she doesn't know if she's crying or laughing.

'Ssshhh, Jellybird,' he says, 'ssshhh.'

When he finally tells his story, it is brief, as simple as a two-dimensional stick drawing. At first she thinks he's hiding things. When she realises he isn't, it makes her sadder still.

They are lying on his bed, sharing the single pillow and duvet recovered from the sofa. Through the curtainless French doors which lead onto the back garden, Jessica watches the horizon crack open in purple velvet. She glances at her watch: almost six o'clock in the morning. A new day.

Six a.m. in London. The deep, nesting sleep before the alarm. And when it sounds today in less than an hour, will Jacques leap out of bed to turn on the coffee machine for her morning cup? Then stop, catching himself, as he sees the bed empty beside him?

She and Thomas. It had seemed right, overdue, a natural progression from the point where they had been torn apart. Now, blood and skin cooling, the grounding, itchy trickle of wetness, of hairs on sheets, he seems strange to her again. The blond hair of his leg is tickling her thigh. She shifts so abruptly he opens his eyes and continues with his story.

'I took the first train as far as it would go, then jumped on another,' he's whispering into her ear. Her left arm goosebumps with his feathery words. Reaching over the side of the bed, she retrieves her jumper, her nakedness shaming her. What has she done? A new day – in a different world, with a stranger, when yesterday it was Jacques. She has tumbled by mistake into someone else's life.

'Hunger stopped me at Stollingworth.'

Trying to focus on what he is saying as a rigid wall of panic builds about her chest. 'So you found a job at the fish market, and . . .'

He nods, says nothing but she can fill in the silence. A job at the market and this – an empty house surrounded by endless fields like a moat keeping him safe. Cutting him off from the rest of the world.

His hand slips under her jumper, fingertips drifting along her stomach. She rolls onto her front.

'And women?' She grins, to lighten her mood as much as his but he doesn't smile back. Years ago, back in Selcombe, he hadn't smiled much either though she could often sense the humour beneath the surface.

'Some.' He looks away. This Thomas has no joy left in him.

'And love?' Love. She is here, and Jacques is in London with Libby and their secrets. Love cannot hold a life together any more than a cloud can catch a falling stone.

'There was a girl who hung around for a few years, but I just . . .' He trails off, closing his eyes as though falling asleep.

A shrill ringing cuts through the house and they both start, glancing at each other in bewilderment before Thomas leaps out of bed. 'That's my phone.'

The call lasts minutes, Thomas's voice contributing little. When he returns, he pulls on his trousers, sits on the mattress with his back to her.

'Is something wrong?'

He doesn't look round. 'Who knows you're here?'

'No one.' But even as she speaks, it occurs to her that she bought her ticket with her card. She pictures police officers at the train station asking questions at the ticket office — her red hair makes her stand out — and the receptionist at the Midway who shared his bottle of Jägermeister with her. She has left tracks. 'Only . . .' Jessica turns cold, pulling the covers to her shoulders. 'Your father. He gave me a postcard. That's how I found you.'

'Who else?'

Her mouth has gone dry. 'I'm sorry, Thomas.' She tries to touch his shoulder but he springs up and away towards the glass doors, face averted. 'I went to the police officer who—'

'Nilson.'

The dry click in her throat as she swallows. 'I never connected your accident with Bloody Russian's death. I thought you were dead. Nothing else mattered. The papers were full of you — a local boy — going missing. When they found the Russian's body a month later, it barely got any coverage. A not-so-tragic accident, was the general feeling.'

'Nilson's here.' Thomas drops his head in his hands. 'He was asking questions about me at the fish market yesterday afternoon.'

Is it possible she has led Nilson straight to Thomas?

'What will you do? You can't go back to the market.'

Thomas shrugs with a resigned sigh. 'No one knows my name. I'm Gabbler, remember?'

'But your employment records?'

'Tom Byrne.'

Despite the severity of the situation, she is flattered that he used her name. 'But how did you get away with that?'

'Someone down the market knew someone who got me fake National Insurance, bank account, the works.'

'He'll recognise you.'

Thomas shakes his head. 'Not after all this time.'

'I did.'

'You weren't looking for a monster.'

'He'll recognise *me*.' Jessica's thoughts are still chasing trails like spilled coins. 'You have to leave.'

Thomas falls back on the bed, running a hand along the sheet, looking for her. Snakes his cold fingers along the base of her spine. She draws away.

'Are you listening, Thomas? You have to go before he finds you.'

'I didn't do it, remember?'

'As far as he's concerned, you did. Case closed.'

'There's the cross.'

'With *your* fingerprints on it, Thomas.'

'Why are you here?'

The question throws her. 'Because I had to see you again.'

'What about your great life in London, your jewellery and all that?'

Jessica hugs her knees to her chest. 'My great life fell

to pieces. Everything I trusted was built on lies. Then I found out you were alive, and—'

'You thought it would be the two of us, like before. Thomas and Jellybird.'

'Maybe,' she whispers, staring at the blotched light above the fields.

Thomas hauls open the sliding glass door. Icy air sweeps through the room like a hungry dog. 'So you have nothing to go back to, and I have nothing here.'

His face, for the first time since she found him, is animated, his eyes fixed with longing on the horizon.

I have nothing here either, she thinks.

He turns to her. 'Are you going to come with me?'

His question betrays nothing of his wishes. She can't even tell if he has a preference for which way she might answer.

Jessica looks into his eyes, pale as the weather-bleached bones of a lost boy, and shakes her head.

'I'm not Jellybird any more.' It is time to stop running.

43

Jessica sits on the floor in the hallway, unable to watch Thomas picking through the minutiae of his life; the weary process of judging which item has meaning and which does not. There's something in his shuttered practicality that reminds her of herself, barely three days ago. Fleeing rather than confronting the situation.

'All done.' He walks into the hall, tucking a few loose photographs into the inner pocket of his coat. Jessica bites her lip. The fact that he is calm, that her refusal to go with him did not devastate him, only proves it is the right choice.

Glancing about the hall, taking in the aluminium-framed mirror by the door and the otherwise bare walls, he almost looks bored. 'I always knew I'd have to move on.'

'This is my fault.'

He shakes his head, helping her to her feet. 'Thank you for finding me, Jessica.' Cupping her face in his hands, he presses his lips to her forehead. 'It's enough to last me a lifetime.'

'Will you be all right?' She reaches for his hand, which slips through her grasp. Can't bear him just to walk out. 'Where will you go?'

He smiles for the first time. 'That's a secret.'

Jessica wanders through Thomas's empty house. Finds his unfinished collage packs in a neat stack on the table as though someone might take up his work where he left off. Apart from that, she can't find a trace of him, as though he had existed only in her imagination these last seventeen years.

She wishes she could cry to ease the pressure inside her chest. It is not so much a loss as a realigning of herself, as if her body had grown up and around the memory of Thomas in the same way a sapling can grow to incorporate the fence it leans against. She leaves the bedroom till last, knowing she will allow herself to lie on the sheets and breathe him in one final time.

When she reaches the bed, she finds Bloody Russian's crucifix lying in its centre.

Will you be back?

Jacques' question had startled her. In the heady, livid rush to leave the flat, to hurt him by walking out, Jessica hadn't been thinking of long-term consequences.

The train is an hour out of Stollingworth before she finally dares to turn on her mobile. It has been switched off since finding Thomas. Texts and voicemail messages arrive in a procession of electronic beeps. Not as many as she'd anticipated. Three messages from Libby, begging to know where she is. One from William

Mansion's saying she'd left them with no choice but to terminate her contract. Her mother, then Hannah. In her impatience, she cuts the messages off before they're finished. Scrolls through her texts and finds nothing. Jacques has not tried once to contact her. She bitterly regrets deleting her unheard messages when she arrived at the Midway Hotel.

The train stops at a station with a single platform. A young mother expertly tilts her baby's buggy over the gap and into the carriage. As the train rocks into motion, she takes her time removing layers of blanket, a glow of anticipation on her face as though she were unwrapping a present. She picks up a pink-swaddled baby, who stretches its little fists in the air, bottom out, tiny legs tucked under. The mother irons out the little body against her shoulder, resting her cheek against the fine down of hair. Jessica can almost feel the warmth of the baby's head against her own face and with a jolt – something close to panic – she remembers how she struggled with the idea of having her own baby. Fending it off as a pleasant but distant notion.

She checks her mobile again, knowing there are no messages.

Jacques, she remembers, had abandoned his mission to clear the box room, sensing her uninterest. Jessica sits up in her seat. When she gets home, she will pick up where he left off. She'll empty the crates of outgrown furniture and clothing, paint the walls a buttery yellow and stencil patterns, the colours of boiled sweets, across them. A way of saying sorry for running away, for giving up on their marriage. They would thrash out the issue with Libby. They would get over it.

A few seats away, the mother settles the baby into the crook of her elbow and Jessica has to look away, a curious, empty ache in her own arms; a feeling she has never before been conscious of. That foolish, selfish fear of sharing Jacques' love with her own baby has vanished under the turmoil of the last year. Now she can't think of anything more blessed.

The remainder of the journey passes in a blur of suspended anticipation. She can't think about what is waiting for her at home, or what she will say to Jacques when she sees him but even with her mind blank, her homecoming reels her in, an ever-tightening rope. When the buffet cart stops by her seat, she struggles with the notion of food.

'Who's the lucky fella, then?' asks the slight girl manhandling the cumbersome metal cart through the aisle.

'What do you mean?'

Flipping long, thin hair over her shoulder, the girl leans in. 'I can tell from the way you hummed and ha'ed over the Kit Kat. Us women only hesitate over chocolate when it's about a man.'

'I'm going home. To my husband.'

'Good for you,' she says, handing Jessica the Kit Kat. 'Glad there's still a few of us out there who believe in marriage.'

Jessica pays, feeling like a fraud.

When she is alone once more in the carriage, she

places Bertie's notebook on the seat beside her and the bloodied cross – now sealed in a plastic sandwich bag she found in Thomas's kitchen – on the fold-down table. Black crusts of dried blood litter the bottom of the bag. She notices an empty, round eyelet in the centre where a ruby is missing and all of a sudden remembers the gem she found in the bed of Caravan Nineteen on the day Thomas disappeared. It explains the twisted knife used to lever the stone from its setting. She wishes she could ask him why he left her the stone seventeen years ago, and why he has now left her the cross. Unable to divine his intention, she shoves it deep into her bag once more and turns her attention to the notebook, flicking through the pages out of habit.

Something drifts to her lap. A photograph. Picking it up, she is confronted with herself and Jacques, sitting in the Longhaven Bay Café grinning awkwardly for the unfriendly waitress. Or rather she was, because Jacques was looking at her. The camera had caught him smiling both at her and to himself. As if it had just struck him that he might love her.

At some point in those last awful days in London, Jacques had taken the picture out of its frame and placed it in the pages of the red notebook.

By the time the train pulls into St Pancras, a sense of urgency fizzes through her. The taxi queue is long, a domino trail of businessmen heading home. She imagines giving the man in front a shove and seeing them all topple over so she can reach an empty cab. The wait drags on for ten minutes until she's ready to scream with frustration. Once in a black cab, she distracts herself by ticking off old, familiar sights. The Planetarium's domed roof on Euston Road; an alien glimpse of the BT tower rocketing through the skyline; the aquatics shop on Great Portland Street where sometimes she ducks out to lose herself in the languid motion of fantailed fish; the circular green of Cavendish Square; the Phoenix pub on the corner of John Prince's Street, her road. Home.

She gets out and has to be reminded by an irate driver to pay her fare.

Inside the hall, she notices a stack of letters bound by a rubber band on top of their postbox where the postman couldn't cram any more in. She sprints up the stairs and struggles to get the key in the lock.

The apartment is dark, and the smell is wrong. Cleaning fluids and unstirred air. Not a trace of cooking or coffee grounds. Dropping her bag, Jessica heads straight to the kitchen. Without turning on the lights, she opens the fridge door. A waft of bleach hits her, the shelves empty and gleaming as new.

Her legs buckle, the floor tilting up to meet her.

~ 44 ~

October 2012, Seasalt Holiday Park, Selcombe

In pyjama bottoms and a vest, Jessica inspects the bruises on her shoulder in the long mirror tacked to the back of her bedroom door. The discoloration has mellowed into jaundiced yellows. She tries to count back on her fingers how long she has been there, but winter days in the park pass by in bland hibernation. The fading bruises are her only way of marking the passage of time.

When the door opens and Grannie Mim appears, she scrambles for a jumper. 'How about knocking?'

Mim's hand on her arm is surprisingly forceful. She frowns at the bruises. 'Is this why you left London?'

'No. How can you think that? You know Jacques.'

'People are damn good at hiding their ugly bits, let me tell you.'

'I fainted, that's all. Hunger, exhaustion.' Pulling on her jumper gives her an excuse to hide her face.

The refrigerator cleaned out with such finality. Jacques gone.

Suddenly she's too tired, too raw to hide anything. 'Actually, I think it was shock.'

'I can read it in your face.' Grannie Mim's nodding. 'You, my girl, need to start talking. Come and help me with my chores.'

Jessica looks at the snow falling in sleety clumps. 'Birdie makes you do chores?'

'I set my own, thank you very much. Today I'm clearing litter from the gardens across the road.'

'Can't we wait until the weather's a bit better?'

Mim slides Jessica's boots across the floor. 'City's made you soft.'

As they walk through the park, Jessica tells her about finding the flat empty and how, once she came round, she hadn't the will to get up. Lay on the floor, drifting in and out of sleep, never changing position even when her shoulder became a piece of dead meat. She doesn't mention the vague memory of warm liquid trickling over her thigh as her bladder emptied itself.

'It felt like I was dying.' Jessica tucks her hair inside her collar to stop the wind whipping it in her face.

Her neighbour double-blinks. 'Possible, I guess.'

'I let everything go. I felt my body giving up.'

She stops talking. Afraid to tell Mim how detached she felt, experiencing the agony of recovering circulation from far away. She has cloudy memories of showering and packing a bag. Of rushing back to the sitting room as she was about to leave her home.

Taking the cuckoo clock off the mantelpiece, she had removed her wedding ring and left it in its place.

'I am feeling better here, though.' Which is true. Bit by bit, she feels herself coming back together.

'You're still rake-thin.' Mim's eyes wander back to Jessica's shoulder. 'Why *did* you run away?'

They are approaching Birdie's caravan, so Jessica doesn't answer. Her mother is gouging clumps of leaf and moss from the roof guttering with Joss, the gardener, steadying her ladder. Though he keeps to himself, it is clear he's now a daily visitor to the park. Jessica and Grannie Mim wave as they pass. Her mother nods back; Joss, too, giving them a quick bob of his head.

'Are you going to tell Birdie what I say?'

'Nope. That's your business.'

She looks over and catches a glint in the old woman's eye. It reminds her of Grannie Mim leaning out of her caravan door with a glass jar of hundreds and thousands, saying *Hold out your hand but don't tell your mother.*

'You used to give me sweets.'

Grannie Mim shrugs, trying not to look pleased. 'You were always poking sticks in rabbit-holes and hiding under the caravans, getting wet and filthy. I had to bribe you out of the cold. Little wild thing, you were.'

They walk through the main gates of the park and cross the road into the council gardens. Jessica grimaces as she looks about. 'It's a miserable place now.'

They find a dead seagull half submerged in the lido's

shallow water, its feet cramped into scaly fists as if it clutched at the sky as it fell.

'We used to play here, me and the caravan kids,' Jessica says, and she sees herself, the leader of a ragtag band of children, devising games and avoiding her chores. Then she remembers Libby had been one of those children, and that they had probably played together. Biting the inside of her cheek, she waits for the swell of anger to subside.

Grannie Mim tosses the seagull behind a tree, tutting at a burned-out tyre surrounded by empty beer cans. She takes a bin liner from her coat pocket and starts feeding them into the bag. 'Back to your story. We were just getting to the good bit, I believe.'

'Do you remember the boy who used to hang around my house? Tall with messy blond hair and light-grey eyes.'

Mim considers it before nodding. 'One of Finn Quennell's boys.'

Jessica picks up a scrap of soggy newspaper between her finger and thumb and drops it into Mim's bag. 'Well, I went looking for him.'

Grannie Mim glares at her. 'Why on earth did you do that?'

'Jacques and my friend, Libby . . .' Her voice trails off. She doesn't want to explain about them but then from the look on Grannie Mim's face, she doesn't need to. 'I couldn't face it, so I went looking for Thomas instead.'

The bin bag makes a tin clatter against the ground as Mim lets her arm drop. 'That was your solution?'

'I wanted desperately to believe it was.' She starts hunting about for litter, suddenly too angry to look at Mimosa. 'The situation was making me ill. I kept catching them whispering together. She was always in my house, always knew what was going on with me before I told her.'

'What did Jacques say in his defence?' Mim holds open the bag for the single beer can she's collected.

'Nothing. I didn't give him a chance to.'

She senses Grannie Mim biting down on her response. They wander towards the boarded-up pavilion, eyes on the ground as they search for rubbish and avoid looking at each other. Jessica sits on a peeling step leading to the pavilion's porch.

'It felt like I'd lost Jacques and was being offered Thomas in return. It made a terrible sort of sense. I persuaded myself it had been Thomas all along.'

'Did you find him?' Grannie Mim joins her on the step with a grunt.

Jessica starts to nod, then stops. 'No.'

Because she hadn't found the boy she'd known, just a stranger with his likeness.

'So you didn't find what you were looking for, and decided to go back to Jacques?'

Jessica shakes her head. 'Actually it helped me find what I needed. It turned out to be Jacques all along.'

Grannie Mim takes her hand between hers, which are somehow warm and dry. 'You know what you must do then?'

'He's gone. I don't know where . . .' Catching the plaintive note in her own voice, she stops.

Mim gets up, straightening with minor jerks as her arthritic joints pop into place. 'Birdie knows. He left a number.'

Closing the door, she heads for the bedroom and strips down to her t-shirt, pants and socks. Climbs into bed. The urge for numbing sleep is never far away. Having drifted off, she hears a knock and thinks it's a dream. Until her mother walks in with an expression so grave, her desire for sleep vanishes.

Nilson, she thinks. It was only a matter of time before the policeman tracked her down. She is unprepared; hasn't even found a hiding place for the crucifix yet.

'What is it?'

'I didn't mention it before because, well, I didn't feel it was my business.' Birdie has her hands pushed deep into her skirt pockets. 'But Jacques was here.'

'When?' The word rushes out.

'About ten days ago.'

She scrambles her legs out of the sheets as though preparing to run. 'Ten days?'

'Well, I can check the register for the exact date but he came here the day you disappeared.'

'I didn't disappear. I called you.'

'As far as your husband knows, you disappeared.' Birdie's voice rises – a glimpse of the determined woman she once was. 'He stayed here. In this caravan.'

The question she is both desperate to ask and terrified to have answered is singing in her head. 'Where is he now?'

'He was going back to America. To his folks, I believe.'

Jessica mutters a thank you, lies back down and pulls the covers up to her ears. The sound of the closing door as Birdie leaves spurs Jessica into action. All at once, she's rattling between the walls of her mobile home like a bluebottle. Spreads her fingers, touching and smoothing sofa seats, countertops and handles, searching for evidence of Jacques as though his presence might be written in Braille across the surfaces of the caravan. She hauls the sheets off the bed, pushing her face into the denuded pillows and duvet desperate to catch a scent of him. Scours the bare mattress for a single dark hair, a hollow in the shape of his body. She finds stray hairs, possibly his or not, dust-bunnies, a pound coin. Jacques is gone. Jacques has gone over the seas to the other side of the world; so far away he will soon become unreal. Like Thomas.

The caravan stifles her. She tugs her clothes on again. Flinging back the door, she takes the steps in a leap. Jessica runs to her mother's caravan, lit from the inside against the grey afternoon. Without knocking, she opens the door so hard it bounces off the wall and the place shivers. Her mother freezes in an awkward position, head turned back, body intent on continuing forward.

'I don't know what I'm doing,' Jessica says in a quiet voice. 'I'm lost.'

Her mother lowers her head for a moment, then closes the door.

'Now you come in and sit down.' Her fingers are cold

as she takes a light hold of Jessica's wrist, leading her to the foldaway table. She opens the drawer under the sofa and lifts out a bundle of material that keeps on coming like a magician's trick. 'It's just as well you're here, you know.'

Jessica can only swallow, her voice untrustworthy.

'Sewing night,' Birdie continues. From another secret drawer comes a battered tin with pictures of the Royal Danish biscuits it once contained. Jessica remembers it from her childhood, how she used to poke among the shiny spools of thread for hatpins and silver needle-threaders.

'You'll have to mend the seat covers because your hand is neater than mine, and people always look before they sit.'

Her mother disappears into her bedroom, returning with a black bin bag full of damaged cushions. The first one has a hole like a puncture wound. Jessica looks through Birdie's tin for matching thread. This is the mother she remembers. As if she'd been hiding in the sewing box all along. The way she would take a distressed daughter and give her a task, something for her hands, talking at her in that bossy, no-nonsense tone until the woes of the world started to look fanciful beside the practical necessities of mending, chopping, cooking.

Jessica threads a needle, finds a blue and gold porcelain thimble and starts to mend the hole while her mother flaps out a curtain, clucking her tongue.

'The damage people do. Nice people, as well.'

Jessica lets her mother talk. It doesn't make the storm

inside her go away – she's not five any more – but it grows calm, sitting heavy and still like a bowl of water.

'Thank you, Mum.'

She is surprised when Birdie reaches out and touches her face. Sitting over their sewing, Jessica thinks that perhaps there's a different quality to the silence between them. Less saturated with their lost years.

45

December 2012

They spend the morning twisting multicoloured Christmas lights through the perimeter hedges. A winter sun shines from a cut-glass sky. Through the open window of the office, carols are playing on the radio.

By lunchtime, Jessica's arms and shoulders are aching. 'Remind me again why we are doing this?'

'Because it looks pretty,' Birdie replies. Which is exactly what she used to say as she attached lace edging to caravan cushions which would only be ripped and stained by the end of the season, and stayed up late icing cupcakes for the school fete.

'Mum, I just want to say that . . .' Jessica pauses. She wants to find the right words to explain that this is exactly where she needs to be. That being with Birdie is – against all previous expectations – making her feel better.

Her mother gives a good-natured tut. 'Just because it's Christmas doesn't mean we have to get all silly.'

For the first time in weeks, Jessica feels hungry. 'Why don't we go for lunch? We could try that new café on the promenade by Whitehead.'

She anticipates an excuse but then Birdie nods. 'A walk would be good on a day like this. It does a nice panini, I hear.'

Jessica raises her eyebrows. 'Next you'll be ordering a skinny mocha latte.'

As her mother goes back into the office to lock up, the telephone rings. The call is short but when Birdie rejoins her, she is quiet.

They walk without speaking, and Jessica tries to empty her head; to walk along and be part of the present, watching tiny birds dart in the gorse and tracking fox prints in the narrow strips of snow that line the cliff path. But as their walk continues, her mother's silence becomes a stiff finger in her side.

'What's on your mind, Mum?'

As they reach the steps leading to Selcombe Bay, her mother stops and gives Jessica a searching look. It unnerves her; she catches herself trying to think what she has spilled or broken.

'Why would the police want to speak to you, Jessica?'

'The police?' The blood drains from her face.

Her mother's sharp eyes widen. 'What have you got yourself mixed up in?'

'I haven't done anything wrong.' She tries to sound indignant but her mother's anxious expression waters down the conviction in Jessica's voice. 'Was that the phone call you just took?'

'From an Inspector Nilson, yes.' Birdie's frown deepens.

'He's looking for a friend of mine.' She needs to get her story straight. Is suddenly afraid of returning to Seasalt in case Nilson's waiting for her.

'Your friend from up North?'

Grannie Mim. Jessica bites down on the sore spot inside her cheek. If her mother can make these assumptions, then Thomas doesn't stand a chance against Nilson and his obsessive hunt. He only has to open her rucksack sitting inside the bedroom cupboard to find the murdered man's cross with its telltale forensics.

'Did the policeman ask to speak to me?'

'I told him you were out,' Birdie says. 'Come on, we'll miss lunch at this rate.'

Her mother continues past the bay steps, keeping to the narrow path which curls steeply towards the broad shoreline of Whitehead Beach. Jessica is grateful they are forced to walk in single file so that Birdie's observant eyes aren't on her. She needs to plan what she will tell Nilson.

Thomas believes the cross will exonerate him, even though his own fingerprints smudge those of his father's. Finn Quennell will fabricate a plausible reason for his marks being on the crucifix but Thomas – still running – can't defend himself. With a sick realisation, Jessica understands that this alone is all the evidence Nilson requires. And of course there is the question of her role. What will happen to her if she comes forward with a crucial piece of evidence?

There is only one person she can discuss the crucifix with. As soon as they return from lunch, she will make a phone call. In the meantime, she has lost her appetite.

As they reach the promenade, Jessica eyes the crowded tables through the café's misted windows. 'I'm not really hungry.'

'Well, let's breathe in a bit of sea air before we head back.'

They sit on the beach, the sand cold but dry. Jessica lets the crash and roll of the surf distract her. She'll think about Nilson later.

'Oh, lord,' Birdie says after a while, sounding amused. 'Would you look at the inappropriate foot-wear.'

A figure is stumbling across the beach, high-heeled boots sinking into the sand and catching dry ropes of seaweed.

'Someone's had too many white wines over lunch,' Jessica says. Then her mouth goes dry. She gets up. 'Let's go.'

'What's the matter?'

The figure calls out and Birdie stops. 'That woman just called your name.'

'Can we just walk?' Jessica tries to keep going but her mother stops her, squinting at the approaching figure.

'That's the woman who was asking after you the other day.'

Jessica shrugs off her hand. 'I have nothing to say to her.'

'Please wait,' Libby shouts.

'Be brave.' Birdie reaches again for Jessica's arm, her fingers snatching uselessly at her coat sleeve. 'You used to be my fearless child.'

Jessica works her jaw, watching Libby curse and lurch across the sand.

'Thank God you didn't run away. I'd have broken a leg.' She's breathless by the time she reaches them, touching the back of her hand to her brow. A smudge of mascara underlines one eye. 'Where the hell have you been hiding? Jacques went looking—'

'Don't say his name.' The volume of her voice makes both Birdie and Libby straighten.

Libby drops her head, still gasping for breath. 'That's why I'm here. You never let me explain about Jacques and I.'

Birdie suddenly steps forward, placing herself between the two younger women.

'I know who you are.'

So Jacques had spoken to her mother. Had told her about Libby. Jessica's head is starting to throb. 'Mum, it doesn't matter.'

'I know exactly who you are,' her mother repeats, voice shaking.

Despite the urge to cover her ears and walk away, there is something about the way her mother has caught Libby in her glare that also holds Jessica.

'You look just like her,' Birdie says.

Libby nods. 'I know.'

'Does Jessica know who you are?'

'Not yet.'

Jessica grabs her mother's hand. 'What's going on?'

Her mother sighs. 'I don't know how you got to know each other but she' – Birdie jabs a finger in Libby's direction – 'is going to tell you exactly who she is.'

Nilson, Libby, Jacques. Weariness, like a familiar craving, sweeps over her; she could simply lie down on the sand, close her eyes and sleep.

Libby's voice is barely more than a whisper. 'He was desperate to see her. He hoped you might relent when he got ill.'

'Selfish to the last.' The words snap from Birdie's jaw.

'Stop!' Jessica shouts. 'Stop talking over me.'

'This is what I have tried to protect you from.' Birdie takes her hand, which further unnerves her. But worse, so much more frightening, are the tears in her mother's eyes. 'From the day your father left us.'

~ 46 ~

They watch her walk away, Jessica's thoughts like a sandstorm and Libby still catching her breath. Birdie's ankles kink over the uneven surface of the beach. It pains Jessica to recognise her mother's ageing; she doesn't want Libby to see it too.

'What's going on?'

Libby, trying to steady herself on sinking heels, says, 'Here. I have something of yours.'

She rummages in her bag. Her hands are shaking as she places something pink and sparkly in Jessica's hand.

A plastic brooch that spells TRUE LOVE.

'What is this?' Jessica knows it but can't place it.

'You left it at my home.'

The brooch winks in the pale sunlight. Jessica closes her fingers over it. She sees it now – the jewelled bower where a beautiful woman lived like a bird of paradise. Her mother, Daniel's plain brown robin, hadn't stood a chance.

She has the oddest sensation of time stretching away like a length of elastic connecting her teenage self – young and naive, letting a stranger play with her hair – to her present self, standing on a wind-torn beach, legs weak with shock. As though she has spent her life running away from this moment only to be caught and snapped back.

'Jessica, I'm your sister.'

'Don't be ridiculous.' She needs to sit down. Turns on her heel and staggers towards the bench with the sound of Libby's heels clipping the pavement behind her. 'How can you be? You're the same age as me, for God's sake.'

'I know.' Libby says it with such gentleness that Jessica falters.

Then out of nowhere, anger blasts through her. She has to grip her elbows, digging her nails in to stop herself from grabbing Libby's shoulders and shaking her.

'What kind of sick game are you and your mother playing? She steals my father, you steal my husband.'

'Is that what you think?'

Jessica slaps Libby's proffered hand away. 'Don't touch me.' Her words start to pour out, stumbling over each other in the rush. 'Sister or not, it means nothing to me. You just couldn't let Jacques be. You had to have him. All those times I walked in on the two of you.'

'Doing what, exactly?'

'Talking. Whispering.'

'About you.' Libby glares back from her perch at the

far end of the bench. 'Your erratic behaviour. Your secretive trips away. We were worried.'

Shaking her head, Jessica says, 'My first exhibition. You were there. You and Jacques already knew each other.'

'No. We didn't.' Libby pauses for an elderly couple to shamble by with their portly Labrador. 'I didn't have the courage to say who I was. I pretended I was an interested customer and asked him a few questions about you. I wanted something to take home to Dad.'

'Dad.' Jessica spits the word, tears popping up in her eyes. She turns her face away, staring at the far horizon so she doesn't blink and let them fall.

'I'm sorry.' Libby's voice wavers. 'Do you want me to carry on?'

All Jessica can do is shrug. She will not cry in front of Libby. Her sister, her father's hidden daughter.

Libby clears her throat. 'Dad kept trying to get in touch with you. Your mother wouldn't let him. She threatened to sell the caravan park and move away with you and your sisters if he tried to contact any of you behind her back.'

Jessica closes her eyes. She sees herself at fourteen, cocooned in a lost place with Thomas while secret conversations and decisions circled and passed her over like currents in the air.

'And then one day I came home and told him something I'd heard about you from a girl I knew at your school.'

'What?'

395

'That you were hanging around with a boy, a trouble-maker.'

'Thomas.'

Libby takes in a long breath. 'Of course. Your Thomas.'

'So you were going home with playground gossip.' Jessica wipes her eyes. Anger is good. It makes her strong.

'At first. Then we realised between the two of us we could find out all sorts of things. How you were doing at school – he just called your school office, actually. We nearly lost you when you ran off to Bridge. Then it turned out one of my friends had got to know your sister Hannah through hockey, and it was easy to get information. She liked talking about her tearaway sister.'

'Good old Hannah.' Jessica can't sit still any longer. Getting up, she starts to walk back towards the cliff path leading to Seasalt Park. The sun is already low in the sky and the wind rises off the beach, skimming sand into the air. She thinks about her father befriending Finn Quennell. Telling Thomas he was going to watch over her; a guardian angel.

'This still doesn't explain how you ended up being my friend.'

'Jessica, I'm trying, I really am but I can't talk to your back.'

She stops walking. 'Go on then.'

Libby's face is pink with cold, her eyes watering in the stinging breeze; far removed from her usual, polished self. 'I built a fantasy life around you. You were my lost sister, my missing twin. I wanted to meet you.'

Jessica thinks back to the night at the shop, Belladonna, with Libby crouched over the spilled lilies daring her to ask Jacques for the truth. 'Jacques knows who you are, doesn't he?'

Libby nods. 'I was desperate for you to come to the funeral. The fury of your reply . . .' She breaks off, shaking her head. 'Someone had to let you know that your father never intended to walk out of your life.'

At this point, Jessica is unsure how she is feeling. There's anger at her core, but layers of emotion have started to smother it like tree rings – bemusement, curiosity, disbelief. 'So you contacted Jacques?'

'I googled him and turned up at his office two days before the funeral.'

'He should have told me.'

Libby reaches out and touches her arm. 'He said the notice of the funeral made you sick. That you lay in bed for days afterwards. You'd made your decision, and there was no way he was going to persuade you to go. He was afraid of how you'd cope if you learned about me.' Libby sighs, running her hands through her hair, and Jessica feels the tension in her chest giving, stitch by stitch. There follows a post-race silence, both of them recouping, gathering themselves.

'Then you bought my jewellery.'

'I couldn't help myself.' Libby bites her lip over an apologetic smile. 'I can't tell you how furious Jacques was at the flower market that day.'

Jessica sighs, rubbing her forehead. 'I felt something between the two of you. It ate away at me.'

'I guess you picked up on the tension between Jacques and me. It was an ongoing discussion between us – whether or not to tell you who I was.'

Jessica shivers as a shoulder of sea wind hits her. The café has finished its lunchtime trade and the staff are upending chairs on tables. 'I'm going to go home.'

'I have the car here.' Libby goes to hug Jessica, then stops herself. 'You could come back with me now.'

'I meant back to the park.'

Jessica takes wide steps up the steep shale path, relieved not to hear the sound of following footsteps. The sun is reaching the white-whipped sea, its settling reds and oranges spreading over the beach. It's only now, having returned, that she is realising how beautiful the place is.

'Jessica,' Libby calls after her. 'Have you spoken to Jacques?'

Lying in her unlit caravan, Jessica tries to unpick the threads of Libby's story.

When the birds start to sing, her mum brings her a cup of tea. From the shadows on her face, it is clear she hasn't slept either. Placing the tea on the windowsill, she fusses about the room, refusing eye contact. The Birdie of Jessica's grown-up life, struggling to connect. But still, she is there.

Jessica sits up, bunching the covers around her knees. 'Mum, why don't you sit down?'

'It's laundry day, and there's more snow on the way.'

She tugs at a corner of rumpled sheet, tucking it under the mattress.

'Birdie. I need to know something.'

Her mother stops moving. She stands still, hands folded like a penitent child. 'Ask me, then.'

'Did Dad try to stay in contact with me?'

Birdie doesn't answer at once, her chin trembling. Then she lifts her head and faces Jessica, eyes glittering but steady. A glimpse of the old Birdie, full of spark and bluster. 'Yes. He begged me. For years. Until you moved away, in fact.'

Jessica scrambles to her feet, hands clenched. She opens her mouth to rail against her mother but suddenly she can't find any anger. Her shoulders slump. 'Why?'

But she knows. She can see the grey ghost of her mother all those years ago. Silenced by the truths she was protecting her children from.

The strength it took had sucked the life out of her.

Before Birdie can answer, Jessica throws her arms around her mother's neck. 'Oh, Birdie. My poor mum.'

Her mother hugs her back; the same fierce embrace with which she used to scoop up an unaware child, eliciting shrieks of laughter and protest. Always followed by a moment of surrendering to the comfort of each other's arms.

'I still think it was the right thing to do,' Birdie says as they sit together on the bed. She dabs her eyes with a thumb knuckle. 'But I have wondered over the years if I should have tried to stop your father from leaving.'

'How? He just vanished,' Jessica manages to say.

She's shocked at how casually her mum mentions her father, after a childhood with his unacknowledged shadow in every corner of the house.

'He didn't vanish. He only moved as far as Rormonton.'

Jessica looks away. Wonders if he lived out the rest of his life in the house furnished like a theatre dressing room.

'I could have fought a bit harder to keep him.' She raises her eyebrows. 'Do you understand what I'm saying?'

'It's too late to fight for Jacques.' Jessica flops back onto her mattress and closes her eyes. Finds sleep waiting for her.

'He left his number.'

Jessica shakes her head. 'I was so sure he'd let me down that I didn't consider my own behaviour. In the light of what I thought he'd done, my own actions seemed . . .'

'Justified?' Birdie offers.

'Irrelevant.' Jessica lifts her head. 'I've destroyed everything.'

'It's a very human talent to distort things to fit your own perspective.' Her mother's voice grows even quieter. 'Your father mastered that particular skill.'

'If I can't forgive myself, how can Jacques?'

Birdie gives a long sigh, sinking down onto her elbows then tipping her head backwards onto the bed. Her mother, who even in her years of silent misery never stopped moving and doing. Jessica curls up beside her and Birdie reaches out to cup her cheek in her hand.

As they lie there, her mother fumbles a folded yellow Post-it note from her skirt pocket and hands it to Jessica. 'Just in case.'

47

Nathan looks tired. The scraping light through the caravan window pools in the deep sockets of his eyes, his skin stretched thin over the pebble of his cheekbones. His usual smile has been put to rest.

'So. Here I am. Having called in sick for the first time ever.'

Jessica pulls up another stool and faces him across the breakfast bar. 'I found Thomas.'

The coffee mug in his hand slops brown liquid over the countertop. 'You saw him?'

She nods and stares hard at the hedge through the window as tears rise in Nathan's eyes. Pulling off his red bandana, he wipes his face with it, blows his nose. 'Shit. Sorry. I just didn't expect that.'

She tells him how she found his younger brother, fills her story with every detail she can, stalling the inevitable subject of the crucifix. His tears keep rising, along with a watered-down version of his smile. He shakes his head, incredulous.

'A born survivor, that boy.'

Then she reaches the point at which they walk into the woods and stops.

Nathan's face sobers. 'Everything. I need to know everything.'

'Wait here.'

When she returns from her bedroom with the crucifix and lays it between them on the table, Nathan shifts in his seat.

'What's this?'

'Thomas pulled it out of Bloody Russian's mouth when he found him in the woods behind your dad's house.'

Nathan squints at her. 'Found him?'

'He told me what happened that night, Nathan. He didn't do it.'

'But who, then?' He swallows, his body sagging.

'Your father. That's why Thomas took the crucifix and left it with me, I think. Because Finn's fingerprints are all over it.'

A pause, followed by a vigorous shake of the head. 'Not possible.'

It takes Jessica considerable effort to keep the frustration out of her voice. 'How could you so readily believe it was your brother but not your father? With his history of violence?'

Nathan mops the coffee spill with his bandana, then his sleeve. 'Because for the first time in my life, I saw my dad cry.'

'When?'

'A couple of days after Thomas disappeared.' He lifts the mug to his mouth but replaces it untouched. 'The old man broke down and sobbed, saying Thomas had killed the Russian.' Nathan raises his fist to his mouth, his face sickly white. 'And that he'd helped hide the body and then taken the boat out with Thomas. I hadn't even realised it was gone. With the storm and all.'

He looks ragged with despair but Jessica can't bring herself to comfort him with a touch.

'You never questioned your father's story? You just went straight to the police and told them your brother was a murderer?'

Nathan shakes his head. 'No, no. I'd already *been* to the police by then. To file a missing person report. I told them about Thomas and my dad's violent row and how he'd not been seen since. I knew my dad was hiding something. I thought he'd finally lost it and hurt my brother.'

'What did the police do?'

'They went round to question my dad. I was there, panicking, having just learned what really – what my dad said – had happened. Knowing if they searched the area they'd find a man beaten to death. I meant to save my brother but instead I'd ruined his life.'

'Your father did that, not you.'

He doesn't reply, staring out of the window as his fingers knead the stained bandana.

'I take it the police didn't search the place then?' Jessica prompts him.

Nathan sighs. 'I apologised for wasting their time; said I'd been drunk and overreacted to the row I saw. Then we told them about my missing boat.'

'And your father got away with murder.'

Nathan folds his arms on the table, resting his forehead against them. 'Finn Quennell. Grand puppetmaster.'

'Thomas thinks he got in a rage over the Russian stealing tools and—'

'It doesn't matter now,' he interrupts, his voice still muffled by his arms. 'Lives have been lived, Jessica.'

Jessica walks Nathan to his car on the boundary road. Waits until it has disappeared over the dip of the hill and the sound of his engine has thinned into silence.

Back in Caravan Nineteen, she shoves the cross into her rucksack and runs through the pleasure gardens and all the way down the slippery beach steps. When she has checked once, twice to ensure she is alone, she rips the sandwich bag open and hurls the crucifix far over the open water.

Afterwards, she scrubs her hands with sand and icy seawater.

48

Later that day, Jessica borrows Birdie's car and drives into Bridge. She is surprised to find the art supplies shop she used to visit after her lunchtime shifts at the Tea Chest, whiling away the hours until Jacques left the library or finished a tutorial.

Except for the staff, it is unchanged. She spirals up the metal staircase to the paints section on the mezzanine and finds a small pot of Liquid Sunshine.

The rest of the afternoon is spent dipping eggshells in golden lacquer, hoping her mother won't notice one of her collection jars is missing. The varnish preserves every hairline crack and chipped fragment, emphasising its fragility while lessening it. Transforming it into something a foot couldn't so easily crush beneath it.

Jessica is lining the birds' eggs up to dry on the windowsill facing the hedge – so Birdie doesn't spot them – when there's a knock on her door. It's not Birdie because her mother no longer knocks. All the same, she shouts, 'Stop. Don't come in.'

'It's me again.' Nathan's voice is muffled through the

crackle-glass of the caravan's front door. 'Sorry to bother you. Is this an inconvenient time?'

His formality alarms her. She can just make out the shape of a man standing behind him on the porch. 'Is it important, Nathan?'

She sees him shuffle round to look at his companion. Strains to catch their voices, but they exchange a look rather than words.

'I guess so.' The sudden weariness in his voice gives him away. He is here against his will or better judgement. Then he knocks more urgently on the door, pressing his face to it so that she receives a distorted vision of an eye and nose.

With a vicious yank, she flings back the door to find Nathan and his dad. A painful smile of apology tweaks Nathan's features while his father glowers at his feet, cane stabbing the ground as though squashing a beetle.

'Why is he here?'

'He insisted on—'

'You saw my boy.' Quennell bares his teeth as he swings his injured leg up each step, shouldering his son aside.

She tries to remain in the doorway but the sheer collapsing bulk of the man forces her back.

'Well?' Quennell plants himself round his cane in the middle of the room. 'I want to know what happened.'

'Thomas told me the truth.' She slips behind the breakfast bar, a flimsy barrier between herself and Thomas's father.

'Come on, Dad. Let's have a cup of tea first.'

'Don't want tea. I want to know if she apologised for ruining my son's life.'

'Dad, please. We can be civil about this.' Nathan slips between Jessica and his father. It's the acrid smell of acute discomfort rising off Nathan that makes Jessica slam her open palm against the countertop. His shoulders hiccough at the sound. The old man doesn't even flinch.

'Just how exactly did I ruin his life?'

She catches a glint like the flash of fish scales beneath the watery surface of his eyes. Relishing a fight. But she's sick of being afraid of an old man, of the truth. Afraid to voice the things circling endlessly in her head. She pushes Nathan gently to one side as she steps forward. 'Because I'm pretty sure he said *you* were responsible for that.'

Nathan groans as he turns away.

The old man takes a step forward. 'You riled him about Nikolai. Incitement to murder, that's what it was.'

'Do you remember the Russian's cross?'

'Jessica, wait.' Nathan rouses himself, tries to defuse their battle stance by encouraging his father towards the sofa. The old man backs towards it, holding out an arm for his son's assistance. She barely recognises the solemn, hunch-shouldered man who hesitates for a moment before lowering his father onto the cushion. Aware of her scrutiny, Nathan refuses to meet her eyes. 'My dad just wants to know how Thomas is doing.'

With a disdainful flick of his cane, Quennell silences his son. 'What cross?'

'Bloody Russian's. Huge thing, it was. You can't tell me you never noticed it.'

Quennell's jaw works away, chewing over his thoughts. 'What about it?'

She has his attention now. He must have wondered what happened to the crucifix.

'Thomas pulled it out of the man's broken jaw as he was trying to save him.'

'Save him?' Quennell flaps a scarred hand in the air. 'He beat that man to death. For you.'

'He took the cross to protect you.'

She looks across at Nathan, white-faced on the edge of the sofa, an unwilling spectator having removed himself from the event. 'Isn't that so, Nathan?'

His father doesn't even glance in his direction, so Nathan merely gazes helplessly back at her.

'That crucifix is covered in your murdering finger-prints.'

Quennell flails his cane in the air, his face turning deep red. Still, his voice doesn't rise a decibel. 'As much as it kills me to admit it, my son is a murderer. I have protected him and I have lived with that knowledge.'

Jessica smiles and notes with gratification how it unsettles the old man. An odd calm fills her. Joining them on the sofa, she takes Quennell's hand. She can feel him resisting the urge to pull his hand away. Grips harder.

'If he'd left it there, you'd have been jailed for murder.'

As she speaks, the truth of it hits her. Whether or not

Thomas admitted it to himself, part of him had been protecting his father.

'Preposterous lies.' Quennell makes a half-hearted attempt to stand before slumping back onto the cushions, breathing hard. 'I had nothing to do with it.'

'Personally I don't understand his loyalty to you. He knew the boating accident was to save yourself, not him.' Jessica leans over Quennell. 'That's how badly he wanted to escape you.'

Nathan's breath hisses out in the silence. His father is frowning at his hands resting on the dog-head cane, his face caving in on itself as he shakes his head, once, twice.

'I saved Thomas.'

'No. He saved you.'

Quennell's eyes bulge. 'I didn't do it.'

'You condemned your son to a life of running.' Jessica's words are soft as a mother crooning to her baby.

'Well?' Some of the bullish strength returns to Quennell's jaw as he snaps his head in Nathan's direction. 'I don't hear you saying anything.'

'Jessica's right, Dad.' Nathan can't meet his father's eyes, but he continues in a stronger voice. 'Thomas was taking the blame for you.'

'He still is.' The image of Thomas packing his few meaningful possessions brings tears to her eyes. 'He lives alone, separate from everything and everyone because he's afraid of being found.'

Quennell shoots his arm out, staggering as Nathan

helps him to his feet. He regains his balance before stalking to the front door. Where he stops.

'I heard Daniel Byrne died last year. Apparently he was desperate to see his girls before it was too late. Only one of his daughters even went to the funeral.'

'That's enough.' Nathan picks his father's crabbed hand off his arm.

'The one he had behind your mother's back, I believe.' Quennell shakes his head. 'Ah, the pain of a father's love.'

Jessica stares straight into his rheumy eyes. 'What would you know about a father's love?'

The old man juts his chin and yanks open the door. Nathan looks back at her, nods and blinks once like the shutter of a camera, and she understands he is saying goodbye.

49

The next morning Grannie Mim, Birdie and Jessica are having coffee and toast in Caravan Nineteen when there is a knock on the door. Through the frosted glass Jessica can see a tall, slim figure with light hair. When she makes no move to get up, Birdie opens the door.

'Ms Byrne.' Nilson ducks his head as he walks through the doorway. 'There you are.'

Jessica replaces her mug on the table with steady hands. She is prepared, having decided to tell as much of the truth as possible, giving him enough material to build a conceivable story in the hope that he will not notice the single missing brick – Bloody Russian's crucifix.

Then she'll pray Thomas has run far enough never to be found.

'What a funny coincidence, I was planning to visit you today.'

Flanked by the two older women, Jessica feels strong and certain. Her mother indicates the stool at the breakfast bar and Nilson sizes it up, taking in its height. 'If you ladies don't mind me towering over you all.'

Once seated, he reminds Jessica of a daddy longlegs, all awkward limbs and sharp joints. She is no longer afraid of him.

'I have some good news, Ms Byrne.'

Jessica nods and smiles but her mouth has gone dry. Grannie Mim's eyes flit between Nilson and Jessica like a robin pecking at crumbs. Birdie stares into her coffee.

'We've had a confession for the murder of Nikolai Galitzine.'

She closes her eyes. It is too late. They've found Thomas.

'Nicky who?' Mim's voice is shrill.

'Nikolai Galitzine. Bloody Russian to the locals. He was beaten to death seventeen years ago. Horrible case, it was. Unsolved until now.'

Jessica has opened her eyes enough to see her hands clenched into a ball of white knuckles under the table. The room is rolling on waves and she's afraid to look up in case she blacks out.

'I don't know what the relevance is of this murdered Russian.' Birdie straightens, pulling back her shoulders. 'Say your piece and kindly leave us to our breakfast.'

'Fair enough.' Nilson jumps off the stool, which wobbles and tilts but remains upright. He walks up to the table. 'Jessica, do you remember Finn Quennell, Thomas's old man?'

Jessica glances up, the blood leaving her face. 'Yes.'

'He came to the station this morning and gave a

written statement. Apparently Nikolai had assaulted one of his son's friends. A young girl. He was outraged and when the Russian taunted him with it, he lost control. I don't have to go into further details; you'll recall the photographs, of course.'

'Finn Quennell, a murderer,' Grannie Mim exclaims. 'They were always a troublesome lot.'

Jessica stares at Mim, then back to Nilson, feeling as though she's running through sand. '*Finn* Quennell?'

'You seem surprised?' Nilson smirks at her but his eyes are unsmiling. It's the anger in them that persuades her to trust what she is hearing. Thomas's father has taken the blame. After all these years, he has finally saved his son.

'I'll see you out,' she tells Nilson. She follows the DI outside, closing the door behind her. 'I trust I never have to see you again.'

Nilson leans forward, his voice dropping into a tone of confidentiality. 'There was one small detail in Finn's confession that interested me.'

'Really?' Let him have his say; he can't touch her or Thomas now.

'Thomas's little friend, the one Nikolai attacked, had red hair, so Finn said.'

Through the thin caravan walls, she can hear the scrape of chairs moving and the clink of crockery as Mim and her mother clear the breakfast away. But their voices are indistinct. If she can't hear them, they can't have heard what Nilson said.

'There are lots of us redheads around.'

Nilson taps a Marlboro Red out of his cigarette packet. Runs it under his nose. 'Did you find him?'

Jessica smiles. 'It doesn't matter now, does it?'

50

Two days before Christmas, Jessica is walking through fresh snow, frost crystals glittering under a sky of blue glaze, when she hears Jacques' voice.

Nothing sweeter than a bluebird day.

The longing to speak to him halts her footsteps, damp towel in her arms, the points of her wet hair stiffening with ice.

'You not feeling well, dearie?' She turns to see Grannie Mim approaching.

'A headache, that's all.'

'Why don't you call him?'

Jessica gapes at her.

'Yes. I can read your mind.' Grannie Mim laughs. 'Nothing to do with the misery on your face.'

'He'll hang up. He might not even be there.'

'All true.' Grannie Mim nods, shrugs. 'Life's shit.'

She waves over her shoulder as she walks off. 'Remember the time difference.'

Later, in Caravan Nineteen, after she has taken a walk, picked at a turkey and cranberry panini in the

Whitehead café and helped Birdie scrape moss off Caravan Three, Jessica is cursing Grannie Mim for planting the seed in her head. Just call him. So simple and terrifying, it takes her breath away. But it's taken hold and grown into a jungle of possible conversations in her head.

Just to hear his voice.

She looks at her watch. It is barely eleven in the morning and Connecticut is five hours behind. She makes herself a promise. Come two o'clock she will call Jacques. By then he will have woken, had his run and be back for breakfast.

Two o'clock arrives, and she lets it pass. Then Libby is knocking at her door, Birdie like a ferocious terrier behind her, muttering warnings.

'Please let me in.' Today she has dressed for the countryside. Shiny leather Dubarrys and jeans. She's never seen Libby in walking boots before. 'Just for a minute.'

Jessica nods. It will distract her from her broken promise.

To her credit, Libby waits to be offered a seat, in contrast to her proprietary behaviour in Jacques and Jessica's home. She doesn't say a word as Jessica makes tea. They sit on the sofa, the foldaway table between them with the remains of last night's dinner – a plate with two lamb-chop bones, her wine glass, dirty cutlery. Jessica pushes it all to one side.

'Why are you here?'

'I want us to stay friends, Jessica.' Libby spoons sugar into her tea, stirring in slow, deliberate circles.

'But our friendship was something you engineered.' Not so much an accusation as a testing of the notion now that the landscape around her has shifted into something unrecognisable. 'It wasn't real.'

'Don't you feel a bond between us? If you're honest.' Libby taps a nail against her mug. Thinking. 'How do you take your tea?'

Jessica gives a small shrug of frustration. 'What's that got to do with anything?'

'Three sugars, right? Just like me.' Libby gives a self-conscious smile; all drama set aside. 'Not that you ever noticed.'

'So, we like sweet tea. What does that prove?'

'Did you ever make Dad a cup of tea?'

Jessica starts to shake her head then, like a switched channel: she sees her mother in the kitchen dropping sugar cubes, one at a time, into her father's favourite mug. Laughing about the extra hours she'd have to put in at the park to satisfy her man's sweet tooth.

'That's our bond?'

'Of course not.' Libby sips her tea. 'But you thought I was chasing your husband, and I thought you were suddenly and inexplicably cold towards me . . . and still we stayed friends. That means something, I'm sure of it.'

Jessica gives a short, unconvinced *hum*. A cold draught of adrenalin sweeps over her as she prepares to ask a question that has been hibernating in the back of her head. 'Is there anything he wanted to say to me . . . at the end?'

Libby presses her lips together, tears rising. She shakes her head, breathing loudly through her nose. When she is ready to speak, she says, 'There was nothing new to add.'

Jessica stands abruptly, her chair scraping against the floor. She empties her cooling tea in the sink and washes the mug. A task for her hands.

'But I promised him I would speak to you. So you'd know how much he suffered in losing you.' Libby joins her at the sink. She slips her hand under the running water, prising the mug away and taking hold of Jessica's cold, soap-coated fingers.

'He said, maybe you'll be friends.'

After Libby leaves, Jessica stands in the shower until her fingers welt with wrinkles and the water runs cold. She allows herself to cry for him. For the man she adored as a little girl, and the stranger he'd become. Her father and Thomas; caught in the receding tide of years, drawn further and further away until they were lost.

The same thing would happen to Jacques, if she let it.

The sound of pebbles against her window wakes her from a dream. Pushing the curtains aside, she sees only caravan shadows broken into squares and rectangles by a full moon.

It is two in the morning. Nine o'clock at night in Connecticut. With just a jumper over the shorts she was sleeping in, she runs through Seasalt Park, her naked feet breaking the frozen skin of snow.

'Mum,' she calls, knocking softly on the office door. 'Can I use your phone?'

It's Joss who answers, shocking Jessica with his bare, white-haired chest and sleep-electric hair. 'Birdie's asleep.'

Jessica apologises, backing away.

'Use the phone, love,' he says. 'Just let yourself out when you're done.'

She unfolds the Post-it note Birdie has given her. Recognises the number of his parents' home. The first Christmas after they met, he went back to see them and she worked extra shifts at the Tea Chest – the ones no one else wanted on Christmas Eve and Boxing Day – so she could afford to call him every day. He never complained when she forgot the time difference, jumping out of bed to answer the phone before it had rung three times.

In the second bedroom, which her mother has converted into an office, she sits in the swivel chair by the desk and dials the number. A long tone sounds, like that of a broken line, then it falls into regular rings which she counts. On nine, he answers.

His voice trickles through her like warm milk. She can't speak.

'Jessica?'

'Yes.' Suddenly she's afraid he'll slip away in the silence so she adds, 'How are you? How's Ma Larsson?'

'All fine.' His voice, in contrast to hers, is slow. Reluctant.

'I'm staying at Seasalt. With Birdie.' The thawing pain of her feet burns up her calves. She hitches her knees, pulling the jumper over them. 'It's funny because I'm staying in Caravan Nineteen. Which is where you stayed, isn't it?'

'I don't recall.' The line crackles and sighs as though they're communicating across outer space.

'How are you?' she asks again.

'I bought a kayak. For springtime.'

'Have you tried it out?'

A long pause. She can feel him wrestling with the urge to hang up. 'It's a little cold. Took a walk up to Cornish, though, following the river by Mount Ascutney.'

Cornish, Mount Ascutney. Those distant, alien places delivered in his thickened accent take him even further from her. She sees the two-dimensional brochure pictures still taped to her sitting-room wall, glorious but unreal.

'Sounds like a long walk.'

Again the silence. She has to keep him speaking. 'You and your dad used to kayak along the Connecticut River when you were a boy, didn't you?'

'I should go now,' Jacques says.

'I know.'

The next night, again at two in the morning, she finds a note from Birdie on the office door.

No need to knock. Just go in, Mum.

The blessed relief as he answers. 'Jessica?'

'Did you go out again today?'

'Sure did.' Tonight the line is clearer. She hears him swallow, a clink of ice against glass. The fact that he has poured himself a drink fills her with hope. Perhaps he was waiting for her call.

'Where did you go?'

'I drove to the Quechee Gorge to see the frozen falls.'

'It sounds beautiful.'

'It's pretty peaceful. I caught sight of a peregrine falcon.'

She's not sure what it looks like but she pictures a bird with golden-brown feathers catching the sun as it lifts above the pines.

I have a picture of you in my head, he'd said in another life. *Sitting by the campfire, your hair wet from swimming, freckles on your shoulders. Just you and me.*

She buys a map of Connecticut and calls him every night, trailing his excursions with her finger along the blue artery of water. He tells her about snow blizzards, ice glittering in the air, an old grizzly at the water's edge. She listens intently and with a new kind of freedom, now that all the inner noise is gone. A few days into the new year, she buys an open-return ticket to the States from the travel agency in Barnestow. When she calls Jacques that night, she holds it in her hand for courage.

'I have something I need to tell you,' she says. 'It's about a boy called Thomas.'

And Jacques says, 'I'm listening.'

Acknowledgments

I am hugely grateful to everyone at Orion, especially my editor Kate Mills. I still remember being bowled over by her warm and uplifting response to *Jellybird* and I cannot thank her and her team enough. A special thank you to Louisa Macpherson and Gaby Young.

To my agent Rowan Lawton, a big thank you for brilliant advice, for always having the time for yet another 'quick question', and above all for her boundless enthusiasm and energy.

I am also grateful to Helen Corner and Kathryn Price at Cornerstones; the first people to read the book cover to cover and respond with such encouragement that I forged on rather than shoving it to the back of the drawer (as I had promised myself).

My thanks also to Anne Aylor, friend and tutor, whose creative writing workshops I have returned to over the years for her singular insight and inspiration. Without Anne I would never have had that 'light-bulb' moment.

My husband Mark, for his love, support and belief,

and for the many impromptu excursions with our children so I could scribble in peace for a few hours. A heartfelt thank you.

Never forgetting my mum, Elizabeth Maltarp, for being as excited as I am about the publication of my book, for always having the time to listen to my short stories and never failing to love everything I've written.

Finally, but never least, a thank you to my friends for their support, for very necessary coffees when I was missing human contact and for never forgetting to ask how the book was coming along.

Jellybird

Reading Group Notes

About the Author

Lezanne Clannachan was born in Denmark before moving to England when she was fourteen. After university, she lived in Singapore for several years before moving to London to work in marketing and event management. Married with three children, Lezanne lives in West Sussex in a haunted house.

The Story Behind *Jellybird*

Jellybird germinated on my way home from my last day at work, thirty-eight weeks pregnant with my first child. I remember taking my seat and watching Surbiton station slide by, then nothing else of that journey.

The setting came first.

I grew up surrounded by water. From my Copenhagen flat, it was a ten minute drive to one of the many beaches nibbled by the icy Øresund. We holidayed in Skagen, on the west coast, against which the stormy North Sea breaks itself. The ocean was always going to be the backdrop to this story.

By the time I reached home, I had an image of a young woman looking out over the sea. She felt lost. And I had Thomas – a damaged, young man whose life played out in moors and empty bays, away from the judging eyes of society. I knew I wanted to write about first love.

On my first morning of maternity leave, I bought a writing pad. The two weeks that followed were a privilege of uninterrupted writing time. I had been scribbling stories since I was six, but apart from my immediate family, had shown my writing to no one. My inexperience showed. Like a flourish of mould, the story burgeoned in all directions. By the time my first baby came along, I had the foundation of *Jellybird*, but it took a further eight years of learning and re-writing (plus the birth of two more babies) before it took its final shape.

The title was the last thing to fall into place. My youngest daughter, at three years old, was babbling to herself over breakfast and I thought she said something odd. It sounded like jellybird. I got goosebumps. I had Thomas's nickname for Jessica. It spoke of her flightiness and their mutual affection, and in doing so captured the core of the narrative.

For Discussion

- What emotions does your first sight of Seasalt Holiday Park evoke?

- 'Her mother is the only person she knows who can pass a car crash without a glance.' What does this tell us about Birdie?

- To what extent is *Jellybird* about how we deal with secrets?

- 'Its true form is hidden because the eye is distracted by all that colour and glitter.' Why does Jessica make jewellery in the way she does?

- 'Libby bestows her friendship like a gift.' What does this tell us about Libby?

- What does *Jellybird* tell us about loss?

- 'You're not living if you don't experience pain at some point.' What does this tell us about Jessica's father?

- 'It's facing your own secrets that takes the greatest courage.' Do you agree with Jessica's father?

- 'Every time they're alone together, Libby wins her over.' Why?

- 'The way to inflict the most pain is to walk out of someone's life.' Is this the core of the novel? Do you agree with Jessica?

- 'It's a very human talent to distort things to fit your own perspective.' To what extent is *Jellybird* about perspective?

In Conversation with Lezanne Clannachan

Q Any of you in Jessica or Libby?

A Personality-wise, no, though I loosely based some of her experience on my own. My father died after a short illness and I tried to convey the gaping emptiness that remains after someone integral to your life disappears. There is also the assault scene, which – whilst I have been lucky enough not to experience it myself – was informed by moments during my teenage years, when I realised the potential danger of a situation I'd put myself in. Recalling that dawning horror helped me write a difficult scene.

Q 'White lies don't count.' Do you agree with Jessica?

A Only when used for good! However, I have a compulsion to honesty that's bordering on pathological. The fear of being caught out in even the smallest of lies makes me feel like a five year old, standing over a broken vase.

Q How did you set about creating Seasalt Holiday Park?

A Seasalt Holiday Park is a collage of different settings. An Italian campsite on the outskirts of Rome provided the functional austerity; the perfect setting was waiting for me when I rented a holiday cottage on the cliffs above Sennen Cove in Cornwall. Smaller details were added every time I happened to pass a campsite or holiday park, my long-suffering family waiting in the car whilst I had a quick scout around.

Q 'You can't help what you feel. None of us can. Keeping it in only makes you sick.' Can we help what we feel?

A No. I don't believe we can. Emotion comes from the gut – be it love, lust, hate and all the grey areas between – and the gut is nothing if not honest. You can try to corral an emotion or a response through the strength of your will, but you can't exorcise it. I'm endlessly fascinated by the struggle that arises when a person tries to deny what they want.

Q 'Everyone has secrets, even those closest to you.' Always true? Always damaging?

A I had this conversation at a party recently. I suggested to an acquaintance that everyone has secrets, or at least shades of their personality they keep to themselves. My acquaintance looked horrified. So perhaps he is the exception. I think many of us adapt our personality to suit a new situation. That's a form of secrecy. None of us reveal our every thought or impulse, not necessarily because it is damning or shameful, but because it is private and belongs solely to us. I think it's vital to retain a little of yourself, just for yourself.

Q 'Something happened to people when they got old; they started seeing everything through dirty windows.' Do you agree with Jessica?

A I did as a teenager. I had several experiences where an adult interpreted my behaviour in a negative manner. It seemed to me at the time that adults were always nosing for dirt. Now, especially as a mother, I think it is less about negative expectation and more about anxiety. We know too much about the bad stuff. I think it can make you look for problems where there are none.

Q Is the keeping of secrets at the heart of *Jellybird*?

A Definitely. The secrets kept in *Jellybird* are damaging. They deny both Thomas and Jessica a safe childhood. If Jessica's mother had been open about her father's departure, Jessica could have made her own decision whether or not to stay in touch with him. I believe she would have grown into a more confident adult, one who might have been better prepared to confront the secrecy she senses between Jacques and Libby. Jacques also makes a decision to withhold the truth – well-intentioned though it is – in an effort to shield Jessica from Libby's true identity. In doing so, he keeps a secret that destroys their marriage.

Q 'Blood-letting, she thinks. Letting the bad blood flow away.' Why does Jessica harm herself?

A Jessica is extremely self-contained. She is not a screamer or a plate-smasher. The strain I was putting her under needed a release. Even I was feeling the pressure when writing her scenes! Something had to give and it evolved from her character. Self-harm was not something I had considered when creating her character but it felt in keeping with her need to take back some form of control.

Q How would Jessica's life have been different if her first love had faded naturally?

A The violent ending to her friendship with Thomas kept Jessica tied to her past. It left her unable to commit fully to Jacques and offered her an alternative – albeit a false one – when her current life became difficult. If that first love had faded away without drama, Jessica would have confronted Libby and Jacques long before her marriage deteriorated, because she would have had no choice. There would have been no one to run to.

Q 'Running away is in your blood.' Is it in Jessica's blood to run?

A Jessica and her father both run away to avoid confronting a painful situation. I find the notion of bad blood interesting because it suggests a doomed sense of inevitability. Thomas is convinced he will become his father, whilst Jacques bitterly suggests Jessica can't help running away. However, both Thomas and Jessica manage to break the pattern of their parent's behaviour. Jessica, through her determination to fight for her marriage despite Jacques's return to the States, and Thomas by escaping the shadow of his bullying father.

Q What constitutes infidelity?

A This is one of the central themes of *Jellybird* and yet I'm still not sure I've found the answer! I was fascinated by the idea that Jessica might suspect Jacques of harbouring feelings for Libby, whilst trusting in his innate sense of right and wrong. She knows deep down he wouldn't physically betray her. But without a physical betrayal, is there a 'case' against him? His betrayal – as she mistakenly sees it – is in thought only. Personally, I think infidelity is in action. I think it begins the moment two people recognise a current of feeling running between them, something more than flirtation or appreciation. Perhaps it's a kiss or a secret conversation. Perhaps it's simply a look.

Suggested Further Reading

One Day by David Nicholls

Life After Life by Kate Atkinson

Atonement by Ian McEwan

Where'd You Go, Bernadette by Maria Semple

The Shadow Year by Hannah Richell

The Sick Rose by Erin Kelly